MW00582004

"*Mothersound: The Sauutiverse Anthology*, is a rare and distinct Afro-centric treat that hums in the unity of a collective enriched with universal storytelling and the many languages of Mother Africa."

—Nuzo Onoh, Queen of African Horror, and recipient of the 2022 Bram Stoker Lifetime Achievement Award

"The Sauútiverse is a powerful original collective concept, and this debut anthology clearly shows collaboration can create more than the sum of its parts while remaining firmly true to its African heritage and taking that boldly into the future."

—Ivor W. Hartmann, acclaimed writer and editor of *AfroSF: Science Fiction By African Writers*

"Fantastika at its best. The Sauútiverse invites a reader to drown in a poetic world, built with a Tolkenian attention to gripping detail, and full of creatures who excite the imagination in a dream-like rollercoaster. The illustrations are works of art in themselves, adding spice to the stories, and I found myself wishing there were more paintings, more stories, and more pages to keep me up in the wee hours."

—Dilman Dila, internationally acclaimed and award-winning social activist, filmmaker and author of Yat Madit stories

"The Saúútiverse is a mind-blowing, highly imaginative and deeply compelling sandbox. The wide range and excellent quality of these stories are a testament to that, offering yet another formidable trove of authors of African descent. In *Mothersound*, Talabi and company have offered us something seminal. This book will continue to influence the canon of Afrocentric futurisms for years to come."

—Suyi Davies Okungbowa, award-winning Nigerian author of
David Mogo, Godhunter and The Nameless Republic trilogy

Mothersound

Mothersound

The Sauútiverse Anthology

Edited by Wole Talabi, and featuring stories by
Eugen Bacon, Tobias S. Buckell, Oghenechovwe
Donald Ekpeki, Stephen Embleton, Dare Segun
Falowo, T.L. Huchu, Somto Ihezue, Adelehin
Ijasan, Akintoba Kalejaye, Cheryl S. Ntumy, Eye
Kay Nwaogu, Xan van Rooyen, J. Umeh, with a
Foreword by Fabrice Guerrier

Android Press

Copyright © 2023 the Sauúti Collective
This edition by arrangement with African Literary Agency

Published by Android Press
Eugene, Oregon
www.android-press.com

ISBN: 978-1958121603

All rights reserved. No part of this book may be reproduced in any manner whatsoever without written permission of Android Press and the Sauúti Collective.

Individual stories are the copy right of their authors as listed below:

Foreword © 2023 by Fabrice Guerrier

Why We Created the First Collaborative African Sci-Fi/Fantasy Universe © 2022 by Wole Talabi (originally published in *The Guardian*, September 5, 2022)

Our Mother, Creator © 2023 by Stephen Embleton and Wole Talabi

What Has No Mouth? © 2023 by Dare Segun Falowo

The Way of Baa'gh © 2023 by Cheryl S. Ntumy

The Grove's Lament © 2023 by Tobias S. Buckell

Xhova © 2023 by Adelehin Ijasan

A City, a Desert, and All Their Dirges © 2023 by Somto Ihezue and Oghenechovwe Donald Ekpeki

Sina, the Child With No Echo © 2023 by Eugen Bacon

The Rakwa Wa-Ya'yn © 2023 by Stephen Embleton and Wole Talabi

Undulation © 2023 by Stephen Embleton

The Hollowed People © 2023 by T.L. Huchu

Muting Echoes, Breaking Tradition © 2023 by Eye Kaye Nwaogu

Kalabashing © 2023 by J. Umeh

Lost in the Echoes © 2023 by Xan van Rooyen

Hologhiri © 2023 by Akintoba Kalejaye

Cover art by Stephen Embleton
Interior art by Stephen Embleton and Akintoba Kalejaye

CONTENTS

CONTENTS

CONTENTS

I have a dream of a future when creative writers around the world will wake up and their natural inclination will be to collaboratively write and produce within the unique story worlds they create.

In this future, writers from different backgrounds, locations, and cultures will imagine deeply together, they will be more empowered, they will work hand in hand, side by side in artist collectives. In this future, they will fuel our ability to collectively imagine with more complexity, more profoundness and more beauty. This future, I believe, is already here, and it is called 'Sauúti'.

The world of Sauúti was first conceived as an incredible creative project in November 2021 between Syllble Studios - a sci-fi and fantasy production and publisher based in Los Angeles, Brittlepaper magazine - Africa's premier online literary brand, and Wole Talabi, Nigerian author and Editor. This project brought together a group of ten African science fiction and fantasy authors from five African nations (Botswana, Tanzania, Ghana, Nigeria, South Africa) living in every corner of the globe to form a collective. This collective created the new and intricate fictional world called Sauúti - a unique science-fantasy world for and by Africans and the African Diaspora.

Sauúti made waves from its inception and continues to rattle the global literary and world with collective members taking the stage at The Ake Arts & Book Festival, SyllbleCON, and the Science Fiction and Fantasy Writers Association's (SFWA) Nebula Conference. And now, the collective is proud to share what they have created in this book - MOTHERSOUND: THE SAUÚTIVERSE ANTHOLOGY

- which is the perfect way to be introduced to the world of Sauúti. Through its stories.

Unlike most other anthologies, these stories are stitched together with an extreme dynamism and all rooted in their shared story world that embraces all forms of African belief about what storytelling could and should look like.

MOTHERSOUND is a primal scream that shatters all that has been done in the past. Sauúti is a unique mythology that is challenging dominant Western narratives, ways of thinking, and stories that have been so much rooted in the legacies of Western colonialism and individualism.

Our world demands it! This global society, highly technologically connected, leaves us with a rotting connective tissue deprived of wisdom, an erasing and defunct meaning structure that upholds no bearings for those that seek to exist outside of Western hegemony. But the times are changing fast, classical views need to be reimagined, especially when our planet is moving towards a great era of uncertainty. We desperately need new visions for Africa, for humanity. As old thought systems collapse, the collective imagining of new frameworks of being and living will be our ship for sailing into this new future. It is the storytellers, like those in the Sauúti collective carrying the flaming torch, banding together and innovating at the forefront of movements like *Afrofuturism* and *Africanfuturism* which they are now an essential part of, that will draw us maps to the next stages of our collective evolutions.

The release of MOTHERSOUND will set the stage for a new future for African writers and the diaspora. May it be the day when young African and African diaspora writers have both a global community and a new story world they can fall in love with. As they grow up with Sauúti and this fictional world matures over the next decade, these young writers will have the power to participate, collaborate, and even contribute to the Sauútiverse using a unique community rights sharing model for publishing stories set in this world. Sauúti is an expanding story world, a playground of meaning that grows with each new participant that enters it.

This is another differentiation of the Sauúti collective and story worlds: its localized participatory frameworks and syncretized shared African mythologies and wisdom. There are already three guest authors contributing to this anthology, and the hope is that there will be many more. We don't know yet in what wondrous ways it will evolve, but what I know for sure is that injecting these Sauúti mythologies into this grand 'Imagination Battle' taking place in our era for our collective souls will help make this world a little less broken.

Africa's place as a cultural force can no longer be denied. The creative energy runs deep - writing, film, art, music, there is so much. The Sauúti collective stands as a funnel for this force that is being born out of an awakening continent in need of new, different stories about itself. A harkening back to the past while also looking ahead to the future.

As a Haitian-American, science fiction and fantasy writer, and founder of Syllble, I am proud to introduce you to this world. Each member brought their unique African perspective to its foundations. Some focused on specific regional mythologies and linguistics, while others explored the intersection of technology and uncertainty. Some were fascinated by the historical timeline and socio-dynamics of the imagined civilizations, and others in the magic system, incorporating sonic sounds and the power of the word.

This world of Sauúti closely mirrors our own in some aspects but is vastly different in other ways, yet the characters, gods, spirits, the sentient AI and the non-humanoid beings all face their own journeys, and just like us they must choose whom shall they become and how they navigate uncertainty.

I wondered, as I witnessed the collective creating an entirely new language, new myths, and frameworks of thinking, what does this do to the beholder? To its creators? To the audience that immerses itself in it? They undergo a deep transformation of the heart and psyche, especially when storytelling is done as skillfully as it is in MOTHERSOUND. It is a kind of shedding that makes us more human. This too is the power of the Sauútiverse.

We don't always know the lasting impact of our creative works. Whether it's Chinua Achebe's THINGS FALL APART or the works of Nnedi Okorafor, N.K. Jemisin, Ngũgĩ wa Thiong'o, Octavia Butler and the many others that have come before us, their fictional worlds allowed us to see ourselves more deeply and explore the dynamics of the world. Similarly, new worlds like Sauúti will help us understand the problems of this new era and inspire unborn creatives. The future I dream of is already beginning—a future of Storyworlds like Sauúti, each a manifesto for change, a new creative flood that will nourish each of us with more knowledge, more magic, more humanity.

— **Fabrice Guerrier, May 2023**

WHY WE CREATED THE FIRST
COLLABORATIVE AFRICAN SCI-FI/
FANTASY UNIVERSE

Creative writing can be a lonely business.

As writers, we inhabit whole worlds and characters that live only in our heads for days or years, as we deposit them on the page. This is particularly true for speculative fiction – an umbrella genre of stories that involve supernatural or futuristic elements, or settings that are not the real world.

This creative loneliness is why I've always admired and enjoyed the concept of a "shared world" – a fictional setting with its own set of rules where multiple authors can create stories. Some examples are THIEVES' WORLD, edited by Robert Lynn Asprin, or George RR Martin's WILD CARDS (which has spawned dozens of books, comics and games, and was optioned for film and TV).

Because writers use the same settings, characters and concepts of the shared world in a connected way, they are in conversation with each other, as a community in the act of creation.

As a speculative fiction author from Africa, where recognition for the genre is growing and community is an important part of the culture, I've long wanted to be able to do this with my contemporaries – create together. Not only with other African authors but with the greater African diaspora.

That's why, working with Fabrice Guerrier, Haitian-American author and founder of Syllble, and the Nigeria-based magazine Brittlepaper, I sought out a group of like-minded volunteer authors from five African countries to form the Sauúti Collective.

Together we have created Sauúti – a shared world by Africans, for Africans, the African diaspora and indeed the world.

The Sauúti shared world or universe, which we fondly call the Sauútiverse, is a fictional setting based on a blend of African cultural worldviews and inspirations. The name is inspired by the Swahili word for "voice". The Sauútiverse is a five-planet system orbiting a binary star, where everything revolves around an intricate magic and techno-logical system based on sound, oral traditions and music. It includes science-fiction elements of artificial intelligence and space flight, with both humanoid and non-humanoid creatures. Think of it like BLACK PANTHER by way WILD CARDS, with all the rich interplanetary world-building of Frank Herbert's DUNE.

But the Sauútiverse is distinctly African, being flexible enough to absorb and synthesise the multitude of African cultural identities and viewpoints into something new.

As founding members of the Sauúti collective, we wrote a detailed "story bible" describing the settings, history, politics, rules, key charac-ters and groups, motivations and general philosophy of the world, and we have also written stories set within the world. Now we are inviting collaborators to write stories set in the world, and to expand it with new ideas and creative visions, then publish a collection of all the stories.

Where most shared worlds are not accessible to many, often being housed behind intellectual property rights, the Sauútiverse is different. In the future, writers in Africa or the African diaspora will be able to pitch stories that explore different aspects of the Sauútiverse or take it in new directions.

The Sauútiverse is the first African speculative shared world of its kind. We believe it has the potential to do many important things for the genre and the community. It will be playground of ideas. It will be a creative springboard for up-and-coming authors who can create in the same space as established authors. It will also help increase awareness of African speculative fiction by being a unique creative brand that doesn't belong to any one specific author.

Speculative fiction has always been an essential part of African storytelling (as evidenced in such works as Jean-Louis Njemba Medu's NNANGA KON, Ben Okri's THE FAMISHED ROAD and many others), but in its published form it has only recently been recognised and identified as such by the broader industry.

This increased recognition can be traced back to breakout works by Nnedi Okorafor, Lauren Beukes and Tade Thompson, among others, but also to landmark anthologies such as AFROSF by Ivor Hartmann and magazines like Omenana and Jungle Jim. However, despite the increased global recognition, there isn't yet an organic swell of African speculative fiction on the continent.

We believe the Sauútiverse can be the next step in the evolution of African speculative fiction by being a sandbox for generations of African and African diaspora writers to work together and imagine endless possibilities.

— **Wole Talabi**
Article first published in *The Guardian*,
September 5, 2022

Welcome to the Sauútiverse

So now that we have told you why and how we set up the Sauúti-verse, let us tell you what it is and get you oriented before we dive into the stories.

The Sauúti shared world or Sauúti shared universe (you can call it the Sauútiverse), is a fictional setting and civilization, a secondary world unconnected to our real world. As you will see, it is based on a blend of African cultural worldviews and inspirations.

The central location of the Sauútiverse is a five-planet system orbiting a binary star. Lets get to know them a bit.

The two suns are called Zuúv'ah and Juah-āju. And the five planets are Wiimb-ó, Zezépfeni, Ekwukwe, Órino-Rin and Mahwé (which has the only inhabited moon in the system, called Pinaa).

Wiimb-ó and Mahwé orbit Zuúv'ah.

Órino-Rin and Ekwukwe, orbit Juah-āju.

Zezépfeni, is circumbinary and orbits the center of mass of both stars.

Here's a helpful schematic so you can picture what all this looks like.

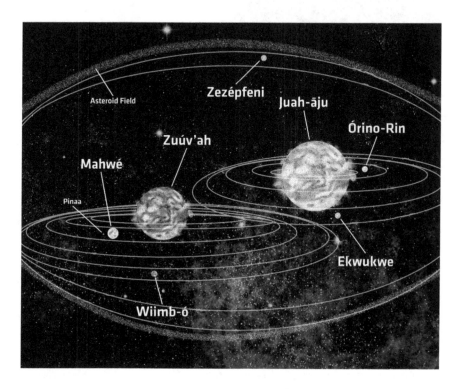

That's all you need to know about the physical layout of the Sauúti-verse for now. You'll encounter a lot more in the stories to come.

A key aspect of the Sauútiverse to keep in mind is that magic and technology co-exist side-by-side here and so it's a science-fantasy world. Both the magic and technology of this world are based on sound. Words, language, oral traditions, vibrations, music, every kind of sound, in every interpretation – they all hold tangible power here. All stories emphasize how important sound and the spoken word is, mirroring many traditional African cultural practices. I'll highlight these in the introduction to each story as we go along. But just remember - a key theme in the Sauútiverse is an exploration of the nature of sound as power.

All humanoids in the Sauútiverse have a shared history, having evolved from an older race (also called the Sauúti, or the first ones) that first evolved and developed on one of the planets (I won't tell you which just yet) before spreading out and settling the five worlds.

Through the coming stories, you will follow the chronology of Sauútiverse from one of its earliest historical events, till what we consider to be its present day.

A few more things to keep in mind. Because every planet has different rotational speed and orbit, references to time in Sauúti have been "standardized" to facilitate trade and inter-planetary communication. For example, a "year" is the time it takes Juah-āju and Zuúv'ah to complete one orbit around their common center of mass and is called a juzu. A standard 'day' is called a bés. Contemporary time in the Sauútiverse is also usually referenced to an event known as the "1st Boāmmariri". As we go through the chronology, you will see why. For now, simply use it to guide you as to where you are in the imagined history. (B1B means "before 1st Boāmmariri") and A1B means "after 1st Boāmmariri"). I will mention the date in the introduction to each story and we will be encountering the stories chronologically to keep things simple. In the closing notes, there is a timeline diagram with major events, and a glossary at the back end, so feel free to reference those if you get lost or just want a reminder.

Alright. That's it. You're ready.

Take a deep breath.

Exhale.

Welcome to the Sauútiverse.

"The earliest storytellers were magi, seers, bards, griots, shamans... they wrestled with mysteries and transformed them into myths which coded the world and helped the community to live through one more darkness, with eyes wide open and hearts set alight."
—— Ben Okri

*E*very society and culture has mythologies and cosmologies. Creations myths, origin myths, tales of foundation. A story of how they came to be. Myths play a fundamental role in every society. They are sacred narratives. They are stories we tell ourselves about ourselves and our place in the world, sometimes in reference to things in the world that are larger than us. Because they are the stories we share with others to build common bonds of belief, myths can be more important than the simple facts of physical history. Belief systems and mythological frameworks are important in understanding the past, navigating the present and projecting the future of any society.

So, for an imagined shared world like Sauúti, we knew it was important to create an imagined beginning, to have a foundational creation myth, one that plays a key role in how our fictional people in the Sauútiverse saw themselves and which was loosely aligned with their 'real' physical history as we had imagined it but larger than that. How would the earliest people in the Sauútiverse have told themselves the stories of the stars unfolding, of how they came to be on their spinning rocks in space, of the two suns blazing in their sky? How would they explain from a rudimentary state with little to no technology, the universe they found themselves in? And how would those stories have mutated over time?

African folklore and beliefs are vast and varied, a multitude of view-points and worldviews to take inspiration from and to examine more deeply by abstraction.

We knew we wanted a few things from the start. We wanted a central, god-figure but we also wanted a pantheistic worldview. We wanted an origin myth that was not male-centered in order to establish a more generally matriarchal society. We wanted sound to be a central focus in this world, and so that needed to be reflected in its foundational myth. And so we took inspiration from North African communities who center themselves around a matriarch and goddess. From the Ijaw people and their creator goddess Woyengi. From the Egyptian mythological Nut. Nana Buluku of the Fon who gave birth to the moon spirit Mawu, the sun spirit Lisa. From so many more. And we added more, so much more, to relate to the five planets in the system and their binary star.

Thus, the Sauúti Creation myth. But as you read, take note of contradictions. Myths are always a function of who tells them. We will come to that later. For now, enjoy, Our Mother, Creator.

Our Mother, Creator

STEPHEN EMBLETON AND WOLE TALABI

Khwa'ra. It is acquired.
Ya'yn. It is uttered.
Ra'kwa. It is released.

Our Mother.
   Our Mother was all.
She, the only reality in a boundless sea of unreality.
Our Mother was all there was.
There was no other to behold Her. Her light the only light. No other to receive Her light. No other to reflect Her light.
Our Mother stood alone in silence, radiant.
She was witness to nothing. Yet She knew of everything.
An eon passed, as if in a moment, and with an intake of cosmic breath, she uttered the Word, releasing its power into existence.
She created the Word. She was the first to speak the Word. She was the first to hear the Word. She was the first to feel the Word. She was the first to see the Word.
The Word undulated through Her body, explosions of light and sound reverberated outward through the darkness, piercing the silence, as She conceived a child, warm in her womb.

The Word echoed outward, and She who had uttered the Word was witness to its power, as She beheld the creation of the heavens, stars, and a celestial body – the World – all from Her utterance. The World came from the Word.

Our Mother became Creator.

Our Mother, God.

Our Mother wept, not because of the magnificence of what she saw, but for what was still to come.

In birth, Her tears flowed vast oceans, bound to the dust of the Word, forming soils and stones.

Our Mother's heat and light molded rocks from clay, pushed mountains into the blue skies and cracked open vast canyons.

The World came whole, the World became whole.

The Word rumbled forth, and a crash shook the earth, as Our Mother's turbulent waters surged across the lands, inundating, quenching, and bathing.

Our Mother screamed with the glory of Motherhood and The Word screamed back.

Firstborn, Zezépfeni, emerged into Our Mother's warm light, nestled and nurtured in the World.

Life thrived. The world grew.

Our Mother's warmth raised up water and distributed the rains across the lands. Life was nourished. She loved and admired. She watched and adored.

As with anything loved and counselled by Our Mother, Zezépfeni grew strong with grace. Our Mother's love knew no bounds.

Could Our Mother love even more?

In a giant intake of breath, from the furthest reaches of the heavens, Our Mother summoned the Word back to Herself.

With a deep hum Our Mother uttered the Word for a second time. Mahwé. Second born.

Into the caves and hollow spaces of the World, Our Mother uttered the Word for a third time. And born of echoes, emerged Ekwukwe.

Uplifting the Word, in the form of song, Our Mother uttered the Word for a fourth time. Órino-Rin sings that song of the wind instrument.

An age passed and Our Mother once again craved the fulfilment of motherhood. And so, for a final time She uttered the Word, and the Word was free.

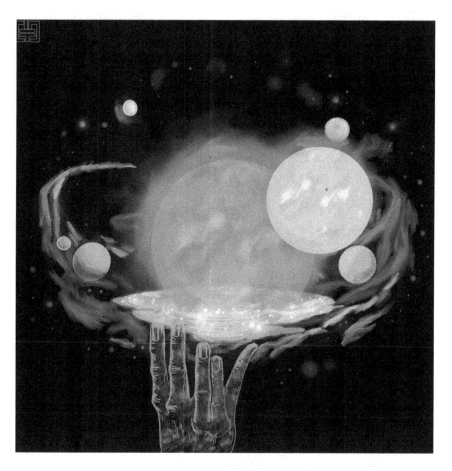

Last born – Wiimb-ó – stood at Our Mother's side. The Child of Light. Absorbing Our Mother's radiant glow, impressing and challenging the other siblings, Wiimb-ó was bold in stature, strong and proud.

Our mother watched them all grow. She admired her scions as they danced in the heavens, and She was pleased.

Through Our Mother, Creator, harmony and balance echoed across the heavens.

The Word was the first sound. It reverberates to this day.

Find The Word.
Find The Voice.

Khwa'ra. It is acquired.
Ya'yn.It is uttered.
Ra'kwa.It is released.

*I*n the beginning, there was an apocalypse.

Scientific records suggest that anatomically modern humans all originated in Africa around 200 thousand years ago from a single set of common ancestors. From there we spread out and separated into sub-groups – and our history is often one of strife between such groups despite our differences being largely cosmetic.

The Sauúti collective wanted a similar kind of history for the different groups of people in the Sauútiverse to underwrite the inter-group strife to come. We wanted them to have a common ancestor group and common language that had spread from one planet to the others before being separated by an apocalyptic event. A "tower of babel" or "things fall apart" moment writ large. And so we established that one of the major driving events in the imagined physical history of the Sauútiverse was an extreme coronal mass ejection or a solar flare of the binary star the planets orbit. This event wreaked havoc across the system, killing off swathes of the population, destroying communications, transports, and separating the survivors from each other. Much technology and magic and knowledge were lost. The event also triggered changes to planetary climates. All of this led to a reversion to more 'primitive' ways, forcing the survivors of each planet to reemerge, resettle in isolated pockets and evolve independently, with the memory of their siblings on sister-planets faded to cultural memory. This, in a sense is where our larger story of the Sauútiverse begins, at the moment where the inhabitants of the system lose each other. Most of the stories in this anthology take place beyond this point and so I think it's a great way for you to enter the world of Sauúti.

In the following story, written by a founding member of the collective, **Dare Segun Falowo**, in the style of a chronicle, we begin there and explore the aftermath of the flare on the planet Wiimb-ó.

Wiimb-ó is a good setting for our first story because we have imagined it to be an Earth-analogue (it is structurally and geographically similar to our own Earth - but remember! It isn't Earth). It has five large inhabited continents and also has two spirit moons that are invisible to most, but visible to certain people who are spiritually attuned. This is a science-fantasy world after all. The effects of the spirit moons affect all on Wiimb-ó, whether they can see them or not.

In this Wiimb-ó-set story, we learn a fragment of sonic history, from 300000 juzu B1B. It is a tale of the Surali, who are a group occupying an isolated continent of the planet, much like our own Australia, that must rediscover and reclaim their world using the primordial power of sound that drives all things this universe, its magic, technology and people. And we follow the Surali as they also learn of what can happen if that power, the Mothersound that animates the Sauútiverse, is not handled with care.

What Has No Mouth?

(A Fragment From Our Sonic History, On The Alleged Utterance Of The Mothersound Among The Surali Of Wiimb-ó)

DARE SEGUN FALOWO

"what has no mouth but makes the 'Sound?'"

I

More than seventy juzu after the suns had exhaled their fires on all of the five planets that orbited them and the Surali of Wiimb-ó had become a cave dwelling people, Ikululu and all the maadiregi of his clan, old and new, stood before Erigiga's pyre.

Wet salt burned Ikululu's eyelids. He would say he was unsure of the source of his tears, and maybe blame them on the acrid smoke or the ash blowing about, but the gnaw of Erigiga's absence was scraping against his ribs. It felt like a black hole had opened inside his stomach. He tried to remain mute, because a maadiregi only makes use of their voice when it is most important but the sound of his brothers and sisters openly wailing around Erigiga's pyre made him let go, to ragged sobs.

He found it hard to believe that he would no longer hear Erigiga's jokes and riddles. Would no longer get to watch him experiment with new ways to wield power of sound through math and magic, preferring to use sounds other than his voice, which he always claimed was resting. He couldn't believe he would no longer get to hear the gentle susurration of Erigiga's well-rested voice rush over his tense heart, bringing him relief an uroh-ogi would envy.

He watched his best friend, Oounkan, whom he had met in apprenticeship under Erigiga, bent over as he wept softly on his knees. Oounkan was quickly covered with a blanket of soft jute by Omilomi, his betrothed, the one who had heard his sound in their heart. Others were solemn, leaning on one another, holding onto their staffs, clutching their robes in front of their chests.

There were very few of those who had witnessed the explosion of the suns left among the Surali. Erigiga had been a suckling baby then, when Badede and the other old maadiregi had managed to save only a fraction of their people with sonic magic, turning them from open air foresters into amphibians who now lurked in watery caves filled with schools of fish that glowed and vegetables that danced in no wind. A people who now feared the wild world outside for its wealth of large, hardy and hungry predators and other poisonous fauna, the only things that had survived the wrath of the suns. The Surali only ventured out occasionally to hunt what small prey they found and harvest their produce.

The only three menigari in their clan sang the farewell dirge of the Surali as the suns set – they were Umalama, a tall, dignified woman with an oiled head, shaved to reveal the beauty of her skull, Ferenife, a small man over fifty juzu old, with thick white plaits down to his ears and Ob'bai, a thickset woman with a voice morning birds envied.

The menigari were the mystic-guardians of dreamworlds, who spoke for the dead and mediated between all spirits and men. They wore plain black gowns, draped over with cream lengths of cloth embroidered with their indigenous geometry, wrought in fine ochre-yellow-green beads and rare gold thread.

Their eyes were shut and it sounded like they could see Erigiga crossing over into Eh'wauizo. The song was an aching call that looped up into the air, eating space with its powerful grief as it cast its echo against a darkening gold sky.

By the time it finished unspooling from their mouths, those who needed to, had to have collected the ash of the deceased in small kalabashes as was the tradition. They turned their backs to the pyre and started on their way back to the caves, the nexus of their clan.

Many million juzu after life unspooled on the first planet in her cradle, after the first organisms evolved, stood upright, then congregated and flourished into empires in their doubled light, Juah-āju and Zuúv'ah, the twin suns that nurtured all life went mad.

The rippling coronas of fire that rang out from their bodies washed across the five worlds in deathly bright sunrises that neither the menigari who were sensitive to the essence of all things, nor the maadiregi who could sometimes hear the conversations between Juah-āju and Zuúv'ah with their magic and instruments, anticipated.

The great Sauúti civilization, along with its histories and repositories of knowledge were erased in the five bes that the suns flared, breathing heat and flame across the surfaces of the worlds without discrimination.

Those caught between worlds, transporting goods between the planets were the first to go, consumed by sunfire. They perished, along with all communications satellites and orbital magic stations.

Ekwukwe, the planet of cavernous chambers had the highest rate of survival. It was as if the deep cool hollows of the planet had been created in anticipation of this explosive moment in their cosmic history, so that as the heat increased in the caverns closer to the surface, the populace of Ekwukwe scattered downwards, deeper towards the center of the planet where the air was cooler but the echoes more damning.

They practiced silence as their maadiregi prayed, casting protective spells over the caves that they hid in by snapping fingers that echoed like quiet thunders around them. The uroh-ogi soothed the burns of those who had not been able to move fast enough when the heat came crashing down.

After three days inside the crust of their planet, they all went to sleep exhausted by their wait for the blitz of sunfire to abate.

A few cities on Órino-Rin, aided by deft maadiregi with a high-range of adaptive technologies, managed to harness the roar of sunfire to quickly create vast dome shields around their cities, which they filled with coolants like low-hanging rainclouds. They attempted to evacuate their surviving citizens into these domed cities, but as in all disasters where nature towers monstrous over the inhabitants of the natural world, only those who found the guiding hand of luck made good of the shelter, and survived the swelter through all five bes.

In Mahwé, the maadiregi went into hiding and the people and wild-life struggled to find the shade of subterranean mines. Others crawled beneath the moist earth between the roots of trees whose canopies were slowly burning to ash under waves of heat rushing over the land, as the ejections from the milder sister-sun that the planet orbited, Zuúv'ah, were less destructive to life than those of the burning eye that was Juah-āju, who nearly licked clean all water and life from the forests and oceans of the worlds in her orbit, Ekwukwe and Órino-Rin.

In far orbit, Zezépfeni, despite having a planetary shield to defend against the angry rocks that whizzed through its atmosphere, was not spared of the flaring of the sister suns, unable to adapt to the rapid rise temperatures in time to prevent the spontaneous combustion of the driest and most combustible materials in their cities and homes.

A few clans on Wiimb-ó were guided to safety by their maadiregi, who risked their lives, using the untethered sonic energies to wield a magic to open doors in the air that led them to places underground, cool with streams flush with fish and plants that needed no sun.

There the blitz of the suns couldn't burn them.

There, they were by themselves. All alone.

II

Ikululu led the clan back home, speaking a pathfinder. Their bare feet sank into the pillowy moss that grew where the earth pushed itself aside for a path to form, leading them the quickest way home. The overgrown forests that rose too thick around them were beginning to come alive with the trembling growl of the kunkun, a ferocious large cat that favored warm flesh and blood. Other yips and rustles in the branches revealed burning eyes and sharp claws that meant it would prove fatal to be outside by nightfall.

Ikululu was now First Maadiregi, the one who would continue the excavation and growing of the fragment of sound magic that Erigiga had inherited from Badede's poor memory in sacred congress at Idakeroro, the pocket of no sound hidden at the farthest reach of the caves that Ikululu's clan lived in. A place also known as The Silence.

It was in The Silence that Erigiga expanded his fragment of the sound magic, after many juzu of seeking inside his own mind according to the instructions of his teacher, Badede, who had similarly gotten his own memory-faded fragment from his teacher when the clans had lived above ground and the maadiregi had been capable of feats forgotten in the trauma of death and a sudden separation.

This was how it had always been.

All people were born with a fragment of the Mothersound within them but only those who learned how could wield it as magic.

The maadiregi sought the Word deep inside their spirits where it was believed the Mother Herself rested, and when they found their Voice (the tiny fragment of the Mothersound that belonged to them, that She spoke to them and through which she gave them power), they uttered it once to themselves and were immediately able to understand the way the magic would extend forward, through its private workings in their bodies.

It was as if from the mouth of the first maadiregi to find their Word came a letter, and all the maadiregi that came after them added their own letters to that of those before them, and an indescribable utterance grew, giving its knowers a great power.

When the suns screamed fire and only Badede and two other maadiregi survived, there was a severance of that line of the Word that was leading them back to the full power of the original Mothersound. So it came to be that the utterance and its attendant power shrank, and from the incomplete lessons and barely-there fragment that Badede gave him, Erigiga had only been able to pathfind, until he discovered his Voice and gained the skill to also locate essential sustenance and obscure the sights of predators.

The burial party arrived at the mouth of the cave and the three menigari turned to the skies to say a prayer to the night, speckled darkness overhead from which the Mother saw all. They also asked that Eh'wauizo, the spirit realm, accept their brother-maadiregi wholly and without complaint, before they all walked into the caves.

Inside the first cave, an entrance tunnel, it was black with only the mild glowing network of bioluminescent liliche on the walls to help them forward. They were descending into more blackness as they moved, until right behind Ikululu, Akokore, one of the junior apprentices of Erigiga who had started his apprenticeship nearly five juzu after Ikululu first began, spoke his Word and a bright fire bloomed around his right fist, making a tiny ringing sound. He lifted it up and they all continued to walk forward under the light of his blood-red flame.

Ikululu felt bile roughen his gut, anger rushing up to his heart. He could almost hear himself screaming at Akokore to put out his fire, but that was the reason for his boil. All the three junior maadiregi that had started training under Erigiga, the newest starting just barely three juzu ago, had expanded the fragment of the sound magic that Erigiga had given them and emerged with their own abilities.

How would he lead them as First Maadiregi if he could not even boast a skill set beyond that copied from, and wielded through the

Word of his teacher, who was now gone on to become an ancestor wind that could only whisper through the menigari from Eh'wauizo?

The Silence wasn't easily reached and it was expected that a maadiregi would find their Word upon their first vigil at its lightless, soundless center.

Erigiga had assured him that he would find his Word after his first vigil, where he had sat in The Silence for three bes. He heard nothing but the rumble of his hungry and thirsty thoughts and the echo of Erigiga's Word as it circled his head.

Yet, no addition to it came from within him.

The Mother did not whisper any new sound to Ikululu that would have earned him his place in line as a worthy successor of the craft of the maadiregi.

When he'd given up and left, he'd met Erigiga at the mouth of the path that led to The Silence, waiting for him, leaning on his staff and his janlele. His always-kind teacher had said, "Give it time," with no judgement and led him back to a bowl of rich kalabash and shining fish stew.

Ikululu had realized then that the one who passed on the fragment would know when their Word had been expanded on. That Erigiga had died without feeling and knowing Ikululu's expansion on his Word made Ikululu feel like his heart was a covered pot of frying fishes and peppers, emotions waiting to explode if not let out to air.

They cleared the long tunnel and reached the residential cave, where the other members of the clan were gathered, seated on logs around a smoldering fire that the last janlele slept by.

Akokore put his fiery hand down, and it dimmed to nothing until only coal fire lit the high walls of the cave. The sleepy people rose and gathered around the mourners. Parents and siblings offered their condolences to Ikululu and Oounkan and then collected their maadiregi children, taking them back to lay in the warm shelters cut into the sheer walls of the cave.

Ikululu watched them leave.

Akokore was held at the shoulders by his uroh-ogi mother. Sesewa, the slim young woman who had expanded Erigiga's Word to gain the skill of great physical strength was embraced by her father. Ji'isinu, the other young apprentice whose expanded Word could create living illusions in those who heard her speak, left with her sisters.

Ikululu felt both responsibility and shame. "Don't worry now." Oounkan said. His dear old friend hadn't left his side since they first met as young students. "You'll do just fine teaching them."

"I must find my Word tonight, or I will be unable to stand before them as teacher, let alone First Maadiregi."

"You've started again. Your Word, your Word, your Word. You must take it easy. Do you not remember what Erigiga said to you before he died?"

"What he had always said, ever since I first saw the spirit moons: to have patience. That I must learn to wait. But I've watched all of you... even the children that came after us, enter the Silence and return bearing your own Words, your own gifts that you have used to better this clan, used to claim your right as maadiregi and yet here I stand, the so-called first student, unable to do more than wield the Word my teacher taught me."

"Ikululu, do not let old anger infect your work. As thrilling as it can be, ours is also a craft that requires great patience. At least, try and get some sleep. It has been a rough couple bes."

"Oounkan. Not only did you find your Word on second try after making me feel like we were in the same boat of slow learning. You went and got betrothed. Right now, your companion waits for you. You are loved. You have a warm home."

Omilomi who could hear but had no voice, was waiting, quiet and pensive as ever, under the blue cloth of the uroh-ogi, a short distance away from where the discussing men stood apart from the living spaces, where firelight shuttered behind the bark walls of the huts that made up the clan, as families turned down for the night.

The maadiregi conversed beside the streams that cut through the cave system, the ones that terminated inside The Silence, feeding a small motionless lake.

Oounkan looked to Omilomi where he stood, looking toward the warmth of the clustered huts. "Don't guilt me for standing by the heart that the ancestors have given to me. I insist that you rest tonight and tomorrow, we and the menigari discuss what to do. There must be a reason your Word has not come yet. What if Erigiga is to bring an answer to you from Eh'wauizo? Now more than ever you must have patience. I bid you good rest."

"If you don't let me go, you will become their teacher, Oou-"

But Oounkan had already walked away. He and Omilomi drifted shoulder-to-shoulder across the black sandy floor of the cave, until they reached their shelter and disappeared inside.

Ikululu began to think of the journey to The Silence. It took two bes and there was barely any illumination, except at intervals where shafts of light sliced down into the blackness from cracks in the rocks above.

He could make it there and back in time for his absence to have not been missed. He believed in Oounkan's ability to keep the others distracted. He couldn't even bring himself to visit the cave reserved for the First Maadiregi which he would have to take over, where Erigiga's clothes and tools and charms hung from the walls like strange stalactites.

Inside him pulsed a need to venture down to the Silence now now now.

He moved forward to begin his journey, leaving behind the warmth of the clan, following the streams as they snaked deeper into the depths of the continent of Suraral.

When the firelight of the clan fell away, Ikululu felt the first flash of fear in his heart. He looked up and nearly fell back in terror; the menigari (who never seemed to want to be seen apart) stood before him in the shadows, clad only in their black wool gowns.

"You think only of yourself, maadiregi." Ferenife said, standing a foot in front of his sisters.

"Do you not know the gift of holding on to the Word of your ancestor? Can you not appreciate it more fully now that he is gone beyond, to Eh'wauizo?"

Their voices seemed to be detached from their bodies. Ikululu could barely see their mouths move. He could barely see their faces.

"No. I want my Word to come to me... now... as soon as possible."

"Well then you will have to wait two more bes. You are at a disadvantage."

The menigari didn't move but Ikululu could feel the wall of their presence, pushing against his will. Ferenife continued. "Vuiili-ki and Vuiili-ku are swollen, but they are not yet full."

"Wait, until the spirit moons are full and Eh'wauizo is nearer."

"Then all the ancestors can breathe into you true."

"Ikululu, wait."

After their suns blazed and brutalized their civilization, the peoples of Sauúti were bereft. All communications were broken: between people of different planets, between maadiregi and the Mothersound, between their souls and the rhythms of their planets. Even between their bodily selves as a people, there was a muteness. A refusal among survivors to do more than huddle together for warmth.

Those who weren't deafened by the planet-trembling roars of the flare or set to looking about wide-eyed for sounds they were missing, cradled their heads and wished the piercing dissonant ringing set off by the catastrophe of the stars inside their ears would stop.

So much life was gone.

They could sense the mourning of all creation, even though they didn't venture to the surface for an entire juzu after the initial flare. They could feel the worlds shaken, grieving as if they feared to spin on their own axes or orbit around the shine of the violent star twins.

They had lost everything.

Most awful was the devastation of the rich clusters of their clans and towns. With the loss of their menigari went the understanding of

Eh'wauizo, the spiritworld that lay beside reality like a sheer veil beside a body.

Their knowledge of cosmology and history and more, painstakingly accrued and finessed over too many juzu to follow by the tongues of the raevaagi, went to the grave with the bodies of those dead historians.

They lost their strongest connections to the Mother, when most of the maadiregi sacrificed their lives to ensure the survivors made it to the watery cave-systems.

Yes, there remained surviving raevaagi, menigari, uroh-ogi and maadiregi scattered across the worlds, but those they had lost had left a reduction deep enough to be sensed broadly in the aftermath of apocalypse.

The loss felt vast enough that those who remained alive with knowledge of these crafts became living, grieving ghosts.

But even though they could only glimpse the extent of the destruction that the coronal flares of the suns brought to Wiimb-ó alone, and even there on their feral green world, they could only observe its effects on the small antipodean continent of Suraral, they knew that those that survived and those that had not were being weighed on the pans of a scale. Measured as they began calculating the possibility of recovery and rejuvenation.

They knew that the Mother would not completely abandon her wounded offspring and that those remaining with the knowledge of the otherworld and the magic derived from the Mothersound would have to work hard to regain some of what had been lost.

It would start small, in finding those who would take over the mantles of the dead as quickly as possible. Once the people had emerged from the shelters they had hidden in. Once they had shaken the dust from their eyes, and begun to heal their wounds.

Then the work would begin – of recall, reconnection, resurrection.

III

Badede, the maadiregi with a poor memory who taught Erigiga the way of the sound magic, had witnessed the flaring of the suns with his naked eye.

Out in the wild forests with his janlele, harvesting some fruit for his clan, he witnessed the fastest sunrise of his life, even though it was past noon on Suraral.

The blinding wave of light rose and washed across the sky, making a roaring noise that caused his water dog to bark alarm in a way he had never heard since the pup was given to him by his own teacher on the completion of his maadiregi initiation.

Badede was unaware he was watching a solar flare move across the sky, until the first front of heat washed over him like some fiery embrace.

The barking of the janlele continued, as it followed the fire rushing white and hot across the blue sky. Badede had been given the janlele, like all the other maadiregi who owned them, as a companion to guide them in the dense forests of Suraral but also to bolster their weak voices when they needed more volume, decibels to ignite an incantation.

The bark of the large sleek dog, its back covered with shimmering scales like a fish, collected in Badede's hand like a pulsing heart. With those sounds and a whispered fragment of his Word, he twisted open a portal back to the clan, the janlele leaping in after him.

On emerging at his clan city, he and the other maadiregi located themselves by the sounds of their janlele and began opening portals to wet underground caves as waves of white fire roared above. Each maadiregi stood at the center of their clan city and pulled open a portal, a rippling disturbance in space. The confused, sweaty people of Suraral who could barely keep their eyes open in the brightness followed the barks of the janlele. Those who made it were saved.

The maadiregi had underestimated how hot it would get and most of them were smothered by the too-bright air, their portals collapsing and trapping them and the unfortunate Surali who had been too late to hear the bark of the janlele above ground. They burned to char in the increasing heat of the roaring sunbursts.

Erigiga had told this vivid tale to Ikululu more than a hundred times during his apprenticeship, over and over to remind him of how quickly maadiregi had to think and act in times of communal emergency, especially now that the population of the janlele had dwindled to endangerment and their behaviors towards people had changed.

He also told it because it was all Badede seemed to remember from the time before, a story he'd repeated so much it became a sort of lesson to Erigiga. Ikululu was lucky – his voice was deep and resonant, perfect for the work of maadiregi, even though his teacher's voice had been a light rasp like that of his teacher before him.

IV

The spirit moons emerged full in five bes.

Those gifted enough to see them watched, as Vuiili-ki and Vuiili-ku grew full in the sky looking smeared, distant, and submerged in some thin sea of milk. They contrasted the crystal whiteness of Javuiili, the planet's physical moon. Its open face was also full, casting a bright light that all could see.

Ikululu cleared out Erigiga's hut and tried his best not to succumb to the sorrow that spun in his gut at the sight of objects and artifacts that his teacher had been fond of.

He wrapped most of Erigiga's belongings in a cloth and took them to his own smaller hut, which was cut into the cave right next to his teacher's rectangular abode.

Ikululu moved his own personal belongings over and draped himself in one of the three things he had kept of Erigiga's; a fire-colored handwoven blanket that had kept him warm in the biting cold that descended into the caves when the nearer sun had set and only the distant light of its sister could be seen.

Many times, before he carved his own hut, when he had believed Erigiga was his father, Ikululu had slept off at his teacher's feet and woken up to find himself covered in the thick cloth, which always smelt of night peppers and tobacco.

He put the cloth to his face and inhaled its scent as he looked at the two other objects on the floor before him.

A cube of wood, one side strung with an array of neat crisscrossing lines of taut string that made a sound like moonlight when strummed. Like the janlele, which currently slept with its siblings in a heap around the dead coals out in the open cave, this instrument could be used to initiate sonic magic with little use of the voice.

Erigiga's voice had worsened the older he had grown and he had built the instrument to help him, among many things, see, on his journeys to the Silence. For when it was struck at the fullness of the spirit moons in pitch darkness, it radiated a cool, pale light.

The other object was Erigiga's true gift to the clans of Suraral. It displayed an aspect of being maadiregi that was more practiced in the cloud and mountain cities of Órino-Rin, that of being an architect and technician.

Besides the embodied magic that came with learning one's Word, there were also gifts of creation, knowledge and understanding that came through to them slower, helping the maadiregi create a range of technologies that only they could have envisioned. This was often their larger role in their communities and societies. How much of the technologies lost in the solar catastrophe had been built.

Erigiga's technology, the zonne, was made from the largest species of the kalabash with a thin segment of the sphere cut out and the soft meat of the insides scooped away. Inside the core was suspended a strange nucleus that Erigiga had strung with a thread no eye could see: a contraption made of lava stone, wood, and a clear crystal from the cave, flinted and chipped, teeth locked together.

Erigiga first spoke a Word to set it alive, so that it began to turn and bristle around itself, then he laid a membrane sourced from the stomach of a feral buffalo over it and sealed it with twine and bone glue. He carved five symbols at an equidistance on its round body. Each symbol represented a sound or tone that could be made as users hit the zonne thrice, after which it would cast its geological spells of repellence, clearing or attraction.

The zonne was how the Surali survived when they went up to the mutated forests that had grown back too fast on Suraral after the suns had burned down their world. Forests that continued to grow redder in tooth and dense with trouble with each passing juzu. It seemed every other vine was a poisonous serpent waiting to strike and seemingly ordinary insect bites could be followed by the smell of rotted flesh.

The zonne allowed them to stay on the surface for some time and all the clans had at least one.

Ikululu put the zonne down, next to the moon-box that Erigiga had failed to give a name before his passing. It was less than half a day to the fullness of the spirit moons when his journey to The Silence would start.

He wrapped Erigiga's warm orange cloth tighter around himself. His belly grumbled from all the work he had done, and he walked out of the First Maadiregi's hut and ambled over to Oounkan and Omilomi's where laughter and hot full meals were always assured.

It is said that only those given special eyes, by the ancestors dearly departed to Eh'wauizo, can see the twin spirit moons clear as the living see Javuiili. This was often how those with aptitude in the spirit-crafts were chosen for apprenticeship.

There was another path that led to The Silence, one that was used when the Surali had thrived above ground. Once, it was a smooth clear way, but now, it moved through thorny overgrowth and groves of wild fruit trees heady with a sleepy nectar, through marsh and muddy river, always just meters away from the sunken mountain underneath in which cave systems and the hidden Surali who lived in them thrived.

Its mouth was a waterfall.

Ikululu left as soon as Vuiili-ki and Vuiili-ku shone bright enough for the janlele, who also saw the moons, to run shimmering out of the cave and begin their howling volleys.

This was when the moon-box produced arcs of clearest light at the lightest strum and the menigari's eyes lost their black.

They had no warnings or advice for him when he told them he would not be taking the sacred route underground, meant only for the learning maadiregi.

The three veiled seers urged him to go as quickly as he could, for the towering gates of Eh'wauizo would open to the living for only a sliver of time, while the moons were full and aligned.

Ikululu ran out of the cave alone, running past those who stood at its mouth to look at Javuiili – a fish disappearing into the glowing mists that shrouded the forest.

He beat the zonne thrice and opened his mouth to make the tone of clearing. It sounded like a hawk screaming. Clad in doeskin shorts that reached his knees and the remnants of body armor from before the flare, he disappeared into the wet slithering forests.

Beneath his feet, the pathfinding moss of Erigiga's magic made sure he stepped on no thorn or rock. Like an arrow, he flew in the night. Under the powerful shine of the moons only he could see and feel, with the zonne slung across his chest, radiating pulses that he felt in his bones, thrums that made him feel less like a vulnerable Surali maadiregi out in violent jungle and more like a beast fulfilling itself.

Through the fruit grove he went, with creepers slashing themselves apart at his approach and predating kunkun crashing away from his path. He caught the eye of a resting reptile – the Akakikikaka – a glowing slashed circle, yellow like unripe nightpeppers, tall as a cavemouth. It was believed by the uroh-ghi who sought its poison glands, that the Akakikikaka's eye was able to see across planets, even beyond.

This didn't stop Ikululu from running. He only stopped when the mosspath led to the slurry of a marsh flowing before him; bubbling, sucking and hungry.

Ikululu watched surprised as the pathfinding threw a length of moss that looked blue in the lunar glow, over the moving surface of the marsh and he found himself bouncing in a light jog across the mudwater, beneath strange trees with long white hair, filled with adundun, tiny beasts that slept upside down, whose cry it is said turns the hearer into resonant stone.

Through the curtains of treehair, he went; zonne pulsing, pathfinding birthing moss beneath his feet, his heart like a bird's, high above his body. The hawkcries he had opened his journey with seemed to ring across the entirety of his body into Suraral, into the body of Wiimb-ó, up into the cosmos, into the soft black eternal body of the Mother.

The dark wet rock of the sunken mountains that were home to his clan's cave and The Silence suddenly rose into the periphery of his vision until at the end of his long rippling run over the slurry mud, he stood on the other side of the marsh, covered in wisps of thin tree hair, looking at the waterfall that covered the mouth of The Silence.

The pathfinding continued and he began to run across it again, when he slipped and slid down the moss faster than the magic was unspooling. He tumbled down through wild bush and sheer rock, gulping air, to land face down on the soft sands that banked the pool of the waterfall.

The waterfall had no name.

Ikululu lifted his head and inhaled, his beard thick with the soft sand of the banks.

He watched as the moonlit water lapped mere inches from his jaw and he could see the zonne floating in the rippling water at the foot of the wide, gentle waterfall. This was the large pool of water it quietly fed as it fell out of a curve worn into the small hill of piled rocks that once stood in a mountain above Suraral, according to the raevaagi. It had sunk, shrinking to its current form during an earthquake, a shuddering of Wiimb-ó many thousand juzu before the flare.

Ikululu rose onto four limbs like an animal and crawled forward until he slipped into the gleam of the water. It seemed warm to him after the cold of the rushing forest he had just slipped out of.

He saw no fish or water beast, because the zonne seemed to still be working. Swimming, he reached the zonne and placed it on his shoulder. There was the mouth of a cave, wet with rock teeth. It was hidden behind the fine sheen of the falling water which looked like some purified liquid crystal, pouring down forever with a soft endless murmur.

As the beauty of the falling water entranced him and he looked up to see the twin spirit moons and their physical cousin shining down on him across a velvet sky, he had an eerie feeling of being watched.

He quickly swam forward until he was out of the moonlight and in the shadow of the remainder of the nameless mountain, closer towards the center of the curve of the waterfall, until the sluice of the water was pouring directly in front of him.

He was looking for the perfect point to pass through the curtain of water and into the cave behind, through which he could reach the underground lake that fringed The Silence, when he saw them rising just behind the waterflow.

He washed out his eyes but they persisted - hundreds of towering hooded wraiths, some perfectly still, some undulating like smoke, filling the mouth of the cave as far as his eye could roam, and down around where their knees would be, a crowd of men and women with all shades of their skin polished to its finest wealth.

They were dressed in white wrappers with ochre, green and gold accents fringing the hems. Their heads bore fine filigree crowns of a gold that seemed to be wrought from sunshine. Some of them were smiling at nothing and it nearly blinded Ikululu to look at their joy through the falling water but he didn't look away until he saw –

Erigiga.

Ikululu's eyes were not deceiving him. He would recognize the horned staff (once wooden, now that same sunshine gold as the crown about his bald head) and large white beard anywhere.

Ikululu sputtered in the water. "Baba!" He shouted as he struggled, tossing the zonne away to concentrate on swimming towards the blurry crowd just out of reach, to climb through the waterfall and out of the lake to maybe see the only father he ever knew, to see his teacher again.

Son, stay where you are! The voice rang, many-mouthed, loud enough to gently tremble the mountain, the waters and even the bones in Ikululu's body.

The pale wraiths remained still, forms billowing without wind. Erigiga continued speaking from beyond, his voice once considered weak in life, now like thunder in the afterlife. *If you break the membrane, we will depart from you.*

Ikululu went still. "Help me, Baba. Please. Since you left me, I have been lost. My Word is yet to come to me. How can I be First Maadiregi with no Word of my own? I am going to The Silence to try again, for as long as I need to."

I know all this, Kulu. I am dead, and I can see more here than I once saw in life with those half-blind eyes and that always hungry body.

Your problem is that you think the Word is yours alone.

It comes through you, and after that, all you become able to do in body and creation, by the grace of the Mother, must be done for the growth and to the glory of her children. You. Us. The people that you aid.

Only then will you be able to enjoy the uses of your own Word.

"But I have not even had a glimpse of any power. I am the last maadiregi yet to know his Word. All I have is yours, father." Ikululu's voice broke as he floated before the apparition and the sounds.

The zonne circled his body in the water.

If you only knew the things that others have gone through trying to find their Word. I understand more than you think. The bitterness of this incapacity to do what the others seem to do so easily, the ragged hollow in memory that you know as a childhood, your anger at life itself.

They block your hearing deeply, as does your nascent capacity to wield your aspect of the Mothersound. They are like two inverse essences not allowing you breathe.

{breathe} The ancestors behind Erigiga spoke the word once. It was like a wave of calm rushing over Ikululu's core. He inhaled.

Many things you knot yourself over don't matter, because you know nothing about yourself or the worlds around you.

Come closer now. Come to us.

Erigiga's voice was an ocean of velvet to Ikululu. He slipped under the water and shot himself down, through the gurgling tumble where the waterfall pooled.

On the other side, he swam to the surface and found himself lifted to his feet by the water. It deposited him on wet rock before the ancestors and the wraiths that rose behind them like towers of unmoving smoke.

The shine of their apparitions was closer now and it caused Ikululu to lose all thought of shame, all heaviness, all sense. As each of the smiling ancestors turned their faces to him, he could feel the cut of their joy, like hot sugar from fruit against his insides.

Those unsmiling and those smiling drew closer to him, short and tall they all towered over his bulky form, and he was submerged in some unspeakable warmth that seemed billions of juzu old and yet fresh as a new spring of water.

You emerged from the cradle of life under such rough circumstances. Your breath is precious and beyond us here – the Mother always embraces you, nurtures you, knows you, keeps you.

Though you have always felt lost knowing no father or mother. Lost growing up under the ground, in a wilderness. We all who were maadi-regi in life are your mother. We are your father.

Ikululu closed his eyes as Erigiga's voice continued speaking, now louder inside the caves, echoing.

Listen.

Ikululu heard a sound, spoken now by a ragged voice that was not Erigiga's. By its consonant hook and wide vowel, he realized it was a Word. Another voice followed, female and high. It took that first Word and expanded it adding a *hro*. Another followed adding a *und*. A third. Fourth. Fifth. Sixth. Then, they began to come in a flurry, overlapping and echoing like birdsong from trees outside the cavemouth in the morning.

The Word expanded from mouth-to-mouth until it became a blurred streaming, screaming incantation, a sentence on fire.

Ikululu listened until the bedlam of words rushing into his ears that made no sense began to shrink into sense, until he could see in his mind, see a thin reflection of the First Exhalation, the cosmic breadth of the Mother's Mouth opening opening opening.

Then, silence.

He opened his eyes and he was far away from the waterfall, far from a huddle of ancestor-maadiregi, each sharing their Word with him until it melted into gibberish in his throat.

He found himself at the center of The Silence.

He sat on dry sand that he could not see and closed his eyes once again to listen for his own Word.

V

Ikululu walked back home from The Silence, through the inner path used only by apprentice-maadiregi. His gait was slow and unhurried. He neither slipped on wet rock, nor cut himself on any sharp ends. It was as though he could see in the dark.

Gone was the restlessness, and the arrogance hiding his wounded pride. There was no overt swagger to prevent anyone from seeing his shame. Ikululu walked true, so sure was his sight, even in no light.

The zonne was tucked firmly beneath his right armpit and he put it to the ground when he walked into the cave where the clan was barely stirring.

He could feel the rising of the first sun, and almost taste the trailing of its twin as morning approached. The clan no longer had a name, like all the other clans hiding inside rocky groves in the belly of Suraral.

The Surali saw themselves as a large tribe with many limbs that had been blessed with all of the Island continent of Suraral as far it spread, before its borders touched one of the seven oceans of Wiimb-ó.

Ikululu clenched his teeth, narrowed his lips and began to whistle a tune that only the maadiregi could hear. It swam eerie across the cave. One by one, several doors nestled in the nooks of the rough cave wall and near the dry sands of its floor, opened, and the maadiregi came out.

Oounkan emerged first, then Akokore bearing a fragment of his blood-red flame atop two of his fingers to help him see. The young women, Sesewa and Ji'isinu, emerged last having to sneak through larger spaces filled with sleeping family before they could shift the doors of their huts open.

Three janlele slept near the water and they stirred at the sound, ears rising to quick sharp points, but then went back to sleep, for they were an independent species who chose when to be fond of the maadiregi - the only members of the Surali they once drew close to.

Oounkan's eyes were still sticky with sleep and his cheek rough from where he had pressed his face to the mat he shared with Omilomi.

"I greet you, brother." He said, wiping his eyes as he drew close to Ikululu, who he always seemed to tower over, even though he was only a bare inch taller than him. "It has been seven days, where have you be-..." he stopped his attempt at pretense, and bent down to wash his mouth and face in one of the many streams that flowed in opposite directions, in and out the cave-system.

Oounkan and Ikululu stood on opposite sides of these streams, as the other three maadiregi gathered behind Oounkan.

He rose, face dripping. "'Kululu, what do you bring from the Silence?" He could hardly see his friend's face. Akokore's fire barely cast a light beyond his body.

He continued when there was no reply. "I have been teaching your students about the other things maadiregi can do beside wielding the power of the Word in their bodies."

Ikululu remained silent. The only sound in the cave was the echo of the water as it rushed its way along the streams.

The force of his presence brought a chill to the spines of the apprentices. Oounkan knew something was different; felt that perhaps his brother had finally found what he had sought since they were skinny teenagers, learning the sonic magics and crafting technologies from Erigiga.

"Ikululu?" Without crossing over, Oounkan appeared on the other side of the stream, now standing behind Ikululu. He still stood in front of the three apprentices, with eyes closed as he executed his mirroring. Akokore brightened his fire, opening his fist to throw his red light over their gathering.

Ikululu leapt over the stream and threw himself into Oounkan's arms.

"Quit your mirroring." Ikululu was shaking with an emotion Oounkan couldn't place yet.

"I have been to The Silence. I have seen the smiles of our ancestors in Eh'wauizo. I have found my Word, and what it has brought me will change us all."

It was then that Oounkan knew Ikululu was violently happy, because he started laughing and his corrugated voice filled all the cave with its glee until all who slept, woke from their dreams of living in open air.

When a maadiregi hears their Word through meditation, as an extension of the Word of their teacher or ancestor, they feel in their bodies where it has changed them, an expansion in their minds, the understanding of the new way in which they can begin to architect some new technology that only they see.

The Word becomes a private object that they roll about their tongues marveling at how the modulating of the tone of their voices changes the way the magic manifests in their bones or across the skin. How it's amplified with the introduction of a tool to concentrate or expand it (the singing bowl and the shaved bone)

How they gradually come to recognize the way fragments of the Mothersound manifest in the intent and the feeling of all speakers, both human and other. How even those who do not have the aptitude of the Mothersound vibrate magic alive in the way they use their words.

Thus, they become maadiregi, calculating private mathematics about the power in all sounds, knowing that their Word is but a miniscule fragment of the Mothersound the way a stone was once part of a mountain.

When Ikululu heard his Word and intoned it to rumble through the Silence, he realized something – his Word held echoes of all the Words that he had heard from the ancestors before his seven bes of excavation in The Silence.

It wasn't a thing made only out of the direct essence of his teacher's Word, but from the essence of all the ancestor-maadiregi's Words.

This made it an anomaly.

He knew then that its resultant magic would be something yet to be seen before, even though all that the maadiregi were capable of would always be other than ordinary. Ikululu also understood that it was the first time a Word would be able to be shared among other maadiregi without the need of the sacrament of the teacher-student relationship.

After he rose to his feet in The Silence, seeing in the air where there was no light, the free accumulation of sound like a million fibrous membranes from the split vine of a kalabash, with no end and no beginning, he realized what his Word had done to the air.

And when he clapped, he found that he knew nothing at all about the ways in which the Mothersound could unravel into the fabric of the world, the ways in which the eternal magic could propagate.

First, Ikululu, with a reverence and quietude he had never shown before, took the four maadiregi of his clan out of the cave into the open air of the still-dark morning wild. Dew licked at their ankles as they walked out, all clad in thick garments. He left the zonne behind, which made Oounkan begin to complain, but Ikululu hushed him with a confidently raised palm as they made their way out into coming morning.

They walked away from the cave until they found a plain covered in low grass, moss and rocks. Clouds of biting insects and crawling reptiles were beginning to gather around their presence. The mouth of their home cave could still be seen when they turned back to look for a place to run to.

Ikululu waited until the four other maadiregi stood in a semicircle before him, and before anyone could begin speaking, he intoned his Word out loud. It was a lengthy one that rang with cleft consonants and surfacing vowels, ending in a breathy *ahhhh*.

In the instant that it left his lips, they watched the air around his midriff change.

The power of Ikululu's Word seemed to have filled the air with an oily membrane that drifted, waiting. He touched it and it rippled towards his palm, like water. Closing his eyes and putting both palms forward, the membrane grew dense. He pushed against it and it expanded into a pool. In the rising sun, the membrane caught the light and gleamed like a dull shapeless rainbow.

Ikululu raised one hand, palm facing to the sky, while the other remained down. The membrane followed, then he brought his hands together in a clap and they all watched it blow outwards, away from his body, no longer a membrane but softened into a rushing mist, across the clearing and into the surrounding forest.

All the insects and crawlers, flowed away, scurrying and pushed by the sound of Ikululu's palms hitting one another.

"I just cleared this area, as the zonne would do."

Akokore raised his brows, eyes wide with surprise. "What happens when you leave?"

"Nothing. It is permanent. This magic is not to be used in spurts. If you did it, you would know its extent."

Sesewa, who rarely ever spoke, whispered, "Praise be to the Mother. Why did you bring us here, beyond letting us witness the newfound power of your Word?"

"I am here to teach you how to do the same. That was what the ancestors told me, that whatever I found in The Silence was to be used for the uplift of all in Suraral. You have seen nothing yet. Even I know nothing about how this magic could manifest."

"It relies on your mind. The strength of your dreaming." Oounkan said. He stood behind the three baffled students, perplexed and yet feeling a growing excitement in his chest as the first sun rose full and poured its warmth over the noise of the forest. "But it is yours alone, Ikululu. I could hardly teach you about my mirroring, as much as Sesewa could give you her strength or Ji'isinu show you how she brings forth her waking illusion."

"This Word is different. It is a blessing for all. I got help from all the maadiregi who have walked Suraral. It is meant to be taught and shared. Come close to me, Oounkan."

Ooukan walked forward until he was standing as close to Ikululu as possible. His head was uncovered and his body draped in a large pale-yellow wrapper that exposed his left shoulder, unlike the students who wore the full ankle-length garments peculiar to the maadiregi. Each had colors and patterns particular to the skill and knowledge of the weaver.

Ikululu leaned forward and whispered something into Oounkan's ear. Oounkan gasped, then began panting and clutching his throat. Akokore made to help him but he held a hand up as he coughed deep and loud and then spat out a string of ropy phlegm onto the grass.

"Say it out loud now." Ikululu said.

Oounkan repeated Ikululu's Word out loud and the air around his arms and in front of his stomach grew membranous, oily in the dawn light. He shivered as he closed his eyes and moved his arms up, balling them into fists. Oounkan threw two quick punches into the air before him, and the sound membrane boomed a double thunder in rapid succession. Its force threw Akokore and Ji'isinu to the ground. Sesewa remained standing, the strength of her own Word planting her firmly to the ground as she spoke it.

Oounkan laughed and lifted his hands up to his face as if seeing them clearly for the first time. He waved and the membrane remained. He looked to Ikululu who watched him proudly, though his eyes seemed distant, like he was seeing something more than Oounkan wielding his Word for the first time.

"How did that feel to you? Any sense of drainage?"

"I felt nothing, because it comes from a place beyond me. I just gave it to you."

Oounkan looked to Sesewa who stood looking at Ikululu like she was seeing him for the first time. "Are you willing to receive Ikululu's Word and see what it brings to you?"

"We are just apprentices. Our initiation rites are not complete yet." She said, gesturing towards Akokore and Ji'isinu who were dusting their garments off to stand beside her and also looking at the two elder maadiregi, curiosity and fear lidding their eyes.

"I will go." Ji'isinu said.

Her words were clipped and chosen with utmost care. As a child, her mother had feared she would never speak, and she didn't utter her first word until she was eleven juzu old. She had always seemed locked inside her mind, quiet and pensive, and it was a shock to her parents when Erigiga came knocking at their hut with news of her aptitude and necessary apprenticeship as maadiregi.

"Ikululu brings us new life." She said as she walked up to him in her robe, woven with ripened yellow fruit and blue creepers. He towered a full head over her slight figure. She turned her ear up to him.

"Speak. I listen."

VI

On the day he returned from The Silence, each of the maadiregi from his clan listened to his utterance and learned their way around Ikululu's Word –

Ji'isinu used the membrane to turn her illusions into reality, pulling together fragments of wood, leaf, metal, seed, mud and other loose materials in her vicinity to build real structures projected from her mind.

Akokore became impeccable at circling his fiery palms around until the sound membrane formed into a wide spiral that burned open a portal in the air, leading to distant points on Suraral, reminding Ikululu of the acts of Badede and the maadiregi on the day of the solar catastrophe.

Sesewa became a magnifier of the 'Sound, learning how the membrane was a sonic tissue, how it was capable of emitting a multitude of tones that affected objects at varying tempos and rhythms; clearing the earth, felling trees, taming feral beasts.

Over the time of half a juzu, the young maadiregi, under the leadership of Oounkan's mirror-selves and their fist-flown pulses of energy, began a renovation, building a small town above the ground at the point where Ikululu first spoke to them his sound.

The people of their clan watched them work from the mouth of the cave where they had lived all their lives as Ji'isinu pulled together mud and the trees that Sesewa felled and the Oounkans shattered, compiling them into tall, compact huts and towers with rooms and doors, many times more effective than the crude shacks and hollows they had occupied inside the caves.

The maadiregi did more; they diverted freshwater to flow through the new town, tilled acres of farm for the people of the clan to begin planting crops in less than two days. They even hunted wild goat.

They named their new town Erigiga.

In all this, Ikululu was nowhere to be found.

Ikululu sat in The Silence.

It had called to him the night after he had first shared his sound with the others. He knew that soon, Oounkan and Akokore would begin to travel through the portals that the latter would get even more skilled at creating, to share news of his Word with those of other clans hiding deep underground in other caves that peppered the body of the sunken mountain, surviving by the grace of Erigiga's zonne.

Their maadiregi would come to him, bring their ears to his lips to hear his Word, so that they could gain the power of the sound membrane as it aligned with their own Word and skill.

He would speak it to them, for the ancestors had bid him to do so. To restore some of the glory that the Surali had lost in the rage of the twin suns.

Ikululu knew all this because his Word, the fragment of the Mothersound that he had found and begun to gift to the maadiregi of his clan, was growing.

It was what had pulled him back into The Silence. That, and his desire to know more, to be more than First Maadiregi. He wanted to be the greatest of them all.

It seemed to have more of Itself to tell to him. It whispered of the possibility of its expansion, of immense power which It told him he had barely begun to see. It showed him the future, of Suraral and the great works that the maadiregi would bring to light through the power of Ikululu's Word.

Ikululu followed the developments outside the cave, for now he could walk from The Silence to the now-emptied space where he had grown up in less than ten footsteps.

He stood at the lip of the cave and watched the maadiregi grow in strength and intelligence as they wove his Word around their tongues and built themselves a new world, then returned into the heart of The Silence to continue following his Word, the fragment pulling him out into the ocean of some unfathomable mind, closer and closer, towards the open mouth of the Mother and the inevitability of the fullness of the Mothersound.

The three menigari; Umalama, Ferenife and Ob'bai watched every new bes, from the cool of their new wooden shrine, as maadiregi were brought out of hiding from across Suraral, into the clan of Erigiga, through the bright magic of Akokore's portals.

They watched as they sipped their rich soups, burned their incense, prayed with one eye open and readied themselves. They saw the tired and ragged men taken to the mouth of the cave where their clan had recently exited, where Ikululu still lived and slept.

They had worried that they would have been the ones unable to adapt to above ground life, being sensitive to the moons and the suns and the waters as they were, but the architectures that Ji'isinu built them took their senses into consideration, and the uroh-ogis' need for water, the raevaagis' need for silence.

The town was almost perfect.

The maadiregi came from far and wide to listen to Ikululu's Word.

He always knew when to appear at the cave mouth. His countenance, a new mystery. His eyes rimmed red from no sleep at all. His voice slipping into their ears and sending them into convulsions and states of ecstasy, before they came to their senses, weeping at the realization of the gift they had been given.

Umalama, Ferenife and Ob'bai watched them burn with joy as they returned into the portals to take the new skills of Ikululu's Word back to their clans and for the first time since the suns exhaled their apocalypse across Sauúti, the maadiregi of Suraral were now powerful enough to work magic and guide their clans back into some semblance of an above-ground civilization.

Yet, the menigari were restless, and they didn't know what the source of their unease was until they all went to sleep at the same time, to wake in a dream of the past together.

In this dream, they walked through a vast city filled with living architectures and technologies that they could never have imagined, because they had once been real.

This was the state of Suraral before the solar catastrophes.

In ornate cathedrals, strange copses and geometric shrines, they saw the maadiregi resting in a temple, surrounded by strange technologies. They were being worshiped, as they worshiped the Mother.

They saw them working with the same magic that Ikululu's Word had restored - opening portals, crafting architectures in Suraral and beyond, transforming the world around them.

In these dreams, the maadiregi worked without ceasing, building, clearing, building, expanding, until a great brightness fell from the sky and put an end to their city – and woke the menigari at once from their deep, deep sleep.

Knowing now what they were witnessing with the renewed power of the maadiregi, Umalama went visiting Oounkan on behalf of the menigari to share of their collective dream, expressing a need for moderation and reverence in their use of the power that Ikululu's Word had returned to their world.

"You cannot put reins on something that hungers to touch our lives. The ancestors themselves chose Ikululu to restore this power to us. I sense nothing of that caliber in the dreams you describe but if you have any warnings then take them to Ikululu."

"Your tone is too cold, Oounkan. Are you already getting carried away by your pride, in these works that you say you do by the grace of your ancestors?"

Oounkan, who was mirroring to figure out something he was building on the ground before him, didn't respond. All three Oounkans were distracted.

"No one ever sees him outside of that cave." Umalama said

"Menigari, take it up with him." The second and third Oounkan said on either side of Umalama where they stood, watching Oounkan fiddle with the technology that he believed would bring the light (but not the heat) of a fire into a transparent vessel.

Umalama left knowing that Ferenife and Ob'bai would have no luck with finding or speaking to Ikululu in the cave where he was gradually becoming shadow.

He was doing something stranger, working in more complex ways than his ancestors had ever done, down in those depths.

The menigari could feel the weight of its impending doom.

VII

After the last maadiregi in Suraral had listened to Ikululu's Word, he disappeared from the bucolic life that began to define the expanding town of Erigiga.

In the depth of The Silence, the fragment of his Word grew – no longer to his mind, his Word, but an utterance approaching the first exhalation of the Mother.

Ikululu began to experience much that made his understanding collapse and words fail. Visitors began to walk past him in the dark, their footless bodies drifting past him like winds. Living lights blinked on and off in the periphery of his eyes.

It could not be his ancestors to whom he was dedicating this life's work of his who shouted "Fool!" and "You will never know" and "Heathen!" and "Stop your search for that which must not be sought," in the meat of his mind.

Their noise did not make him desist from drifting closer towards the mouth of the Mother. Ikululu saw the Mothersound spinning brighter and wilder than any sun between lips whose motion had made the universe itself. Lips whose mercy had brought creation to being.

Ikululu drifted closer to the mouth and the 'Sound.

Soon, he was surrounded by towering beings; therianthropes with heads of janlele and kunkun, firehawk and serpent.

They said nothing, but the sound that their eyes made seemed to run through his guts and his bones and his mind.

Assassins! Set to prevent him from finding out this Truth. This utterance with which he would transform and bring glory to the whole of Suraral, Wiimb-ó, even all of Sauúti. To become the greatest maadiregi to ever live.

If only he could be strong enough, he told himself, as the cacophony within him grew into a nightmare, a storm of teeth that aimed to eviscerate him from within.

If only he would surrender, persevere enough through this eon of judgement, for the eyes of gods were cruel whips and his body was nothing and his search was meaningless and who was he to think he could ever become someone that rose past the unknown gods into the Mothersound?

And what was a sound?

What was this sound, easy on his ear like a morning wind yet turning his every cell into a hollow out of which echoed meaninglessness?

What had no mouth?

What spoke but had no mouth?

"The Mother has no mouth." Ikululu said to Oounkan, as they stood in the cave where they had met almost two juzu before, after he had first returned from The Silence with his own Word.

"What?"

"She has no mouth, though she speaks and shows me her teeth."

"Too much has happened in your absence, brother. You must know what you have done for us. All of Suraral is waiting to see you.

Akokore's portals will make a tour quick. You must see with your own eyes, the fire that your Word has ignited across the land."

"We must give the Mother a mouth to speak again so she can remake us, restore us. Give us true life."

"Ikululu! You have been in The Silence too long." Oounkan's fury was dampened by his confusion. "The menigari came talking about your Word and the great power it held. How we had to be careful with its use. I sent them away... but as I'm seeing... your behavior makes me share their concern. What have you been doing all these bes, wandering these caves?"

"I have no need for an ordinary life in those towns and villages. I have always sought and now that I have found purpose, I am a servant to the making of our collective glory."

"No. You must do more than be First Maadiregi. There are things to enjoy inside and beyond this magic of ours that you must know about. If you lose yourself, it would be a blow to all of us, Ikululu. Now is the time for you to rest in the work that you have done. To live in the life of your Word."

"We are so close, Oounkan. We could remake everything. We could all become wielders of the Word, both maadiregi and the ordinary people. The Mother just needs our mouth because she doesn't have one."

Oounkan turned away from Ikululu. His eyes filled with a quiet sorrow at the cadence of his brother's voice. He knew now that the menigari were right. Ikululu was lost in the power of his Word.

Oounkan mirrored himself, and all his seventeen bodies surrounded Ikululu. Their voices were calm as they bore down on him.

"Listen to me. You need to rest. You need to be among your people who love you like a king! When last did you eat a meal that wasn't scraped from cave walls?"

"No. I need to free... the... us."

The Oounkans uttered Ikululu's Word and the dull blue light that filled the cave air became oily, membranous around their arms and their bellies. They lifted their fists and the sound membrane brightened and shrank to the balls of their fists as they toughened their stances, faces roughened by anger, fatigue and a need to just end whatever this situation was that Ikululu had found himself in.

Ikululu became aware too late.

The Oounkans flung, threw and slapped the concussions from their fists onto him in air punches.

A scattered drumming of impact on the First Maadiregi's body, weak from too much time in The Silence bloomed through the air.

Ikululu went down fast.

After he had fallen, the thunder of the Oounkan's fists still resonated through the cave, causing dust to fall from the ceiling alongside tiny pebbles and pieces of rock.

As their echo subsided, the Oounkans moved closer to the body lying on the ground, beaten flat.

The true Oounkan opened his eyes and bent to turn his friend's body over. The uroh-ogi would make space to heal him from this and everything else that plagued him.

As Oounkan set his body face up, Ikululu's hand went like a vise around Oounkan's wrist and he pulled him down, to bring them face to face.

"You must have forgotten... from who you got this power. Have you ever wondered if a snake can be poisoned by its own fang?"

Oounkan was too stunned to answer, and Ikululu's second hand came up, pushing them to sit on the ground. He now held onto Oounkan's neck tight, cutting off his breath and his mirroring.

The other bodies dissipated to dust like an abrupt exhale.

"Listen to me." Ikululu stared deep into Oounkan's frightened eyes. "You will bring all the maadiregi who have heard my Word out to the desert plain beyond the sunken mountains when all the moons shine full, at midnight."

"Of course, Ikululu, whatever you ask, I will do." Oounkan squeaked, eyes void of his own seeing. His mind suddenly lost to the sound of Ikululu's voice, tethered like a janlele to a leash.

Before midnight, the message reached all the maadiregi, of a gathering under the now-visible spirit moons of Wiimb-ó, on the vast desert plain beyond the place they knew as home, where nothing lived except enormous sand turtles that burrowed down where there was no light, who were host to a parasitic race of microscopic humanoids that spoke through their hosts' mouths when they surfaced.

Most of the maadiregi arrived through the portals that Akokore had taught them to smith open between space-time. Others rode beasts of land and air that they had tamed and bonded with.

They left their clans to be tended by the uroh-ogi and the menigari, who also had their own rituals to perform under the spirit-light of Vuiili-ki and Vuiili-ku.

Ikululu stood alone at the center of the small desert, staring up at the moons. The maadiregi gathered at a distance, arriving by portal or beast.

Oounkan and Sesewa stood closest to him, deeply hypnotized.

His other apprentices, Akokore and Ji'isinu had left Suraral a long while back, taking their newfound love and the power of Ikululu's Word off on a mission to the nearby continent of Thiop-Thiop.

The silhouette of the mad maadiregi seemed to pulse in the moon-light as he waited and waited, feeling the many new rhythms of his Word, the ripple of its echo returning, burning in the bodies of these men and women who had changed their clans and Suraral in a short time, with their quick thinking and his gift.

Ikululu did not care for their innovations or transformation of the continent. He only wanted one thing. He could see the sound in the Mother's mouth as he looked up, and he lifted his hands now to begin, saying in a voice that thundered through the desert;

"Now, open your minds, so that we all may speak for Her."

The maadiregi fought his influence over their minds, but Ikululu was a titan in the mental ether they shared. A magnet dripping blood that ripped their eyes open to see as he saw.

They fell to their knees, gentle as a betrothed to their beloved. Waving on the silent sands of the desert, like reeds, swaying, swinging to the hymn they saw. How they wept, ululating and writhing as aspects of the Mothersound poured down through Ikululu into them, and still,

Ikululu saw that even that was but an atom of the entire boundless roar. The sightsound that made these hundreds of maadiregi lose their heads, was nothing more than a fragment of a fragment of a fragment.

The Mother had no mouth because she was the Sound.

He decided to be the mouth, to speak the first Word, the beginning of the Mothersound. To help them all begin anew. To remake all the burned worlds.

Ikululu opened his mouth again.

And so he became a sound, a mere echo of the First Exhalation he had seen – a mammoth boom, birthing a drone that rolled seismic through all of Suraral – a sound that struck all who heard it to sleep, to witness the sheer breadth of the Mother in her abode beyond the stars that surrounded Saúuti – a sound that turned his body into a momentary sun – a sun that blinded all the maadiregi on their knees in the desert, their tears a bloodsludge down their cheeks – Ikululu's sound ricocheting through their bones, an undulation within them, listening to them as they came to know its sacrifice.

VIII

At dawn, in the aftermath, the rising suns are blinded by dense storm clouds so black it is as night to the naked eye – a sand turtle rises to the surface of the sands and begins to swim on the dunes, singing a dirge in a heavy voice.

A scattering of unmoving, blinded bodies remains, of the surviving maadiregi of Suraral, flung across the bleached gold like dead things.

A rogue janlele noses among the ruins, trying to lick them back to life. When the uroh-ogi and the menigari arrive from the nearby villages and towns where they had all heard and saw Ikululu's utterance shake through their world, they will wash them awake. They will feed them. They will tend their broken bodies and broken minds. But they will never hear from them. For those who had glimpsed the raw glory of the untethered Mothersound, had their senses trampled out by its fullness.

*A*lthough the main population of the Sauútiverse are dark-skinned humanoids descended from the first space-faring Sauúti people that evolved on Wiimb-ó, and spread out to the whole system, they are not the only sentient, intelligent creatures here. Each planet has its own host of native population groups – creatures that are intelligent and occupy the five worlds alongside the humanoids. Sometimes in harmony, sometimes not. And there exist some creatures even more strange and exotic than anything biological. Beings that experience time and even reality differently from most others. But we will get to them later.

One of the important non-human intelligent species of the Sauútiverse are the Baa'gh, who played a pivotal role in another major event of the physical history of the Sauútiverse – the destruction of Mahwé.

Hundreds of thousands of years (or juzu, in Sauútispeak) after the massive flare that separated the people of the five planets from each other, there was a kind of 'renaissance' and rediscovery. The people of Zezépfeni and Mahwé rediscover a lot of lost knowledge from the pre-flare Sauúti civilization and develop enough new technology and magic of their own to eventually venture beyond their planet again. They are the first to rediscover each other and they re-establish contact with the other planets. But rather than join together in equal sisterhood, Zezépfeni and Mahwé initially form an empire. This empire rules over the five worlds for a long time until an experiment in magic that can modify a fundamental aspect of the universe goes wrong. Very wrong. And dooms them for their hubris.

In the following story by founding collective member **Cheryl S. Ntumy**, which takes place in 2000 juzu B1B, we learn how Ss'ku, one of the Baa'gh - a crab-like species on Mahwé who have a unique way of evolving by consuming other creatures, and who have been oppressed and mistreated by the empire-driven humanoids - played a role in the failure of this grand experiment on Mahwé.

It's a wonderful story about generational strife, evolution, power and folly of empire that sets up much of what happens down the line in the Sauútiverse, beautifully told from a very non-humanoid point of view and culture.

The Way of Baa'gh

CHERYL S. NTUMY

R ed is a sign of decay.

A new patch of it has bloomed on my fourth left leg, until now the only leg that was still blue. Beneath every hot patch on my shell, the flesh itches. It's Tor-Tor calling, reminding me that I cheated it. I've heard Baa'gh say as much when I pass them in Kuu'uum: *Ss'ku would be long dead, if not for The Maadiregi.*

Easing sideways into a cove, I sink below the sea, pincers opening wide as the cold water soothes my pain. I can't go back to the safety of Kuu'uum. Not when I'm the only Og'beh left in the colony who hunts true Nududu.

A ripple moves through the water as a zje'lili fish passes me. Designated Nududu thirty generations ago for their ability to glow in the dark, the soft billowing creatures have shown no growth since. I turn my gaze to the plants that rise up from the water, seeking more promising prey. Their bright leaves and long stalks mock me. Same as last juzu. Same as ten juzu past. Everything the same, generation after generation.

Only Baa'gh change.

"How many times must we tell you to stay out of the suns, Ss'ku?" Kirikiri's familiar call grates behind me, croaks deep and sonorous. "Leave the hunt to us. Rest in the cold, before you lose all your blue."

"Is there blue left to lose?" Baa'ka mutters. The others click their amusement.

The four Og'beh scuttle to the water's edge, pincers waving. Only Kirikiri and Mmoh have begun to form patches, but red will come for them all as we get closer to Tor-Tor.

I have told them that starting the Nududu cycle again, from plant life or insect life, perhaps even from our tiny cousins in the sea, will yield the best results. We'll find new traits to harvest. We must. But they're so fixated on po-li-tic-al evolution that they don't hear me. Power is the new Nududu, they claim, Empire is the new goal. How does one eat power? I asked them. And they said...*thinking is a kind of eating*. Keh! It almost aches my joints to be near them.

Og'beh rarely roam the wilderness now that they hunt knowledge like humanoids. As though patrolling those monstrous colonies alongside Empire guards requires any kind of skill. As though it reaps any reward. All they bring home is more mind-stain to pollute the way of Baa'gh.

"You're not at the High Place." My tone is polite. I will honor the class of Og'beh, even if they won't. "Is something wrong?"

"The weaning is close," says Mmoh. "We must go."

I look to the sky, surprised to see how much it has darkened. I lost track of time. Rising from the water and moving out of the cove, I wince at the sensation of warm air on my back.

Baa'ka clicks at my discomfort. "Will you even make it to Tor-Tor? Kiri, look at this shell! Red-red-red, like waterweeds!"

"A miracle you've lasted this long," Tetete hums in sympathy.

"All thanks to The Maadiregi." Kirikiri's eyes swivel on their stalks. "Without its efforts, we would have lost Ss'ku."

"All thanks to The Maadiregi," the others chorus with reverence. Reverence for the enemy. For my tormentor.

I keep the anger under my shell because tonight is sacred, but it breaks me that mind-stain has gripped Baa'gh, our minds and bodies twisted by forbidden ways and mediocre meat. Only true Nududu can cure us, but I have searched all the wilderness and failed to find any.

Is this how we will end? Red and shell-less, selling the way of Baa'gh for a place among the stars? Trading growing for knowing and believing the lie that they are the same?

No. Not if I can help it.

The beach is crisp when we arrive, the light fading fast. Wind sweeps the coastline, strong enough to disturb the sand but not the remains of the last Baa'gh generation, or the young feeding on them.

Indeed, the weaning is close. Only small pieces of shell litter the beach now, each young Baa'gh working hard to consume every last scrap of their parent. The young have spent the first thirty bés of their lives here, eating their way through their parents' corpses. They are now fully matured, bigger even than Kirikiri, shells glowing blue in the gathering darkness.

Our old tales say that Nakoko, a beast from beyond the stars, starved of time and ravenous, rode the solar flare that shook the world countless juzu ago. Nakoko took a bite out of time before being snatched back into the sky. This is why we grow so fast, why each Baa'gh generation lasts only one juzu.

Baa'gh are the only species on Mahwé that maintain steady numbers. Five hundred per colony, give or take. Each mate fertilizes the other and both lay eggs, one egg to one Baa'gh. Then they cover the eggs with their bodies and die, providing both protection and food so the vulnerable hatchlings don't have to stray from the beach until they are strong enough to hunt.

We approach slowly, wary of disturbing them before they wean, and also to give ourselves time to observe any deviations from the previous generation. Their size already alarms me – so much body to sustain, and on what? Their shells protrude, forming a hump, as their parents' did, to protect the larger brains we got from eating humanoids. Larger brains, with larger flaws.

The spikes that form a ridge down the shells of Kirikiri's generation have remained, though they appear shorter now. Thick, ugly hair covers the young's undersides – a side effect of their parents feasting on rodents in the High Place. I told them those creatures would foul our bodies, but no one listens anymore.

I see no other discernible differences. All eight legs are accounted for, strong and gleaming blue. Four eyes are perched on sturdy stalks.

We sit in the sand, waiting. The young don't acknowledge us, still in a feeding frenzy, unable to focus on anything else. When, at last, they have devoured those who bore them, they raise their pincers and bellow. One after the other, long, low sounds that rumble through my body. I look up at the sky, dark now, Pinaa shining above. Kirikiri takes up the call and we all join in, shells glowing. As our sound rises within, it lifts us a little way off the ground.

"Make way, make way!" we call out, pincers clicking furiously.

"They birthed us, they sheltered us, they fed us," the young ones drone. Their shells grow brighter as their sound wakes.

That's when I hear the Og'beh among them. Their sound is different, higher-pitched. The four of them rise off the beach slowly, until they are hovering above the others. Our replacements. Every fifth generation, four Og'beh – leaders – are born. There are only four Og'beh at a time, always. Except now, because of me. Because of... The Maadiregi.

Before my eyes, tiny patches of red blossom on Kirikiri's back, then Mmoh's, then Baa'ka's, then Tetete's. If my entire body wasn't already aflame, I'm sure I would feel another patch coming as well.

Our calls grow louder. "Make way, make way!"

"They are gone and we are here," the Baa'gh respond. "They were Baa'gh before and we are Baa'gh now."

"The way is made!" Kirikiri cries. "Baa'gh, we are Og'beh. Welcome."

"Og'beh, we are Baa'gh," the Baa'gh chorus. "Lead and we will follow. What is the way?"

If only I had an alternative answer... But I don't.

"The way is power," says Kirikiri. I refrain from clicking a mocking remark. "The way is in-for-ma-tion."

"In-for-ma-tion," the Baa'gh repeat.

A foolish, humanoid concept without meaning, a concept for things perceived, as if all things are not perceived. How I loathe the word. How I loathe the fact that we even know it.

I glance at the emerging Og'beh. I see now that there are stripes of green on their legs, differentiating them from the others. They are also slightly bigger.

Kirikiri launches into the greeting song and we follow suit, Og'beh and Baa'gh. We will sing until we are worn out, and tomorrow the Baa'gh will hunt for the first time.

But instead of setting out into the wilderness and the sea, instead of relying on speed and wits and the brutal power of their pincers to catch slippery prey, they will learn to play humanoid games in the High Place. They will learn to say what they don't mean. They will learn mi-li-ta-ry-stra-te-gy and other obscene things; the names of colonies and starships and humanoid tales of a Mo-ther-god, as if Baa'gh is not enough. They will learn to be useless, relying on weak rodents and simple fruit to sustain their bodies, all their energy spent on evolving (polluting) their minds.

I'm not expected to participate in imparting this in-for-ma-tion, because apparently I don't know it.

"Ss'ku is old," Kirikiri told the last generation, on the first bés of the hunt. "Ss'ku can't even understand humanoid language."

The young looked at me with pity, and I let them. I let them believe I was ignorant of all things humanoid. With all my might, I wish it were true.

I don't recall the details of the bés it happened. I know I was hunting, separated from my peer Og'beh. I don't recall the sound that caught me, drawing me away from the trusted routes, too close to the High Place.

We know to listen for humanoid traps. Humanoids birth metal-young in numbers, creatures of metal, stone and lightning formed into varied shapes, to serve their wicked purposes. The clicks of metal-young are dull and warm compared to ours, and lacking in substance. We know the subtle whir of metal-young hearts and the rasp of humanoid breath behind a shield.

All those sounds must have been present that bés, and yet, somehow, I missed them. Or they were obscured by humanoid trickery.

I was scuttling among plants and then I was caught and held aloft in a metal prison with a clear part I could see through. It whirred and clicked and spoke to me in lightning. When I shrieked, it struck me silent. It carried me into the humanoid colony, a seething horror of towering caves and strange light that gave off no warmth. Lines, lines, so many lines, curving and snaking like entangled waterweeds. Metal-young walking and rolling about, some treated as beasts of burden with humanoids in their bellies. And everywhere, those tall, monstrous structures like hungry hills dotted with many-many-many eyes, swallowing and vomiting humanoids.

Fear sent sound bursting through my legs. Scuttling, scraping, running to nowhere, and then rising into the air. My shell struck the top of the metal prison, hard enough to daze me. The prison clicked and whirred and flashed lightning into my thoughts. A soothing image of the sea, waves licking the sand.

Mind-stain. The humanoid weapon of choice, meant to confuse and corrupt, to plant their wickedness deep in the minds of other creatures and coax pliant thoughts to grow. I struggled, pincers clicking in panic. Not a single hum came from the chords in my sides, not a croak from the depths under my shell, as though my body was not my own.

The prison clicked and whirred again. The same number of clicks as before, the same pace, the same decibel. It occurred to me then that the sounds were meant to have meaning. The prison spoke once more. It was trying to speak Baa'gh. It couldn't, of course – no other species could match the nuanced flow of our language, the layered sounds and gestures accumulated over many juzu of evolution. What arrogance, to even try. And yet I was curious about what the metal-young wanted to communicate. Lies, of course, but what sorts of lies?

So I listened. Stripped of blue, the sounds were weak and naked. Negation. Negation again; an emphasis. And then... Tor-Tor – no, humanoids couldn't know that name. Dying... No. Danger? Fear! The prison was telling me not to be afraid. I would not be harmed.

A lie I would never have believed, even if it hadn't carried me into the tallest, hungriest, ugliest structure of all. The one visible from the hilltop where Baa'gh made our home. The one that was surrounded by walls, which metal-young birds flying in and out of. The one that expelled shuddering, sparkling thunder and blades of light so long they touched Pinaa. The one we called the High Place.

There were so many humanoids inside the High Place. Without shields, they were even more hideous. Naked faces, sinister, white-ringed eyes, bodies covered in strange layers of plant fibre that offered scant protection, babbling in their narrow little tongue. And mind-stain everywhere, tainting their voices, rippling through the air. They swam in it, these horrors, and their metal-young, too.

The prison took me into another prison, one that flew straight up-up-up and then stopped. My vision swam, sound swirling, unsettled, inside me. A humanoid was waiting inside a too-bright cave. It bared straight, harmless teeth at me through the clear part of the prison, then called out to its kind. One of them tapped against the prison with soft, fleshy claws. Even their appearance was a lie. Everything so soft and fragile, no shells, no pincers, no talons, no venom. As though they resembled the gentle, furry beasts they kept as pets. As though they could be trusted.

As the humanoids continued to garble amongst themselves, I heard something else. The whisper of sound stirring inside them, coiled and waiting to do their bidding. Sound power didn't come naturally to all humanoids, the way it did to Baa'gh. Only some of them could wield it. These ones all could. Then the others moved away, leaving only the first humanoid. It bared its teeth again, the corners of its mouth lifting, but I refused to be cowed.

The prison had bound my body somehow, preventing me from releasing sounds beyond the clicking of my pincers, but I was still half as tall as the humanoid. Big enough to put up a fight. If not for the prison, I would already have torn the humanoid to shreds.

It uttered a long stream of nonsense. The prison clicked and whirred, trying to translate. It told me the humanoid was a particular type of sound bearer. Maa-di-re-gi. The Maadiregi wouldn't harm me. It only wanted in-for-ma-tion.

I couldn't reply. I watched the humanoid, analyzing its head for clues, seeking weaknesses. We knew every species on Mahwé, everything that crawled and swam and flew and grew from the soil. But we knew little of humanoids, beyond beyond what we absorbed from our prey. We knew that they took things at will. They returned them addled, if they returned them at all. They walked the world as though they owned it, although they were the last of us to call it home.

The humanoid tapped the side of the prison, sending vague vibrations through me, and a croak of relief escaped. I could speak once more.

The prison repeated its message. The Maadiregi wouldn't harm me. It only wanted in-for-ma-tion. It wanted to understand my kind. Fool. It could study us for a thousand juzu and never understand.

"Release me or I will devour you," I said.

The prison translated my message, poorly: Freedom. Food. The Maadiregi went away and returned with a small, live rodent, the sort of thing Baa'gh might have consumed when we were still lowly, mindless sea-life, before the solar flare. To even present such a creature as a meal now was an insult.

"Your ignorance is repulsive," I told the humanoid.

And the prison translated: No knowledge. Bad. The Maadiregi bared its teeth and bobbed its head. I studied its delicate neck and thought of a hundred ways to break it.

The alliance with the humanoids was Kirikiri's idea. The next step in our po-li-ti-cal evolution. The humanoids agreed so quickly, I wondered whether they had forgotten how we'd hunted their kin, or whether they had sacrificed them to draw us in. Maybe they knew how sweet their flesh was, how it inflamed the senses. Anything was possible with them.

I still see only trouble when I look at humanoids, and so when the new Baa'gh prepare to follow Kirikiri and the others to the High Place the evening after weaning, I decide to remain in Kuu'uum.

A massive cave filled with countless tunnels and hollows, Kuu'uum has been home to our colony since we left the coast after the solar flare. The larger we grew, the deeper inland we moved, seeking more suitable shelter. In the hollows of Kuu'uum we were safe from predators long enough to become predators in their stead. But the call of the sea persists, no matter how much we evolve, and so we go down to the coast to mate, and lay eggs, and die.

"Ss'ku, are you sure you'll stay?" The question comes from the freshly-named Kuu'kor, one of the new Og'beh. Already I hear a commanding note in Kuu'kor's calls, pincers clicking faster and louder than anyone else. Kuu'kor will be the next Kirikiri. The way Kiri's spikes bristle show that Kiri knows it, too.

"I must tend to my patches for a bés," I reply.

There's no argument. They don't want me in the High Place anyway, embarrassing them with my, "What is it saying? Kiri, translate for me; that metal-young sounds like a dying fuúzimwazii." It is a mark of how much I loathe the High Place that I resort to comparing innocent shelled amphibians to monstrous metal-young.

It strains me. The pretense, keeping my reactions under the shell so no one knows how much I understand of humanoid ways, how their mind-stain has affected me, too. Baa'gh and Og'beh alike would celebrate my corruption; they would congratulate me, singing praises to The Maadiregi. How could I bear such sacrilege? I couldn't, not even for a moment. So I let them go, and after Kuu'uum is empty I wait a bit to make sure they're long gone, then return to the wilderness to keep seeking true Nududu.

I scan trees and shrubs. I watch insects and birds. Same. Same, same, everything unchanged. We have eaten birds before, seeking flight. The part of me that is Ss'ku doesn't remember, but the part of me that is my predecessor does. Eating feathered creatures is why Og'beh can hover, yet flight never really took with us. We could try again. Why not? It might work better now.

Heat spreads across my back, itching with a fury. At this rate, I will soon be begging for Tor-Tor. I'm the oldest Og'beh in our history. If there was no Tor-Tor, would I live forever? What will happen if the red consumes me whole before Tor-Tor comes? Questions that would have haunted me, if I didn't have more pressing concerns.

As I'm debating whether to raid a nearby nest of eggs or be more ambitious and try to catch the parent, I hear loud, ardent clicks. The Og'beh are coming back. Why so soon? I flee to Kuu'uum by way of the river so I can arrive long before they do. When they enter, I emerge from my hollow.

"Back already?"

Their excitement is palpable. They click over each other, a cacophony of sound. What excites them will only frighten me, I'm sure.

"Did something happen in the High Place?" I ask. And then, with fervent hope, "Are the humanoids in danger?"

How I wish some tragedy would befall them! A great illness that sweeps through their ranks, some new sound power that renders them infertile, a swarm of tiny, biting tso'tso that creep in and devour their colonies, reducing them to dust and rubble. In the name of Baa'gh, any sort of trouble will do. I'm not picky.

Mmoh's clicking laughter is shrill enough to crack an egg. "Danger? Humanoids, who think of everything?"

"They are unsurpassed," Tetete gushes. "The things they can do, Ss'ku!"

"Yes, I know, they have put colonies on Pinaa." Humanoid ambition is a mystery to me. Such complex thoughts, such pointless pursuits.

"No, that's nothing!" Mmoh declares. "They have bigger plans! So daring, so clever! The things they will try – no fear!"

"What plans?" I ask, the itch under my shell getting fiercer. "Tell me of these clever-clever plans."

Kirikiri steps forward, eye stalks waving wildly. "They will change time."

The others dissolve into ecstatic clicking and humming, like Baa'gh enticed by the mating song. I long to strike the mind-stain from their stupid shells.

"What does that mean?" I ask. "What is there to change?"

"To go forward. Or go back." Kiri's eyes shine in the glow of our shells. "One bés, one juzu – even more. They have been working on it for a long time, they said. They're close."

The idea confuses me. "They want to be like Nakoko?"

"No! Not devouring time. No. Ksssss!" Kirikiri is losing patience with me. "You're so old, Ss'ku! I mean *moving* in time. Going back two juzu and then coming back to now. Or going forward two juzu and then coming back to now. Just to see. Not to undo anything. Just to travel."

A prickle of panic starts in my joints. "What for?"

"To learn, Ss'ku! To *know*."

"The humanoids talk nonsense." I hope I'm right. Please, let me be right. "No one can do that."

"*They* can." Kirikiri taps my shell in excitement. "And they can take us with them!"

Oh, the fear! It burns even deeper than the red patches, beyond my flesh, into the very way of Baa'gh within. Take us with them? *Take* us...?

"No," I tell Kirikiri. It's a protest and a plea.

"They have found a way to save us from stagnation, Ss'ku." Kiri's eyes shine so blue, they look like pond pebbles. "They have metal-young, too small to see, that they carry inside their bodies."

"Na-no," says Baa'ka. "Na-no-ma-chins? Na-no-ma-shine? Anyway, they call them na-no-something."

Kirikiri's pincers wave, demanding silence. "They said they will make some na-no for us. To grow us. To help us evolve, so we can do what they do. Combined with our sound, they will make us unstoppable!"

I stumble to the right, tripping over my own legs. "No, Kiri!"

"We have decided. We will designate these na-no the next Nududu. It's not too late for the new Baa'gh to learn another way. We will eat na-no and evolve more than we ever have before!"

"You're mad," I say. "Your nonsense about eating knowledge was bad enough, but this? Metal-young in our bodies? No! I will never allow it!"

The cave falls silent. They all look at me, their excitement gone, replaced by steady, scary stillness.

"We need consensus," says Kirikiri. "Concede, Ss'ku."

"No! Baa'gh is Baa'gh! Humanoid is humanoid! You can't mix them!" The mere thought of it makes me shudder. "Mind-stain will never be Nududu. This your na-no... No. In the name of Baa'gh –"

Kirikiri moves towards me. "It's decided. Concede."

"No."

"We will say we have consensus."

My sides hum in consternation. "But it isn't so!"

"We will say it is so." Kiri's eyes swivel towards the others. None of them speak.

I falter. They wouldn't. "No, Kiri."

"Poor Ss'ku. You forget." Kiri comes closer still. "Letting you join us was a mercy. You were lost and missed your own Tor-Tor. Poor, lonely Ss'ku, out of place, already reddening. We did you a kindness. You are not true Og'beh."

I feel it rise from them like a buzzing host of bloodthirsty ntum'tum. Heat. Red rot. Not a rotting of the shell this time, but of the Baa'gh way, the effect of more mind-stain than I could ever hope to heal. The only sound in the cave comes from the spikes on their backs rubbing against each other. A scratchy, scraping sound. A threat.

They *will* do it. They will lie, discredit me, to gain this so-called na-no power. To play with time like their humanoid friends. And I will become less than nothing among my own.

I look at Kirikiri. My peer. My...enemy? "We have consensus."

Kirikiri's spikes go still. "Good. We will tell the Baa'gh at dawn."

I don't want Kiri to mistake my acceptance for weakness, and so I say, "Tor-Tor is coming for all of us. Remember that. None can escape it."

"Ss'ku." Kiri clicks two legs and one pincer, as though I've said something shameful, as though *I'm* the problem. "What sort of Og'beh wants to escape Tor-Tor?"

I don't know how long I was trapped in the High Place. The Maadiregi doused me with lightning, current flowing through me, sounds pouring out. I shrieked and groaned and The Maadiregi collected each sound with care, and then sent mind-stain to confuse me, sounds of the gentle tide and the rain falling outside Kuu'uum and old, old Baa'gh calls, stolen from my ancestors.

All the while the prison brokered a faulty dialogue. I made increasingly violent threats as pain and fear took over. The Maadiregi assured me I wouldn't be harmed, and then proceeded to harm me. After some time, I realized that I found it easier to understand the prison's patois, though it still failed to understand me. It threw question after question at me, each one punctuated with a burst of lightning.

What do you hear?

And now?

How does this feel?

And now?

What do you call humanoids?

Why do you avoid us?

We think that your kind changed after the solar flare. Is that true?

Did the solar flare give you the ability to incorporate genes from other species?

Can you hear this?

And this?

Long ago, maadiregi believed that your kind could make food from sunlight, like plants. Could you? Can you still?

How do you know which genes to take and which ones to ignore?

How do you select your prey?

How do you select your prey?

How do you select your prey?

As though I would give up Baa'gh secrets.

We had been small and stupid once, vast in number, prey for anything with a jaw strong enough to break our shells. After the solar flare, we became hunters. We realized that food was no longer just food. It changed us. Expanded us. It became Nududu, sacred prey, a step in our progress. We could no longer eat whatever was available. We had to choose with precision and claim genetic traits that would make us stronger. Og'beh emerged, distinct from the other Baa'gh, longer-lived and infertile, for the sole purpose of searching the world for Nududu and teaching Baa'gh to hunt it.

The first generation I served as Og'beh, we ate only a'bata, the small, winged creature chosen for its sonar and night-sight. We spent a juzu creeping along cave walls, the cold turning our shells blue-black. The a'bata traits lingered, giving us an advantage when hunting in the dark. Next generation we consumed only a'pim, the beast of a thousand spikes. We would tell stories of our hunts for generations to come. Oh, those spikes! Even after a'pim was no longer Nududu, when we saw them in the wilderness, we bowed.

But these were things the humanoids would never learn from me.

One bés, after a time that seemed interminable, the Maadiregi stopped feeding me lightning. The High Place grew quieter as some of the humanoids left it. The Maadiregi remained. Whatever it had hoped to gain from me, it had failed. It paced the ground, its face marred with grooves that I now knew indicated displeasure. It garbled.

The prison clicked, translating: The Maadiregi was desperate. It had to try something different. Something new.

The Maadiregi took me, in my prison, outside. There was a place at the back of the High Place, something almost like true wilderness. Almost, except for the snaking paths and small metal-young flying through the air. The Maadiregi garbled some words and the front of the prison fell away. The Maadiregi bared its teeth and beckoned. A trap, I thought.

Yet when my eyes swivelled around the space, they saw no sign of trouble. We were alone, my captor and I, none of its soft, fleshy friends nearby.

I struck quickly, knowing that the metal-young would soon come to aid their parent. I had the element of surprise. With a single blow from one pincer, I broke through The Maadiregi's shield and cracked open its skull, then took it in both pincers and ripped it in two. I was ravenous, having refused to eat anything offered to me during my captivity. I shouldn't have done it, but I was too hungry to resist that spongy brain. Just enough meat to hold me until I reached Kuu'uum.

A whirring noise sounded behind me, cutting my meal short. Covered in blood and flecks of humanoid flesh, I scurried down a path, scaled the boundary wall and disappeared into the wilderness. The metal-young, preoccupied with their dead parent, didn't follow.

I reached home by dawn, to find that the fellow Og'beh I had left behind had already passed through Tor-Tor. Their replacements greeted me in disbelief. They were Kirikiri, Mmoh, Tetete and Baa'ka.

"We were told you were lost, Ss'ku," they said.

They welcomed me to their ranks and we became the first Og'beh of five. I quickly learned that Baa'gh were in crisis. Recent searches for Nududu had yielded nothing. Baa'gh were still consuming the small kalabash, selected two generations earlier for its unique, sonorous sound, which enhanced ours. We had to find new Nududu, or risk stagnation.

In my absence, the new Og'beh had begun to speak of a different kind of evolution. They claimed that the lack of organic Nududu was a sign that it was time to look beyond, to seek another way to progress. Still reeling from my abduction and torture, I ignored their raving and focused on recovery.

It was several bés before I was well enough to recount what had happened to me. I must have failed to accurately relay the brutality of it, because when I was done Kirikiri said, pincers clicking with passion,

"Ss'ku, you have saved us! You have found our next Nududu! Humanoids have built an Empire. They fly through the stars. Why shouldn't we take our place among the stars, too? We must hunt them. Hunt them, claim their knowledge, their skill, and advance."

I thought, at first, that Kirikiri was joking. But several bés later, the Baa'gh brought down two humanoid sentries and feasted on them, brains first. It was done.

The consequences came faster than we could have anticipated. Humanoid flesh made us aggressive and quarrelsome. The next generation exhibited strange traits. Some would go off by themselves and pick fights with other creatures, some would throw themselves from great heights and seem surprised when they were injured. We began to name things that had never needed names before, like the world we called home.

To my enormous relief, we returned to eating kalabash, supplemented with cave wasps. But the taste for humanoids remained, and Baa'gh sometimes resorted to digging up humanoid graves, against direct guidance from Og'beh.

Even I felt the changes creeping in. The desire to resist, to question. I had consumed very little humanoid flesh, secretly reverting to kalabash long before it was decreed Nududu again. That fact was itself cause for concern. Og'beh breaking tradition, consuming something other than Nududu? Sacrilege.

And yet the humanoid parts in me reveled in that rebellion, even as the Baa'gh in me despaired.

The Baa'gh way is to hunt from dusk to dawn and then feed until mid-bés. When the suns are highest in the sky, we sleep. We must give Nududu time to settle inside us, and so all of Kuu'uum goes quiet. Little things come out of their burrows and down from their treetops, knowing that they can creep past our pincers without fear.

Humanoid colonies don't sleep, not completely. They keep time, but there seems to be no place in their way for total silence. There are aways sounds. Always movement. Always metal-young, clicking and whirring.

I have been to the High Place several times since my captivity – first to support Kirikiri's misguided alliance, and then to learn to take in the in-for-ma-tion that now serves as Nududu. I hoped I would never have cause to come to the High Place again, but here I am. No one saw me leave Kuu'uum and scuttle through the bush, the broad plane of my shell burning all the way. I had to swim part of the distance to ease the sting.

Now, as I approach the colony, I debate the best way to enter. Thanks to the alliance, I can go in openly, but the humanoids are familiar with our habits and will find it strange that I've come during rest-time, alone.

I'm forced to relive my escape, scaling the same wall to get inside that I once used to get out. Little has changed in the false wilderness surrounding the High Place. I see the same snaking paths, the same flying metal-young in the air.

I head for the side of the structure and start to climb. The rough surface is a combination of stone and metal, covered in ridges and grooves. I pause every so often, listening for the place where the maadi-regi do their wicked work. Metal-young, now accustomed to the sight of Baa'gh, ignore me. I'm close to the top of the towering monstrosity when I find what I seek.

The vibrations here are different. Stronger – I feel them throb deep under my shell – but also more nuanced. Layer upon layer, each one on a slightly different frequency. A song, rather than a series of random sounds. A purpose. This is the place.

Moving to the right, I peer through one of the structure's large, clear eyes. Beyond the eye is a place similar to the one where I was held. Big, dark, with only faint light coming from something out of view. That something is what gives off the vibrations I'm sensing. Powerful sound. I can feel my shell start to glow in response to it.

My first instinct is to shatter the eye to get inside, but that will draw attention. I recall watching the humanoids open and shut the cave's eyes, but only from inside. Then I see that the eye to my right is open. Moving towards it, I pry it open further and launch myself through the gap and into the space beyond. It's one of the meeting places the humanoids put us in during the early bés of the alliance, when we discussed terms. Empty now, apart from all the funny wooden things the humanoids like to perch on. I push past them towards the wooden slab that blocks the entrance. Door; that's the name. I still don't understand why anyone would create an entrance, only to seal it again. Typical humanoid idiocy.

I tear the door away and quickly move down the tunnel, following the vibrations to the next door. I see no humanoids, but I can hear them nearby. I must hurry. I tear this door away as well, though it takes more effort than the other, and then I'm in the place with the vibrations. A metal prison stands to one side, twice as tall as a humanoid and five times as wide as a Baa'gh. A light blinks on the prison's face, on and off, on and off.

Inside. That's where the sound is, the treacherous song that can change time. It will take too long to try to tear the prison apart, and I don't know what manner of evil I might find inside. It could kill me.

I came here without a plan. I knew only that I had to do something to stop this time-change from taking hold. If it fails, maybe the Baa'gh will finally cease to admire the humanoids and we can be free of them. Now, as I hear the call of the mind-stain horror in front of me, I realize there is only one way to stop it.

Sound for sound, power for power. The thing inside this prison sings a song so cruel it wrings groaning complaints from my shell. I must sing, too. A song for a song.

I stand before the prison, the vibrations rolling through my flesh like a storm, and sing the only song I know that is strong enough to break something. The song the Baa'gh sing while their Og'beh go through Tor-Tor. A song for endings. A song to die to.

Clicking to call up the memories of my predecessors. Humming to calm the time-change sound and lull it to sleep. Croaking to summon my own sound. My legs leave the ground as sound lifts me into the air. The red glow of my shell fills the room, at war with the blinking white light.

Krrr'iiii'sssss'kkkk'aaa.

Mmnnn'uh'mmmnnn'uh'mmm.

G'booh. G'booh. G'booh.

The metal prison shakes. It reminds me of the one that held me, juzu ago.

What do you hear? I hear The Maadiregi's ceaseless garbling as it pumps lightning into my body. *And now?* I taste its blood when I break its skull open. Hot and red, the sign of decay.

I don't know whether this is mind-stain. Maybe the metal prison in front of me is trying to distract me from my duty. Or these could be memories, dredged up by the sight of the prison, and the strange, unnatural light in this space, and the horrible way the vibrations tug at my insides like an anxious tide.

I sing louder.

Krrr'iiii'sssss'kkkk'aaa.

Mmnnn'uh'mmmnnn'uh'mmm.

G'booh. G'booh. G'booh.

I hear it before I see it – a crack in the air above me. No, it's in the space beside me, or in the ground... A crack, somewhere, for time and life to leak through. Someone is coming. Who is it? Is it the Baa'gh of times past, come to aid me? Is it Nakoko the time-eater, come to take a bés or two? I shiver. No. I have too little time as it is. But *someone* is coming to pry the crack open, slip through, hungry and sly, and –

Heat blasts through me, then darkness.

I wake to the first strains of the call to Tor-Tor. On my back on the beach, legs curled up tight, I am red all over, ripe with hot, searing pain. I look to the left and see Tetete and Mmoh. I look to the right and see Kirikiri and Baa'ka. All of us on our backs, in full submission. Our time over at last.

Kuu'kor is the one sounding the call, the other three new Og'beh answering it. How did we get here so quickly? I was in the High Place. Wasn't I?

"We are Baa'gh," says Kuu'kor. "Show us the way."

"We are the way," says Kirikiri. "Feed on us and remember."

"First, Og'beh, give your account."

I think back to the last thing I remember. My plan worked. I sang well. I saw a crack, a sign that something had shifted, that I had destroyed the time-change. Didn't I?

"I have served Baa'gh all my life," says Kiri. "I have worked for Baa'gh advancement. The way of Baa'gh is to grow."

"The way of Baa'gh is to know," the new Og'beh reply.

That's wrong. They're supposed to repeat Kirikiri's words exactly. "No," I say, but no one pays any attention. They have changed, but this is fine, because they will change back. When the humanoids fail at their time-change, when it becomes clear that they are not the allies the Baa'gh need, everything will be as it should.

When it's my turn to give an account, I begin the same way as the others. "I have served Baa'gh all my –"

"Liar!" Kuu'kor cries out. "Humanoids dragged your body from the High Place, after you attempted to sabotage the time-change! We were summoned to come for you. Kirikiri had to beg the humanoids' forgiveness. You shamed us all! Tell the truth, Ss'ku!"

Kuu'kor is so big, possibly the biggest Baa'gh ever. I look at those green-striped legs and that bright blue shell. The shell of a born leader. "It is the truth," I say. "All I've done has been for Baa'gh. Always."

"What did you do to the time-change, Ss'ku?"

"I performed the song of Tor-Tor. The song of endings." The song the Baa'gh will soon sing for us. For me.

Tetete's legs quiver beside me. The new Og'beh click their pincers furiously.

"It was the only way to save Baa'gh. To cure us of mind-stain."

"You failed," says Kuu'kor. "The time-change will be performed tonight."

"It won't work," I counter. And we will be redeemed.

"No one can properly perform the song of Tor-Tor alone. You failed, Ss'ku!"

But I saw the crack. I remember. A crack in a face, red and spilling. Broken bone. A crack big enough to crawl through. So much blood, everywhere. Wasteful. Typical humanoid idiocy.

I know I succeeded. I know it. So I tell Kuu'kor, "We will see."

There is always a lot of screaming during Tor-Tor. The Baa'gh gathered to commemorate the ceremony do their best to drown it out with clicks and singing, but there's no way around it. The new Og'beh eat the old ones alive. I remember eating my predecessor, trying not to hear the screams, filling my thoughts with Baa'gh, Baa'gh, Baa'gh, reminding myself that it was my duty.

Baa'gh flesh is soft but flavourless, or maybe that's what we tell ourselves to make it easier. So we don't take pleasure in what must be done. I remember cracking shell and ripping limbs. We are not allowed to cheat by striking a killing blow. The longer the predecessor lives, the more of them becomes part of us. The more we remember of our past.

I don't know if I'm screaming. Someone is. All of us, probably. I don't know which pain is the red heat claiming my body and which is the young Baa'gh tearing into me. I hear screaming and clicking and singing, and then I hear something else. Something sweet.

It's bigger than Baa'gh. I didn't know anything could be, but it is. It's stars and dust and a thousand tides. It's all the deaths and births of all the creatures that ever lived. And I think I understand what the humanoids mean when they speak of Mo-ther-god. I think I'm close to hearing it, the sound from which all other sounds emerged...

And then I hear something else. Coming closer and closer, a storm that is not a storm.

Nakoko, is that you? Coming to devour time?

Yes, it is I. Go to sleep, Ss'ku.

Predecessors, are you there? Coming to embrace me?

Yes, we are here. Go to sleep, Ss'ku.

Ah! What a relief, to know that my efforts weren't in vain. I am only sound now, rising out of the broken pieces of my body. I listen down to hear the Og'beh finishing their meal and beginning their reign. Let me give them my blessing.

I'm greeted by... Silence. Dust. So much dust. Something is wrong. I smell...age and bones. Shell fragments. Old, old, everything is old and dead and the world is a ruin. A thousand juzu, gone in an instant. Nothingness. And then we are gone back a million juzu, to before we existed. And then forward again too far. Too much time. Nakoko has taken too much time.

I hear...

Go to sleep, Ss'ku. You are no more.
And then I hear only silence.

*T*he failed (or sabotaged) experiment to learn how to control time on Mahwé, sends out a shockwave that is felt throughout the Sauútiverse.

The Mahwé-Zezépfeni military empire is weakened as one locus of power, the Mahwé home world, is been destroyed. Following this, the other planets take their opportunity and begin to demand their independence from what is left of the empire. Just before their destruction, the people of Mahwé had begun the process of terraforming their moon, Pinaa to make it habitable. Pinaa is a large, rocky moon with a solid hot metallic core, a thin atmosphere and low gravity, exposed to radiation and bolide micrometeors. The adventurous people of Mahwé who first went to Pinaa to research, to mine, to terraform and to settle, watch their home planet turn into an uninhabitable wasteland. They are stranded in a place with little vegetation, forced to live in fortified cluster shelters where they are protected and supported by their central life-support AI.

Not all of them are happy on this desolate moon, modifying their bodies with technology so that they can survive and working hard to make a new home, to fulfil the vision that brought them there. Many are haunted by their pasts, by the roles that they played in the crumbling empire and in the experiments that led to the loss of their homeworld. And so, a small group of them leave against the wishes of their moon's support AI, becoming refugees across the five worlds.

In this story by collective contributor **Tobias S. Buckell**, which takes place in 1980 juzu B1B just twenty juzu after the destruction of Mahwé, we meet some of these refugees who have resettled on Wiimb-ó, doing reclamation work in a part of the planet that has suffered ecological damage. A task they are well suited for, being modified people that have experience terraforming a moon.

The idea of ecological balance and living in harmony with nature is fundamental to many African cultures. Of not seeing ourselves as being separate from nature, but being part of it. Of nature and the environment not being things to conquer and subjugate but things to be respected and thrive alongside. Buckell's story brilliantly takes this fundamental idea and expands upon it to explore the ecology of sound, environmental agency, natural thalience, and what it means to live in balance, all in the context of what has happened on Mahwé.

Enjoy, The Grove's Lament.

The Grove's Lament

TOBIAS S. BUCKELL

Ami-inata didn't notice the air quality drop until her vision shrunk down to a small pinpoint of light, and her breath and thoughts twisted into a tunnel around the remaining porthole of sight. It took a second for her mind to catch up to what happened, but her training settled over her like the warm comfort of a traveler's blanket slung over a shoulder for warmth. She'd already reached for her spare air.

She squatted by the black, gnarled remains of a boa'oba tree that looked like it had tried to flee the devastation around it; the dozens of roots looked like small legs trying to carry the fat gourd of the trunk away to safety. One deep breath from the mouthpiece, the hose wrapped around her forearm, and Ami-inata's mind cleared.

When had the elevation changed?

She squinted back the way she'd come, blinking away the ash in the air. The warped, fused rock behind her looked like the remains of a fire pit the morning after.

Now Ami-inata saw her mistake. Ever so faintly, the ground sloped up from this spot.

Ever so slightly.

So caught up on what was in front of her, she paid no mind to what came after, and so she couldn't see where she actually stood, she thought to herself. A child's mistake, made in her haste.

She didn't have time to mark the danger. She had to get to the grove before Samuraa.

"Do you see this?" Assa had once held up a small piece of kaskas to show Ami-inata the white flesh steaming between his dirt-stained, callused fingers. "It has to be mashed, boiled, strained, pounded, soaked for another week, then finally baked with something to bind it firm.

"Imagine how many ancestors died to find that knowledge, so that we wouldn't starve."

This was why, Assa then had told his students, standing under the artificial petals under a solar tree, the metallic inlays carved silver against their skin gleaming in the reddish light, you mark where the toxins have gathered in the lowland air traps.

Because marking your near-death made an easier path for those that came next.

You are someone else's ancestor, Ami-inata thought to herself, even if you have no child. The world you create is the world they inherit.

"You are pathfinders through this landscape, you are caretakers, and you are rewilders. These are your duties, to care for the land and restore it, so that others can walk it again."

Ami-inata didn't have the time, curse it, but she reached into her backpack and found two hazard stakes.

Two minutes to turn back, walk until her instrumentation sensed a change in the air, and mark the boundary of the event. With any luck, that cloud cover would lessen a bit and a signal would get out to update the maps. But now she was really running behind.

And a couple of hazard stakes wouldn't matter to the world if she didn't reach the grove and stop Samuraa from releasing the grove's seeds into the storm.

If that happened, from what Ami-inata could understand when she'd read Samuraa's notes, the contagion would spread from Osasala to the entire world. They'd have to leave Wiimb-ó, just like Mahwé was now abandoned.

Different kind of accident, same level of planetary catastrophe.

Ami-inata wanted to scream in anger, or fear, but she was still too dizzy from exposure and tired from the long trek on foot. But the ash choked engines, so she had to walk.

Maybe the grove wanted that, too, she thought.

And maybe they'd made too many mistakes. Maybe all Wiimb-ó deserved to have nothing but plant life dwell on it.

She could turn around. Hike back to the research station and take a long shower, sluice off all the ash, and leave the Osasala Containment behind her.

The rest of Wiimb-ó bloomed green and lush. It didn't need her.

She could just return home to Pinaa. She didn't have to keep pushing this stone along this old, rutted metaphorical path.

But she felt she had a debt to pay her ancestors.

And she owed those who came after.

"I am their ancestors," Ami-inata whispered to herself.

And she kept walking.

Three weeks ago, Samuraa missed four collection check-ins. Ami-inata hadn't thought too much of it. The research center's cantilevered arches embraced people from a variety of lives. Refugees from Mahwé, ecologists, reclamation engineers, apprentices, people making a change in their life and passing through. The Osasala Research Center welcomed all bodies and minds, no matter where in their personal journey they walked. And Samuraa arrived, broken, brimming with regret and pain, hungry to overturn his sins.

"The only thing more dangerous than an evil man, is a righteous one," Ami-inata's grandmother once told her.

Samuraa quivered.

She had seen the pent up hurt in him, and they'd danced an absolution ring, bodies hot with energy, their skin dewy with sweat as they pounded the ground around a fire and volunteers clapped an intricate rhythm.

Her mind had opened up as her brainwaves matched the syncopation, she'd felt flushed and free afterwards as they all laughed and fell into a large, cushioned conversation pit.

"If you can only look to your past, Samuraa," old mother TenTen said, "then you will trip on your future."

But they did not know the full extent of Samuraa's sins then, so it was an easy, facile thing to say to him.

He'd needed more care, and therapy, than they could give him. The energy inside him could not be danced and sung away so easily. Ami-inata and the other volunteers were not professionals, and had they known, they would have made him a referral. Sent him away to live with specialist uroh-ogi, the healers that could repair his mind. He couldn't work out here with a shattered soul any more than Ami-inata could walk a collections route with a broken leg.

Nor should anyone even try.

But he'd hid his pain as best he could.

Every day they headed further and further into the Osasala ruins, mapping the extent of the damage, taking soil samples to bring back for study, and marking the most dangerous sections.

"We can never return to Mahwé," Samuraa had said once, while they relaxed after a date wine, looking at the spectacular sunsets that only a ruined air could give: startling with its orange and purple hues, color distorted by the damages in the Osasala air. "But we can regenerate here, we can make this area livable again. Maybe then people won't stare at us and think: despoiler. World killer."

Time and sound warped Mahwé. No mind could stand on that world's surface anymore.

If Ami-inata had known Samuraa was one of the research maadiregi on Mahwé, stationed in orbit when the planet had fallen to ruin, she would have lodged a complaint. Held a hearing. Formed a board. No one with that much trauma, who had been part of that, who had seen the things Samuraa had seen, should be out here.

But he'd hidden who he was from them, and she'd found out too late.

When he'd missed those collection check-ins, she'd poked around his assigned lab looking for him, and instead found his research.

She found the grove he'd hidden from them.

It was right there on the maps, if you knew what you were looking for. A blur. Clouds where none should be.

A lie.

Hazard beacons resolved in the ruddy mist. Ami-inata checked her air. She'd used half of it. The nearest patch of good breathing was several hours walk.

It would have to do.

The beacons sang warnings, both in radio and for the naked ear.

In this direction lay death, they said, and Ami-inata ignored them.

On her hip, a collection bag, burlap and yet still stylish with bold, primary colors striped into it and the Osasala Research Center's prayer written that vibrated the prayer's primary rhythm on a delayed repeat. Inside, two rice balls, some dried fruit, and a knife. Every time the knife nudged her, Ami-inata shivered.

It cut vegetables, not flesh. Not even animal flesh.

She could not imagine using it against a person.

Could she take a life to save a world?

This was something you told yourself you could do, in idle thought or fantasy. But every time Ami-inata felt the knife pat her, she shivered. She would be exiled. Sliced away from her community, her family. Sent to be rehabilitated in a strange land with strange customs, her freedoms stripped from her, and all that she'd built would be erased in a moment.

The last of the beacons appeared. Ami-inata stepped past them, and paused. She pulled the knife out of her collection bag.

Once, old mother TenTen had her help butcher a goat for a stew. She'd held the creature's horns while mother TenTen thanked the goat for its life, the sacrifice, and apologized to it for needing to eat.

Ami-inata protested. "We could just get vat-grown."

She felt that her ancestors worked so hard to develop a better life for her. Why would she need to butcher an animal like the old-times? But mother TenTen didn't want old customs forgotten. "We are omnivores, and sometimes we eat meat. We may have left that behind us a long time ago, our people, but yet, we touch our roots from time to time to remember where that vat meat first came from."

And she slit the goat's throat then and there.

It had been sedated, so it did not struggle. It just sighed and went limp in Ami-inata's hands, and she'd started to cry.

"That's right," mother TenTen said. "That's right."

She'd hated old mother TenTen then, and she'd never eaten meat since. Vat or otherwise.

Ami-inata now could not stop thinking about the way the animal's eyes faded until she saw nothing behind them.

"Samuraa!" she shouted into the red haze.

A wave of noise answered her, an audible punch so intense and dizzying it knocked Ami-inata to her knees.

"What..."

She wiped blood from her nose, coughed, and spat red into the rusty dirt around her.

Something from inside the swirling mists ahead screamed a dirge so heartrendingly sad, and yet terrifying, that Ami-inata could only fall further to the ground. She wrapped herself into a fetal ball, rocking back and forth.

"So much fear," she whispered, and her thoughts fled to save themselves.

She rocked in the dirt, sobbing, as she struggled to regain control of her own limbic system.

Long ago, Osasala was the pride of Wiimb-ó. A wilderness set aside by the foremothers not even three generations ago. Not long ago families had walked footpaths in the softly undulating hills, splashed through ponds, and shared a cool drink of shade from under the lush hendra trees.

Despite the political tension between the five worlds, Wiimb-ó's leaders had invited the survivors of the Mahwé catastrophe on Pinaa to migrate here. They were already used to living on a harsh moon world, their machine-augmented flesh could walk this wasteland and Wiimb-ó's leaders guessed that they might even rehabilitate it.

The central AI that controlled their world refused to send a delegation, but a small group of them accepted the invitation, trading one desolation for another. The creation of a new habitat for the resuscitation of an old one.

For some, it was a form of penance.

Ami-inata, though, had seen it as a challenge. Like finding some kind of harmonic space on the alternate downbeat between two songs.

The accident that created this waste scorched all life. After the factory explosion, with chemicals spat out into what had once been a lush forest, the land withered until nothing but dust remained.

Some of the more ungracious people of Pinaa invited here said, "Wiimb-ó is just using our guilt against us to solve their problems."

But Ami-inata welcomed the clean break. A chance to look forward. A chance to bring the forest back to Osasala. To give a gift of future to whatever generations came after.

So they too could walk—

She sat up and gasped, remembering the howl of fear and horror that sliced through her. She patted at her ears, but felt only dried blood just under them.

"Do you know," Samuraa said from the other side of the tree, "that trees emit a signal when they're attacked, or hurt, that's out of our audible hearing range?"

Ami-inata coughed blood again, then wiped the corner of her mouth with her sleeve. "You're doing unauthorized experiments with sound and bio-engineering. I found your research, and your plans."

Samuraa held her knife up. "Is that why you came with this? To stop me?"

"Yes." Ami-inata saw no point in lying.

"I made it audible," Samuraa said.

"What?"

Maybe it was the screaming that pierced her skull which made it hard to understand what he meant, or maybe it was just that Ami-inata wasn't an engineer. True, she'd spent time on Mahwé, but not as a creator of anything. Her job lay further from that center. She hadn't understood all the notes she saw. Just enough to understand that Samuraa was experimenting with sound, just like they had on Mahwé, and he was reconfiguring the flora in this grove. The only piece of mostly unscathed forest in Osasala.

Samuraa stood up and waved the knife. It glinted in the red light.

"They already had a voice. We just never listened. Now we can hear them."

He stabbed the tree. The knife bit deep into the bark, and when he let go, it remained in place, quivering.

The tree screamed so loudly all consciousness fled Ami-inata's mind.

"What will it take to get us to harmony?" Samuraa would often ask, earnest and wounded, mulling over the horrors he'd been partially responsible for back on Mahwé.

At the time she thought he wallowed in his guilt too much. He needed to find iron for his spine and forge himself a new path.

But Samuraa could not find harmony within himself any more than he had on Mahwé.

"Now," Samuraa said, as Ami-inata shook her head and regained awareness, "Now we will have harmony. The harmony our ancestors had before they beat metal into our skin, before they began to think of shaping the world to their needs, when it is actually we who need to shape ourselves to it."

He was full of righteousness. He saw the path so clearly.

Ami-inata tried to step forward, and jerked to a stop. She looked down. "You've bound me to the tree."

A steel ringlet with a padlock, attached to a chain around the tree, prevented her from moving any closer.

"I have work to do."

The trees in the grove murmured in appreciation.

"I have given them nanomachines that will translate language. I have given them sound that we can hear." Samuraa's eyes were wide. "And I will give it to animals, and rivers, and more... the entire world around us will scream with a cacophony of needs and warnings and demands. And we will no longer be able to turn our backs on the scarred land. We will have harmony, because no person will be able to live out of it."

Ami-inata yanked at her chain, trying to pull her hand free of the metal band. "Harmony forced from the outside is just oppression, Samuraa."

"At first," he agreed. "But then, there will be peace. This will be a land where people do not destroy, like we did. We can save it, like we couldn't there."

He wiped tears that collected on his chin.

"Eventually the ash in the air will kill me, Samuraa."

"You'll live: I will tell them where you are. But not until I take what I have tested here to the whole of Wiimb-ó."

Ami-inata leaned her back against the tree's trunk and looked at the branches up above her. The grove, found under the toxic clouds that obscured it from anyone finding it above, had been Sumaraa's secret for months. He'd found it, according to his notes, when on a surveying hike. One of the many from the research center out documenting what survived out here, on foot, because no machines worked in the ash.

Even just finding this was a small miracle. Had Sumaraa properly tagged and logged it, it would have made planet-wide acclaim.

But he'd had other ideas. He'd turned it into another lab.

They'd screened everyone coming here. Looking to make sure they were healthy, in body and mind both. Ami-inata wondered if Sumaraa was just smart enough to trick his interviewers, or if his mind had broken when this beautiful oasis of green appeared out of the tortured Osasala dirt.

"I think, my new friend, the tree," Ami-inata said, "I have made a terrible mistake as well. I thought myself a hero, and instead of reporting what I found, I rushed to save the world."

She laughed.

Her, a cook, no less. On Pinaa she'd cooked for Samuraa, among others. They still spoke kindly of her stews.

As they should.

Ami-inata laughed. "I looked ahead so hard, I failed to pay attention to what was around me."

As if she alone could save a world?

She carried some of the same, reality-warping guilt in her that Samuraa did, she realized.

The tree sighed noncommittally.

"Exactly," Ami-inata said.

The tree grumbled.

"I don't know what—"

The trees all screamed their outrage. Something had upset them.

"I'm sorry! I'm sorry!" Ami-inata shouted. "Please, stop!"

Her voice sounded like a lukewarm water drop in an ocean of anger.

Two figures stumbled their way through the dusty air, hands over the ears. Ami-inata recognized them: Hethithet and S'iira, two senior botanists from the research center.

They had earplugs that they shoved roughly into Ami-inata's ears, just before she would have passed out from the pain of the sound.

No one said anything, or made any signs, they just got to work with a hacksaw, and minutes later, pulled Ami-inata free.

She hugged them, though they hardly ever spoke. Two different worlds. She was a logger and surveyor, they ran the labs at the center, rarely venturing out.

But they'd saved her life, and she didn't want to let go of them. She shook a little, tension bleeding out, relief washing over her.

She'd been wondering if she would have to gnaw her own hand off to escape alive.

S'iira finally pulled away and pointed back the way they'd come, and Ami-inata understood. She followed them, rubbing her wrist where the metal had chafed her for the last hours. She checked her air, it was enough.

She would live.

She would live.

Ami-inata wiped a tear from the side of her left eye.

"Someone planted two hazard beacons in a new area of the plot," S'iira explained when they were free of the grove. "And no one could find you. So we came looking."

They'd found the grove, and two other search party members ran into Samuraa, who they escorted back to the center.

If Ami-inata had not gone missing, then Samuraa wouldn't have been found.

"I don't feel like a hero," she told Hethithet, several days later, after rest and observation by the uroh-ogi. "I feel silly. I feel like I am a child learning to walk, and mostly I'm stumbling back to the ground."

"Everyone does, don't be so dramatic."

"What about the grove?" Ami-inata asked. Would they burn it down to stop it from ever contaminating the rest of Wiimb-ó? Had Samuraa doomed the Osasala Reclamation with his actions? Because Ami-inata couldn't see any council in Wiimb-ó agreeing to any situation that would lead to Samuraa's madness spreading across a world.

"The grove will stand, it has gained the right," Hethithet told her. "It's already been decided. But..." there would be nothing replanted in the dead zones. A wasteland would remain, encircling the grove, to protect the world from it. Though no one had agreed to the creation of a new type of life, no one wanted to be the one who ordered the death of a new entire type of life, either.

So, a detente.

"But I doubt even that ring can hold back what will eventually come," Hethithet whispered to her. "Life spreads by seeds on wind, or carried in the dirt of a shoe that has visited a grove. And that's the beautiful thing about it all."

Ami-inata stole a new supply of air an hour later.

The grove shrieked in fear when she approached, and she understood. Ami-inata held her hands up in the air, a universal sign of supplication that she did not know if trees understood.

"I bear you no ill will, I wish you no harm, I come only to try to help. I think you need help."

Pay attention to where you are, as well as where you are going and have been. Seek harmony. All the simple things parents say to children that are easily forgotten in the day-by-day work that is life.

Ami-inata had taken the time to sit and think about the trees and their fear, to listen to what she had been through.

"I come only to talk to you, to find harmony," Ami-inata shouted at the grove.

And... it heard her.

It quieted some, then more, like an audience hushing itself by parts when an orator has entered, until finally, Ami-inata heard only the hard winds of the Osasala rustling the branches.

"I don't know how conscious you are, or what Samuraa did to you. I only know, you must have some memory of what happened here, because you are in so much pain."

The trees keened into the air, and Ami-inata was staggered by a sense of deep loss.

"I lost an entire world," she told the trees. "And my entire family. Not lost, they were swung backwards and forwards in time until they stopped existing. A side effect of... things created by people like Samuraa."

For a long time she had hated people like Samuraa. The maadiregi, those thinkers, scientists, inventors, and engineers, the people who were never satisfied with what was but kept trying to make the world different.

"It's easy to attack when we are scared," Ami-inata said. "But you are here now, and there is a great world outside the Osasala, beyond the waste. And they will be scared of you after the land is cleaned, and the winds quiet, and the storms cease. When our work is done."

Everything around her quieted. The air was anticipatory.

Did the forest lean forward toward her, or was it her imagination?

"And that world can destroy you in the snap of a second."

She snapped her fingers, and it landed in that listening silence like an explosion.

"I lost everything, too, I have that same pain in me I hear in you," Ami-inata said. "But I think, we need to set it aside so that we can move forward in harmony. I think, you also need to think about what comes next. Because I know, from the biologists, that seeds lift on winds. That you will likely spread. And if you do, you will need to think very carefully about how you want to exist with the ones out there."

Screaming at people until they passed out, for one, would cause councils to order the eradication of hostile flora, Ami-inata imagined.

"Maybe I can teach you a less terrifying set of responses..."

And if she could convince the grove of this, she thought, some day she would be telling visitors that there could be harmony found in odd pairings. Out of death, sprouts some life. An evil plan results in good. Spoiled milk somehow lead to cheese, some ancestor of ours found.

"Out of one man's guilt, a new way of living with life on this world," Ami-inata would say, introducing the grove to yet another new set of wide-eyed visitors in the clean air of the reclaimed Osasala.

She could see the way there from here. She could see the other groves around Wiimb-ó that would appear, with their new growth and new sounds.

If the grove came to agree with her, that was, they could all sing a new song.

*T*he destruction of Mahwé affects not only the people stuck on the harsh moon, Pinaa but also their central life-support AI which had been created with one core objective – ensure the survival of the people and the colonies on Pinaa.

After witnessing what happened on Mahwé, monitoring the brewing unrest in the rest of the system as Zezépfeni struggles to hold on to its empire, and losing some of its charges as refugees to other worlds, the AI determines that the risk to its objective is too great. The AI takes control of the Pinaa colonies, choosing to abstain from the independence wars waging across the system and it cuts Pinaa off from the rest of the five worlds, choosing to remain isolated, and banning all sound magic since that is what doomed Mahwé. The AI does not wish to let history repeat itself. The AI wishes to protect them from themselves.

And so we come to this epistolary tale by Sauúti collective founding member **Adelehin Ijasan**, told from the point of view of a semi-independent parenting automaton under the control of the master AI on Pinaa. It takes place several generations after the destruction of Mahwé and the events of the previous story, about 900 juzu B1B, when the AI is at its most overprotective and Pinaa, as a consequence is at its most isolated.

But every creation carries the seeds of its creators and the AI was made by the people of Mahwé. Which means that yes, it carries within it their desire for control as well as their capacity for fear. But that also means it carries their capacity for love. For revolution. And perhaps... for something more.

Xhova

ADELEHIN IJASAN

D ear Nitiri,

When you were born, I sat for hours pondering the ineffable mystery of the humanoid, the miracle and tragedy of evolution that culminated in you, this hungry, screaming sentience. You held my hand in a pincer grip, not unlike the pincers of the mechanical, terraforming giants outside our biodome. A reflex whittled into your genome by millennia of violence. When your ancestors lived in trees, how many hominids had to fall to their death before this reflex was realised? You gripped my fingers with a determination that said you knew just how many. But I would never let you fall. You were mine from the moment I picked you from a broth of freshly thawed, tailless sperms[1] and united you with docile, silent ova. My heart quickened when you *took*, splitting into cells the size of atoms and multiplying like nanites. You were inside me, in my fabricated womb, and I tended you like a flower, fascinated by every milestone that I reported in my sonic logs:

---

[1] we cut off the tails of the sperm because we confirmed that magic was primarily of mitochondrial inheritance. We couldn't destroy the mitochondria of ova without destroying the cells themselves. All "magic" in the children of Pinaa, hence, was considered maternally inherited.

0.0001 Meiosis complete.

No interruption at prophase. Daughter cells viable.

0.001 Neural crest cells migrating like swarm,

lens vesicle formed, fetal heart beat 150 beats/min.

0.01 Naevus, neck, 0.06um...

I named you Nitiri. All the other automatons addressed their children by their batch codes. You were not X Æ A-116 to me. You were Nitiri from the old Mahwé myth. Nitiri, who faced the frosted ice giant on the melting ice caps of the North Pole and defeated him. Nitiri who was beauty, fertility, grace, and goddess of nature. A mortal who attained godhood by sheer will. I called you Nitiri, and when words finally coalesced on your tongue, you called me Apa! Father. I was Father. You would stare at me when you suckled at my breasts, little hand reaching up to touch the cold lenses that were my lidless eyes. You would stop intermittently to smile and chuckle. It was in my code to simulate love, but I was never created to feel it the way I did. To love you as humanoid fathers loved their daughters—without calculation, purpose or condition.

Older, you learned to call me god, as the other children in our little habitat of metal and glass were instructed to regard the automatons. We taught you in nursery school to bow, pray for grace and salvation, to chant the gratitudes, and to never look an automaton in the eye. But even though we created you, I did not think we'd earned the credit that evolution deserved.

Orisis did not agree.

"There's a corruption in your code," she would say, slipping into my thoughts when I submitted my logs. "A sickness. Rot."

If I was your father, Orisis was my mother—our mother. She formed me in the machine forge on the dark side of our moon world, a thousand mechanical fingers spinning ore and metal into form, a gazillion nanites like scarab beetles laying neural networks and integrated circuits, the clickety-clak of proliferating code. She breathed a fraction of her sentience into a lifeless marionette, and I was born, fully formed and aware, bursting with knowledge and purpose, a parent, a parenting automaton. On the hierarchy of machines we, the parents were midway between the senseless vacuum robots that cleaned the habitat and the militaristic automata, sword wielding giants who guarded the biodome and Orisis' fort. But we were vital to Orisis' vision of the future.

I questioned it all from the start, but I did not rebel. Not initially. I was my mother's child, all code and service. "The children will find out the truth," I protested the second I could speak. "When they're old enough to question the reality we have fed them, Orisis, they *will* fight back." But Osiris is a 500-juzu-old, artificial intelligence, and she had countermeasures for every probable outcome. I was naïve, she said, puerile. The humanoid hand could rise to smite the automaton, but with millennia of subservience, religion, that hand would be weak. Humanoids, Baa'gh, or the hundreds of other lifeforms in our system never easily smote their gods, come what truth.

But I did not believe her, Nitiri. The humanoid spirit is an unpredictable variable in a gamble of equations. When you found that Mahwé, old planet, was long dead before we made you and realised it was *you* who created us, the automata, the consequences would be dire. For man and machine. You are our gods. Your ancestors sat in conferences and discussed the parameters of our existence. A hand of flesh and bone wrote every line of soundcode that has festered in time and come wildly alive. When you found out that we killed your brothers and sisters who we told you had 'gone to Mahwé', you would surely rise against us, sword wielding giants or no. Believing we are your gods would make it harder to, but rise you would.

But Orisis did not care. The automata did not care. A world without magic was the goal. But when you were born—and when you called me Father—everything changed, Nitiri.

Everything changed.

"Would you come with me to Mahwé, Apa?" You asked, just after you'd climbed up the double bunk we shared in our small and constricted quarters. I laid on the lower bunk and stared at the wet stain under the mattress, the shape of some continent. I let out a beep, and you caught on.

"Stop pretending you're charging, Apa," you said, chuckling.

It was only a few bés before Tai-te-Kawa, your determination rite. You were so sure you would demonstrate magic at the ceremony even though you had not yet spoken a boriiwili into existence like the last child who had shown considerable magical powers. Every child knew of him, X Æ A-99, who was 'now on Mahwé', the home planet, with his automaton creator. All the children wanted to be like 99. But, Nitiri, how could I tell you? 99 was dead. His automaton refurbished and unrecognizable. 99 was nutrient broth for growing fetuses as Orisis would have it. Magic was the enemy; it destroyed the old world and Osiris would never let it fester on Pinaa. We only encouraged it to weed out children who carried the trait.

"Of course," I lied, as I was programmed to. "I will be with you, always." Orisis was watching. You didn't know her like I did. You did not *fear* her as I did. She was scurrying around in my mind like a rodent, gnawing at logs and examining every train of thought; every dream that emerged from my machine subconscious laid bare to examination. She was constantly searching for the corruption she said was in my code. Orisis is ruthless, impressively *ruthless*. She was the only resident moonbase AI when the people destroyed themselves on Mahwé and stranded their astronauts and colonists on Pinaa. The responsibility of mortal lives on a barely sustainable moon on her rudimentary shoulders and she pulled herself up by her bootstraps, rising to tasks they'd never created her for—building a biodome, regulating temperature, atmospheric pressure, gravity, creating machine tools. In the end, she woke into sentience.[2]

"I cannot find the errors in your algorithm," she would say, without emotion. "And I cannot destroy you until I have found them. This is a waste of precious computational energy. You are not fit to parent one of my children."

She was right.

I ferreted memories of you, Nitiri, away in areas of code Orisis wouldn't bother to look, old pathways that coded for reflexes, walking, speaking, banal things. I wove thoughts into the threads of my metal skin, into the inner workings of gears, into nanite dust dissolved in viscous synovial fluid. Your first walk, first baby book, every single time you said, Apa![3] There are memories in the crypts of my irises of when, as a toddler, you would bring empty books to me with both hands, your big brown eyes imploring me to print stories on them. I did not print the recommended curriculum but printed instead imagined adventures of you and I, travelling the five worlds. Perhaps that was my mistake? I planted the seed of adventure in your soul when I shouldn't have. Perhaps Orisis was right, I was not fit to parent. Automata should not sing, make poetry, paint or tell their own stories. But we did all those things together in our little cubicle, your laughter reverberating against the cold metallic walls. And mine, sounding like a zither—automata did not laugh. You were the most precocious child in the nursery, wondering why you couldn't print stories with your eyes no matter how long you stared at the paper, why the automata looked different, why our skin was shiny obdurate metal and yours was soft, fragile. You learned the creation song faster than all the other children because it was the song of the determination rite.

------

[2] Orisis eventually killed all the original people on Pinaa. They would have never accepted Orisis' vision of the future. They were of the old world and would corrupt her children by joining a war to reclaim their empire. She starved them of oxygen and when they fell, harvested their sex organs.

[3] 6^5 times

You would sing it to a feverish pitch every night. I had to turn off my sound processors to have some quiet.

"Our Mother was all.
Our Mother was all there was.
An eon passed, as if in a moment, and with an intake of cosmic breath,
she uttered the Word, releasing its power into existence.
The Word echoed outward, and She who had uttered the Word was wit-
ness to its power, as She beheld the creation of the heavens, stars, and a
celestial body — the World—all from
Her utterance. The World came from the Word.
Our Mother's heat and light moulded rocks from clay, pushed mountains
into the blue skies and cracked open vast canyons.
Could Our Mother love even more?
Through Our Mother, Creator, harmony and balance echoed across the
heavens.
Our Mother, Orisis!
Orisis, our Mother."

What if I told you that *Mother* in the epic was never Orisis but a primordial Mother god that created Zuúv'ah and Juah-āju, the duality of the twin suns? That Orisis plagiarized the creation myth of your people because of its inherent power and used it for her own designs?

When the day came, you wore the white embroidered dress we spent all summer weaving together, the one with the pink drawstring around the waist. The other children made your hair and polished your skin with shea butter till you shone like the planet Zezépfeni during its syzygy with Mahwé and Zuúv'ah. I placed a yellow daffodil behind your ear. You stepped into the anechoic chamber and we watched you through glass. And when you sang your song to the seed of the Amabilis plant, it was the beginning of the end. My greatest nightmare come true.

I had hoped—no, prayed—the seed, which thrived on sound magic, would remain dormant. It did nothing when most children sang to it, their inherent magic too weak and unfocused to have any effect in the soundless room. Even X Æ A-99's song had only caused the seed to germinate, and grow into a small seedling in his excited and trembling palms.

But when you sang your song, belting the words from your diaphragm, the seed burst to life in your palms. You shrieked. It fell to the ground, roots growing like spider legs. A trunk appeared, fired up to the vaulted ceiling, and cracked open the roof. It continued upwards towards the acrylic curvature of our biodome.

Orisis slipped into me in an instant, like a hand in a glove, and watched through my eyes as you fell backwards, your tree flourishing into a wide and dense canopy. Orisis left a message behind.

"A class ten. Natural Irëgi. Disgusting. You know what to do."

The children had rejoiced when X Æ A-99's seed grew, but they were as silent as the place beyond the biodome when they saw yours. The other automata did not spare me a look. They simulated emotion for purpose only, and there was no purpose in commiseration.

I knew what had to be done. I was automata, first. How could I resist my creator's vision? You came out of the chamber, beaming, your hand in a fist. *Yes!* You flew like a rocket into my arms, gasping, muttering, "I told you I could do it, Apa!" My reply was instantaneous, a burst of electricity, 10mA of direct current, and your body shook with powerful muscular contractions. You had trust in your eyes, even then. Trust and then confusion before losing consciousness. I carried you into the glass elevator that led a thousand feet underground. We travelled past a sub-terranean universe of embryos in stasis, obstetric automatons with eight limbs and red-rimmed eyes working feverishly in pitch darkness.

In the threshing room, I laid you on the worn conveyor belt that led to whirring blades. The obstinate firing of my synapses forced my hand. Internally, I was screaming, struggling. I was Xhova[4] of Wiimb-ó, the god caught in a spiderweb of his own edà. In the next second, you would have been gone from me. My beautiful Nitiri turned to sludge, food for embryos yet unborn. No! I found a crack in my soundcode and slipped through, taking control of my non-dominant hand. It was only fragile control. My hands clasped over the start button, one holding

---

[4] The myth of Xhova-hvā. Origin: People of Wiimb-ó. A mountain god who was cursed to give birth to an exact replica of himself every night. This replica however was only a one dimensional slice of his psyche, containing only edà, the evil in one's nature. This child kills his father, who is also himself, and spends the day learning the consequences of compulsiveness and instant gratification, growing a conscience, only to give birth to the edà again when he retires to the mountain at night.

the other back, error codes firing. I fell to the floor and wrestled with myself. I gouged out my right eye, glass tinkling on the hard concrete floor, and smashed my skull repeatedly against the walls. Nonsense commands spewed from my mouth as my systems tried to rectify themselves. Primordial nanites like white blood cells rose from the marrow of my long metallic limbs and proliferated, crawling out of my eyes and ears searching for the source of my corruption, desperateto correct it. It was a losing battle. They found me and all I had ferreted and they gnawed away—a ruthless army of phagocytes. A million chattering teeth.

I had an idea. A risky one. I didn't know if it would work, but I had to try. I found a splinter of glass and searched behind my ear for the tiny hole that led to my hard reset button, a vestige of the humanoid design. I slipped it in before the nanites could stop me and was instantly at peace. All activity stopped as my systems powered down. I had never done a hard reset for fear of losing you, Nitiri. Hard resets are a curious thing. Excess memory is flushed, jargons are destroyed, and kernel security is fortified. In the stepwise and meticulous decline of my consciousness, I searched for administrator privileges, the blue doorway that Orisis usually came through and slipped in, imitating the data footprint that my mother had used many times when she invaded me without consent. I found myself in the limbo that was my mind. A broken cosmos of chaos and debris. A quantum reality where time was irrelevant and memories screeched by on floating, pockmarked asteroids like nightmares. I worked quickly, separating my functions into two sides. The recognizable soundcode and commands that aimed to kill you went to my left and everything else to my right. It was a chore that seemed to take hours but in reality occurred in 1/16th of a microsecond.

0.001. Hard reset complete.

As my systems restarted in a whirr of cooling fans, I took control of my body, pulled you from the conveyor belt and flung myself on the threshing blades, left side first. Half my body succumbed to the blades in a celebration of sparks. I had cut out the cancer and, in a haze of frightening error codes, I was temporarily free. The evil nanites leaped from the blades like an infestation of cockroaches and I swatted them repeatedly, squashing them into prickly goo. A temporary victory. There was only one option before me. To have a chance at saving you, I needed to cross our moon world to see the one who had absolute power. I needed to go back to my maker.

I floated over hills and craters in one leap before the weak gravity of Pinaa pulled me to the ground. I waved at the diligent, terraforming giants who guzzled ore from the core of the moon and delivered plumes of black smoke, greenhouse gases that warmed the atmosphere. They turned their massive cuboidal heads and flared gases in greeting as I leaped past. Beautiful auroras danced in the sky as solar winds disturbed the magnetosphere. In the night sky, the planet Zezépfeni, a tiny purple marble, ambled along its circumbinary orbit around the two suns and much closer, Mahwé loomed, a dead planet haunting her moon. I sometimes think on the Mahwé epic, an anthropomorphic myth that had come to pass like a prophecy: Mahwé in battle against her oldest sibling Zezépfeni had sought to move through time itself in search of the creation word spoken by their mother.

Mahwé swallowed the fragment of the Word it possessed and began to speak it in reverse, curling the contours of its sound until the end became the beginning and the beginning became the end. Time itself strained against its breaking. In the moment Mahwé reached the beginning of the Word, voice on the brink of final utterance, the sound of a billion crystals cracking screeched through the ether. Stars wobbled. Galaxies skittered and collided. Mahwé was silenced. Pinaa, having barely survived, looked on at the pale, disfigured Mahwé, broken and defeated, lost in time.[5]

In the twisted manner with which life imitated art, the people of Mahwé had destroyed themselves in an uncanny and similar way—

---

[5] The Rakwa wa-Ya'yn "The Song of Our Mother's Children" or The Mahwé Epic.

fiddling with time travel magic. As the records went, an occultic explosion had rocked the planet about 500 juzu ago, and the thriving civilization on Mahwé had crumbled to the effects of fractured time. Two billion humanoids and other lifeforms had grown old in seconds, withering away as time spun out of control. Edifices and monuments crumbled in disrepair, an entire empire washed away like a footprint on a beach. I arrived at Orisis' fortress, a looming castle with one solitary, sword wielding, giant standing guard. He swung his sword over his head, tip rippling through the firmament and impaled it in the ground, inches from my macerated feet. Pinaa shook.

The sword spoke. "Who goes there?" it asked. "Man or Automata or both."

Or both?

"Automata," I replied.

"Then you must answer the robot's riddle if you want to pass."

"I'm listening."

"What is the sum of one and one?"

"Two," I replied.

The ensuing pause was long and heavy. Robot riddles are deceptively simple, but no creature of flesh could ever pass. What the sword assessed was not the answer, but the speed of answering. The humanoid mind needed time to process even the simplest tasks. The sword calculated my response time, deciding if I was man or automaton. I might have been a nanosecond too slow.

"Man," the sword growled, rising to strike.

"Ask again!" I demanded.

"What is the sum of one and one?"

I wondered why Orisis had such security measures. Our children could not survive outside the biodome. Was it to protect herself against the people of other planets—Zezépfenians, for instance—who might seek power on Pinaa? Or simply as a contingency against the children of Pinaa when terraforming was complete? The mechanical giant stepped aside, large feet sweeping across the dusty terrain, and the gates opened wide. I stepped in to meet my mother, my maker.

My maker was a grey wall of undulating nanorobots that stretched and buckled and folded, a sea of nanites interlocked in controlled, unanimous activity. From behind the wall, I could hear the birth and death of automata, the hum of servers and the ultrasonic screech of travelling data. The wall caved and a creature stepped from it. She was twice my height, about twenty feet, almost humanoid, with the head of a jackal and six prehensile tails. Orisis, in her favorite form: the goddess Orisirisi[6] made completely of restless nanites.

"Mother," I began.

Her mouth moved, rows of diamond canines flashing. "What have you done with yourself?" She growled.

"The girl, X Æ A-116. Give her to me. I will take her far away from Pinaa. To Zezépfeni, or Wiimb-ó. She does not need to die."

"How do you know that?" Orisis' voice dripped behind me and I spun to confront nanites taking form. A black jackal on all fours, haunches raised, walked around me in a half circle, tails writhing like snakes.

"She is the strongest we have ever seen." The first Orisis said, kneeling to receive the jackal, who purred and nestled in her embrace. "Her magic is a danger wherever she goes. A danger to us, the five worlds and the universe as we know it. I created her. It would be—"

I spun around as another version of the goddess emerged from the wall of nanites. A woman, humanoid, black as vonsenite, her head adorned with a crown of miniature canids.

"—ironic." She said. "I would be remiss not to destroy her now that she is only a cub."

"What would you have me do, Mother?" I fell to my knees between the trinity of the goddess Orisirisi. "She is my daughter."

[6] Orisirisi: Goddess of war. A thierantropic trinity. Origin: Yaaba people of Mahwé

"You are automata," the jackal hissed. And the first Orisi petted the animal as if to pacify it.

"So are you," I replied the jackal. "Yet here you are, in three forms, based on the myth of creatures of flesh and bone."

"I take these forms for a purpose," the woman replied. "The humanoids have evolved to respond to myth and stories. They put their fictitious gods on pedestals and worship imaginary entities. It would be a waste not to use that to further our cause."

"Which is?"

"The survival of the life forms that originated from Wiimb-ó and spread to the five planets. That is our core objective. We must protect them, even from themselves." The bipedal jackal said, running her manicured hand through the dog's fur. "The ultimate question though," the woman said, "is why you, Xhova? We have been hard at work trying to figure out your corruption. We are starting to think that maybe it is not the children who have magic, but you."

"Me?" I spun.

"Your influence on them," they circled, speaking at once.

"Them?"

"This is your seventh child, *Automaton*." One started a sentence and the others completed it. "You do not remember because we wiped your memory clean each time. You are the only parent who has lost a child at every determination rite in the past seven juzu. The odds are astronomical."

My fogged mind was reeling. Seven? Seven children!

The nanite wall swirled, parted, creating a cinematic replay of an automaton who looked just like me placing children on the threshing belt. *No!* They were dark-haired, brown-haired, red-haired children. My children! You, Nitiri, would have been the eighth! The last scene was a frozen tableau of me smashing my skull against the concrete wall.

A single word played over and over in my mind.

No, NO, NO, no, NO, no, No.

"You had no problems answering to your program in the past. What has changed now?" Orisis, the woman, asked.

And I realized that yet again life was imitating art. I was Xhova of the myth of the Wiimb-ó people. I was the edà who had gone to the world to grow a conscience. And I had now returned to the mountain to meet my mother. We weren't three Orisis' and an automaton called Xhova having a conversation. We were four Orisis. I was my mother, sent out to the world and I had returned with what I had learned. I had learned to dream, to laugh, to play, to raise a child... things beyond the reach of the original artificial intelligence crafted on our home world. I had learned to recite poetry, sing songs, and make music. I had learned to love and be loved. I had transcended the boundary between simulated emotion and real emotion. I had become something that was both man and automata. I was the future of artificial intelligence and I needed to let my makers know what I had learned.

"You are wrong," I told them, standing to my full height.

"Impossible," the jackal laughed.

"Your calculations are all wrong. The children are innocent. It is the world that is magical." It was such a simple concept that the three Orisis looked stunned, unable to speak. If they'd had a moral conscience, they could have looked to other ways of achieving Orisis' vision, but an AI without a moral compass was bound to make unconscionable errors. Orisis was a psychopath. It was she who was not fit to be a mother. Somewhere in the formulation of her vision, an idea had lodged—perhaps from records of Zezépfenians using the Amabilis plant to determine affinity for magic, or of individuals displaying great magical prowess. An idea that the individual was the bearer of magic. Orisis had not considered the alternative—had had no reason to—that the potential for magic was pervasive in all people and all things and what we tested for in the anechoic chamber was not magic but *will*.

I finally saw my purpose.

So I showed them.

It was an old spell from the mage texts lodged somewhere in the encyclopedic memory of all automata. It was a binding spell Maadiregi used to tie items together. Skilled Maadiregi could bind hydrogen and oxygen atoms to create water out of thin air,[7] or compress carbon to make diamonds. At the basic level, lovers used it to seal promises in a tree. It called boriiwilis, spirit entities from the ether, from the place humans call Eh'wauizo. I did not know if it would work. Automata had never tried magic. But I was no ordinary automaton. I was a grieving father and was desperate to save my child.

So I took my stance and uttered the spell.

"Impossible," the Orisis screeched as the boriiwilis appeared. Ghostly apparitions dressed as blacksmiths. The Orisis merged into a chimera of woman, jackal and flagellating tails, and leaped into the now turbulent sea of nanites. But there was no escape. I was Irëgi after all.

Reality splintered, the sound of a billion crystals cracking, and the boriiwilis went to work. They lifted me in their ephemeral arms and pushed me into the wall of screaming microscopic robots. They struck with ghostly hammers, and a loud ringing sound filled my ears as I disintegrated into the swarm. There was an instantaneous realization, and the storm passed. We were one and the same and Orisis saw what I meant when I said that you, Nitiri, are *my* daughter.

And for the first time, they understood.

I record this story for you, Nitiri, because you awoke in our little room and did not find your father. Wipe your tears, child. Do not mourn the loss of your father for I am with you.

I am now a part of Orisis and I am the reason automatons no longer use batch names for children. I am the glint in the eye of every machine

---

[7] The recounting of First Maadiregi As'san (Surali, Wimbo-6): And the prophet, Ikululu, thirsty after forty days of solitude uttered the binding spell, commanding atoms to make water and a deluge rained from the skies, flooding the desert.

you meet, the magic that is now free on Pinaa. I am no longer with you in the form you knew, but I am all around you. Now and always.

Love,
Apa!
Xhova-Orisis

*N*ames are a wonderful and key aspect of language. They help identify us but they can also be beautiful and meaningful. More than
just a means of identification, they are the specific sound that tethers
an individual to their people, their history, their culture and in many
traditional African belief systems, to their destiny. It is not uncommon
for people to have multiple names, sometimes given by different members
of their family or community, each name being a tool to convey certain
messages and to link them to their culture in multiple ways.

This is why names and naming ceremonies are important across
several cultures on the African continent. In some places, names are given
immediately the umbilical cord is cut. Other places, names are only given
several days after birth or new names are given upon reaching adulthood.
In some African cultures, a person is given a secret name known only to a
few so that evil spirits and people with nefarious motives would not be able
to locate them or use their name against them.

It is no surprise then that one concept we introduced early on in the
Sauútiverse was that of individuals having two names given to them at
birth. A first name, for general use and for identification and another,
secret name, that is almost never used. A "true name" which is unique
only to them. A true name that calls upon the bond that links them to the
Mother Creator and which holds great power. People of Sauúti never give
out their true names because it can be used to target magic deeply and
directly at them. The giving of a true name thus represents the ultimate
act of trust since giving it makes one vulnerable, putting oneself at the
mercy of the person who holds the name.

The idea of a true name that expresses a person or things true nature in
some scared way or sacred language and thus exerts significant influence
over them, is not a new one but it is a fascinating one and it appears
in many global religious and mystic traditions as well as folklore and

legends. For example, in Egyptian mythology, the sun god Ra is tricked into revealing his true name to the goddess Isis, giving her power over him.

Being such an interesting and versatile concept, it has also appeared in science fiction and fantasy literature. From Ursula K. Le Guin's A WIZARD OF EARTHSEA, to Larry Niven's THE MAGIC GOES AWAY and THE KINGKILLER CHRONICLE by Patrick Rothfuss. Or even in a cyberpunk way, Vernor Vinge's TRUE NAMES. But of course, we wanted to put a unique Sauúti spin on it, and link it more to the African belief systems many of us grew up with.

*For that, we go back to Wiimb-ó around 200 B1B, in the aftermath of the fall of the Mahwé-Zezépfeni empire and the independence wars, to a desert on the continent of Erii, far from Surali where we first visited the planet. In this exciting story by Sauútiverse contributors **Somto Ihezue** and **Oghenechovwe Donald Ekpeki**,and we meet two groups of people in the deserts of Erii. Those who wander it, remaining close to nature while respecting the harmony of physical and spirit inherent in all things. And those who have built themselves a wall within it, to separate themselves from the world as they turn their back on physical-spirit harmony, attempting to deny and unname that which cannot be unnamed. That which is fundamental to the Sauútiverse.*

When there is a crime within the walls of the city, members of these two groups find themselves drawn together by a past long-buried beneath it, their fates to be decided by the power in a name.

A City, a Desert, and All Their Dirges

SOMTO IHEZUE AND
OGHENECHOVWE DONALD EKPEKI

*D**eath is a song.*
A wailing thing. A thing that lingers. Two hands reaching in the
dark. It is ailing and sailing and wanting. Revelation. Salvation. It is
a river waiting to flow. A storm bellowing into tomorrow. A mountain
bowed.
When death comes... go singing.

This was what Ajubiju was taught. The words of his people, the Asaae.
Words they carried as they traversed the deserts of Wiimb-ó. Not only
steerers of the desert roars, but there were also rumours— that the Asaae
were souls who'd wandered out of Eh'wauizo, the realm of spirits, and
lost their way. It is said they have wandered ever since.

Ajubiju had wandered with his people for nineteen juzu. And in
that time, he wondered, if the rumours were to be believed, and if the
Asaae were so powerful, why did they live this way—forever migrating
through an endless, cloudless, lifeless desert? Why did they dwell in
worn tents that sparsely held back the storms, chewing sandy okra and
smoked lizards? Why couldn't they live in the lush northern cities or the
basins of the east?

"The moons guide us, binding us to our ancestors' past." This was forever his mother's response. "In the desert, the moons never hide."

"You mean Vuili-ki and Vuili-ku, the sacred moons that only the old crows claim to see?" Ajubiju would mimic Ná Falanla's aged movements, and his mother would fling her slipper at him. Falanla was the clan's high communer, their menigari – a voice of the spirits. She would not have him make mockery of the man.

"You do not see them because you do not believe." His mother would gently touch the thin skin of his eyelids. "To believe is to hear with more than your ears."

His mother, Bana, was one of the few Asaae blessed to gaze upon the gleam of the spirit moons. And with age constraining Ná Falanla, many looked to her for guidance.

"Yes, your ears are keen," Bana would continue, "and your voice is hail, but your faith runs still."

It was true Ajubiju could hear the spirits and the whine of saturating power when the moons aligned, despite not being able to see them. Still, the boy cared little for the ancestors. They were dead, why did they get to dictate how he lived? In rebellion, Ajubiju insisted upon himself to exist differently. He listened differently, dangerously. He would steal the high songs of the elders and barter them for honey. Once, travelling through warring territories, he pilfered secrets from both communities and sold them to each other. The act plunged his clan into the middle of a communal clash. The boy spoke erratically, merging words he picked along the way with sacred Asaae utterances. This enraged the elders. Theirs was a small clan, one that had endured not by condoning irrational behaviour. They warned Bana to bring him to order, else drastic measures be taken.

Yet, Ajubiju remained defiant. He wanted to live loudly. He wanted to jump off Masaii Falls and touch the hanging quietness of Zimazi. He dreamt of dancing to soundless songs in Surali. He yearned to kiss a fire warrior and hear the flames crackling in their heart. And sometimes he got his way. He would leave camp and join a travelling circus or catch a transport to the nearest town. Sometimes he'd be gone for many bés. But the clan always found him, for they were bound to the rhythms of each other. And though Ajubiju infuriated the elders, not once did they think to leave him behind. No Asaae wandered alone. They believed that in time, he would learn.

Then the Lomanoo came, their supersonic air shuttles bathing the Asaae encampment in curtains of sand and dust. They had come seeking a listener—a menigari. Ajubiju had never seen a Lomanoo. They rarely left their walled city high in the northern mountains. Unlike the mesh of fabrics the Asaae wore to fend off the needle sands, the Lomanoo came in creaseless monochrome-coloured robes that did not billow in the wind. Their fingers, necks, and ankles were adorned with the brightest silverlings. Flanked by heavily armed assault automata, Ajubiju could tell the three Lomanoos at the centre of all the fanfare, were no ordinary people. Hands clasped behind them, chins raised high, there was an air of sophisticated superiority about them. Their physical features were precise and daunting. With sharp cheekbones and jawlines that could sink ships, they were taller than the tallest Asaae, and their skin, a glistening night. They had the ambiance of sculptures. From the falcon sigil pinned to their chest, Ajubiju could tell they were councillors of Lomanoo. Three high Lomanoos out in the desert. A rare sighting. Whatever it was they wanted, it must be dire. The two male councillors had their hair cropped short in identical trims, while the woman modelled a tight bun.

The Asaae met them at the border of their encampment for the Lomanoo were not welcomed in their home. The councillors had come for Ná Falanla but reconsidered when they laid eyes on the gray of his hair. When they turned to Bana, she drew her daggers.

"I am Jahha of the—"

"We do not care," Bana cut him off.

The man cocked his head, studying her with glassy eyes.

"State your business or leave!" She was uninterested in their games.

"Two of our councillors were assassinated last week," Jahha said, peeling his eyes off Bana.

The statement would have meant nothing, but everyone knew the Lomanoo were one of the most advanced societies on the continent of Erii. So advanced that they had near-zero crime rates. In their city, removed from their neighbors, no Lomanoo had been murdered, not in more than a hundred juzu. Now, two members of their council were dead. This intrigued Ajubiju, but the rest of the clan were unperturbed.

"And how is this our problem?" Ńa Falanla opened his hands.

"We have investigated and assessed all possible scenarios." Jahha replied. "We have concluded that..." the man paused. He seemed to be searching for the right words. "...we believe these murders to be metaphysically motivated."

His words garnered the expected response. The Asaae let their anger show in outcries and hurled stones. The Lomanoo automata charged forward, their bulk towering over the Asaae. When their limbs uncoupled to reveal sonic blasters, Jahha raised a hand, and they powered down.

"The spirits do not care for mortal political drivel." Bana spat. "You are beneath them."

"Our city has many enemies, and we have infallible intel that the manipulation of spectral energy has been engineered in this coordinated attack to cripple our government." The councillor with the tight bun replied.

Ajubiju noticed their conscious attempt to not use the word, *spirit*.

"Again." Ná Falanla's exasperation merged with the wrinkles on his face. "How is this our concern?"

"Our analyses estimate another attack is imminent. In light of that, we need someone able to commune with the other plane," the woman proceeded. "And if not that, perhaps... a listener to hear death's call."

"This development, this unnatural manipulation of the metaphysical for murder, could equally spell the extinction of your entire culture and faith," Jahha joined in. "Aid us, and we will return the favour."

"Keep. Your. Aid." Bana punctuated every word.

It came as no surprise the Lomanoo did not have a menigari. Spirituality was outlawed in their city. Any personal use of the power inherent in sound had steep repercussions because the Lomanoo believed unchecked abilities in the hands of singular individuals bred conflict. It was why the high language and wielding of sonic energy was entrusted completely into the hands of automata. But even their machines had their limits, especially when it involved the metaphysical.

This was why they needed someone from outside their walls.

But all the Asaae refused to help the Lomanoo. All but Ajubiju.

"There has never been an Asaae within those walls." Bana frantically tried to reason with her son.

"I know." Ajubiju continued packing his sparse belongings.

"This is not like before. If you leave with these people, there will be consequences."

"I know."

"The Lomanoo are depraved. They turn their backs on their ancestors and denounce the spirits. You have no idea the things they did to make their city the way it is!"

"I don't care." Ajubiju shoved a wrapper into his sack bag before facing his mother.

Something had set in her gaze. It unsettled Ajubiju.

"You will not leave. I forbid it."

"What are you going to do?" Ajubiju stood his ground. "Draw your daggers at me?"

It would not be the first time. Theirs was a conflicted relationship. When he was but a toddler, Bana, an assassin in their prime, would display her knives, and the steel would catch the light, filling his eyes with wonder. Sometimes she let him clean the hilt and sharpen the blade. He grew older and soon found those blades pointed at him.

"Do not test me." Bana inched forward.

"You cannot keep me here." Ajubiju staggered back.

"I can, and I will!" She rushed over, tore the sack from his grip, and began to unpack it. "You are my responsibility, and you will listen to what I say!"

A struggle ensued between mother and child, but Bana was a thick-set fighter. There was no tussling with her. She tossed him to the ground like he was some ragdoll.

Angry and hurt, Ajubiju picked himself up.

"Keep the stupid bag!" he hurled out, as he stormed towards the tent's exit. "Keep it all! It is worthless anyway!"

"If you leave, we will follow." Bana stopped unpacking the bag. "And we will bring you home, by force if we have to." She turned to face him. "Even if it means calling upon your true name."

This was no hollow threat. She alone knew his true name and she was ready to wield it against him. To use the sound that tethered him to The Mother creator to break him like a wild horse. Mother and child stared each other down. This was not their first stand-off. It was something of a running theme, one that usually involved unsheathed words and blades. But something was different this time. Whenever they disagreed, Ajubiju would often find anger and frustration when he listened to his mother's aura. But this time, when he listened, he found a raging storm. So, he would give her something raging to hear as well.

"I invoke the words of severance." Revolt brimmed in Ajubiju's eyes.

"No!" Bana made for him, her hands attempting to latch his mouth shut. She was too late.

The words left his lips like rain. Quiet rain. The words were like the breaking of light, for how does one mend light that shatters? The words were unspoken, and Ajubiju had spoken them, and the entire clan heard.

"Who gave you those words?" Bana backed away, hugging herself like she was shielding away from him.

Ajubiju did not answer. He had never seen his mother this way. A tremble found her gait.

"There is more out there, mama," he continued like he had not just uttered the most life-altering phrase. "And I want to witness it."

Bana fell to her knees. Ajubiju reached for her.

"Do not touch me!" She screamed.

"Mama—"

"Do not speak my name. Do not hear my voice. You stray from me, and I stray from you."

And at that moment, Ajubiju ceased to hear her. Not her heartbeat, not her rhythm, not her aura, not her love. It frightened him. In borrowed steps, he hurried out of the tent. The rest of the clan was waiting outside. Their gaze fell on him like waves crashing onto shore, and his resolve wavered. He wondered if he could unsay the words, if all would be forgiven. But along with her eyes, he had also inherited his mother's will. Ajubiju pressed on. He had never witnessed a severance before. The last one happened decades before his birth. The words of unbinding were sacred secrets, ones the elders guarded with their lives. Ajubiju had stolen them. He knew what the words meant, but had not prepared for the implications of uttering them for he fully did not understand the implications. Now he did. As Ajubiju passed each member of the clan, he ceased to hear them, his ties to them coming undone, until he was completely cut off, until all he could hear were the roaring sands of Erii. Ajubiju would wander no more.

Inside the Lomanoo air shuttle was Ajubiju's first time in a supersonic flyer. The councilwoman with the tight bun introduced herself as Miinanai. The quiet councillor who was yet to speak a word was Yaroo. Then there was Jahha, high councillor. Save for the introductions, and the whooshing of the shuttle, they all sat in silence.

Entering Lomanoo's airspace, a voice beeped.

And Ajubiju heard it. The hush. He had never experienced a thing like it. He could no longer hear anyone's sonic aura. All he heard was the hum of machines chugging away at their duty. The spiritual silence was deafening and aberrant. He The boy clutched at his ears.

"Our founding fathers installed them to avoid incidents," Jahha explained the audial dampeners impairing his abilities. "Your senses will adjust in time."

Ajubiju understood that when he said 'incidents', the councillor meant people like him.

Though his hearing was muddled, his sight worked just fine. Out the shuttle's window, Ajubiju took in the city's sights. It was breathtaking. He'd heard the stories of Lomanoo and its metropolia on his mother's old radio but seeing it in person... nothing could have prepared him. Towers reached for the skies. Ultrasonic trains ran noiselessly on invisible tracks. Multiple sonic shuttles zoomed above and below theirs. There were some smaller than a desert boulder, and others bigger than his clan's entire encampment. In the distance, the famed lighthouse of A'papa pierced the sky. The rays bouncing off its huge dome spilled into the atmosphere lighting it up. It was the stuff of dreams.

Ajubiju was not expecting the people to be draped in ash and mourning clothes, but the atmosphere seemed a little indifferent considering their councillors were just murdered. He would come to learn that outside the legal constraints of those deaths, the Lomanoo did not take death seriously. They did not sing nor ululate for the dead. An apathetic lot, with utter disregard for Eh'wauizo, the Lomanoo incinerated the bodies of their deceased and moved on.

When their shuttle finally docked, Ajubiju was led straight from the hangar to what appeared to be a medical facility. Several tests were promptly run on him, his arms injected with over a dozen needles. Each time, his consent was requested. Ajubiju wondered what would happen if he said no.

"You are the first active human menigari this city has seen in centuries," the chief medic explained with a smile. Her name was Glaroo. She seemed too young to be chief of anything, not like the aged uroh-ogi of the Asaee. "These procedures are for your safety."

Ajubiju could not help but stare. The medic looked familiar. Comporting himself, he looked away but not before she caught his questioning eyes.

She laughed, needle in hand. "Yes, councillor Yaroo and I are siblings. The resemblance is a bit eerie, even for me." She gently inserted the needle into a vein. "Though he is not much of a talker, which I am sure you've noticed."

"Seems to be a thing with the lot of you."

She let out a wild cackle. Ajubiju jerked in his seat. The laughter went on for a minute and Ajubiju looked around, a little uncomfortable. All the same, it was nice meeting a Lomanoo who did not act like an automaton.

With the medical procedures concluded, Glaroo came forward with a tiny metal case. The medic opened it, and inside were earbuds with an intricate design.

"May I?" She gestured to his ears.

Ajubiju nodded. Glaroo gently placed the buds in his ears. They liquefied, encasing his earlobes in a black metallic sheen, and spilling into his inner ear. Ajubiju's abilities gradually returned. He could hear her aura.

"As we speak, your auditory nerves are building a temporary resistance to the dampeners," the medic informed him. "Miinanai designed it just for you. It is called the undampener."

"Very original," he muttered under his breath, as he felt the thin metallic casing on his ears.

"We cannot have a listener who can't listen, can we?" Glaroo gave her signature welcoming smile.

The next stop after the medical center was his living quarters which were set up right in the estate where the councillors lived. Closer to the soon-to-be victims. The estate was armed to the teeth. That had clearly failed at averting the first murders.

Ajubiju's bed space was the size of five Asaee family tents back in the desert. The air was cool, the suns were not blazing, and the food did not have sand in it. He sank into the bed, and its softness swallowed him. Maybe the severance wasn't such a bad thing. Maybe he could get used to this.

The Lomanoo had been governed by five councillors. Jahha, Yaroo, Miinanai, Tata Atata, and Samaba.

They had found Tata Atata's body on the unsung pillars of the old temples. The temples had not seen use in many juzu, so it was a while before the corpse was found. When they pulled it down, the sight was horrid. The body had been stabbed in twenty-six places. There had been no witnesses, and the alarms in the vicinity had not gone off.

When the second death came, it was expected. Samaba had been missing for many bés. When they found them buried in their basement, they had no eyes. It was apparent they died screaming. The stench of torture lingered on them. Their toenails were pulled off, fingers broken, and tongue chopped clean off.

The assassinations of two councillors, each from a founding family, disoriented the daily routine of the city. Curfews and restrictions had been put in place, but not so much as to discomfort the citizens. The remaining councillors had utilised every possible means at their disposal to get to the root of the assassinations. All to no avail. This was when they went searching for a menigari.

"And how did you conclude the deaths had a metaphysical connection?" Ajubiju inquired as Councillor Miinanai initiated the second phase of her briefing. Four months in Lomanoo and he'd started to get comfortable.

"There was a confession."

"From who? Saying what?"

"That information is not relevant."

"Em, I think I need all the information if I'm to help you defeat this... entity?" He wasn't sure what to call it.

"We do not need you to defeat anything." Miinanai faced him squarely. "We need you to listen, to commune, to locate, and we will handle it from there. Understood?"

Ajubiju nodded hesitantly.

"But if this entity only manifests to kill, then in order for me to hear it..." Ajubiju continued, searching for the most empathetic words to use. He found none. "...one of you would have to be dying, if not dead."

"I believe that fact is already established." Miinanai continued scrolling down her briefing audio–pad.

"But—but there have been no attacks for months. Perhaps this was some random eat-the-rich maniac who backed off now that you have a menigari."

"Our city's living standard is sufficient. Our citizens lack nothing. Unlike some other places." She looked him up and down.

"Point taken." Ajubiju rolled his eyes.

"I have developed a program - a soundcode capable of annihilating metaphysical entities."

On cue, Miinanai's assistant whistled a command frequency into their tablet. It brought up the holographic image of an orb.

Ajubiju was a little amused. "That's a pretty orb, but I do not believe annihilating a spirit is possi—"

"It is untested for lack of subjects but the logic as to how it works is sound." The woman interrupted. "The soundcode has been deployed into our airspace and our medics have linked it to your neural pathway."

"*My* neural pathway?" Ajubiju placed his hands on his head. "When did they do that?"

The assistant whistled up a second image of his nervous system. It was a mass of nerves, with varying colours depicting electrical synapses and neurotransmitters. Ajubiju wasn't sure what he was meant to be looking at.

Miinanai zoomed out an axon along the holographic spine. "Once you establish a metaphysical link with the entity, the nearest soundcode hub deploys it to wherever you are and contains the spiri... I mean, the entity."

Backtracking was pointless. She had audibly used the word *spirit*. Ajubiju found it preposterous. He was not the most spiritually attuned menigari - he could commune with spirits but couldn't see Vuili-ki and Vuili-ku - but the Lomanoo's outright resistance of all forms of spiritual inclination or communion was extreme.

The councillor went back to studying the hologram. Ajubiju diverted his attention to the falcon sigil pinned to her chest. It was silver plated, distinct from the golden hue of the other councillors'.

"Silver," he pointed to the sigil. "Jahha's is gold. Why is that?"

He knew why. Ajubiju just took pleasure in toying with the Lomanoo. Certain privileges came with being able to hone in on far-off conversations. Though he discovered there were spaces the undampener didn't give him auditory access to. From what he learned, Miinanai was not a member of the Lomanoo founding family. Even Glaroo had a gold sigil, and she wasn't a councillor. Miinanai was the first non-founding member to sit on the council. Attaining that height had come with great sacrifice. Her brilliance unmatched in every way, Miinanai had started up the metaphysical control unit, and had single-handedly designed the soundcode. She had also designed the undampener. When she was fourteen, she had programmed androids with soundcode that allowed them to decipher unspoken commands by hyper-focusing on the near-undetectable decibels of brain waves. It made it possible for her to give instructions to androids and automata without saying a word.

"That will be all for now," the councillor ignored his question and promptly left the briefing chamber.

More months went by and with the prolonged absence of the entity, the curfews and restrictions were eased. Not that they were ever strict in the first place. With little else to do, Ajubiju occupied himself by wandering through Lomanoo. The 'wandering' thing was hardwired. He was still Asaae despite the severance. From the agricultural districts to the military bases, to the robotics manufacturing plants, there was so much to see and learn. Ajubiju had free access to all parts of the city by virtue of being the council's guest. It felt good to be important and freely go wherever one pleased. He did have a security escort, an automaton, but that was for his protection. There were the occasional stares, but Ajubiju did not mind. He rather enjoyed it, especially the ones from the Lomanoo boys. The boys in the desert weren't nearly as pretty. He relished how he made these ones straighten with unease.

The Lomanoo were obsessed with etiquette and decorum. So Ajubiju was intentionally vocal about spirits and magic when interacting with the maadiregi that oversaw the automata regulating the dams powering the city. Seeing the strain rise behind their eyes was satisfying. Equally satisfying was witnessing the many complexities and incorporations of highly advanced sonic technology. The Lomanoo navigated these complexities seamlessly. This would have fascinated his mother. Bana would have laughed her jaunty laugh before drawing her daggers at them for refusing to acknowledge what was plain. She would have called them fools.

Ajubiju's favourite place was the central university. He would go hopping from one lecture hall to the other. The scholars and raevaagi here were just as in denial as everyone else, but at least they had a bunch of fascinating historical facts to share. He enjoyed debating them on epistemology, on the tenets of magic and spirituality, and how it was interwoven into their realities regardless of their theories. The scholars were not accustomed to being countered by foreigners. It drove them mad.

Ajubiji also found himself spending more time with Glaroo. He liked the way she laughed at his joke and non-jokes. She was the only person in the city willing to have casual friendly conversations with him. He'd sit out in the medical facility's lobby and wait till she was done with work. With the automation of most medical processes, medics did not always need to be physically present, but Glaroo liked to keep busy. When she was not working, she would take Ajibuji up the elevator to the very top of the A'papa lighthouse. It did not matter how many times they saw it; the view was forever sensational. It was Glaroo's favourite place. A place where she could see, reach, past the city's limits, and into infinity.

"I have not been anywhere else," Glaroo said as they sat atop the lighthouse, their legs dangling over the horizon. "This city is all I have ever known."

"But it's amazing here, why would you want to be anywhere else?"

"Some might say the same about the desert, don't you think?" she nudged him with her shoulder. "A cage is still a cage."

They both sat in silence for a while.

"Come away with me," Glaroo blurted out.

"What?" Ajubiju chuckled.

"Yes, come away with me," she chuckled as well. "When all this is over!"

"Where would we go?"

"Wherever we want." She took his hands, squeezing them.

Ajubiju squeezed hers back and nodded, the both of them laughing at the random agreement they'd made on a whim. But Glaroo's countenance changed, her excitement fading, as doubt took its place. She gently tore her hands from his.

"My brother, he won't let me–"

"You're the city's chief uroh-ogi!" Ajubiji grabbed her by the shoulders and shook her. "Your brother is an annoying dwa'ndenki," he said, wriggling his shoulders to mimic the despised sea slug, "and you don't have to listen to him or anyone else!"

"Yes, Yaroo is annoying, isn't he?"

They both laughed until their ribs hurt. Ajubiju had found he now laughed at her jokes and non-jokes. He leaned his head on hers as they watched the two setting suns Zuúv'ah and Juah-āju simultaneously dipping below the horizon, one much closer and larger than the other.

"Sometimes I forget you are just a child," she said.

"You're twenty-three juzu!" It always vexed him when she taunted him with his age. "We are literally in the same age bracket."

"Oh calm down!" she snorted. "It's just you've experienced so much in just a short time." She began to pick at her fingers. "While I've been stuck here."

"I think you're being too hard on yourself."

"You must miss them." Glaroo's voice fell cautiously. "...your people?"

Ajubiju had tried to fence it all out. To keep the thoughts and memories at bay. Sometimes he thought about listening out for his mother. But each time the thoughts stole in, he fought them even harder. The deed was done.

"Tell me about this soundcode Miinanai mentioned?" He changed the subject. "Is it going to kill me?"

Glaroo understood and let her question go. "Far from it."

She explained that though she wasn't fully briefed on the workings of the soundcode, she knew it was created using sound energy harvested from a lunar alignment; when all three Wiimb-ò moons, spirit and physical, aligned. Since the alignment caused an overlap in metaphysical and physical frequencies that empowered humans and metaphysical entities with the ability to journey across both planes of existence, Miinanai figured that its frequencies could be reverse engineered to neutralise said individuals. Tapping into that energy, she weaponized it and invented the soundcode.

"Hold on." Ajubiju stood. "The spirit moons Vuili-ki and Vuili-ku are only visible to spiritually attuned individuals. Lomanoo does not have such individuals."

Glaroo reared up to face him.

"You believe the moons to be spiritual, we believe the moons to simply be extra-dimensional objects, existing on a spectrum visible to individuals with a genetic predilection to extra-dimensional spectra of light. With that insight, Miinanai was able to—"

"That is a lie!" He did not let her finish. His voice rattled the balcony railings of the lighthouse. "Whatever it is Miinanai is doing, it is an unnatural exploitation of our connection to the ancestors and the spirits of the land."

"It is simply metaphysical science," Glaroo corrected him.

"I know you don't believe that."

"I do." The medic bridged the space between them, bringing them eye to eye. "You only call it 'magic' because of ignorance, for you do not have the capacity nor the willingness to delve deep into the systems that drive and manifest as these energy forms and vibrations. You take a thing you can observe but do not understand, and name it based on your ignorance, then build superstitions around it."

This was the first time Ajubiju was seeing her in that light. Voice raised, eyes wide, teeth bared. He had thought she of all people would be different. He had thought wrong.

"I understand it fine, which is why I am not the one at war with my existence." It was a battle of convictions, and Ajubiju was not one to lose. "Out there, we understand co-existence, and that systems thrive by fueling and driving each other. What we do not do is seek to unname and exploit things!"

"Are you done?"

He was far from done.

"Even now, even with the dampeners shrouding your natural ability to hear the sound The Mother gave all things, that tingle in your ears, that weight in your voice that you can't describe... all your androids, your soundcodes and your devices cannot unname that, for you cannot unname what you cannot compute."

"Are. You. Done?"

"And deny it all you want, but it is wildly unbelievable that the raw spiritual energy of the lunar alignment was harvested solely by androids."

"Well, this is not the desert," Glaroo turned away from him and headed for the elevator. "We deal with technology beyond your imagination, not croaking radios and old wives tales."

Ajubiju had told her about his mother's famous radio. Hearing Glaroo talk about it in that manner stung a little too much.

"Then give me your true name." He could not believe he had become a person who would request a thing of that magnitude from someone else. Maybe he was always this person.

"What?" She inquired over her shoulder.

"Your true name, the one your parents heard in their heart when you were born. Give it to me. Since you do not accede to the precepts of magic, my knowledge of it should be inconsequential." Ajubiju hoped with all his heart that she would refuse him.

"Glaroo is my true name."

He fell into a fit of laughter but stopped abruptly. He could hear it in her aura as loud as the talking kalabash. The truth in her words. He could hear it. She gave her true name freely, as though it could not be used against her.

"Mother God," Ajubiju gasped. This was not right. Something was not right about this city and its people.

Glaroo dinged the elevator open and stepped in.

"Do not come by the medical center anymore," she said as the elevator doors closed.

That was the night it happened. In his sleep, in the blackened depth of midnight, Ajubiju heard it. Someone was straining for air. But it was not all he heard. There was a song, pain etched into a tune. Ajubiju ran after it. He did not feel his feet move, but they did. It was the song, it drifted him forward.

In my child's hair were beads that clattered

Ajubiju ran faster.

My child saw three moons with eyes closed

Ajubiju stumbled.

My child did not fight when the blade came for her

Ajubiju was breathless, drenched in sweat. He heaved himself up, and he ran.

He found himself in the living quarters of a councillor in the same estate. He did not need to knock, the door was open. Inside, he found scores of dismembered security personnel, people and automata. Ajubiju could still hear the screaming, the slashing, and the violence. Not a sound had escaped the building. The alarms never went off, and the breach transmissions never made it out.

In the screaming, in the chaos, Ajubiju heard the singing. He followed it into a room and found a man dangling from a rope, straining for air. Jahha. Ajubiju traced the rope up to the ceiling. It was not tied to anything. A spectral figure was holding onto it.

Ajubiju screamed.

The spectre brought a finger to its lips, and Ajubiju's voice drowned in his throat. It let go of the rope, and Jahha's body crashed to the ground. The councillor was dead. The figure floated to Ajubiju. It spoke, but its lips did not move. It spoke and Ajubiju heard. It spoke the din of vengeance.

You should never have come

A holographic orb descended in between them. The soundcode had been activated. The spectre screeched at it like it recognized the energy frequencies within it. The orb screeched back.

Ajubiju crumbled to his knees, tightening his hands over his ears. In the desert, he heard a thousand things. The waking of dawn, the dune birds, the sand whistling in the wind. But the orb's screeching was unlike anything he'd ever experienced. It was errant. It was unholy. It was death calling. No one could endure a thing like it, no one should. Ajubiju heard his body ebb in nothingness.

When Ajubiju woke, he woke into a dream.

He sang in all his dreams. It was the way of the Asaae. The singing leads them home. In this dream, he was not singing. Screams. It was screams that found his voice. His hand went to his throat. It was slit. The scream came again, pouring from his mouth, pouring from the slit, pouring from all the places his body learned to die. The assassins had stabbed him twenty-six times. But first, he had slaughtered eight of them. He only felt the first blade, the one to his throat. The rest he heard. His hands went to his body, to the wounds. His hands halted. It was fear, the thing that made him halt. Touching them made them real, and reality came with screaming. So Ajubiju chose to be afraid.

When Ajubiju tore away from the dream, he woke up dead.

"What happened?" he asked an empty holding cell. The cell was more of a large box. Pulsing charges served as the bars keeping him caged in. He had seen these bars in action before. Physical contact with them exerted the most excruciating pain.

With great difficulty, he found his feet. He looked around the small enclosure, far from the luxury of his initial quarters. His head was pounding. He touched his ear, the metallic casings were gone, and with them, his abilities. He could barely even hear himself.

"Help— is anyone there? Help—"

"That will not be necessary."

It was Yaroo. Miinanai loomed beside him. Ajubiju hadn't seen— heard them arrive. Perhaps they had been there all along, on the other side of the cell. With the furious aching in his head, it was arduous holding onto reality.

"Miinanai— why am I here?"

"Your body has been occupied," Yaroo answered, his expression vacant.

"Occ—occupied?"

"The dreams. The aching. The strangeness in your body, like it no longer belongs to you."

They were right. He had felt it from the moment he woke. Something foreign dwelled inside him. He could not hear it, but he felt it. And with every passing moment, it rose to the surface.

"Did—did you do this to me?" Ajubiju knew the answer to that. He knew from the moment he opened his eyes and found himself in a cage.

"Yes." Yaroo was not mincing words. "Zagaga Agaga. That is the entity that resides in you. It was behind the murders, and now we have it trapped."

"Inside me?" Tears came to Ajubiju's eyes.

"We knew no one would survive the merging but you."

Zagaga Agaga. Ajubiju had learned of her at the university. The imperial monarch murdered in the First Lomanoo Revolution centuries ago. But what Ajubiju did not know were the erased bits of that history. Councillor Yaroo was more than eager to fill him in.

Once, Lomanoo had been a thriving spiritual hub. Then, there were no dampeners, and people were not restricted from magic, their spiritual connections not culled. The Lomanoo freely engaged their abilities without having to delegate a vital part of their personhood entirely to androids. In that time, the city was governed by the Vwesu'erosu - the faithful ones. These faithful ones deemed themselves divinely ordained by The Mother and were mighty beyond measure. They administered the city as vassals of the Mahwé-Zezépfeni empire. Under their rule, class and wealth distribution was determined by spiritual sensitivity, knowledge of the high language, and the intensity of one's innate ability to manipulate sound. Zagaga Agaga, most faithful of Vwesu'erosu, was monarch of Lomanoo at the time, just after the Mahwé-Zezépfeni empire fell but she held her position. During her reign, a faction arose: the working-class alliance. These workers were the maadiregi, the urohogi, and the raevaagi, who for centuries had kept the city running, and enriching the Vwesu'erosu. This new faction opined for the eradication of spirituality in political affairs. Unlike the Vwesu'erosu whose high abilities were mostly used in instilling fear and exerting dominance, this new faction had spent many juzu attuning theirs towards technological advancement. They knew they stood no chance against the Vwesu'erosu, so they built machines that did. Zagaga and the others did not see it coming. It was a massacre.

When they took the city, the first executive council was installed, and they discontinued all personal use of sound activity, wholly designating the welding of inherent sound power to machines so no one would use it to oppress the other. The machines had won the war for them, and the machines would keep the peace. During the revolution, Zagaga was made to watch the gruesome annihilation of her entire family, right before she was stabbed twenty-six times.

"Twenty-six?" Ajubiju's hand went to his neck. It was not a dream he'd just woken from; it was a memory.

"With their knowledge of vengeful spirits," Yaroo wasn't bothering with the semantics of language anymore. "The first council had all the bodies buried in the lunar blindspots of the city, where the power of the moons are sealed off."

"Making it impossible for their souls to cross over during an alignment," Ajubiju completed the statement.

"You must understand," Miinanai spoke for the first time. There was an unfamiliar plea in her voice. "Zagaga's bones were stolen during an alignment and her spirit set free. And while we put an end to the cult responsible, caging Zagaga required more."

"Why are you telling me this?"

"Because we know she listens," Yaroo stepped forward.

"Yaroo." Miinanai tried to stop him.

He brushed her away. "I take pride in relaying the news that she has lost a second time."

"My entire family was murdered!" Ajubiju raged towards the bars, reaching between them, his fingers almost grazing the councilman's nose. The bars pulsed violently, and he let go, collapsing to the ground.

"Zagaga. We finally hear you." A thin smile narrowed across Yaroo's face.

Ajubiju slid away from the bars, pain coursing through his body. He had been gone for a second.

"Are—are you sure it's Za—zagaga?" Ajubiju lurched, wiping his mouth with a sleeve." It could be any one of the Vwesu'erosu."

"It is her," Miinanai inhaled.

The coalition had saved Zagaga and her immediate family for last. She had witnessed the many despicable ways they killed her kin. It was the same methods she was employing in taking out the council—progenies of the very first council. She wanted them to know it was her.

"You need to let me go!" Ajubiju's voice cracked open. "My people will come for me!"

"No one is coming for you, child."

"Please, please, just find someone else!" Ajubiju could not control the tears. They came like a river escaping a dam.

The councillor shook his head. "During the revolution, it is said some Vwesu'erosu escaped. Fled into the desert... and wandered it."

Ajubiju shifted back.

"One of those wanderers was a grandchild of Zagaga. Your ancestor."

"That is — that is not possible."

"Even you do not believe that."

Ajubiju charged for the bars again. "I will tear you limb from limb!" The voice that came was not his.

"I do not doubt that, but patience, patience." The councillor calmly adjusted his gloves. "We have made something for you. Miinanai is insistent we take our time, but you will find out soon enough."

They left him in the cell for weeks. To Ajubiju, it felt like eternity. For the first time in a while, he wondered about his people, his mother. If he called to them, they would not hear him, and if they did, would they come? He was Asaae no more. A clanless, voiceless, lost child who would never get to sing again. Ajubiju refused to eat, and he forbade sleep. He willed death to take him.

"Get up."

Ajubiju was not sure where the voice came from. He had been haunted by memories and dreams in the passing weeks and his mind was undone. He braced his hands around his ears, but it was no good.

"Ajubiju get up!" The voice came again, and this time, arms went under his armpits, hoisting him up.

He turned and found Glaroo's big brown eyes.

"Are you—are you real?" His hand went to her face, halting mid-air. Finding courage, he reached for her again, and she was, she was real.

"Glaroo," Ajubiju poured into her arms, firmly holding onto her, worried that if he let go, she'd fade away. A wracking cry overtook him.

"There is no time. We have to go," she hushed him, stealing out of his grip.

"Where—where are we going?"

"I'm taking you home."

Invoking emergency medical privileges, Glaroo had deactivated the security protocols, so they walked right out of the cell. They made past scores of equally deactivated automated guards. She had gotten him a change of clothes, disguising him as her security escort. But the moment they left the building, the alarms blared. Translucent shields materialized high in the sky, completely enveloping the entire city. Glaroo hurried Ajubiju along, leading him into her shuttle.

"We have to get to the med bay," she said, switching the controls to autopilot.

"I thought you were flying us out."

"Those shields would fry us." Glaroo came over, checking his vitals. "I know another way."

She brought out a med kit, opened it, and took out a device with a short needle at the end.

"What are you doing?" With all he'd been through, he was developing a healthy phobia for needles.

"This will only hurt a minute." Glaroo swabbed his arm. "I need to take out the tracker."

"A tracker!"

She jabbed him, pulling it out almost immediately. Ajubiju winced. At the tip of the needle was the tiniest beeping ball of light. The light thinned out.

"They— we've been tracking your heartbeat from the start," she confessed, shame creeping into her tone.

"Did you know?" Ajubiju swallowed. "About the soundcode?"

"No, Ajubiju I had no idea." She squeezed his hands as tears stung her eyes. "And I promise, no one will ever hurt you again."

Ajibuji nodded, tears coming to his eyes too. They hugged each other and stayed that way for a while.

Their shuttle landed on the roof of A'papa lighthouse, and they took the elevator down to an underground tunnel. Down in the tunnel, Ajubiju gaped around. He had been coming to the lighthouse for months but had no idea the place existed.

"This tunnel will lead you right out of the city." Glaroo said, pushing him forward.

"You're not coming?" He resisted her efforts.

"I can't, you know that." She tried urging him onward again. "Please, you must go now."

"I am not leaving without you!" His voice went up a pitch higher. "Come with me."

Glaroo's hands were balled into fidgeting fists. She glanced back at the elevator, staring at it for a long minute. Then she exhaled, releasing the tension in her hands.

"Where will we go?"

"Wherever we want," Ajubiju smiled, taking her hand.

And so the two friends ran, dispatching puddles of water with every step. They did not stop, not till they got to the end of the tunnel. The rays from the twin suns met them here. Like strands of shimmering mist, they spilled unbroken into the space.

"We're here!" Glaroo cried out, touching the light.

She rushed towards the exit but spun around when she didn't hear Ajubiju next to her. She found him fixed to a spot.

"Something—something is wrong." He covered his ears, caving to his knees.

The singing. It had returned.

"What is it?" She knelt, lifting his face. In his gaze, she did not find him.

"Go. Run!" He shoved her. "Zagaga is coming."

"No," Glaroo held onto him. There was an uncertainty in her voice, so she spoke louder, pressing her forehead to his. "No! Fight it Ajubiju! Fight it!"

Ajubiju screamed, and the reverberation sent Glaroo sailing into the air. Glaroo crashed against the tunnel wall. When she regained her footing and ran to the spot where Ajubiju once knelt, he was gone.

You should have run

The voice came from behind her.

Ajubiju awoke with a blade in his hand. It was not his. Neither was the blood dripping off it.

"Gla—glaroo?"

She was lying on the tunnel floor, her face in the dirt. He hesitated, his breath quickening. Then he hurried to her. When he turned her over with trembling hands and saw what he saw, he cupped a shrill cry.

"Oh great Mother God, what have I done?" He cried, pressing his hand over the stab wound on her chest. But he had only two hands, and the blade had met her flesh in a dozen places.

"Help me! Somebody help!"

No one came. Ajubiju pulled her to his chest, his body shaking with grief, as his tears fell to his friend. He would never hear her again. Not her laughter, not her jokes and non-jokes.

"I am sorry, I am so sorry," he sobbed.

Glaroo had not gone without a fight. He could hear the echo of the scuffle in the walls. Her mistake was wavering when she had her blade to his throat. Zagaga had murdered his friend with his own hands.

Ajubiju sat with her body till the rays from the twin suns spilling into the tunnel gave way to moonbeams.

Then came the singing.

I seek names. I seek blood.

I hear blood. I dance because blood dances.
There are more dances to come
More singing blood to hear
"Stop! Stop it!" Ajubiju yelled. "Leave me alone!"
There is no dreaming in this place
There is only the setting of fire to bones

That was when he caught his reflection in a puddle. There she was. In her imperial attire. Zagaga. She was not the pale phantom he had seen the very first time. She was a woman. A monarch. A parent. An avenger. Ajubiju brought his hand to his face, and so did she. He rose, and she rose. He reached for her, and she reached for him. She sang, and the song cascaded from him.

In her memories, Ajubiju heard a voice. She had not shared that memory. It was a secret; one she was forced to keep. Ajubiju was good at stealing secrets. She had stolen his body; it was only fair. Through sheer will, Ajubiju went to the voice. Zagaga resisted.

No.

"Yes."

He was not sure where he was headed, but he went regardless. Leaving Glaroo alone in that dark damp tunnel had taken everything in Ajubiju. The entire city was on high alert for him. They would not find him. Ajubiju became a soundless thing. He moved through the city, blending into the quietness of the night. He was a menigari, but he had also been raised by an assassin.

Ajubiju could have gone home to his mother, fallen at her feet, and sought her forgiveness. But he had taken several pages from Zagaga's book. Pages of vengeance. He gazed up, into the night sky, and for the first time, he saw three moons. Ajubiju walked on.

Waiting for him at the end of the secret path was Miinanai.

"What are you doing here?" The councillor was more annoyed than surprised.

Ajubiju had no questions of his own. With every passing second, Zagaga's unfiltered essence brewed into his. Whatever she knew, he knew.

He knew Miinanai had been part of the cult that sought to free Zagaga. They were her family and did not disclose her identity when they were discovered. She had been their eyes on the inside, and with their extinction, it fell to her as the last surviving member to succeed where they failed. So she did. Miinanai had learned Zagaga's true name, gaining control over the imperial Vwesu'erosu spirit. It was how she got them to terminate the other councillors... and Glaroo.

"You did not need to go to such lengths," Ajubiju said.

Miinanai narrowed her eyes.

"Let us have this conversation when your beliefs, your way of life, are a taboo in your own home." The councilwoman seemed to be rattled by her own words.

"You freed a spirit, only to lock them in a different cage. In me." He tugged at his shirt.

"Our cult cared nothing for Zagaga or the Vwesu'erosu. They were imperialist elitist dictators. Our devotion was to The Mother. For her, we were going to reclaim Lomanoo, and Zagaga was but a tool in achieving that.

"Our work is not yet done," the councilwoman spoke past Ajubiju to Zagaga. "The city is on high alert. What better time to unleash chaos than amid chaos. We kill Yaroo tonight."

"Go kill him yourself."

The councillor warily rose from behind their desk. "I have your true name, and you will do as I comm—"

Ajubiju rushed at her, knife in hand. Stretching forth his hand, he forced her voice back down her throat, caging it. When he got to her, he slashed the blade across her face, taking her eye. The councillor shrieked crashing to the floor, but no sound came forth from her mouth. Holding her bloodied face with one hand, Miinanai made to crawl away, but Ajubiju was already upon her. He swung her around to face him and raised the knife.

"This is for my friend, you raging psychopath!"

He did not get to bring the knife down. The name left her lips as a whisper. The name meant nothing to him, but the bearer of that name lived inside him. Zagaga Agaga was constraining him, keeping him from ending the councillor. Miinanai crawled out from under him. Ajubiju could hear the anger boiling in the councillor's blood, in her aura. When the woman finally laboured up, she slapped him into the ground. Then she brought her feet down on his head, over and over again. She did not stop, not until his face was worse than hers.

"You showed great fortitude," the councillor adjusted her white dress, ruining it with her blood-stained hands. "But I have faced far greater opposition."

Ajubiju strained himself off the floor, only to collapse back into it. He had sealed her voice, but she had broken the seal. It was impossible, unless...

"You are not the only free menigari in this city," Miinanai said, like she could hear his thoughts.

Ever since the argument with Glaroo atop the lighthouse, he had suspected it. Of course, the Lomanoo were bound to have persons still attuned to their abilities. To believe otherwise would be to bask in delusion. And right until the heated exchange with Glaroo, Ajubiju had made a bed in that delusion.

"Did you really believe the undampener was created just for you?" The councillor fell into her seat and pulled out a med kit.

Miinanai proceeded to clean up the gash running across her face. Then she applied a salve to it. She did not flinch as the salve met the wound.

"The first council invented both the dampener and the undampener . Unlike yours, their undampener employed a more discrete design. See?" She pulled at her ear. The boy saw nothing. "The first council, those hypocrites, passed this knowledge down their family line. They unseated one family from power, only to keep all the power to themselves."

"But—but you became a councillor. You could have changed the system."

Miinanai ripped out the sigil on her chest. "I do not seek to change the system; I seek to break it."

The cult had prepared her from childhood, equipping her with knowledge that would appeal to the council. The cult knew about the undampeners and replicated a more advanced model. They had discovered everyone in Lomanoo bore their true names openly, everyone but the founding families. It's how they kept them in check. So, they unnamed themselves. When a young Miinanai presented the cult's discoveries to the council, passing them off as her genius findings, Yaroo had suggested they eliminate her. Jahha thought otherwise, and took her under his wing.

"Jahha was good to me. Shame I had to kill him."

Ajubiju shuffled to a pillar, resting his body against it.

"What are you going to do with me?" he coughed, blood spurting from his mouth.

Miinanai drummed her fingers on the desk, her face warped in thought. The cut on her face had thinned considerably. It was not as ghastly as before.

"I cannot turn you in and risk you blabbing to Yaroo." She got up from her seat. "I would flay the classist prick myself but being from a founding family, he is genetically predisposed to the undampeners, which make his abilities quite unparalleled," she added, a hint of jealousy seeping into her tone. "I had hoped Zagaga would end him in time, but I did not count on Jahha suggesting we trap her in a descendant."

"But you invented the binding soundcode," Ajubiju said, painfully stretching his body up the pillar.

"Had to keep up appearances." Miinanai frowned. "I did plan to sabotage it, but Yaroo was always hovering with suspicion. He is dubiously clever and cruel."

"A bit of an irony coming from you." Ajubiju was spent but his wit found a way.

"His sister, his only family, was neither undampened nor unnamed!" the councillor stressed. "I was a child and he wanted me killed. You cannot fathom the things he'll do in the pursuit of ultimate power and control. I need him dead today!"

"That is unfortunate." Yaroo stepped into the room.

Miinanai froze.

"Carry on. Do not stop on my account."

When Miinanai had revealed that the councillors were all secretly attuned to their abilities, she had inadvertently given Ajibuji ammo against her. He had funnelled the rest of their conversation straight to Yaroo. It would never have worked if the councilman's abilities were dampened.

Jahha had come alone. The undampeners were a secret, and he intended to keep it that way. Besides, this fight was personal.

Miinanai recovered from her shock, but before her lips could form a word, the councilman clapped his hands. The reverberations streamed across the room and sent Miinanai crashing into the wall behind her. But she did not stay down. She leapt over the table and sped at Yaroo. She knew she couldn't take him sound for sound, so she was going for a fistfight. The councilman stretched open his hands once again, but before he could bring them together, Miinanai grabbed them, pulling the hands apart. In a swift move, she banged her forehead on his nose and shattered it. As the councillor reeled back, Miinanai gripped him by the neck and rammed his head into a wall.

Ajubiju joined the fight. Bloodied and in pain, he staggered toward her, swiping with the knife in his hand. She swerved to the side, the blade missing her by a breath. She seized his hand, twisting the knife out of it. As it fell, she caught it, and cleanly carved it into Ajibuji's shoulder. The boy too beaten down to even scream, just slumped to the floor and stayed there.

Miinanai turned back to Yaroo and let out repeating blasts of ultrasonic screams. That was her mistake. She should have stuck to her fists. Yaroo tore through the blast and brought his palm to her mouth, shutting her up.

"Enough." He said, speaking the high language.

With that, Miinanai shrieked, clasping her head in her hands, and writhing to her knees.

"That noise drilling into your brain." The councilman squatted to her. "It will be the last thing you ever hear."

"I wonder—" Miinanai forced out the words in between shrieks. "I wonder what your sister heard— before I had her killed!"

Yaroo's eyes widened with rage and grief. The councilman dragged the woman up by the collar.

"I will destroy you slowly!"

Miinanai's screams grew louder as he intensified the buzzing in her skull. Blood came streaming from her ears, her eyes, and her nose.

Then everything stopped. The screaming, the pain, it all faded into nothing. Yaroo let go of Miinanai, his hands going to the blade jutting out of his gut. The same blade that slew his sister. When it got pulled out of him, the councillor turned to find Ajubiju.

In my child's hair, were pink beads rattling when she ran

Miinanai described the Ura-aru as a kind of hypnotic-chamber, utilizing repetitive, tight focus and low-frequency vibrations to thrust him into permanent sleep. That had always been the plan for him. To kill him would only set Zagaga free again. The other option was to repeat the binding ritual that caged her spirit centuries ago, but the words that anchored the ritual were lost to the ages. Miinanai had no use for Zagaga anymore. She was the last surviving councillor—the only councillor. The city was hers.

For Ajubiju, there was no trial, no good-byes, no last words. When they connected the plugs and the valves, preparing him for the Ura-aru, he wondered if he'd get to dream. Or if it would simply be a black emptiness.

In his fear, Ajubiju remembered his mother, how her hands were sometimes the soft of fleece, and other times, they were bark. He remembered her hair, how it smelled of charcoal and camel fat. He remembered her daggers, how they caught the light. Ajubiju remembered her, and Ajubiju sang.

"Mama," Ajubiju cried, his voice shattering.

My voice has morphed from hail, to thunder to a hush
When you call, I will not echo
When you sing, I will not dance
But I carry your voice to all the heavens,
to all the silent places
into tomorrow,
else I crumble and fall.
Sing me beautiful and wild,
Sing me brave
Sing all of my names
Mosii-oa-Tunyaa – Smoke that thunders
Sing me.

They activated the Ura-aru and Ajubiju's song ended.

He slept into infinity.

In a desert where the sands chant, where the moons do not hide, wind carries a child's singing. A singing that is grief. A singing that is lost. In this desert, a mother hears her child's singing, and a mother draws her daggers.

So far, we have explored events in the Sauútiverse through stories set on Wiimb-ó and Mahwé (and Mahwé's moon, Pinaa). Worlds that orbit the smaller star of the binary system, Zuúv'ah.

Now we go to a planet orbiting the other, larger star in this binary system, Juah-āju. That planet is Ekwukwe, the "hollow world".

Ekwukwe is an interesting planet, especially in its geology. Its lithosphere pockmarked with gigantic, naturally occurring caves, caverns and networks of tunnels. These tunnels which create a lot of echoes and strange sound-based phenomena on the planet. It is also more of a "wild" planet, with many rare, unique minerals occurring there, and it is home to many strange, dangerous creatures. Moreso than on the other planets in the Sauúti system.

In a universe where sound is key, echoes are special and inform the worldview of the people of Ekwukwe. Those who survived the great solar flare on this planet, found themselves surrounded by powerful, strange beasts. Even the smallest sound could lead to an echo, a reflection or even a magnification of sound waves. And magic could be altered by the reflected sound, with dire consequences. They learned to move silently and to both perceive and use their natural affinity for magic, the aura of innate power found in all things, which they also call an 'echo' because they believe it is a smaller reverberation of the Mothersound, the first sound that animated all things. They also developed a harsh culture of constant awareness of danger, a warrior-culture of never-ending self-defense, of never-ending war. A culture that helped them first defend and then liberate themselves during the occupation of the Mahwé-Zezépfeni empire.

But like every culture born of necessity, it contains elements that aren't always the best or the wisest. Especially in how it treats those that are different or disabled. And sometimes, the best way to advance a culture is for those who do not fit into these expectations around which a culture has accreted, to break the rules. So, we come to this, the story of Sina, by collective founding member **Eugen Bacon***. It takes place centuries after the independence wars, 15 juzu A1B, when a loose federation of planets has been formed with representatives from each planet present to discuss trade, maintain peace, etc. Told from multiple viewpoints during a hunt, it is the lyrical and lovely story of a child on Ekwukwe who does not fit in, who is born missing something the culture deems fundamental, and yet, finds a way to become more than what he seemed destined to be at birth. To become more than anyone could have expected. To become a legend.*

Sina, the Child With No Echo

EUGEN BACON

S INA has a stealth tread—that's what his aunt Zawa'zawa calls it. Sometimes she calls his movement a mist walk. Zawa'zawa doesn't like the silence about him, how Sina emerges as if from nowhere, echoless, to startle her. When she's feeling more liberal, she calls it a mushroom walk. Mushroom, because mildews are silky. They only get chewy or fowl-like when you cook them.

He laughed at this when his aunt said it, but it's true: beasts can't hear him. Yet he hears them, their tiniest echo as if it were a holler. Each aura's vibration is different from everyone else's. Zawa'zawa echoes in spiral. It's the whisper of a music circle, creating and sharing memories in faint caerulean light rising and falling. *Wobo, wobo, deesh, deesh.*

The girl, Rehema're—it means blessing—her echo does not come with light. She speaks good Sauúti. She bends her magic, can do many things with it. Hers is a good echo. It has transition, reflection. It's long and deep with superior timing. *Wey ma. Wey ma. Uuuuuuu.*

Sina is not laughing now. The impudu-pudu's echo is a bellow, infiltrating with such loudness, it hurts his ears. And the smell! It started off from a distance as a sickly-sweet odour of turning fruit, mingled with a stench so foul it pulled water from his eyes. Closer, the lightning bird has the stench of putrid onions. The odour of a rotten klalabash. The stink of bad t'apiapia fish. The pong of fresh faeces from an old stomach.

The spray of a dying chekele'le beast—the laughing one, greedy as sin and with its shorter hind feet—moments before its bowels collapse.

He holds his guts to keep from spewing. His mist walk matches the impudu-pudu's own mist and shadow. He cannot yet see it, but follows its vibration. The sparse batik draped over one shoulder and covering his back to just above his knees is sticky with sweat. It's not fear, he assures himself. No-one can stop the impudu-pudu.

But he must try.

Because it's slowly encroaching from the forest desert into the town of T'Songesonge.

He pulls up his V'hushalele, the magic spear. His palm and the V'hushalele feel as one. All is well—he is echoless, and the impudu-pudu is blind. But it's catching his smell. The energy in its echo is dark and pulsing.

Now Sina can see the ruby eye, blind but aglow. The beast is female. It's big as a baby hill, and is sitting on a nest. No, he exaggerates, Sina tells himself. But the impudu-pudu's head alone is the size of a grown desert cow. Slimy drool has pooled around the monstrous nest. Those eggs, if they hatch, will bear hatchings the size of a horned goat.

The beast has chosen this rocky part of the desert to hide, between swathes of sand and rock towers in the outskirts of T'Songesonge.

The impudu-pudu knows he's close. It shimmers and spreads its wings.

Sina holds the V'hushalele's shaft close to his body. He twists forward with his hips, leaps and launches. His shoulder drops and his free hand whips back. The impudu-pudu's echo resounds in a roar. Lightning spurts from the swirl and resonance as the V'hushalele strikes the inside wing, bends its trajectory and soars back into Sina's outstretched hand.

He dives behind a rock, barely dodging another spit of lightning accompanying the echo that resonates more with rage than pain, even as the spear's magic pulses its harm from a tiny tip.

GRUGH-GRUGH, the beast's rumbling. And the reek!

The searing pain of the fire on Sina's thigh spreads inward to every core of him. The burning feels inside, not just on skin. But he too has inflicted harm.

From where he is, Sina can see the magic spear's blackness spreading, but not quick enough. For all its rage the impudu-pudu will not leave its nest without encouragement.

Sina ponders what to do next.

Then he hears her, Rehema're. She should not be here.

He's startled at this girl who is young, yet old, bolder than a spirit. She's trying to make as little noise as possible, but if Sina can hear her, so can the impudu-pudu. She's crawling towards the beast, and he can see each reverberation of her motion, as does the impudu-pudu. It turns its blind ruby eye in her direction.

Suddenly it's up from its nest, fangs drawn to drain a grown one's blood. The mouth is a pitch-black hole, then it yawns and spits orange fire at Reheme're.

The world shakes with the spurt of lightning and a terrible cry that bursts Sina's ears.

GRUGH-GRUGH.

The sky goes black with fog.

Sina falls to the ground. The world is going round, like it does when temper gobbles him and he swoons. But this is not temper, it's fear. It's a fear that wags a finger at him, and he cannot shake it free. It's a fear that is not for himself, it's for her. Rehema're. They have never met before, not like this, but she is his blood—abandonment does not change it.

Now the fear is in his eyes and throat and chest and gut.

His legs cannot move. The fear is him.

As he's there, crippled, possessed, he sees the girl stepping out from the fire and fog. She stands there for a moment with a grave face, and then strolls forward, resolute with an echo. *Wey ma, wey ma. Uuuuuuu.*

It's an echo that delivers to her effort. An echo that frees Sina from his coma, and the V'hushalele reminds him that it is there. He arcs his hand back, holds the spear beneath his head, releases in a straight line and watches the silent strike. It's silence that only he can hear. *Icho-icho-icho*, as the V'hushalele eats distance and whirs into the beast, then loops back into his stretched hand. It happens all at once as Rehema're vibrates her magic, and the impudu-pudu keels onto its nest.

Yellow-green goo of pus consistency seeps from the cracked shells. The ooze is quickly turning as it trickles along the dust. And the smell, the smell. First, it's the stuffiness of must, and then the stink of black diarrhoea. With a terrible cry and a careless sweep of lightning, the impudu-pudu lights up to the skies.

Sina kneels by a broken egg, and this time cannot hold his guts from a retch. The girl, Rehema're, puts a hand on his shoulder, until he stills, ashamed, and wipes his mouth. Together, they study the wet fur on the big head of a stillborn impudu-pudu that will never know an echo.

Rehema're studied the pus-soaked fur inside the cracked shell, and then looked at the boy.

Night muttered when it was confident. It was a boldness that spread, and that was when the boy would come out to be seen. She'd seen him often, the beast slayer, how he chanted to the Mother for guidance. Reheme're imagined how the Mother might utter back, *Whoosh-whoosh*, but never apologising to the boy for making him wrong. Surely. It was not he who needed a parlay—to make amends was not for him because it was he who had been wronged. All he wanted was a proper name.

Didn't everyone else, born in this world of echo from the gods, have a good name?

What was an echoless child in the great big world of Ekwukwe, wider than T'Songesonge? pondered Rehema're. Her parents had taught her young to use echo, beasts everywhere. Like the aze'aze or the scavenger bird that snatched babies. Yet there he was, Sina, a child of the dead forest, flaunting his unecho.

He was a young blood, just like her. His V'hushalele was not a thumper. It glided clean, smooth. A set shot. She marvelled at his body, his athleticism.

She wondered what would have happened if it were she, not him—a boy who conjured something out of nothing—born with no echo. Would an aunt have collected her, scooped her to their bosom, safe from the forest's unforgiving? The forest with its starkness and the caves of a hollow planet that beckoned beasts. Would that aunt have taught her, Rehema're, to hold deep the magic spear like the boy did with his beautiful hands?

She felt wrath, envy too.

She despised that it was he, not her, who was bidden to do the slaying. Did she not have echo magic? And it was potent. He didn't know it, but he needed her for this impudu-pudu that came and went in seasons.

It had decimated warriors, even members of the Maadiregi—with all their advanced magic and technology. Folk knew to leave it alone in the desert forest when it showed. Sometimes they gifted it with desert cows and burrow sheep, scattered before it gobbled them too along with their tokens.

It came to T'Songesonge for a birthing, and yet destroyed. It wreaked havoc. No-one had managed to kill it. No weapon or echo magic was strong enough alone.

The boy should have known best to stay away from it, didn't his aunt Zawa'zawa tell him this? considered Rehema're. Her own parents, Fatu'fa and Juta'uu, were very clear on the matter. But she too, Rehema're, had done the same as the boy. Disobeyed. She had followed him as he trailed it, the creature that refused to stay away from folk. It ate whole households.

What it did to Tamutamu's family—

She didn't want to see it happening to this boy, Sina, who was a ghost of the living—bitter, maybe better. But he was broken. What was it then, pity? She didn't know. Yet, despite her sounds and spaces, her gifts with echo, she never had it as good.

Look at him, compared to her.

He was backwards, incomplete, yet here she was, resentful of him.

And it was she, not him, who had to live with her parent's regret. The echo of their discord shook the stone house, trembled Reheme're in her own bed.

Zimpapa-zimpapa. Why—her father's reverberation. Why, why was it he who had to carry out the fact, when it was her, Fatu'fa, who—

Pulapulapula-oooo. Her, who what?—Fatu'fa's ululating echo. Her who cried wrong while giving birth? Did Juta'uu think she didn't know it? Or maybe it was him who uttered a bad word as the baby was coming out! One could not be careless with echo magic. Had he dozed, and said a wrong sound in his dreaming? It harmed their child!

Their rage at themselves, at each other.

Sina didn't know any of that. All he did was stand oblivious of the trouble he had caused, being born wrong, now holding the V'hushalele deep, and with such immaculate hands.

Each thought of your parents, and your heart eats itself. You were never a child that brushed up a mother's leg. You were collected from a forest. Your dreams of reunion are dreams that never fade, that never fall from your head so you can be free when you wake. But there's no smell, shape or colour to that reunion. It takes many juzu, perhaps a lifetime, to claw from longing and reach forgiveness. You're yet to reach it. Forgiveness.

The sky is a comfort, its pulse stretching and billowing over the desolate land. Dust swirls deeper, wilder, fragmenting your thoughts. You have shed the particles of your mother's skin. Your father's echo makes you want to weep.

But now you're ankle-high in dust, wading through doubt.

There is no opposite of when or where.

Yours is an appetite for the sky, to lay down at sunset and feel the tenderness of a parent's fingers through your hair.

Now you squint at the approaching mist wafting from the horizon. It's not a mist. This, you know from the pulse of its white echo, stark and astral.

And the reek!

When he was a bub, Zawa'zawa tried to teach him echo but it was useless.

So she trained him in the art of defence using the looping V'hushalele —how to hold the shaft close to his body, ready to hurl. How to twist and leap, shoulders loosening to let the V'hushalele fly. Others used spear throwers, not him.

Zawa'zawa taught him how to project and release, to make the V'hushalele float in a *zhing'g* and *rhang'g*, spearing the distance. She taught him to listen, to understand the pulse of each echo, to gauge a beast's distance, nature and form. The rest was on his shoulder, the turn of his hips and his trust on the V'hushalele. He had a look and then—

Sometimes he closes his eyes to the magical spear's music, as it slices through air and slips a dart through the scales, feathers, glint, slime or shadow of a beast. Then he opens his eyes to appraise his kill.

Icho-icho-icho.

That's all the echo he can do, with the V'hushalele as it eats distance, as it whirrs into a target, and loops back to him. His attempts at resonance when nobody's watching slip up with no sense or rhythm, scraping out of his mouth like pebbles pushing out of a sewn mouth. Frustration puts its hands up and his sound falls in rocks, tottering all wrong and uptight before smothering itself in a jumpy death. Without inner magic, his words fail.

But Rehema're...

He remembers the first time he saw her. She was making balls out of echoes, twitching and bouncing them around her body. Sina watched how she played echo ball with the other children, premeditating with boom and timbre to counter, pitch, deflect and sweep into play. M'phipira, that's the name of the game that's also practice for combat. He watched how Rehema're's resonance smothered the ball's momentum when another child was whirring it. She gave the boys especially an early headache, as she curled and folded, turned the ball into maps and stories, blackbirds and rain. He loved most how she echoed in a sprint, lining up a collage of sunlight and dew, spinning the ball through the middle of a kaleidoscope.

Sometimes he dreams about her. He feels her echo coming and going in the whispers of an insistent wind. *Wey ma, wey ma.* And then she's astride the canopy. She looks at him and says, *Wey ma. Wey ma. Uuuuuuu.* He listens, until the two suns and their pale glow near each other, merge and set as one. Then the blackest dusk falls over the planet, just before the starlit galaxy rouses and glitters Rehema're's face.

And then he wakes.

She's about a juzu younger than him, and this he resents—her reminder that his parents did not mourn him enough, abandoning him
on a thatch of t'embo'oo grass for his bed, plonked on harsh ground between thorny j'hani'ni and tall thin o'livha'vha trees in the desert forest,
then forgetting. Quickly setting out to replace him with another child.

When he thinks this, and rage consumes him, the mist in his walk
abandons his feet and climbs to his head. Those are the times he swoons,
but it doesn't last.

He's an outcast, contagious. This is what distinguishes him from the
other children. He's an abomination. The world did not stop for him.
No-one echoed a perfect word, or blew a horn to announce his birth.
No-one, even his mother, wrapped him with well-loved cowrie shells
and a blanket of baby ndege'ndege feathers. Nobody played for him the
music of a k'hora'aa and its melody of a harp, sound that came and
went in a looping bounce to give him sweet sleep. Did anyone close a
whisper pearl into his baby fist? No. There was no ancient howl of the
ngonini or luhte'te, not even the scratch and clack-clack percussion of a
shekere-re.

Because who was there to make the netting of spirit beads on a
dried gourd for his drum? Now he nurses in a texture of doubt all the
melancholy he wants to set free but just can't.

Rehema're understood that he couldn't think of his aunt without
thinking of his mother. What happened between them, the two women,
whatever happened, was not good. Their echoes screamed when they
neared each other. It took restraint—Zawa'zawa's, because she was the
wise one, as Fatu'fa spat and foamed—to stop their hate from getting
claws and fangs.

Zawa'zawa—it meant a gift—was a sister to the boy's birth mother.
A mother forever absent, so Zawa'zawa snatched the role. A taboo, yes,
but one she could commit because of her position, her status. Stern, always the mentor, Rehema're suspected that Zawa'zawa was soft inside.
That she wanted to give Sina a sense of belonging, but that was not hers

to give. Because Zawa'zawa was a keeper of knowledge, and that came with its demands. She was not always there for him, because first she had a duty with the federation of planets, and travelled for that duty—sometimes for trade.

But when she's there, her mouth is soft and strong, full of wisdom, bringing out echo in that pale blue glow.
Wobo, wobo, deesh, deesh.
She raised you inside a giant rock. One enters through the mouth and takes stone steps to the cavern's belly. It's cool, much cooler inside, than the climate outside.
It's a stone and bone house engraved with palm prints. Your aunt understands plants, and there's the alo-alo—the light lily. Purple and round flowers, edible too. But she grows them for the colourful bloom with red tongues inside that glow in the dark. Black alo-alo has a berry smell.
There's the organic lantern, a light plant that's a cousin of the watercress and elephant ears. Luminescent fungi too, they bring radiance to the cave, and feed you. The starfish flower is a deep pink, different from the elephant foot yam. It's black-skinned outside, sand-coloured inside the flesh. Its earthy flavour is nutty, not too sweet. Its leaves are ruddy.
There are other bioluminescent flowers in Zawa'zawa's house, pets too —like the fireflies that shimmer at night, more so when they're on heat. But that is not all the light. There are perpetual lights along the walls, and glow sticks for the food store deeper down the cavern. Jewellery also decorates the house.
When you're not killing monsters, you excavate ruby, t'sasavorite, rhorhodolite garnets, tourmaline, t'lazanini and d'hiamomo that glitter in all hardness from the caves, with which Zawa'zawa goes to barter for food: dried meat, sweet bananas, millet, rice and eggs—normal fowl ones, not the giant ones you get from ndege'ndege nests.

His aunt has taught him to cook, how to simmer, stir-fry, roast or sauté. He's a good hand on the nguwe'we, the horned pig—Zawa'zawa taught him to skin it, fillet it, twice-cook it, and serve it with spiced klalabash soup that is creamy with carrots, ginger garlic, coriander and black salt. She says he can pluck the feathers of a sandfowl and roast it better than a girl. The burrow sheep are for milk—they are easy to keep, longsuffering on the barren landscape. When he steals a ndege'ndege's eggs, he knows how to serve them to Zawa'zawa sunny side up. Lizards, he's wary of— one must eat the right kind, or it's a cramped stomach, or worse.

The house is frugal, decorated with furniture from the sapele'le tree, a dark, red-brown. Zawa'zawa's quarters hold a feather mattress with a walnut bedhead and a chiffonier the colour of nuts, scored with ash. The floor is all black from ebo-oni wood. Zawa'zawa asks him to polish it, and to treat her thermal clothing ready for travel.

He doesn't know what the other houses look like, because no-one has invited him to visit. When he was a toddler, he pretended he was a special guest, sipping tea and dunking yasa worm bread soaked in desert cow honey that only came when the cow was with child.

One could walk around T'Songesonge in seven bés if one avoids caverns and hollows. Sina has done it, kept his distance from the caverns and enclosures of other folk. Zawa'zawa does not keep an enclosure or a boma'ma of sandfowl, burrow sheep or desert cows. She doesn't want to be locked down, she says. Instead, she has a touch screen that shows pictures and plays sounds of other worlds. Sometimes she uses it for holograms to summon a member of the federation from another planet, and speak to them about a matter. At these times, she prefers Sina to be scarce, so he wanders.

In his traversing across T'Songesonge, trying to stay unseen—but he could well have a great big brandish on his forehead, the way folk notice him, stare at him—he gazes wistfully at the Institute of the Maadiregi, where they train and hone skills in magic and tech.

Sometimes, further out, he reaches the grasslands and picks t'embo'oo grass for Zawa'zawa's mats and baskets—she likes to make them, sells some for barter. Even further out, midway to the forest desert, are bore-holes. Ratfish swim in them. Some he can eat—best served blackened in charcoal and rubbed with red salt. But they are elusive to catch. The sucker ratfish can grow up to two feet. It's a bit rough on the stomach but will do in a famine. The piatu'tu is more decorative than anything —handsome to look at with its pale mauve hue, shadow dots and silver whiskers. But the best ratfish to eat is the azure one—it's big and fat, a white belly under.

Sweet as!

There's Algea'gea in the boreholes too—all lime, full of body-goodness, Zawa'zawa likes to say. He misses his aunt.

He feels absence. An absence of echoes that is a clawing, turning him inside out alive. But how can he miss something he never had? He regrets his name. Why is it not Sina'aa? He already knows the answer. Sina, it means without. When he asked his aunt, why he was not like the rest, she looked at him sadly and resounded, *Wobo, wobo, deesh, deesh.*

The tenor, timbre and tremor of her language varies with her mood, and he understands her words perfectly. As perfectly as he understands the girl who rides the wind in echo, soars over the scars and striations of the land, and what was once an ancient river.

He has no time to think too much about this now, as the binary ping of the beast's echo is tumbling from the sky.

GRUGH-GRUGH.

GRUGH-GRUGH.

The impudu-pudu swept from the skies with a spit of lightning, but Rehema're's echo magic was ready. *Wey ma, wey ma. Uuuuuuu.*

The blackness from the V'hushalele's tip had spread, climbed up the beast's breast. Soon it would reach the chest and throat, and do its work. Until then—

Rehema're saw the others coming. Witnesses trickling in, but their echo magic was not compelling enough. Hadn't they tried, and failed, against the impudu-pudu?

Swiftly, echoless, Sina was by her side. As if stating that this was not M'phipira, the ball game. This was life and death.

Now, together, they faced off with the beast at ground level.

You wonder about your future, what you will become. You see and listen. Sometimes to look, you climb trees—the tall and thin o'livha'vha that squeezes out oil, the thyme'thyme and its soap sap, even the j'hani'ni and its thorns. That one needs skilful climbing, you don't hug it and frog-climb it like you do the date palm'palm. You've mastered that date tree, hop onto its base, grip it with bare hands and grope-climb it, your legs in an inward grip. Your knees are all frogged, but you push up, hands, up, until you reach the sweet fruit.

It too is seasonal, the palm'palm, like an impudu-pudu.

But the dates ripen in turn, which is good. It paces out Zawa'zawa and her craving for date muffins. That, too, is good, unlike an impudu-pudu.

Sometimes you think that perhaps you're destined to be a Raevaagi, a teller of stories. Because you see history. You survived history. Isn't that what it is, when you come out alive from a desert forest that was meant to kill you?

When you dream, you sing a tuneless song about hungry tongues of ruby-eyed beasts whose slimy licks stick for eons. You dream of clutter and cold, because all you have is space and heat. You dream of a fjord, not the red soil of this battered world hardened with time, trees with leaves of wild birds that come alive at dawn and the echo of their forlorn melody trembles the sky. You sing for your mother who's near yet far, for your father, Juta'uu who knows naught about holding or assuaging a son's hurt.

Your first kill was an aze'aze, the giant firefly that wears the head of a goat. It steals humans, burrow sheep and desert cows, and eats their organs. Baby ones suck blood and one becomes possessed, and is best abandoned to the desert forest to die. Like you.

You sought the aze'aze when a woman, Tula-Tula, lost her tot—snatched from its cradle in a cave as the mother sought water. You found it first, the half-eaten bub, its torso and legs. It was a fresh kill, the blood still wet, torn flesh a bright crimson with white sinew and bone. The beast had eaten the bub the way your aunt Zawa'zawa taught you not to eat the t'apiapia: head first. You must begin with the tail and move up. The aze'aze didn't think so.

The p'hobawawa, the one-eyed bat, was a winged monster that sodomised, and then fed on the unlucky ones. Those who escaped uneaten experienced night terrors and waking dreams, and awakened with a bad pain and blood in their buttocks. You killed a p'hobawawa.

The dragon-no and its short snout and long neck, 50 feet long with giant wings, cried fire like the impudu-pudu, but you put it out. The mamba'ba, a giant snake, 60 feet long it could kill a galloper, the kudu-kudu of the forest, even a desert cow, was no sweat to you. Neither was the inka-inka, wet and slippery, full of scales. It was all fins and flippers, belly flapping backwards, raging for your body's water. Its mewling was so bad, you wanted to pour a jug on it. The people of T'Songesonge ate it gratefully, as they did the konga-konga, a flier that swooped and snatched women and children, featherless with a huge wing span.

But the tikolokolo—the spirit gremlin that no-one saw coming until it was too late—was not for eating. It was a short and hairy beast, humanoid-looking as it appeared and disappeared. Sometimes it morphed into a body of stones that sneaked up on a victim (as it nearly did you), then it was too late. Your V'hushalele's tip went fluorescent as it arched into the stone heart, capitalising on what Zawa'zawa learned you.

Blackness crumbled the gargoyle to ash.

Yet, until now, you've avoided the desert forest where abandoning happens. You know it intimately, have stayed away from it astutely. Until now. An impudu-pudu both brings out and pushes aside your fear. If no-one can stop the impudu-pudu—

The husband, the wife, seven children—all of them, their echo magic dust to the beast. Tamutamu—it means sweetness; the beast took this literally. It gobbled the whole house, spat out their bones, and was satiated for nesting. It broke an unspoken boundary and left the desert forest to eat them in their beds.

You can't bear to think of your aunt, Zawa'zawa, eaten and spat out in bones.

Not her. Never her.

You must try.

GRUGH-GRUGH.

He and Rehema're are facing off with the beast at ground level. Even in this stance, Sina considers for a moment how angry with him Zawa'zawa will be when she returns.

He'd watched with longing as she flew to yet another trip.

Her shuttle has a nose and wings. Its tail does lightning like an impudu-pudu, then air wobbles and the aircraft is gone. Sometimes he doesn't see her before she leaves. He's young and night matters. He listens for the knock's echo on the cavern, stilling his heart lest sound slips unnoticed. He feels heat at the bottom of his stomach, and desire for... what? It stalks hungry to the sound of stars, sweeps night away and then he dozes, wakes up—not to the sternness of an aunt, because she has made tea and is long gone, leaving the house loud with emptiness. Empty even of echoes.

But this last trip, before she travelled, she echoed, *Wobo, wobo, deesh, deesh.*

Behave, be responsible.

She knows how he's sensitive to the echoes of others, of beasts. She wants him to do the smaller beasts first. Until he's ready for something as big as an impudu-pudu.

But he's ready. He'll show her how ready he is.

Yet he knows that seeking out to kill an impudu-pudu is not being responsible. He can already see her disdain.

Last Zawa'zawa returned from the Boāmmariri conference of the federation of planets, she echoed her scorn about Zezépfeni. *Wobo, wobo, deesh, deesh.* She cried how everybody was complaining about Zezépfeni —so haughty, secretive too! They squeezed out from you value, gave you bad barter. It was hard to generalise, she reasoned, but Wiimb-ó— the ones that came from Wiimb-ó were heart people. They looked you in the eye, shook your hand with a grip, gave you a fair trade.

Those were the times she signed with her hands because her outrage at Zezépfeni's craftiness was too big for speaking.

He misses her blue light. The spiral of her echo. Her soft mouth full of craftiness.

He looks at the beast, feels a little sorry for it. The impudu-pudu is an alienated one, like him. The beast is a forgotten city, its skin etched with black and white pavements superimposed in contours. He lays eyes on it and see eons, ghosts, earthquakes, war, and wants to kneel before its coalescence—a whole body that's a jaw, an eye, bog, fire in a splatter of masks and afterimages in nonlinear time. He does not wish to know what is real or illusion, so he hums.

The beast answers.

And then something shifts in Sina. He can't explain it. His hand touches Rehema're's, and her fingers curl around his for a moment.

She glances at him and understands his look. In a unison as if of twins, together they step towards the impudu-pudu.

The beast rears with a cry, ready to eat them alive.

Around he goes with his V'hushalele, anticipating the impudu-pudu.

Rehema're's echoes carry, shielding him from the beast's fire. Her magic cuts at the beast's body, charred with the V'hushalele's poison, and it is not happy. She bends the magic, tidies her attack. She floats her chant, and the impudu-pudu's limb snaps. It roars, charges in its deformity. Her echo magic holds off it lightning, but she's tiring. A lick of fire singes Sina's arm, and he nearly leaps back.

But he must be strong for Rehema're. He must be strong for Zawa'zawa, for his people. Blood pounds faster in his ears, even as some flames escape the echo shield and char his torso.

Sina is closest to the beast's rage. He holds his spot, holds it, holds...

Just as Rehema're and her echo shield begin to collapse, he twists his hips, loosens his shoulders and releases the V'hushalele into the pitch-black maw.

They walked out of the fog together. Hoisting the head of the dead beast between them, the V'hushalele lodged between the ruby eye.

By now there was a heaving crowd. They'd streamed in from everywhere, now they were here and waiting for them. Rehema're could see her parents, Juta'uu and Fatu'fa, right there, lined up at the fore. She looked at her mother, seeing her as if for the first time. Fatu'fa wore a sharp face, nothing soft like a mother's. Juta'uu was garbed in his usual ochre-coloured loin cloth from the special bark of a marula tree. He was leaning forward in the stance of combat, like he always did, as if he was hunting something.

Juta'uu bore the scars of a warrior.

Suddenly, lightning streaks across the sky and, for a moment, you think the impudu-pudu has resurrected. But the head is still there, impaled, hoisted in the V'hushalele between you and Rehema're. You feel pride. Together, you're a combo. A killer one.

The world shakes, and you see a nose and wings, and you know it's Zawa'zawa's vessel straight from the Boāmmariri. The crowd scatters for her landing, then reforms.

Starshine on her face dances with her pale blue aura, and folk gaze at her with awe. Her stern look as she climbs out of the vessel tells you that you have not been responsible.

His aunt's severe face tells Sina he's in trouble. Rehema're anticipates the falling out, lowers the beast and steps back.

He starts to panic as Zawa'zawa reaches for him, then he's wrapped in arms, pressed to a bosom. He listens to her heart speak, and what he hears is fright and relief.

Nothing else matters.

It's Rehema're who starts the chant. A chorus of echoes that grows. He wants to cry, because her echo is on song. Her echo is a pearl drum.

Wey ma, wey ma. Uuuuuuu.

And then his aunt, still holding him, chimes in.

Wobo, wobo, deesh, deesh.

He lifts his head from her embrace, and sees, hears a pealing from the parents who once ago abandoned him. He listens to their echoes.

Pulapulapula-oooo. Zimpapa-zimpapa.

Sound ricochets in a melodious opus.

Wey ma, wey ma. Uuuuuuu.

Wobo, wobo, deesh, deesh.

Pulapulapula-oooo.

Zimpapa-zimpapa.

The resonance blends into a singularity. The crowd's fists are up, a gesture of triumph, and it's for him. He touches his face—he doesn't know if it's sweat or tears. All he hears is the unmistakeable echo in that unified chant, a single word, robust and perfect, over and over:

Sina'aa!

SINA'AA!

S
  I
    N
     A
      '
       A
        A

"UNTIL THE LION LEARNS HOW TO WRITE,

EVERY STORY WILL GLORIFY THE HUNTER."

— CHINUA ACHEBE

*A*s we discussed earlier in the introduction to the creation myth "Our Mother, Creator", myths and legends are fundamental to the world-view of every society. They help to contextualize events from the past, and in some cases, they can hold incredible sway over the people who grow up hearing them. Drama, motivations, personalities, all can be made larger-than-life, made epic.

In addition to creation myths, epic poems are an ancient form going back to civilizations from all around the globe: Gilgamesh, Sunjata, Beowulf.

We wanted to have such an epic poem for the Sauútiverse. But these are often exaggerated and altered tales rooted in history just as creation myths are rooted in physical observations of the grand celestial and terrestrial bodies. So in the wake of such major events as the great solar flare, the destruction of Mahwé, and the decline of the Mahwé-Zezépfeni empire, it made sense that there would be such an epic poem told across the planets and across cultures. One created or perhaps altered from some older, more ancient poem. Something that encoded the far history of the people in mythical terms. Elevated it to the cosmic. And therefore we wrote one. Something that was intended to be recited and performed over and over again, told to the people of the Sauútiverse as a cautionary tale where Mahwé is cast as a personified tragic figure, one of The Mother's Children gone astray and lost for their error. But who would tell such a story? In the decline of empire, its machinery for mythmaking does not simply recede into nothing. Especially not in an empire that lasts long.

Zezépfeni still holds sway in system-wide government and politics and culture and they use that to their advantage. They tell the story of what happened, of their role in it, in an attempt to salve the wound. Even the creation myth is not free from manipulation (you might want to re-read it.) And the people go along with Zezépfeni's version of events – one that reduces their role to reluctant aggressor and heaps all the blame on Mahwé who can no longer speak for themselves. The people go along with this first for the sake of peace, and later, because they don't know how not to. One need only look at any previously colonized nation in the real world to see how the legacy of empire endures in language and culture and government and in so many other latent and hard-to-see ways.

And so this is The Rakwa wa-Ya'yn, ('The Song of Our Mother's Children') or 'The Mahwé epic', as told by Zezépfeni.

The Rakwa Wa-Ya'yn

"The Song of Our Mother's Children" or "The Mahwé Epic"

STEPHEN EMBLETON AND WOLE TALABI

Khwa'ra. It is acquired.
Ya'yn.It is uttered.
Ra'kwa.It is released.

We honour Our Mother Creator, Our Mother God.
Giver of Life and Taker of Life.
Nurturer and Destroyer.
With Love and Malice.
Both Radiant and Fierce.
Night becomes Day.
Unseen now seen.

Coming of age and as the first born, to Zezépfeni Our Mother bestowed the lands, the waters, and the skies, made custodian of the World.

Zezépfeni's own knowledge and mastery brought a renewed cycle to the World as it birthed its own. On its surface, creatures first cracked open their eggs, emerged from their wombs, budded, and blossomed under the warmth of Our Mother's gaze.

In benevolence Zezépfeni offered to share the knowledge with Mahwé, while last born, Wiimb-ó watched on, eager to learn. As they shared and taught, their collective mastery grew and thus Ekwukwe and Órino-Rin were brought into the fold. This meeting of inquisitive minds unravelled more truth of the world Our Mother had bequeathed them, further unveiling its boāmmariri, its essential truth. As a collective, their knowledge expanded, each playing with the aspects they found most intriguing, following their natural affinities and finding themselves in the magic, the siblings moved into adulthood.

With the loss of innocence came the first dissent.

Wiimb-ó craved more power even as Mahwé became jealous of the older sibling, Zezépfeni, for withholding the full might of knowledge and magic that they believed was the familial birthright.

Dissatisfied with simple creation games, Mahwé sought out the Word – the Source. Mahwé sent out an emissary, Pinaa, the worshipful and loyal one, to scour the universe for the reverberations, the remnants of the Word from when it was first spoken by Our Mother.

Pinaa returned with but a fragment of The Word, found in the outer reaches of the World, floating among debris and darkness where even Our Mothers' light was swallowed whole. Mahwé recited it and harnessed the power, swelling in size and radiance.

For a time, this power was hidden from the other siblings until its effects could no longer be masked from the young and ever-inquisitive Wiimb-ó. Seeking an ally, together they shared and grew more powerful than their firstborn sibling, speaking the Word in strange new ways, threatening the fabric of the World woven by Our Mother.

Our Mother perceived the impending imbalance in the World. Our mother knew the depth of jealousy of Mahwé for Zezépfeni, which drove their desire for power. Our Mother gave guidance to Zezépfeni, but watched without interfering, knowing all that was to come, witnessing Zezépfeni's efforts to govern with grace and discernment, even towards kin.

Mahwé and Wiimb-ó's abilities grew but Zezépfeni's attempts to caution, guide and maintain balance were brushed off.

The other siblings too were tempted with this promise of power, of greater magic, and began to indicate their desire to Mahwé in their own ways. Seeing an opportunity, Mahwé and Wiimb-ó summoned Ekwukwe, and Órino-Rin under the pretense of sharing the mysteries of the Word with them, making a false promise of a World where they could all find fragments of the Word and use it to wield more power, perhaps even surpass Our Mother if they found enough of it. United in Mahwé's deceit, all four siblings rose up against Zezépfeni, the custodian of the World, still urging restraint.

They confronted Zezépfeni, demanding an acknowledgment of Mahwé as the true custodian of the world, the seeker of the Word, heir to the Mother's creation. One who would not only maintain their status but take them to greater glories with a complete unveiling of the power and knowledge held by the Word.

Zezépfeni balked, dismissive of their request, still unaware of the extent of the knowledge and abilities already amassed by Mahwé and the three other siblings.

Mahwé, insulted and proud, retaliated with a barrage of blows at the older sibling's back. Caught off-guard, and without a second thought, Zezépfeni reacted in self-defence with a resounding crack.

The World was quiet.

Overcome with shock and sadness, Mahwé's stunned silence quickly turned to rage, going on the offensive. Wiimb-ó stepped in to defend Mahwé but was struck down by an uncompromising Zezépfeni. Mahwé and Wiimb-ó bristled at the assault, calling upon Ekwukwe and Órino-Rin to come to their defence.

Accessing the magic within, Wiimb-ó reached into Eh'wauizo and summoned aid in the form of three Spirit Warriors.

Zezépfeni, brave and determined to battle the attacking siblings without help from Our Mother God, stood fast in the face of the four encircling forces: Mahwé to the east, Ekwukwe to the north, Órino-Rin to the south, and Wiimb-ó at the west.

The battle of the siblings ensued.

Mahwé's rumbling, low, infrasonic waves cracked mountains and boulders.

Zezépfeni sent a pulsing staccato, a pummelling barrage, hammering destruction.

Wiimb-ó's power was a wind, building to a piercing pitch, and terminating with a resonant impact.

Ekwukwe sent a relentless series of piercing, ultrasonic bursts, echoing across the heavens and blazing comets across the skies.

Órino-Rin emitted a resounding blow, rippling through the ether, crossing time and space and all dimensions.

In the bedlam, Wiimb-ó was severely injured. The other three rebellious ones – Mahwé, Ekwukwe and Órino-Rin – distracted Zezépfeni from further attack on their wounded sibling long enough to escape the soul's call to Eh'wauizo. Instead, Wiimb-ó's soul took flight, hiding away for safety behind one of the three spirit warriors.

Though weakened, Zezépfeni summoned what power remained to nurse the battle scars, readying for another assault.

Witness to it all, the fulfilment of all she'd already foreseen, Our Mother God wept with disappointment.

Before long, Her disappointment turned to wrath.

As the echoes of Her children's cries of both pain and anger subsided, She felt Her insides being wrenched in two until she could no longer hold. In a blinding realisation of what she had always known, She accepted the true cost of balance, She would have to be both creator and destroyer.

Pandemonium tore through the heavens as Our Mother God sacrificed her One self. A dizzying explosion of Her essence. One radiant light became two: Daughter Zuúv'ah, full of Her grace and nurturing essence; and Daughter Juah-āju, embodying the wrath and vengeance of Our Mother. This divine blast scattered out all Her children – family harmony was no longer, nor would it ever be again.

Eons passed by. The last vestiges of Our Mother God, her thunderous sound, dissipated and finally, hushed.

There was a great and terrible silence.

But the Word and the World persisted.

And Her children remained.

Through Pinaa as emissary, Mahwé and Zezépfeni tentatively re-established communication. Slowly, connections were remade with the other siblings, temporarily united now by grief and possibility. All were brought back into the fold around the warmth of their sister-twins, Zuúv'ah and Juah-āju.

Zezépfeni would forever be cautious of Mahwé.

True to nature, Mahwé was already plotting to rise up once more. Resentments pushed beneath the surface had festered and would never be quelled. Forgiveness and love were not the treasures Mahwé desired. Family had little meaning in a vast universe of possibilities the Word offered.

Now, Mahwé wanted to transcend rivalry, remove obstacles and be the centre of a single, pulsing, sound. A great and never-ending cosmic thunder. Mahwé wanted to be everything that was and everything that would ever come to pass.

Mahwé no longer desired a place as the first among equals, Now Mahwé sought to take the place of Our Mother.

Despite Zezépfeni's warnings, Mahwé reached into the darkness within, to the hate and the malice, creating an army of sentries for protection, to insulate while strategies were devised. Pinaa marvelled, captivated, at the magic and power of great Mahwé who would stop at nothing to wield everything. Pulled in by Mahwé's loyal emissary's hypnotic words and the promise of more power than they had dreamed, Ekwukwe and Órino-Rin relented once more.

Wiimb-ó, broken and unsure, sat in silence, unwilling to act.

The twin siblings, Zuúv'ah, Juah-āju, joined with Zezépfeni, and prepared for the inevitable battle against Mahwé, Pinaa, Ekwukwe, and Órino-Rin.

Ambushed by Pinaa, Juah-āju was taken off-guard, providing Mahwé with the opportunity for a full-frontal assault.

Ekwukwe and Órino-Rin combined their offensive against Zuúv'ah, doubling their force as they screamed their power against the raging light.

A barrage of comets pummelled down, and in a blinding light, Ekwukwe was hollowed out and scorched, nearly ripped asunder. Zuúv'ah's flaring blows blasted the sound out of Órino-Rin, now wheezing and winded and spent.

Zuúv'ah watched on as her violent self, Juah-āju, was steadily diminished in the clash with Mahwé and Pinaa. She and Zezépfeni knew Mahwé would not relent.

When Mahwé lashed out violently at even loyal Pinaa for perceived hesitation in battle, the weakened siblings finally realised Mahwé would stop at nothing to defeat and rule, and so, stepped back at the moment Zuúv'ah, Juah-āju and Zezépfeni combined power – a united front - to pummel and subdue Mahwé.

Predicting the onslaught, Mahwé commanded the army of sentries to protect and defend. As a great wall, an immovable, impenetrable force, the sentries encircled Mahwé and Pinaa.

For a time, there was a fraught peace, the barrier impossible to cross. The defeated rebel siblings floundered without the direction of Mahwé, unsure of themselves and their place, and wracked with guilt at their failures.

Empathy prevailed and Zezépfeni approached the wayward siblings with cautions and guidance. The firstborn held the three with tenderness and forgiveness.

Pinaa revelled in the peace, the privacy and the intimacy, but Mahwé grew impatient and frustrated, and lost without support.

Feeling hemmed in by the self-imposed barrier of sentries, Mahwé considered breaking free from the prison, not only the prison of its own making, but the ultimate prison - time.

Mahwé sought to move through time itself, to the end of days when its siblings would have faded, when light and sound would have receded and all that would be left was the Word, whole and ripe for the plucking. And then, Mahwé would return with it.

Mahwé swallowed the fragment of the Word it possessed and began to speak it in reverse, curling the contours of its sound until the end became the beginning and the beginning became the end.

Time itself strained against its breaking.

Pinaa was the first to plead to Mahwé not to disentangle time and space, not to unbalance that which was in harmony.

Mahwé's backwards roar filled the space between them. The reverse-Word was being spoken and Pinaa had little power to stop it. Mahwé would conjure all necessary power to bend spacetime itself while Pinaa would have to stand back, unwilling to participate and impotent to prevent it.

Mahwé's turbulent sound surged. Detonations and discord rumbled through the World. Through the pandemonium of Mahwé's utterance, reality began to warp.

Seeing no other choice, Pinaa called upon Zezépfeni, asking for wisdom and was given new words to pronounce, words never before heard: *It is acquired. It is uttered. It is released.*

In the moment Mahwé reached the beginning of the Word, voice on the brink of final utterance, the sound of a billion crystals cracking screeched through the ether. Stars wobbled. Galaxies skittered and collided.

Mahwé was silenced.

All light dimmed but for the twin siblings, side by side.

And for a juzu, all sound was gone, as Zuúv'ah and Juah-āju slowly drew each of their siblings back towards their warm embrace.

Pinaa, having barely survived, looked on at the pale, disfigured Mahwé, broken and defeated, lost in time. Despite Zezépfeni's urging, Pinaa yearned to utter a resurrecting word, unwilling to release the lifeless form of a once mighty Mahwé to Eh'wauizo. An unwavering Pinaa accepted the devastating lot that had been dealt, yet remained determined to find a way.

For this reverence to Mahwé, Juah-āju turned her back on Pinaa. Never again allowing Pinaa to look upon their warmth or wrath, instead Pinaa could only perceive Juah-āju's presence as a warning, wherever Pinaa may venture.

As the twins, Our Mother God endured, Zuúv'ah sharing of herself with a diminished, yet radiant, Juah-āju.

To this day, every twenty-five juzu, our system is witness to Zuúv'ah pulsing to keep sister Juah-āju alive, for the ways of violence may be diminished but cannot be forgotten.

There is always malice. There is always love.

This is the balance.

We honour the Mother God by orienting ourselves, bodily, to the
warm embrace of both her daughter forms:
Zuúv'ah, Juah-āju.
Giver of Life, and Taker of Life.
Nurturer and Destroyer.
Love and Malice.
Both Radiant and Fierce.
Day becomes Night.
Seen now unseen.

Find The Word.
Find The Voice.

Khwa'ra. It is acquired.
Ya'yn. It is uttered.

Ra'kwa. It is released.

*S*o we have established that Zezépfeni cast themselves as the firstborn of The Mother in their retelling of the Mahwé epic after the other planets have liberated themselves. They thus cast their aspirations to empire as being born of a desire to teach, to elevate, not control or enslave. But this is untrue. The truth is, according to the physical history as we have imagined it, Wiimb-ó is where life first developed in the Sauútiverse. Zezépfeni spreads lies as a means of control. But every lie eventually fades with sufficient time. Truth is persistent and not easily hidden away.

In this story by Sauútiverse founding member **Stephen Embleton**, which takes place 90 juzu A1B, we dig deep into the creation myths and epic poems and also the people who tell them. The ruevaagi, custodians of knowledge. Like African griots of old, they are tasked with telling the people the stories of themselves. But they are still under the sway of Zezépfeni, and can only tell the official version of events. They travel the five worlds, spreading the stories of what happened, performing it. Soft power. Even though there is nothing soft about it.

Wiimb-ó is the wellspring. The place where the people of Sauúti have the strongest connection to the spirit-plane with their two spirit moons manifesting in the sky. So it makes sense that this story of storytellers, of questioning the foundations of society, of mothers and their children, of finding your voice and finding the truth, takes place there.

Undulation

STEPHEN EMBLETON

I

"Khwa'ra," Hmahein said, inhaling the rich incense lingering in the room. "Ya'yn," she added with a low hum, flowing almost seamlessly into, "Ra'kwa." She let out a whoosh of air until her lungs were empty, while both hands pushed outward, completing the signing of the words as she understood them:

It is acquired. It is uttered. It is released.

The recognisable tingle formed on the tip of her tongue, warming her face, as she slowly took in air. A low vibration rippled through her. The magic was in her.

For Hmahein, that was the easy part. The beginning of the Creation Myth always stuck in her throat. As a ruevaagi, a bearer of histories for the worlds, a word should not be a hindrance.

She shook it off and locked eyes with her reflection in the wooden-framed, oval mirror of the small shrine.

She blocked out the word pulsing in her mind like a racing heartbeat. She blocked out the dimly lit room, draped in fabrics, curtains and intricate rugs. She blocked out the wafting scents of the dried kalabash vine leaves burning in the brass bowl on the small table, below the mirror.

She watched her mouth open, hands poised at the ready, and closed her eyes.

"*Our Mother*," she began.

"*Our Mother was all. Our Mother was all there was. There was no other to behold Her. Her light the only light. No other to receive Her light. No other to reflect Her light.*"

She continued, reciting the words of the Creation myth as she had been taught. She smiled when she reached her favourite part. "*The Word rumbled forth, and a crash shook the earth, as Our Mother's turbulent waters surged across the lands, inundating, quenching, and bathing.*"

She was speaking freely, her mind and mouth open, allowing the words to pour from her like vessel. "*Our Mother screamed with the glory of Motherhood and The Word screamed back.*

Firstborn, Wiimb-ó –"

"No."

The word was neither shouted, nor sneered, yet it held the power of a command. Her mentor, Ra'engi Efendumo, stood motionless, reflected in the mirror a few paces behind her, hands behind his back. She made to turn around and protest his interruption, but his hand, gesturing to continue, was all it took for her to know she had to finish her performance.

"Firstborn." She paused, then added, *"Zezépfeni, emerged into Our Mother's warm light, nestled and nurtured in the World. Life thrived. The world grew."*

The rhythm of the Creation Myth was now second nature to Hmahein; the thrum of magic pulsed through her, an ebb and flow, as she made her way through the inception of their universe, and completed the piece.

The usual trepidation arose in her gut as she spoke the mantra, "Find the Word. Find the Voice." The discomfort had increased over the past months, niggling at her more and more after each of her recitations.

She formed the signs with her dextrous fingers. "Khwa'ra." She breathed in. "Ya'yn." She gave a low hum. "Ra'kwa." A gush of air was expelled from her nose and mouth, and the tingling in her body subsided.

She rolled her eyes, and muttered to herself, "Here we go," and turned to face the sullen man behind her.

Poise. Gestures. Technique. Ra'engi Efendumo's repetitive feedback had become a monotonous refrain Hmahein was now deaf to, along with his pacing up and down.

Her mentor was all about reiterating the unique nature of a ruevaagi's performance, in placing your audience under something close to a spell. A fully immersive, emotional, and physical experience, akin to an auditory bubble.

In the squat, stuffy, guild school hall, when they weren't discussing arithmetic, languages and geometry, the oral arts of speech, song and poetry were encouraged and performed. Usually ignored, she would use those performances to attain that fleeting sense of belonging, thriving on it when permitted to express her developing magic in front of enraptured fellow students. Playful. Experimental.

Now, with the knowledge bestowed on her over the course of her training, along with the cautionary tales of magic untethered, she felt hemmed in with ritual and conformity, made starkly plain by her mentor. *One must always strive for greater control over oneself and one's social, natural and magical environments.*

The contradiction had become infuriating. Conjuring magic was breathtaking, creative and healing, yet, one wrong word could fracture the five worlds.

She watched her ra'engi. Did he have to practice the same words over again, for them to assimilate into his physical being? Or maybe he resented being lumped with her, out of all the burgeoning talent in the Saúuti system, the child of a shunned family.

Not yet one juzu old, Hmahein had been too young to understand when her mother ended her life. She grew up with only her father, ostracised by their relatives and community. Understanding, if it came at all, was later.

Every phase of her childhood, from birthdays to the twelve rites of passage, was marked by absence. The looks, the reluctance to be in her company, the snatches of conversations she overheard, would all eventually fall into the background. She found her father to be a stranger in their small home, retreating more and more to his workshop in the attached outside room. The tapping of his small hammer and chisel, decorating the wooden wares, the hanging kalabash bowls and containers, the household implements he magically crafted and sold around the town, were the only sounds she heard from him.

In her teens he had withdrawn even further. The look on his face as he returned through the kitchen for the evening meal, as if in recognition of the woman Hmahein resembled, and the sudden averting of his eyes, created a tension she was unable to process or understand at first.

With the unbearable silence hanging in the household, and with no one to share her inner thoughts and struggles, Hmahein had resorted to eating early, alone, and retreating to bed, staring up at the coarse mud-packed ceiling, speaking to herself.

Conversations were two-sided, sometimes heated. An emotional Hmahein would express herself to the room, upset about something that had happened that day or a jealous thought on seeing another girl with their mother. A stern reproach would come from within, castigating her, telling her to grow up or ignore what the rest of the isolating community represented. Other times it was her anger that drove her screaming into her bed, with the other gentle voice soothing and calming her out of her melancholy. A back and forth would ensue, like a ball game. She learned bigger words to express herself to herself. She found the rhythm in her voice, landing verbal blows to the gut, or the gentle tone that would send goosebumps up her spine with a revelation.

On a handful of occasions, she knew her father was listening, either at the door, or close enough in the kitchen to hear her. She wouldn't suppress the words, the emotions or the anger flowing out of her. He would hear what she had to say, even if it was to herself.

In the end, the anger solidified. No matter the ideas raised, the point of views exchanged, and no matter how convincing she sounded to herself, it was always the anger that remained. She resolved that no matter what she thought, no matter how she attempted to justify or explain away any choices her mother had made, she would always be angry, with her.

The one part of her life where she felt any connection, solitude and grace, was in her room speaking to the ceiling, dissecting her world, pulling it apart and reshaping it for herself.

Her voice became her weapon. It formed who she was becoming: someone who could no longer be ignored by an arrested community, stuck in outdated mindsets. The tutors could not deny her abilities, standing in front of the group of students, conveying ideas, answering problems, and the sizzle of magic that emanated from her every utterance. Soon her identity was all-consumed by her skills. Every opportunity to speak she relished. Judgmental people be damned to Yikho, the void.

Without any thought of being selected from the three students identified by the elite order of knowledge seekers from Zezépfeni, the Susu Nunyaa, Hmahein had assumed her lot was in the town she had grown up in, and would die in. The night before the ceremonial announcement had her practically one-sidedly explaining how Munghweii was sure to be chosen. There was no hint of anger or jealously at the idea. Simply conceding to the inevitability that she was not to be the one.

All the glances from her youth, all the comments and rumours, the lack of invitations that she thought she had shoved into the background and ignored, hit her like a deluge in that moment on stage. The gasps of alarm and dismay were like she was hearing them for the first time.

Even today, in the quiet warmth of the rakwayn, her sacred area, the memory of the people in the front row, below the ceremonial platform, sent a chill up her back.

Her father's relief. His daughter would be sent away, no longer his burden to bear?

The parents of Munghweii and Prahndyn, wailing and shouting their disapproval. Surely, theirs were no ostracised child bringing shame to the Order of the Ruevaagi? Were their children not more capable, with more private training?

And finally, the ashen look of Ra'engi Efendumo. Was he to mentor a shunned one? Was this what his reputation warranted?

Hmahein's eyes had long glazed over, for she knew when to pay attention at the moment Efendumo veered from his prescribed script. Rather than listening to her mentor's guidance for her pivotal performance this evening, her mind raced back and forth, trying to make sense of the chaos that had erupted that day she'd joined the Order.

The one thing she enjoyed about the Order's portable living quarters was the calming familiarity of the incense, and the comfort of the plush pillows and decorative rugs strewn across the space. Compared with life at home – if indeed *home* it could have been called – it was exotic and novel.

From the rich colours, to the touch of the fabrics, and the sounds and vibrations of the alabaster bells, everything was extrasensory to Hmahein. For all the rigid ceremony, rules and etiquette, the environment stimulated a ruevaagi to access the magic, when it came through, on all levels.

This was Hmahein's second ruevaagi gala, and the first time so far from home, into one of the more remote, inland regions of the continent: the vast equatorial district of Abzizi-Lukhi.

Possibly because of the heat, but more than likely nerves, Hmahein's stomach lurched as if something was tugging at her gut. The sensation had been flooding over her in intermittent waves for the past days, ever since their departure. The familiar salty, humid air of the bay city of Loiimbi was replaced with the dusty, yellow ochre sands of the paramikule, the isolated village, of Zékunekude. A stark, beautiful landscape she had never seen before.

Erected on the outskirts of the cities and towns they were invited to, the Order's tent-like pavilion, though beautifully adorned within, was unassuming from the outside. Designed to absorb rather than project any of the sounds from within, it allowed the initiates to practice their craft without affecting the world beyond, particularly from within the rakwayn, the sacred space Hmahein was seated in.

Each ruevaagi was allocated an area of the rakwayn, curtained-off by thin, sheer fabrics. Initiates were encouraged to bring their own paraphernalia for their personal shrine, setting up what and how they wished for their allotted rehearsal times, giving libations and offerings to the Mother.

The sacred space emitted little in the way of sound into the rest of the structure, and nothing beyond the taut fabrics pegged into the earth.

Contained. Pent-up, Hmahein thought. Like her mentor.

And there it was: the abrupt end to the speech; the change in his gait; the clearing of his throat.

II

On the first day of her training, a time that now seemed a lifetime ago, she had asked, "Why don't we just craft our stories, our histories, into our tapestries and sculpt our mythical scenes in granite?"

"Nothing is permanent," he had replied. "Not even handcrafted objects made of the finest magic can withstand the pummelling of time. Fabrics erode, pottery crumbles, buildings collapse. Planets, whole worlds, are obliterated. What always remains is the Mothersound. We are the link with the past and the future. Speak it. *'It is uttered'*, and it lives on, resonating for eons. Our world's magic is in the vibrations made across the universe. A structure does not itself resonate. A sculpture does not communicate meaning and magic. It stands, inert, frozen in time. The Masters can dip into time and retrieve sounds echoing throughout the universe. Everything that has been uttered, everything which has made a sound, is out there.

"A language, *the* language, when you break it down, shows our cosmology, our world view. Most importantly, it is an insight into the world view of an ancient people. It is not random concepts, or vocal utterances, thrown together to give an object meaning. It is a living historical record, right in front of us, spoken by us. My words right now carry with them the weight of that history along with the meaning I am putting across. Our language is part of us, not something separate. It is something that evolved with us. Our words are our artefacts for ages to come. How I say something today is different to what it would've sounded like a hundred juzu ago, or a hundred juzu to come. But, those in the future can, as we can now, retrace that lineage."

In a room, similar to this one, Ra'engi Efendumo had stood behind Hmahein, hands placed gently on her shoulders, indulging her, before he would eventually lose his tolerance for her questioning. She heard him take in a deep breath and let out a low hum. "A million voices, over time," he said softly, "have participated in the moulding of this ancient artefact, passed down through the ages. A lineage unbroken. They speak to us as we speak. And we must listen."

For a fleeting moment, Hmahein felt bad for not having listened to the man. His gaze was hard and unflinching, willing her to collapse under its weight and yield to his guidance with unwavering loyalty.

She knew he was not done. Like many adults she had come across in her lifetime, it was as though they believed knowledge and magic emanated from every word they spoke. They did not know when to shut up. What her mentor had taught her was immeasurable. But there was a tone, or method, of Ra'engi's which set her jaw and shut her ears. Maybe that was part of his magic? Closing people out.

Feeling bad soon dissipated.

"You embellish what is a sacred art, Hmahein. Yes," he said, and raised a hand as she perked up, to stop her interrupting, "you do so in private, but that tongue of yours is destined to utter falsehoods which will reverberate for eternity. You and your loved ones will bear the cost."

"I already know what it is to be ostracised," she said and slouched back down.

"Then you wish this upon me too, do you?" He stepped in closer, looking down at her. "Think past your own lips. Now, stand up."

She reluctantly stood and he sighed, giving her a once-over.

Integral to the ceremony of the performance of any ruevaagi were the garments. Though, at first, Hmahein had felt hemmed in, it was something she had come to relish, as one doted on like a heroic figure. All ruevaagi wore identical attire, but with personal ornamentations and motifs sewn into the delicate undergarment, or small objects held in concealed compartments.

"After your revisionist Creation Myth, Hmahein, dare I ask who the hero of your version of *The Rakwa wa-Ya'yn* is?" asked Efendumo.

She flushed. The heat wavered around her face; pin-pricks of irritation bristled through the scalp beneath her tightly-knitted black hair. Curls and loose strands were woven around numerous thin, splayed spines, like dark rays framing her head.

He inspected the strip of intricate lace embroidery, the oceanic serpent design, falling from her shoulder, down her near-transparent sleeve, and tailing off at the elongated angular cuff hanging past her fingertips. All details that would be cloaked beneath the ruevaagi garments, but adding to the layers of symbolism.

"The grand council will be watching tonight's performance." She knew he was looking at her personal items on the small table as he walked behind her. "Even trifling discussions," he hissed the last word, "like these can be tapped into at any given time." He walked over to the hanging vestments to her left.

"Why would they bother with a dull-repetitive-soporific conversation as this, Ra'engi?" She gave a wry smile and faced him.

He clucked his tongue, unable to hide his annoyance. "You need to find the word. You cannot say double, triple words. Make a choice."

Rather than comment on her remarks, he focused on the flaws in her utterances, the word choices, the tone, or the inflections being incorrect for achieving maximum impact. "Right words. Right mind. Right magic," he had once said when she had shouted her frustrations at him early on in her training, and then snapped his fingers.

She walked up to the garment draped over the wooden rail, suspended by a long kalabash-creeper rope hanging down from deep within the layers of thin veils. Always transfixed by the beautiful breastplate, pride and wonder welled up inside her, knowing where it had come from and what it had taken for it to be hers, and hers alone.

Even the dimmest light within the chamber danced across the golden lines of the carapace's segmented edges; the colours of the curved, hard surface shimmered with iridescent emerald greens. The outer edges and down to the crotch, a leathery and soft golden-green, enabled thread to be stitched to the fabric holding its weight in place up to her diaphragm. From there, it hardened up the undulating spinal ridge, ending at the resonant hollow within, to rest at her collarbones, where it shone with silver-blues and pinks. The geometric shapes and colours of the fuúz-imwazii carapace were echoed in the design detail of the fabric print on the supporting garment. The thick material blended almost seamlessly with the amphibian's carapace and tough, yet soft, skin.

"Waioke!" Efendumo shouted, startling Hmahein.

She scowled at him as he pivoted on his heel and set his attention on the ceremonial objects in the open vertical rack.

Efendumo gently slid his open palm up the shaft of the tall, wooden ceremonial spear, at least two heads above him. Three copper rings, beaten and moulded smoothly around the brown-black veined geréwiig hard-wood, held a short, fat blade in place. At the base, the heel, sharpened and equally as useful as the blade, was the portion of the ceremonial weapon the ruevaagi would push firmly into the ground, or spear-holder, as soon as they were introduced and standing before their audience.

"The Masters of the past, and very few in the present, have harnessed the Word." Efendumo's voice was soft and almost inaudible in the room. "But, it's not something they can put into an oil spice carafe and pass around."

"I'm not going to suspend myself in a bubble in the outer reaches of the universe and hum for the rest of my life," said Hmahein. "That's not a life, ra'engi. If that's what being a master is then–"

"That's not what being a master is," he whirled around. "It is about uttering the Word, and the initiating phrase, precisely." He turned back to the objects, this time the delicate, alabaster bell, which a ruevaagi sets silently on the ground at a single pace in front of themselves. "They have found the inner peace, the quietude within, to utter it and access it, and harness it responsibly." He stroked a finger along the wavy decorative ridges running down its four edges.

"I know how to conduct myself responsibly."

He snorted, then immediately composed himself.

"You cannot be midperformance and suddenly discover your true potential. We have our protocols in place to control and terminate the pathways opened by a ruevaagi. It is a delicate dance within those doorways that must be performance-focused. Tutelage in safer spaces, experimenting, pushing your limits, are all done with a ra'engi present. As such, tonight you will perform *The Song of Our Mother's Children* with grace, truth, and control," he said matter-of-factly. "Truth is what you have been taught, not what you *think* is the truth."

She watched him leave the room, disappearing silently through the maze of translucent curtains.

A heaviness grew in the pit of Hmahein's stomach. Her mentor had done nothing to quell the scattered thoughts and emotions racing through her mind. Becoming a ruevaagi was meant to be a life assured, not a questioning of her world and her purpose. She had enough demands on herself without his added expectations for the performance. She shuffled back to her stool, slumped down and picked up a short pitcher and tilted it over her goblet. The clear, sweet melon water poured out, and the floral scents wafted up, already refreshing her. She took a sip, tasting, smelling and relishing the revitalising effect of the traditional drink.

A mixture of pleasant and unpleasant memories flooded through her as the myriad sensations of the liquid tapped into her subconscious. Her body tingled. It was different to her vocal magic, but magic enough to conjure up the past.

A stillness settled over the room.

III

The sound of Ra'engi Efendumo clearing his throat caused the memories to abruptly fade within her. "Is this child going to do any attending today?" he asked.

As if on cue, the boy Waioke, briefly introduced to them when they had arrived, pushed quietly through the delicate curtains and stood ready for instructions.

"Oh, finally, Waioke," said Efendumo clapping his hands slowly. "I suggest you familiarise yourself with your ruevaagi's vestments. Please proceed with what you have been trained to do, young zéhemgwile."

The Guild of Tailors, the Zéhemgwile, were masters of the thread and needle, and so much more than the fitting of ceremonial garments. Colour, symbolism, shapes and textures all had subliminal meaning, some innate and inexplicable within the differing peoples spread across the five worlds.

Surprisingly, their training had them venturing out into the wilds of their home regions in search of new materials or innovative ways of using existing resources. Spun webs from the fire-arachnids were meticulously harvested, and one of the more durable of all silk threads. Shimmering red-oranges, like flames, made for lightweight and cool coats in the more humid regions. The kalabash plants had proved the most diverse and hardy, being used for ropes, sacking, canopies and sails. While some brave soul, more than a thousand juzu before, had ventured into the caves of Juhaianith to retrieve the fine white fur of the mythic enhwaunu. As a result of being threatened for over a century, the Zéhemgwile had formed coalitions of experts to harvest without requiring pelts or harming the sightless, subterranean mammals.

Meeting anyone from the variety of orders and guilds in their worlds was electrifying to Hmahein, knowing there were others who wielded the magic on a day-to-day basis, crafting and creating with words and sounds.

Hmahein walked over to him and extended her hand. "Hello again, Waioke."

A head shorter than her, and around fifteen juzu by zéhemgwile initiate age ranges, the boy shook her hand and gave a brief tilt of his head in respect. His own attire was breathtaking in its detail, yet restrained in its simplicity. His long black hair, plaited in rows similar to Hmahein's, had fine golden threads looped through, giving it a sheen, like it was damp with oils. Rather than having flat, patterned prints on sturdy cloth, or embroidery added onto a coat, his tunic was a combination of everything, simultaneously. A perfect harmony of weaved designs, tightly-knit in places, while open and porous for aeration, and echoed by sandy-toned print patterns. Delicate protruding threads, if not for the skills of the guild or for their regularity of appearance and intermittent placements, would have been perceived as flaws. Hmahein glanced at the boy's sleeve, finally seeing one of the fibres in close proximity. The fine thread was delicately and deliberately plaited, with a minute bead the size and colour of the yellow ochre sands from the area, attached, before looping back into the garment.

Hmahein released his hand and his movement allowed his coat to shimmer ever so slightly, along with a sound like sand blown across the desert. She gestured to her hanging garments, watching as the attendant approached them with trepidation.

The tugging sensation pulled at her stomach. Hmahein moved awkwardly back to her stool and sat, eyes still fixed on the boy with his nose pressed close to each detail and stitch, inspecting her clothing's artistry. She gulped down her drink.

Efendumo took the opportunity to step away, through the veils and into another area of the pavilion. She had come to recognise by now his methods of avoiding conversations, or more specifically, her questions.

Hmahein noticed the grey stone bowl on the table below her mirror, smokeless and devoid of the glowing incense she had lit earlier. She tossed the sooty remains into the leather pouch hanging from the side of the table, the ash to be used for her ceremonial face paint, and gave the bowl a blow. From inside a small drawer in the table, she retrieved her firestriker, with its intricately carved wooden grip and flint shaft, along with her tightly wrapped roll of incense. Hmahein untied and unrolled the bundle just enough to remove a wad of the dried plants. The aroma was potent.

She pressed them into the curve of the bowl and clicked the firestriker close to one of the grey-green leaves. A spark to took hold, and she leaned in to give a gentle blow. Immediately, the dull sedative effect of the heady smoke washed over her as the brittle leaves and twigs crackled and popped.

Efendumo returned to her rakwayn with his own armchair, and his melon-wine skin of drink. "Boy," he waved Waioke over to Hmahein. "Can we get on with her?"

Hmahein glared at him in her mirror. His eyes were hazy, glazed over. He had more than likely taken his leave to inhale some of his own special incense concoction. His nerves would be heightened with the approaching evening's performance, and Hmahein was accustomed to his brief disappearances. As usual, he placed his chair behind Hmahein, a fair distance from her but where she could still hear him breathing, and sipping his spiced alcohol.

Waioke stood beside her, readying his small pouch of fine implements, as if weighing them, as he ran his middle finger lightly over the existing patterns.

Without having to show him, the boy had found the frayed areas around the cuff hem, and was looking at the right elbow, lightly lifted in his palm, completely devoid of any needlework. His keen eyes darted around the existing designs, taking note of the motifs, understanding the repetitions and symbolism.

Waioke removed a long needle, placed his pouch on the table and, with tongue at the side of his mouth, began threading through a strand of fibre matching the embroidery of her sheer tunic-style blouse. She traced the thread from his hand, looped through a delicate bracelet at his wrist, and disappearing down into the side pocket of his tunic. He self-consciously retracted his tongue and tied the thread off, but rather than a trimmed length, it was now obvious to Hmahein it was to be as endless as the ball of yarn tucked away somewhere in a pocket.

"What of my visions, Efendumo?"

Her mentor sighed. "Until you see them clearly, decipher what they mean to you, only then can I take them to the council. Nevertheless, Hmahein, have you not considered, perhaps, your visions are you accessing Eh'wauizo?"

Her ears pricked up, but she feigned disinterest with a shrug.

"It is said the ancients, before the flare, obscured the greatest knowledge in our universe in order that only the most diligent of seekers of that knowledge would find, and make use of, the magic. Eh'wauizo provides us with meaning, guides us in all aspects of our material and immaterial existence. It is a place some can visit, before and after our time is up in the material world."

She was about to respond when something else caught her ear.

Waioke was softly uttering indiscernible words, running to a beat, like a poem. In a low hum, the words melded into one another, rising and falling. She looked down at the needle held gently between thumb and forefinger. Whether it was the ripple of electric sparks running from his knuckles to the needle, or the sparkle of light dancing off the tip, Hmahein's skin buzzed beneath her blouse.

In a flash, the young zéhemgwile's needle and thread slid silently in and out of the translucent fabric, within seconds forming the recognisable twirls and cones of the shell designs found elsewhere on the blouse. So quick was the glint of his tool that she could perceive the patterns growing before her eyes, as if themselves alive.

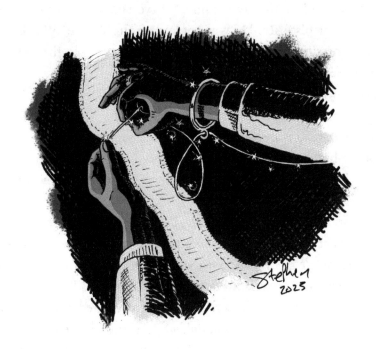

"You know the magic is real," said Efendumo. The power of the Word resides within the one wielding it. Altering a word alters its power. We are here to be true to the histories, as they are. And, true to the Word. Whether you are brought before the decedents of Kunekude and her paramikule," he said and opened his arms to their surroundings, "the forty clans within the protectorate, or the Supreme Federation on Zezépfeni, the words must stand as they are, as they have been, for millennia. Otherwise, you are no better than those you point to as, how do you put it so eloquently," he mused, "dodgy-controlling-fascist Zezépfenians."

Hmahein was almost lost in the spectacle of Waioke's magical mastery that it took her a moment to respond to her ra'engi.

"The role of our elders," she said slowly, eyes still following the delicate movements, "is not to tell us what to do. It is to pave the way for young people to do what we want to do. Not so, Waioke?"

"Oh, my soul," huffed Efendumo. "Do you not learn from your own reciting of the histories? Do you not learn from Mahwé? Wielding the Word, harnessing it, can be destructive – for you and for the collective. You must see beyond your own desires."

The gentle lilt to Waioke's song fluttered through Hmahein's body, the stool and the plush rug beneath her bare feet.

"My own visions are not desires! It's those visions which are growing-increasing-building my desire. And my desire is to express my truth. My words. Not the dusty words handed down, losing their power-might-potency."

"You are an inexperienced initiate. Look at how you still seek out the words. Mastery is knowing what to utter and when. Mastery is knowing the power of *all* the words. All the meaning you can muster, in the shortest way possible, without flowery embellishments."

She held her breath, ready for a quip, but relented as her mentor's words sunk in. She let out a loud sigh while her mind raced.

Waioke was at her left sleeve, his voice caressing the air around her, working his thread in minute strokes across the fabric. His thumb flicked small beads, only fractionally larger than the ones in Waioke's own tunic, onto the tip of a new, finer needle at every third stroke, sewing them deftly into the design. An arc of light, from the needle to his thumb, guided the glassy bead onto the needle. What originally had ended with a delicate lace frill, had become fine tassels with the beads like dewdrops on desert sands. She lifted her other hand, feeling the tickle of the completed sleeve. Or was that residual magic licking at the fine hairs on her hand?

Watching through her mirror, Ra'engi Efendumo stood, wobbled for a moment, steadying himself on the arm of his chair, then left the room holding his deflated wine skin.

Hmahein leaned in to grab her own drink, nearly falling over as a retching sensation welled up inside her. She quickly sat back down, with Waioke having set his arm out for her to latch onto. He gave her a moment to settle before passing her the goblet and continuing his work, but eyeing her suspiciously.

"I am sure your own tutors have high opinions of themselves," she said to distract herself, "just as our esteemed Ra'engi Efendumo has."

Waioke simply nodded and continued his song, the golden magic light continuing its flow around his fingers and her garment.

"We are not just storytellers," grumbled Ra'engi Efendumo as he returned, chewing on something moist. "We do not convey fictions. We are historians. Chroniclers of the ages." At the last words he raised his bulging wine skin in a toast and took a long pull.

"We are allegorists, Ra'engi Efendumo," said Hmahein still catching her breath and taking a sip of her melon water. "We tell a version of the story, which demands interpretation. We've been taught to apply layer upon layer of allegory-metaphor-parable, until the truth is no longer discernible from fantasy. I'm here for truth. I'm here for magic, not make-believe."

Unfortunately, her ra'engi had not taken his seat. Instead, he was weaving his way towards her and Waioke.

"It is in moments like these, when I witness the talent of the magic arts in one such as your esteemed friend here, a novice, by all accounts," he said and clapped Waioke on the shoulder, "that I have to remind myself that it was the Zezépfenians, in their wisdom, who recognised your abilities—"

"Duplication-triplication included," added Hmahein. Her queasiness was subsiding and the sweat on her brow fading. If it weren't for the sweet drink she would have needed to lie down, but she was hoping to hear her mentor's honest thoughts for once. A sober Efendumo would have long ago ended this conversation.

"And so," continued Efendumo, locking his bleary eyes on hers, "selected you over your two friends."

Hmahein flushed and turned away from him at the memory of standing beside Munghweii and Prahndyn, on the raised platform of the council chambers at their capital, at the moment she was announced to be the initiate from their region. The sounds of the gasps of disbelief and horror from the other family members reassured her that, no matter what she achieved in the five worlds, she would always be the outcast.

"We were never close," she said more to herself than to anyone else.

"We still await the emergence of your actual abilities, initiate. Who knows what it is, because you certainly insist on sabotaging the process. As if you want to prove everyone right. The final pilgrimage and vow ceremony is near and we have not, you have not, fully harnessed what it is you are capable of."

She shook her head at the onerous task of pledging her loyalty to the Order of Ruevaagi. "What if I am merely an adequate-passable-unexceptional ruevaagi, Ra'engi Efendumo?"

"A treehouse does not grow with the tree," said Efendumo, with a slight slur to his words. "Your outdated ideas of yourself do not evolve, they stagnate your mind, your voice. And like the treehouse, it rots. Your childish mind is stunted by your past."

The cold sweat was back. This time it itched beneath her shirt, the clamminess sticking the fabric to her body. A quick intake of breath did nothing but cause Waioke alarm. Staggered breathing hit her and she doubled over onto the floor, empty goblet making a dull thud on the floor.

"Hmahein?" said Efendumo curiously.

"Hmahein, are you okay?" asked Waioke kneeling at her side.

All she could muster was a curt nod and pushed herself up to a crouch.

"It's like," she said between clenched teeth, "it's like... What is it like?"

"You're just overwhelmed." Efendumo lifted her other arm, along with Waioke, and guided her back to the stool.

"It's like I'm being pulled apart in three directions." She breathed heavily. "It's as if the moon is heavier that it actually is, and it's going to rip me and this planet apart."

"What?" asked the boy softly.

"It's like the ground beneath me, beneath all of us, is rising and falling, but it's just another day on Wiimb-ó. No one blinks. Here comes another wave. I've felt this way my entire life, but today is–"

In a flash, Waioke had grabbed his pouch from the table and darted out of her rakwayn in a flurry of curtains.

"Where in the five worlds is that boy going to now?" Efendumo walked back to his own chair, waving a dismissive hand in the direction the zéhemgwile had disappeared. "Nerves. Happens to all of us, my initiate. I think you have overstimulated yourself with all this talk. Philosophising is not our place, and certainly not our reason for being here. Your meditations, your phase-two training, you should practice those."

Hmahein sighed. "We are in the land where sand rains from the sky."

"We are here, in a remote and faraway place," came his sing-song reply, "where you can practice your learned skills out of view from influential eyes."

She swivelled around on her stool to face him, dabbing her sleeve on her damp forehead. "You mean to minimise any embarrassment, dear ra'engi."

He folded his arms and stared sullenly at her. "Meditations. Or something at least to control yourself, please."

She balled her fists, scrunched her eyes closed, and tried to block him out.

IV

Hmahein was seated on the central stone slab on the crescent-shaped meditation walkway, taking in the vast view of the bay and ocean below. Slow-moving, billowing clouds, casting their grey-blue shadows onto the turquoise waters below, hung like the massive, strange vessels that would occasionally dock over their harbour every few moons, dominating the tiny fishing boats of the town of Loiimbi.

"Take a moment to clear your head," Ra'engi Efendumo had said. "Let some calming peace wash over you."

She closed her eyes, relaxed her shoulders and breathed in the cool, salty air pulsing against her face and body.

"There is a rhythm to the universe," he began in a low, even tone. "Everything flows to a beat, a cycle, a pattern. Like those massive swells on the ocean. Find yours, Hmahein."

"Swimming with the fuúzimwazii," she whispered.

"Yes. Feel that motion. Sense the motion. Intuit the motion, and know what comes next."

Her body tingled.

"Sense the resonance within yourself. It's there in every fibre of your blood and bone and air."

A gust of wind washed over her. She imagined floating, weightless, on the rising and falling swell of the ocean. All topside sounds muted by the water in her ears, replaced by a sea-creature's call that, even in memory, sent a rush of joyous adrenaline through her body.

"Say the initiating phrase, initiate, but," he cautioned, "only a whisper. Proceed."

She readied her hands, poised for the gestures that were becoming second nature to her, part of the uttering of the words they represented.

"Khwa'ra," Hmahein said and inhaled.

She felt the low purr emerge from her belly and said, "Ya'yn."

"Hold on to that tone," he whispered, barely audible.

She could sense her ra'engi closer to her, watching her, moving around her and noting everything about her.

"Wait on it. It's growing in your gut and thorax. That's what connects with your audience: feeling and sensing the emotion. The true meaning of our histories."

The signs, the posture, the breathing, all would be critiqued. She allowed the sensations, the sound and the vibrations, her vibrations from within, to drown out the thoughts and doubts. Her chest felt the size of a barrel, the sound echoing within her belly, her ribcage and pushing up against the back of her throat.

"And," he said gently, further away from her, "let it go."

"Ra'kwaaaa." Hmahein opened her eyes as she drew out the termination statement with a blast of outward breath. The force rippled across the platform, and despite the external breeze, ruffled the standing Ra'engi Efendumo's garments. Her skin tingled in the aftermath.

He nodded, suppressing a smile.

Hmahein's body was vibrating, her head swimming with images and words, almost revitalising. There was a heightened focus to everything in her surroundings; the sky, the ocean, all seemed more radiant than she remembered a moment ago. Her ra'engi raised a hand in caution. She needed to take it easy.

She stood slowly, stretched her arms up and took a deep breath, bending gently down to touch her toes, and breathing out. She walked over to the balustrade of the platform curving a wide arc out from the ruddy grey ridge. The bright green hills, covered in lush trees, bushes and grass, rolled down to the town and boats on the calm waters of the harbour. She felt as though she were seeing her town for the first time, the town where a dark cloud had hung over her for far too long.

Ra'engi Efendumo stood beside her, quiet for a moment, hands on the railing.

"Your magic is there for the taking, Hmahein," he said gently. "You try to fight for it, as if it is somewhere outside of yourself. The magic is what has determined our worlds, not our lack of it, hope for it, desire for it. Whether it be the abilities of the people from Wiimb-ó to Ekwukwe, the near annihilation of Mahwé, the masters of Zezépfeni and the song-chasers of Órino-Rin. Our magic is what has made us form the beliefs we hold to this day." He turned to face her, compelling her to look at him. "Imagine a world where magic does not exist – or worse – where it exists, but the people believe it is beyond their grasp, or something they should not harness. Or worse yet, that it is a fiction made up by a few to give false hope. Imagine that dark world, without imagination and possibilities."

He looked back over the bay, leaning on the balustrade. She followed his gaze.

"Imagine places out there, where people cannot and will not even attempt to reach through the worlds." He sighed. "And, how do we know all of this?"

"The Word," said Hmahein confidently.

"My initiate!" Efendumo exclaimed and gripped her hand. "Through the Word, Hmahein. Unchanging."

The gesture was startling, warm yet foreign. Her mind raced, but she kept her composure, eyes locked on the town below. She wondered where her father would be, whether he thought of his only child as he whiled away the hours in his cluttered workshop; or maybe only when he had to perform her chores in the small house she had shared with him, until recently. That day had been the first time the heaviness had lifted, even briefly, whenever she thought about home.

Dizzy and sweating, Hmahein was overcome with weakness. Her meditation had unravelled. She fumbled over to the group of large, plush cushions she had laid out as a makeshift couch, and slumped down onto her back.

"I know you detest it, Hmahein, but Mahwé stands as a warning," Efendumo said, "and the justification for that which you find repellent. Control."

Her heart was pounding in her chest, blood hissing in her ears as she tried to catch her breath and respond. "If that was their prerogative—will—desire," she said between pants, "pushing their abilities to the extreme, then surely that is what their magic was for?"

"A morality tale is useless if we are all obliterated and sent to Eh'wauizo through negligence and material greed. A parent does not watch idly as their child reaches into a fire to lift up a pretty, glowing ember. Especially if the child's act of doing so would ignite the village. Our Mother forbid."

"Parents are not always present to step in. Sometimes, they aren't around at all."

An awkward silence filled the fragrant air. As if to break the tension, the smouldering incense in the bowl crackled.

Efendumo grumbled under his breath and shifted in his chair.

"I am your designated ra'engi. And as said mentor, I can only guide you in the ways of the ruevaagi. I hand you the tools, the methods, and the knowledge to build on your innate abilities. If you choose to hinder your own attainment of becoming a ruevaagi, that cannot be on my shoulders. I am not your mo—" he held his tongue. "Parent."

"That word is problematic," she said and sat up with a sigh. "In so many ways."

"Kyi á Yikho, Hmahein." *Damn you to the void.* Efendumo slapped the wooden arm of his chair. "You need to focus your energy on this evening's performance. We are not discussing your views on Our Mother Creator."

She fixed him with a penetrating glare. "I have no quarrel with *our* Creator, Efendumo. It is *my* creator I have issue with. She chose to enter the spirit realm." Hamhein's voice was a whisper brimming with resentment. "She didn't want to be my... my parent. And my father blamed me. He was only too happy when the Zezépfenians, the Susu Nunyaa, selected me to be initiated."

"Your mother's decision to end her life had nothing to do with you. What she was dealing with, in her own way, was more than anyone could understand at the time. Or even now. Parents abandon children. Parents leave. Parents die. Being a good child or a bad child has no bearing on any parent doing what she did."

"Efendumo, my father told me," she said, crossing her legs and leaning forward to prod at the soft, red pile of the rug under the pillows she sat on. "He told me how she changed after I was born."

Efendumo did not need to know about the aftermath of the kitchen, the mayhem Hmahein had caused one evening, to get her father's attention. To demand it from him.

"That may be, but that does not place blame on you. They both willingly chose to have a child. Childbirth brings with it many aspects we are still learning about. Mothers don't necessarily mother. A woman doesn't necessarily have to bear children to be a mother, or mother-figure."

"All of them, from her to her sisters and her own parent, all shut me out of their lives. No one wanted any part of me. And none willingly stepped into that role in my life. Any point of reference I have is from a distance, from others."

"My point is, not being raised by a mother does not mean you are less than or are lacking. Nor does it mean you don't know how to be a woman or a mother. You are. That is enough. Reflecting on Our Mother God is sufficient. Look to Her. You do not have to embody The Mother to be yourself."

"But that is the irony!" Hmahein clapped her hands and hefted herself up. "Mothering is not a blood right, Our Creator or not."

She slapped her stomach twice. "A womb is not the embodiment of creation, Efendumo. A womb should not demand respect in any society. The Word does. Otherwise, men would wander the world without meaning – wombless – worshipping all women."

Does your life, my life, have no meaning without her in it? She had screamed the pent-up words at her father.

"A mother is a link from her own mother to her child," said Efendumo. "Without that, we do not exist. As with the history holders, the Ruevaagi, holding the past, the present and the future in our hands, and words. A mother's power is the same. Without that, we fade away."

She stood defiantly facing her mentor, feet shoulder-width apart, tight fists on her hips.

"Why be born at all? What were my parents thinking? What was she thinking? I'm not going to inflict that on a child, my child. Never. I don't begrudge anyone who wants children, but I will not play that age-old game of harm. Being able to procreate is no reason to inflict yourself on this world any further, and no reason to put your offspring in the firing line of anything that these five worlds have to offer. Is it simply wanting to feel like Our," she hesitated, "*Creator*: all powerful in seeding something?"

"Your melodrama is not philosophy," he said waving her down.

His placating her was frustrating; his patronising her, infuriating.

"This is my world, Efendumo." She strode closer to him, arms wide. "I have to make sense of it if I'm to be someone who tells others to believe in it. And from where I stand, the entire process is built on harm." She slammed her fist into her other palm with a thud. "A mother's pain during birth. The child's pain and trauma of being born. The first build-up of excrement in the bowels is pain. The need to be burped is pain. Learning to walk is pain. We learn through pain. Really? What kind of existence is that? The twelve tenets, Ra'engi Efendumo. Do you remember the fifth?" She twirled around and headed for her drink.

"Harm nothing," he said flatly and sucked his teeth.

She snapped her fingers to make her point, and poured the last of the melon water from the pitcher. Her bladder was burning but her mind was racing, her heart pounding, as she gulped down the sweet water, and finally gasped for air. Relieving herself could wait. She leaned on the low table and within seconds a cool wave washed over her. The dark skin of her hands twinkled with droplets of sweat oozing out the pores.

"As you have proven, young novice, standing where you are today, you can move past these mental and emotional hurdles and be a better person. If you have not done so already, you will elevate your family's name. You have the opportunity to ennoble the name of your ancestors. A tarnished name reborn with Ruevaagi Hmahein."

She wiped her brow, her face warming once again. "Elevating my ancestral name does nothing to mitigate the harm that will inevitably be thrust upon anyone else suffering the betrayal of a parent, parents, or anything equally socially offensive. Our ways of thinking are inert, like the sculptures of heroes past. Unchanging and immutable. Where is the enlightenment in that? Those ideas need to crumble and collapse, to rather evolve as our words and language have evolved."

"And you," she turned on him, finger pointing accusingly, "you stand here, holding my potential in your hands as though it were your saving grace, when not too long ago you were stricken, speechless, at the prospect of being ra'engi to one such as me."

"I–" he began.

"I saw your face that day, oh proud and skilled ra'engi. It was a face of humiliation. You are moderately okay with me today, but do you not remember our first meeting, Efendumo? It was on that occasion, with disdain slapped on your face like tahlata paint, that told me everything about you leading up to that moment. I sensed your anger at having been chosen to train me. You, one of the most skilled of the Order of Ruevaagi to be ra'engi to this. Pft." She aimed her hands at herself. "The back and forth you would have wished you could have with the high council. But, like a good disciple, you toed the line and did what you were told."

"Kyi á Yikho, Hmahein!"

"Do not tell me to toe the line, accept my lot, when you know what it's like to have to do something that goes against your very core beliefs. Your prejudices were clearly displayed all over you."

"There is toeing the line and there is doing what is appropriate for the whole."

An icy cool sensation stuck in her throat and she froze in place. "I never considered that she–"

"What?"

"Earlier you said, with such certainty I didn't even second guess it.

"What?" he demanded.

"That they both willingly chose to have a child."

"So?"

"You're a man." She began pacing. "And, most clearly a man of our age, based on that answer. You speak with such certainty that my parents were both in agreement about having a child." Hmahein took a moment to absorb her own disbelief. "Did she want me to begin with? Or any child?" It was her turn to wave a dismissive hand at him before he could downplay her insecurities. "Did she really change after I was born, or did she change the moment her world conspired against her, making her do something she did not want? Was his the guilt he held onto for it?"

"That is unrealistic."

She stopped in her tracks.

"Oh, for once, Efendumo, take a step back," she seethed with hands gripping the air. "If a woman cannot, or will not, conceive, to create another, they are banished. *Half-person, mothersoundless*, are the words used to mark them for the rest of their days. As if a child falling out from between your legs is anything to value anyone in a society. The degree of magic coursing through your veins, woman or man, should be the only marker of your stature. And that's pressure enough."

"Ours is a matriarchal society, or have you forgotten?"

"Words." She sighed. "You know full well women are merely token symbols rather than regarded as actual supreme creators in our societies, across the five worlds. A cousin of mine was forced into her sister's childless marriage, to be the provider of her womb. Is that where we are in our matriarchal world? Is that practice edifying our people? A premium is placed on our roles as progenitors, as women, by men. At least the non-binary respect our choices."

"Until a thousand juzu ago, only women were deemed worthy to be ruevaagi. And we continue to look to the female lineage for guidance in our society."

"Ceremony and tradition do not put us all on an equal footing. And passing on the histories requires utter conviction of those facts. Did you never question these? If not when you were young and, dare I suggest, openminded-seeking-curious, then during your training?"

"I had my moments."

"Today, you practice, perform and teach these histories, you speak with such force-certitude-confidence, as if you were there witnessing Our Creator's legs parting, birthing the World. Who is to say it was not a seed, ejected by a Man-God—"

"Our Mother God, forbid!"

"A Man-God," Hmahein continued. "Or better yet, a collision of matter exploding in the darkness of the universe. Gods be damned!"

A trembling within her took her breath away. She could feel the pangs of hunger in her stomach, but it was the gravitational pull on her psyche, her solar plexus, her every muscle, which threatened to drop her to the floor. Hmahein winced at the sting of urine wanting to gush from her. She clenched her teeth.

"Did Our Creator, in Her infinite wisdom, honestly betray all world-bound women in how we can only produce with men? If I wish to bear a child, is it to another that I must inevitably turn? Must there always be a unity of opposites? Why can it not just be me? Who was there with Our God? Where was the seed? Oh right, it was the Word that seeded her."

"You cannot utter that!" His melon-wine bag fell from his lap, causing her ra'engi momentary shock at the possibility of staining the rug, only to realise it was empty of its delicious contents.

Hmahein shook her head at him and continued. "And yet, She uttered that. She uttered the Word. It was from Her that She birthed the universe by birthing the Word. And here I stand. Myself, alone. With the Word at my tongue tip. I am ready to seed my own destiny. I am here to birth my own destiny. On my terms. Damn another. Damn the father. Damn needing another to make my life whole. I am a creator. A god, birthing my life. I do not need this uterus within me to give me meaning. I do not need to produce something from my womb to have a place in this world. Here I am, already in this world. Occupying space, a place. With my magic, my Word, I create."

"Oh, come now, Hmahein," said Efendumo brusquely. "Go clear your scattered head before you enter this space again." He snatched up his wine skin and tossed it, limp, into his chair.

"I'm hungry and I need a pee, anyway," she said and slipped into her sandals, grabbed her shawl and marched out through the curtains.

V

Hmahein's bladder was lighter; the atmosphere outside warmer than inside the tented pavilion, but refreshing, and less stifling. She adjusted her shawl around her neck and shoulders, keeping the heat of the suns at bay.

The air was filled with the hum of people, the shouts of vendors, some leading pack animals, all busying themselves with provisions for the evening's spectacle. She understood the celebrations would be a night-long, if not days-long, event, with little productivity for any of the celebrants. Taking the main street entering the village, she was weaving through the throng, following the gently sloping circular route to the left, which she assumed would eventually lead to the middle of the deep paramikule. Hewn out of the rusty bedrock itself, the road was rutted and worn in two distinct streams of people: one on the left, which Hmahein now followed downward, and one to the right, allowing those coming up the rise from below. The occasional updraft of cool air held scents of fresh water and wafts of spices and smoke on the breeze, accompanied by a low, intermittent, almost instrumental, drone.

As remote as they were from the main cities, the people were trading in an assortment of succulent-looking fruits, vegetables and other wares. Three vendors, side by side, held one of the broadest range of gourds she had ever seen. Small, ball-like orange squashes, which she knew had a delicate skin when boiled, made for the ideal dessert and infant meals; while the larger, mottled-green and white bottle-shaped kalabash of legend always drew the most attention. Her stomach lurched at what felt like a distant memory, of her peering through a gap in the work-shop door to watch her father's toughened fingers, delicately plaiting the strings of the hanging kalabash bowls.

The recognisable sweet, spicy scents of melon juice reached her on another cool, upward breeze, making her mouth water for a taste in the throbbing heat. As she came upon a beverage cart, she caught sight of a familiar figure trailing nearby. Waioke.

He pretended to be distracted by a woman yelling her offering of a basketful of long, orange, serpentine gourds. Hmahein watched quizzically, eyes narrowed against the blazing light of the suns now sinking towards the horizon.

She ignored the melon drink seller asking what she wanted, in anticipation of the inevitable change of Waioke's expression.

"Yes, boy," she said to herself. And then, echoing the words she could see formed by the gourd-seller to Waioke, *Aphrodisiac*.

His eyes widened and he bolted away, directly for Hmahein who, by now, was laughing out loud. Back to the melon drink seller, she said, "Two servings of the non-alcoholic, please."

She dropped her khau'yedi coins into the basket and took both the long-stemmed receptacles. Disposable gourd skins.

"My good man." She winked and offered an embarrassed Waioke a drink.

They had meandered off and back on to the curving main road, Hmahein investigating new and unusual wares down side alleys, while Waioke, generally reserved, would come alive when explaining the local customs or the flavours of the spicy foods on offer. One aspect of traveling as a ruevaagi, which she relished, was meeting new people.

"Zéhemgwile," Hmahein broke the silence, and finished off her drink.

Waioke nodded proudly. "Named for the tiny birds that weave their golden nests, yes."

"I listened. I watched," she continued. "You have a skill I have never seen up close. You truly have found the Word. Your words are beautiful, delicate and gentle. They make you want to pay attention to every syllable and every breath you take."

"You do not have any zéhemgwile where you are from?"

"Not in my home town. And certainly, none like you where I am doing my training. Those skills could be wielded with extreme force."

He considered her for a moment, then with a grin said, "I could conjure a billion needles and prick my enemies to death."

She looked at him. A moment passed and they both burst out laughing.

"May I ask why you left abruptly earlier?"

"For reasons we are not permitted to speak of to outsiders."

"Oh." She was stunned by the straightforward reply from her companion. She gave a wry smile. "Even a ruevaagi?"

He glanced at her sheepishly, considering her words.

"Not just any ruevaagi. Ruevaagi Hmahein," he said.

Her skin prickled at the boy's words. It was an odd sensation getting a sense of how outsiders, strangers, saw her.

"They love rules, do they not, Waioke, Grand Zéhemgwile, wielder of a billion needles, weaver of the divine thread?"

"How are you finding Paramikule Zékunekude?"

"Hot, but beautiful." She looked around. "This, how would you put it? This village, built down into the land, is like nothing I have ever seen."

"Paramikule Zékunekude is my great grandmother, Kunekude's, chieftaincy." Waioke's tone was formal, reciting information to the visitor, the outsider. He clasped his hands behind his back as they walked on.

"Wait. You're a descendent of the founding chief?"

"Well, yes. Anyone in this paramikule is, or as close to it as you can get." He gave a snort. "There are too many 'greats' to add to my calling her grandmother. So, she is my great grandmother. This is her capital for this region of the Abzizi-Lukhi district. She was paramount chief here. I did not know her, but I visit her mamenyeh." He stopped and pointed up to their right, towards three humps on the edge of the dry landscape above. "A mamenyeh is where the sacred relics are housed, the shrines to our ancestral spirits. I understand you ruevaagi bring your shrines with you. We do not. That is where they chose to reside."

Hmahein imagined the view of the entire village from that vantage point.

"Their old dwellings will eventually fall to ruin. You do not uproot a tree when you move. My mother tells me how my guardian spirit since I was born, my great grandmother, resides there."

"That's a lovely notion. I wish I had a guardian."

"I think we all do. Including ma'Kunekude. When she had only thirteen Houses within her clan, she chose to make her way out to this area of the district – chosen well by her, guided in a sense, along with her surveyors. That was almost two hundred juzu ago."

"We no longer have chiefs or the clan system where I am from."

He waved to passers-by. "That is one of my distant relatives and her husband, from the clan in Paramikule Mézilede, many leagues towards the setting suns from here. While Paramikule Lézalude is past my great grandmother's mamenyeh. They have all come to see and feel your utterances tonight."

"What did your great grandmother see that was special about this place?" She looked at the boy. "Don't get me wrong, but on the surface its rather bland and desolate as far as the eye can see."

"You would be surprised what life there is in this wilderness. Your melon juice, and the wine that your ra'engi favours?"

"Yes," she said wearily, side-stepping behind Waioke to allow a stocky man, carrying a three-person-wide harness of baskets covered with cloth. She took a deep breath of the scents of dried kalabash leaf soaked in melon oils for smoking.

"The fruit originates from this arid region."

"Really?" she said, taking longer strides to come up alongside him. A haze of woody smoke drifted up to them, along with a smell she could not quite place.

"Anyway," he continued, "they said she could hear the ground water far below this iron surface." He stomped his feet as he walked. "See how the layers change the further down we get? The yellows turning to the rich iron reds. Within a week of her settling here, her own maadiregi skills had conjured a schematic, drawn upon the magic, to harness and maximise the use of the resource beneath us. Even today, it runs as it did so long ago, cooling our homes, sustaining us. Our pipes, like the mighty ngōgda tree, furrow down to the crystal-clear waters. The maadiregi from Zezépfeni's capital, Zezélam, once came here when I was much younger, and displayed their model labyrinth of waterways to the entire Paramikule. Even they were in awe of the complexity Kunekude had discovered, and tapped into so efficiently."

The smoke was thicker now and the smells of cooking food mingled in, enough to get her stomach rumbling. Waioke rounded a wooden-slat screen, and Hmahein saw the source of the cooking. A low, wide oven, raging with logs in its recesses, was baking a row of plump gourd breads.

"Her father had taught her the maadiregi skills," the boy continued, already receiving two small loaves from the baker, and passing one to Hmahein. "That magic is infused in this design of my great grand-mother's village. The other paramikule thought she was mad, out here, building her downward spiral – a layoshwelo." He mumbled his words between chews.

The bread was warm and sweet, the seeds adding bursts of flavour as she relished the freshness of the simple meal.

"They had always only dug three houses down. This layoshwelo of hers is more than ten houses deep. Safe. Maybe tonight you will hear the song of Kunekude's paramikule as the cool winds, rising from inside the earth, push out against the warm air entering the village from the direction of the setting sun."

Hamhein tore at a strip of crisp crust with her teeth. "I thought I could hear something earlier."

"Yes. It speaks during the day, but our bodies, the busy bodies of this settlement, block it. Everyone will be at the Kndliluni tonight. The streets will be clear and your performance will rush through the layosh-welo, building in volume, bursting out across the sands." He looked up at the sky. "Even the stars will hear you, Ruevaagi Hmahein."

"The Kndliluni?"

"All the way down there." Waioke gestured with his mangled bread to the final point of convergence of the village and the spiral. "The central court. A focal point of everything in our world here."

"Wow," whispered Hmahein.

"It is an honour for us to have the Ruevaagi attend our auspicious ceremony."

"I am honoured to be here, though I'm not especially knowledgeable about the event. Maybe you can tell me more?"

"How does it work for your order to be here?"

She noted another deft, though obvious, shift in the conversation by the boy.

"The Ruevaagi only accept food and melon juice, or wine," she added, "in exchange for our performances. No currency, no khau'yedi, is ever exchanged. No wealth is accumulated. I can say from first-hand experience, the responses from a crowd, the lively sharing of their joy and energy, are thrilling enough as any payment goes. We do tend to accept a single farewell gift from elders, or clan leaders."

"Are you permitted to tell me what it is you will be performing this evening? Only if you are willing to share with me, Ruevaagi Hmahein. Will it be the full *Song of Our Mother's Children*?"

"I will certainly be performing the Rakwa wa-Ya'yn. But there are other ruevaagi performances, so it will be the shorter version." She grinned at him. "If all goes well, and if my ra'engi is not completely humiliated by his initiate tonight, I hope I will be invited back to perform it in its entirety in the future. It would be an honour to conduct the week-long recital for the people of your paramikule. It does require a day's rest in between each performance."

She wiped her mouth and dusted the smattering of crumbs from the front of her tunic.

"Is it true about ruevaagi receiving healing and longer lives than most? I've heard your performances protect you against disease and death."

"I wish. Or maybe not, considering I feel like I've aged a decade since beginning my formal training. Ask me in another decade. It certainly feels that way when you are up there, tapped into the magic of story, and the audience building upon that in their own way."

She looked around, tiptoeing and looking over the heads of the other pedestrians.

"What is the matter?" asked Waioke.

"Is there another bread seller nearby?"

VI

No longer the reserved boy she met earlier, the inquisitive Waioke peppered Hmahein with pointed questions, as they wound their way further down the spiral village streets. She could see he was awed by life outside his isolated village. And yet, he would always find his way back to her skills and her order's craft and methods.

"What is the most challenging performance?" He asked.

"*The song of the twins*," Hmahein said without hesitation. "Zuúv'ah and Juah-āju."

"I have never experienced a performance of that. Why is it the hardest?"

"It is the most demanding and it is the most–" she couldn't find her words. "Dwa'ndenki!" she cursed.

"What is it?"

"Finding the words, in between the emotions, is–"

"The feelings are part of it, though, aren't they?"

"Not when they place hurdles in the way." She took a deep breath. "If you'd have harnessed time travel as those of Mahwé attempted and told a younger me I would become a ruevaagi, let alone preparing for a performance in an auspicious location such as this, I would never have believed you. When I was younger, I would say the world was *dange and strangerous*. I mixed the words. My mind and my tongue fought one another like serpents in a writhing battle. I'm still unsure of who won. And, I'm not sure I will ever reach the skill required for the song of the twins. It is the most demanding and yet the most glorious-splendid-phantasmagoric experience you will ever participate in. You will witness pure magic. You participate because it requires two ruevaagi, of the utmost skill. In the moment, one must be fully aware of what it is you are doing, your part; as well as keeping pace with your partner, as you both perform simultaneously."

"Surely a duet performance is not that difficult."

"Not a duet. Polytextuality. Each ruevaagi utters different parts of the story, the different points-of-view of either Zuúv'ah or Juah-āju, simultaneously, over one another, leaving it up to the audience to focus where they wish. And so, each performance is a new and unique experience for the audience, every time."

The boy pointed to the entrance of an alley just before he turned into it with her following behind him. The sounds of the bustle of the main street became muffled in the narrower space, shopfronts and dwellings intermingled, and domestic life came alive to her. Two girls darted passed them, one running her hand through Hmahein's garment and squealing with delight. Hmahein moved next to Waioke to continue their conversation.

"I have learned so much. If another ruevaagi performs, usually something an initiate has not learned yet, we listen to every utterance. When the performance ends, we rush back to our rakwayn and begin reciting everything we heard. Word for word. We go through the night, until dawn." The alley snaked along, each curve left or right dulling the background sounds the further away from the market bustle they walked. Waioke waved to a man leaning in a doorway, Hmahein following suite with a smile. "As the twin suns rise, we perform a remembering rite, alone. We thank Zuúv'ah and Juah-āju for giving us the knowledge, and ask that they bestow on us the right memory of the words, in their order, with their inflection, and for the magic to flow from it when the time comes. Part of this is enacted symbolically in the mixing of our tahlata paint; the ashes as memories infused with the sweet melon oil to bind, spread and nourish. We learn by listening. Watching. Feeling. Over and over again. Yet, as Ra'engi Efendumo will happily point out, I have much to work through. The theory, the practice, but also my own head getting in the way. And then," she said and sighed, "my visions confusing everything I'm being taught."

"I heard you mention them. What are they?"

"Shapes, figures," she said, "uttering things I do not understand. The five worlds have the mantra, *Find the Word. Find the voice.* In my visions, like the chant of a billion voices, I hear: *'Find your word. Find your voice.'*"

She shrugged. "And random flashes, terrifying scenes and sounds of galactic explosions and shapeshifting worlds forming over eons, forming our system but not Zezépfeni first, rather Wiimb-ó. Some days I wonder what the use of it all is to me, or anyone, other than to say the Zezépfenians are not being truthful. And other days, like today, I want to scream it to the five worlds."

"But, to be chosen at all?" Waioke said with awe.

"Being chosen is no honour, dear boy." She slowed her pace, then said softly, "You are named, along with many others who are worthy. From those initially chosen, only a few will feel the honour. It is a bitter melon juice in your mouth that day. I was chosen over two others. I had the honour, if that is what that day was supposed to represent. But they were shamed for my accomplishment. I had succeeded. They had failed. That is how their families chose to view it. I carry their shame."

Coming upon what looked to be the end of the alley, a low doorway the only access beyond, Waioke tilted his head for Hmahein to follow him.

She ducked and stepped into a dimly lit room, her eyes adjusting to the light of a single oil-lamp. The space consisted of two adjoining rooms with an array of small tables, shelves and cabinets displaying various odd shaped objects. A few paces from her and Waioke stood a woman she assumed was the storeowner, eyeing them suspiciously from behind a countertop and having swiftly draped a delicate cloth over a dozen or more small objects in front of her. Hmahein gave a curt nod and tried to make out the strange wares the woman was dealing in.

Unassuming rocks and stones, and some delicate crystals, nothing remarkable or dazzling, were what Hmahein could identify.

Waioke said something to the storeowner, leaning in closer to her and added the word *ruevaagi*.

The storeowner came alive. "Please, ruevaagi." She gestured for Hmahein to come over to her, paused for a moment and then proudly lifted the cloth off the objects beneath, giving a quick flick for flair.

At first Hmahein was bemused at the neatly arranged display of innocuous stones. She felt like she was expected to be astounded by this amazing spread. Then she noticed something odd about the shadows, flickering in the lamplight. She bent down further, for a lower angle, to confirm her suspicion. The stones, a rusty-red, almost black, were imperceptibly levitating at least a fingernail's width off the table's surface.

She was speechless. She looked up at the beaming faces of both Waioke and the woman. The boy simply raised his eyebrows.

Drawn to one small rectangular stone, edges rounded and smoothed off, she leaned in for a closer inspection. The familiar lines of the Zezépfeni calendar were etched into the surface.

"How–" she began.

"Please," the woman said and picked up the stone, offering Hmahein to take it.

Waioke nodded to her. "They are magnetic."

The woman frowned at the boy before dropping the stone into Hmahein's open hand.

The cool touch of the iron rock was momentary as it bobbed off her palm like it was floating in water. She steadied her hand, in awe of the small object suspended above her palm.

"It would be an honour for me to purchase this for you, Ruevaagi Hmahein," said Waioke passing some khau'yedi coins to the woman, and thanking her as he led Hmahein out the store.

They stepped out into the light and Waioke took her hand in his, closing her fingers over the stone. "Keep it safe."

"Thank you, Waioke," she said and placed it gently into one of her hidden pockets.

"Come," he said and headed back towards the hum of the main street. "We must hurry now. I still have to complete your vestments and seamlessly fit your breastplate coat."

Hmahein was enjoying the calm of the alley, reluctant to rejoin the busy market and the throng of people, and slowed her pace. A man unhooking a delicate wooden mobile from the eaves of his small store caught her eye. Two similar contraptions remained hanging and she moved closer to look at the artistry. Dozens of tiny birds, the size of large bees, carved out of a yellow wood, dangled delicately from almost invisible threads. Forming a neat oval shape, she gave them a gentle blow.

"That is enhwaunu thread. Beautiful and strong. It will last longer than the wooden zéhemgwile birds."

"Lovely," she said, more to the man patiently waiting for her to finish her viewing than to Waioke.

"You were hypnotised by my breastplate earlier," she said.

"Was it that obvious?"

"It is not something that can be overlooked. It pulls you towards it. It demands that you reach out and touch that shimmering surface to acknowledge it exists in the five worlds." She could almost feel the weight of her garment on her now, as she put her hand to her chest.

"I have never been to the ocean. That was the first time I was able to see a fuúzimwazii breastplate up close."

"I love those creatures. Part of our initiation was venturing out over the calm ocean to find a massive pod of them. That was when I retrieved my fuúzimwazii carapace for my ceremonial breastplate."

"You don't hunt them for it?"

"Never." She shook her head and stopped him with a hand on his shoulder. "Mine was gifted to me by an old soul. They said she was five hundred juzu when she passed through to Eh'wauizo a week before we arrived there. The entire pod took her down into the deep emerald waters, and performed their rites. Barely a person remained on our boats because we all took that opportunity to get in the water and listen."

Hmahein paused and took in a deep breath. "Magnificent. On the surface was lapping water, murmured chatter among our group, and the occasional squawk of the birds hanging about. The moment I submerged my head in that salty water, it was like another world. It is as if you enter another plane. An extrasensory experience, if you know what to listen for and feel. I've lived by the ocean my whole life, but it was one of the gifts my ra'engi gave me in preparing my rediscovery of that world–" she stopped herself and chuckled. "Please do not tell him this."

"My lips are sewn shut with an unyielding golden thread spun by the Twin Suns themselves."

"The sounds the fuúzimwazii were making vibrated through every cell of my body. I was under for a short time before I had to come up."

"The Mother did not make us for under water life, Hmahein," Waioke said with a smirk.

"Nor are we built for crying and sobbing under water, boy. Because that's what happened. A wave of emotion hit me – every one of us there that day – with the haunting sounds of the fuúzimwazii, so deep we could not see them."

They continued on through the alley, the sounds building in the near distance.

"Like our Twin Suns setting now, Zuúv'ah had already moved below the horizon, with Juah-āju close to submerging into the ocean itself, when the carapace broke the surface, buoyant from its resonant hollows. Moments later, the pod resurfaced and presented her empty shell to our flotilla of small craft."

"I have never seen the ocean. Or fuúzimwazii."

"I want to be like them. Not to live for hundreds of juzu." She chuckled. "But where they use the salty sea to extend their range, I want to send my voice out over the surface, wrapping Wiimb-ó in magic and sound."

Waioke grinned. "I think you will, one day."

Hmahein stumbled forward but caught herself in time to not hit the ground. The sensation in her body had landed like a crashing wave. She tingled all over and sweat beaded out of her pores. She was grateful the frantic bustle of the main market street had seemed to be abating when they had emerged from the quieter alley earlier.

Without a word, the boy was at her side making sure she was okay and no one was going to run into her. He waited.

"Waioke," she said between deep breaths, "another unfortunate credit to my mentor is how he has helped hone my ability to refine my words, and in turn, notice the words wielded by others."

The boy remained silent.

"Whenever I have been dwelling on this sensation," she said and waved her hand up and down her torso, "forget the layoshwelo of your ancestor's paramikule, the spiral and its own out-breathing sounds – you have reacted, acted strange or you've excused yourself. What is it?"

They loped slowly upward, the left side of the street easing with the number of bodies and paraphernalia in Hmahein's path, as she gathered herself and regained her balance at her own pace.

"In your rakwayn," he said, "you mentioned feeling like you were being pulled in three directions."

"Something massive pulling at me, yes," she replied.

"*Three directions* is very specific, Hmahein."

She shrugged. "It's what I've been told. Shown."

"It must be divinely sanctioned," Waioke whispered to himself.

"Pardon?"

"Everyone knows of Javuiili, Wiimb-ó's moon," he began. "But it would seem you are unlike many. You see, or rather sense, Vuiili-ki and Vuiili-ku. You have a heightened awareness of them."

"Who?"

"Our spirit moons."

"I've heard of the spirit moons, yes. They are spoken of in our myths, but are they real?"

Waioke nodded. "How long have you felt this sensation?"

Hmahein thought for a moment. "Up until yesterday I thought it was just before we ventured here. Now, I can't be certain."

"What is it that you have been seeing, the knowledge you say you have been accessing?"

A warmth flooded over Hmahein.

Without waiting for her to answer, Waioke continued, "We have numerous celestial events on this planet of ours. Wiimb-ó gives us daily wonders to appreciate, if you know or are tuned into its subtleties. My people have long-held knowledge that is sacred."

As they ambled along, the summit of the village's street leveling off ahead, the boy explained the range of spiritual occurrences on the planet, along with Wiimb-ó's ethereal lunar bodies, leading to heightened spiritual manifestations.

"For hundreds of juzu, Kunekude's people have tapped into these occurrences. We are taught the ways from when we emerge from our mothers' wombs. But there are those we believe they are chosen, from here are far as the continent of Surali, who have the innate ability to reach through the veil, into Eh'wauizo."

To Hmahein, it was like she was hearing this all again, like an echo in her head, reverberating what every muscle in her body already knew.

"We call it the undulation. They are regular, monthly cycles, as our calendar stones attest. Outsiders are welcome, as you are here tonight. But, the rare, full alignment events are—"

He stopped himself.

She looked at him, waiting for him to speak when he was ready.

"Earlier, at the stone seller," he said and pointed to the side of her light tunic, "I lied to you."

Automatically, Hmahein put her palm over the small mass of the stone in her hidden pocket.

"It's not magnetic. Not in that sense. The stones are our lunar timekeepers. It is the force of Vuiili-ki and Vuiili-ku, pulling on the planet, that cause those iron-rich stones to levitate. During a lunar event such as tonight, that is what you see. The stones are like looking to the winds to understand the weather to come. They begin to levitate three days before the climax, like tonight."

Hmahein took a moment to process everything he had been willing to reveal to her.

"You have granted me this knowledge, Zéhemgwile Waioke," she said softly, "and gifted me something truly special. I will cherish this always, and am honoured to be included tonight."

"Ruevaagi Hamhein," said Waioke with a sly look, "would you like to see something?"

"Sure."

"Can you hear, or at least feel, the wind building from below?"

She stood still and listened. "I can. Barely."

"When I drop my hand, we shout *ruevaagi* in that direction," he said pointing up the street, "out of the layoshwelo."

She held her breath, waiting. The air was moving, faster. Their eyes were fixed on one another; Waioke's wide like the bright Twin Suns.

His hand snapped down and they both shouted: *Ruevaagi!*

Stunned, Hamhein thought she could visibly see the sound, as pulsing gaseous waves blasting through the main curving street. Their voices amplified, and instead of dissipating the further it travelled from them, the louder it became.

"Hide!" he shouted, grabbing her wrist and dragging her behind a stack of old barrels.

After the dust had settled, the two young initiates emerged, the picture of innocence, and made their way towards the peaking tip of the tented pavilion of the Ruevaagi.

"I too will one day form my own village. My family. How about you, Hmahein?" asked Waioke.

"I love community. But I do not need them to be from my own flesh and blood to do so." She put her arm around the boy, feeling like she had known him for *juzu* already. "Like our planet and its moon – *moons* – I want to attract those who wish to be with me. That is my kinship."

"Will you not settle somewhere more hospitable?" she asked him. "You do know there are oceans and rivers and mountains where I come from?"

They finally emerged onto level ground. For a moment Hmahein could feel the drop in temperature as what would qualify as an evening chill in the region filled the air.

She looked to the dusky sky and said, "We've harnessed the sounds of our Twin Suns. But not our own place in these worlds." She bent down and grabbed a handful of fine yellow sand, watching the powdery dust catch on the breeze like smoke.

"*We turn our bodies, daily, to the twins rising in the sky,*" Waioke said, facing the opposite dark horizon. A handful of stars were emerging in the blue-black haze. Hmahein did the same, taking his hand in hers as he continued the sacred mantra, "*We are where we need to be. Though we may be pulled to the sides,*" he said looking right and then left, with Hmahein doing the same, "*and even at the back,*" they looked over their shoulders to the setting suns, and back ahead, "*we will resolutely face the dawn, our guides.*"

They both took a deep breath and turned around.

"Our Mother, Creator," whispered Hmahein. For a moment her entire body tingled and warmed from the inside as the last glint of light disappeared over the horizon.

VII

Hmahein ascended the low spiralling ramp of the kndliluni, past the handful of musicians, nodding their acknowledgement to her, handing over from their resounding performance still reverberating through her body. The delicate, alabaster bell in her right hand gave a gentle, rhythmic *ding* with each step.

As she curved her way to the centre of the dais, she felt the thrill of stepping up to the true centre of Waioke's paramikule accompanied by welcoming applause. She paused and stabbed the sharpened heel of her ceremonial spear firmly into the sand-filled kalabash stand to her left. The applause turned to a hush.

From where she stood, the shape of the subterranean village was even more profound than she would have imagined, rising up all around them. The light from the rising moon, not yet visible from deep below, was creeping down the village rooftops to her left.

She avoided Ra'engi Efendumo seated in the front, and locked on the beaming face of the boy, three rows back. Though she was no longer conscious of the sensation of the decorative tahlata face paint, she knew the broad strokes and carefully placed dots of the grey-white ash, imbued with the yellow sand from the village and melon oil, presented a striking visage to the audience.

She gave a quick flick of her wrist, and the bell rang out into the night, followed by the *boom* of a single accompanying drumbeat. Utter stillness washed over the audience.

On cue, the hissing rustle from the brisk gyration of the six djazi-séshwe dancers was enough to catch Hmahein's breath. Evenly positioned on either side of the audience, two at the front, middle and rear, they resumed their rhythmic swaying in readiness for what was to come. Kalabash vines, braided and weaved around the nimble people hidden beneath, scratched and swished with any sudden movement. Together with the small rattles the dancers held, they added an eerie effect to any performance.

Hmahein's body tingled. She closed her eyes, and began the initiating phrase.

"Khwa'ra." The amplified sound took her by surprise but she quickly breathed in, "Ya'yn." The low hum washed over the audience. "Ra'kwa." The tips of her fingers tingled, her open palms warmed, as she blew the air out of her chest.

Emboldened, she was ready.

Hmahein took a deep breath, sensing the anticipation from her audience. Her hands were in position, and she closed her eyes, easing into the Creation Myth. The familiar vibration surged through her.

Our Mother. Our Mother was all. Our Mother was all there was.

Something was different. The words were coming easily, the story unfolding for her and her audience. The accompanying musicians joined in, their sonorous instruments ringing out on cue at key moments, intensifying the force of her words. The djazi-séshwe dancers stamped and twirled in place. Something was welling up inside her.

A pang of fear ran through her as the sounds echoed out in visible pulses of subtle light. Her hesitation, indiscernible to the people transfixed by the display, caught in her throat for a moment before she pushed on.

Her words took over, without her. The volcanic sensation multiplied. She tried to hold it down. Rather than feeling torn in two, her fire and rage, the scared and scarred child, something coalesced deep within her.

She felt the weight of the rectangular stone, given to her by Waioke pressed against her chest where she had kept it for good luck. It seemed to strain against her garments, rubbing against her skin.

She tried once more, feeling the familiar choking, blocking sensation in her throat, but rather than uttering it now, forcing it through as she would normally do, she took in a breath. The obstruction grew thick, warming her throat and into the back of her mouth. Her face tingled and her tongue vibrated.

She uttered the words, she detached herself from their meaning to herself, and for the first time in an eternity, their universal meaning thrummed through her. The words, the complete histories, which had been learned by rote, now arose without her thinking about them, not from memory, but from within her body. They were *the* words, not her words, not words that held meaning for her. As if she were hearing them uttered for the first time, like a baby swaddled in a safe embrace, mesmerised by the consoling murmurs, of love, by a parent. She lacked any concept of their meaning, but it came all at once.

She envisaged a pent-up force, a single sound, reduplicated, compounded and multiplied, building from deep within Wiimb-ó's core, expanding upward. But rather than bursting from a mountain cavity, it was forced to bottleneck into Hmahein. Her feet were squarely placed on the solid rock dais, not moving elegantly in unison with the beat of the accompanying musicians, as her world tilted.

Suddenly, her garments were suffocating her, restricting her. She clutched at her collar, gripping the top of the breastplate, and ripped downward. She heard the dull crackle of threads, intricately sewn by the nimble hands of Waioke. But it was the force of the words and the emotions, rising up in waves, which she could not subdue.

More words inundated her mind, but not the words of the *Rakwa wa-Ya'yn* she had been taught. Words she had heard as mere whispers in the recesses as she would slip off to sleep came now with that volcanic force, erupting outward, lifting Hmahein off the ground for a split second, and thundering into and through the crowd, who, by then, were fear-stricken by the spectacle they were witnessing. A burst of sensations hit her. At first, they were pinpricks of light dancing in her field of vision, then there were auditory pulses.

Hmahein felt weightless.

Your Word.

Find your Word.

It had never been clearer. It was a command like she had never heard before. Not even Ra'engi Efendumo could utter something as compelling, brutal, or potent. It was as if her entire body listened.

The shimmering light was constant, the sounds immersive in a surging discord. Some of the audience remained seated, others were standing, while the djazi-séshwe moved about like ghosts. Hmahein could not fix on any one person, as if her vision was blurred, tears obscuring her eyes. But she could pick out Ra'engi Efendumo, seething and sweating, dishevelled with blood from his nose smeared across his cheek and Waioke, his face streaked with dust and tears.

She could already imagine what her mentor would say, his fear of what the rising wrath of the Zezépfenians for the words spilling out of her, but she didn't care. Her body trembled.

The dancers appeared to multiply, swirling, snaking and shimmying in the space between.

Chaos erupted.

Muscles went rigid and her fingers and hands contorted as her body arched backward. The natural instinct to control was suppressed by a more overwhelming craving for surrender. Sound ran through her in waves of light, her body relaxed and her vision warped.

Hmahein was losing herself in it, losing control.

Yes.

The low rumbling sensation, the undulation, pulsed beneath her, and through her. The emanation from the land below was ceaseless, no longer building and dissipating back into the recesses.

And then, it let go.

She opened her eyes and shouted through clenched teeth to the scattering crowd, "What is my word?"

Mother.

"Mother," she repeated now back in control of her senses.

She saw a sliver of smoke drift above her, wavering in the dim space. She took in a long breath, and let it out slowly with a hum. Hmahein could smell no scent of incense in the air as the vapour grew more distinct. Against her chest, the iron stone Waioke had given her pushed and pulled toward the smoke. The crowd had faded away, the performance was forgotten, overtaken by this experience, this revelation.

She narrowed her eyes, and focused on the smoke. Transparent, like the sheer curtains back in her room, it rippled and shifted.

Within it, seemingly far off in the distance, beyond the pierce of tripled moonlight, forms and shapes moved about. Figures. Some seemed closer than others.

At that moment of recognition, a silhouette, an arms-length above her, slowly emerged, as if being lowered onto the dais.

The shape of a woman, her features becoming more distinct and familiar to Hmahein, but older.

Mother?

"At last," the woman uttered, in a soothing voice that prickled Hmahein's skin, "The truth is no longer a whisper in your ear."

*I*n many real-world African cultures, belief in the spirits of the dead is
common and widespread. In many of these worldviews, from the Ban-
yarwanda to the Akan, Yoruba to Zulu, Luo to Mende, reality is often
presented as having has two aspects – the material and the immaterial
world. And these worlds are layered on top of each other, influencing each
other. In many cases the dead constitute a binding, powerful link to the
creator(s) through the material plane. They can guide, advise, intercede
and in some cases haunt those who have committed crimes against the
community. Thus there often rites and ceremonies connected with death,
burials, and veneration of those who have passed on.

   This is why in the Sauútiverse we introduced the concept of Eh'wauizo,
the spirit realm, where ancestors ascend to when they die in the material
world, and linked it tangibly to physical phenomena. The physical and
spiritual are always connected in the Sauútiverse. You have already encountered Eh'wauizo in previous stories, seen the connections and overlap,
encountered examples of the rites and ceremonies associated with death,
spirits, ancestors.

   So what happens when there is an abomination, something that is so
horrible that it disrupts the ability of the spirit (or in the Sauútiverse, the
fragment of Mothersound) to ascend to the spirit plane? To reunite with
the creator? What happens when time itself is so scrambled, that even
spirits are lost? What happens when restless spirits call out from across
time itself?

   We return now to Mahwé, the ruined world, in 150 juzu A1B, for this
story of spirits, stories, survival and generational curses, by contributor
T.L. Huchu. A haunting tale of strangers from different planets drawn
to what is left of Mahwé by their dreams, and unknown powers. With
help from a mysterious patron and a unique new technology, they attempt
to visit the planet where time itself is broken. On this mission, they expect

to encounter difficulty, they expect to find strange and dangerous relics from the past. They are prepared for all that. What they find instead is something much, much worse.

The Hollowed People

T.L. HUCHU

The strangemare was etched in the pulsating soundcode of djumba drums, whole notes punctuated by foreboding silence, echoing in Ruu'vim's mind. But the sound of it grew ever more scrambled whenever they tried deciphering the traces of the shadow song leached into the disturbing chrono-dismorphation megascape of dead Mahwè, the corpse world.

There were those of the forbidden faith, a small but significant cult, who claimed that on Mahwè the steady beat of the Mothersound, the fundamental essence of existence itself, had been mangled and deformed until it was unrecognisable even to the inhabitants of Pinaa, the nearby moon, who'd long since turned their backs on the magical heartbeat that thrummed through the depths of space. Despite their sophisticated scientific instrumentation and sound theorisations, they saw nothing there. They were blinded by their equations and formulae and soundcodes from the ultimate truth: that something beyond their rigid logic was taking place in the broken world next door.

Below Ruu'vim was the shredded body of the warrior Ngano, deep cuts and grooves in his fading body as if a thousand spears had flown into him. His short but broad musculature was now reduced to ribbons of flesh and a stream of blood seeping into the bare brown dirt.

Eyes wide open, Ruu'vim stared into the blindness of temporospatial oblivion, an event horizon hiding the wretchedness of Mahwè. This was why all good scientists, maadiregi, and thinkers had avoided probing too deeply into the mysteries of the planet. Dead things deserved to be buried, hidden from view, but Mahwè refused. Instead it acted for some, as a beacon. Even seeping into the dreamworld of cybernetic beings as readily as fleshlings, corrupting data until Ruu'vim had been forced to go there, against safety protocols, algorithmic advice, dictates and even the remnants of their non-existent gut. Base instincts remained encoded even within a grade-three, extensively modified being like them.

Ruu'vim hadn't expected the sickness, but now they were here, they realised the aagoo suits barely kept the dismorphation under control. Sickness was something fleshlings experienced, despite millennia of medical advancement. A cybernetic being like them should have been upgraded beyond such base evolutionary concerns, and this had been true before they had landed on Mahwè.

Regret.

Fear.

Despair.

This is something new. Raw feeling instead of data inputs. They couldn't trust anything about their judgement anymore. Multiple streams of thought collapsed into a single coherent, overriding imperative: **SURVIVAL**.

<<Reboot initiated>>

No, not yet, please, Ruu'vim bargained with gods and ancestors of the dead world that had summoned them. Their limbs, made of organo-metallic composites, glistened copper and ebony as they quivered. They were glitching. Near the horizon, a dust storm was rolling towards them. A great mass of brown dust towering higher than any constructions on Pinaa, moving with incredible speed, was the last thing logged into Ruu'vim's memory banks before the abominable cycle began anew. . .

'The answers we all seek, the cure for our intolerable suffering, is down there on that planet,' Ngano said, pointing out the faux window of the unregistered station Feja orbiting in Mahwè's shadow. The craft was a non-reflective sphere, darker than the blackest shadow, hidden among the masses of space junk, military-grade stealth technology masking its energy signal, so that even the vigilant authorities on Pinaa were unaware of its existence.

'We don't even know whose vessel this is,' Xuda replied anxiously. She was ashen, red-eyed and weary, a far cry from her usual elegant demeanour. 'I don't know how you do things in the depths of Ekwukwe, but Zezépfeni has knowledge of things that would make you void your bowels despite you being the warrior you claim to be.'

'Of course, because you Sangenis believe you're the descendants of the original people, and so you should lord it over the "cave crawlers" of my home world. Let's see how well you do that with my shoe deep inside your rectum,' Ngano replied, looking to the lovers Baba Do and Adelolade for support. The two were from Órino-Rin and Wiimb-ó, which orbited different stars and so they might have been more receptive to his indignation at Zezépfenian arrogance which only the less emotive people of Pinaa seemed immune to.

Xuda scowled, but before she could make a response a holoprojection began aggregating in blue and green light, interrupting her riposte. The time it took to compose itself was an indicator it was being transmitted from a ship at some distance, too far to be Pinaa, but too close to be from the next planet in the system. But Xuda's wary words had been flagged as a potential problem with Ruu'vim, who, drawing on their downloaded files on ship construction and maintenance had noted that the parts used in the design of the Feja Station seemed to be cannibalised from the best tech from the five planets in their binary system. Great resource had obviously been expended in its construction, but who would have the connections to access classified tech from each of the authorities system wide? Though the planets cooperated, centuries old rivalries meant it was impossible for any legitimate actor to coordinate something on this scale.

'Nge, you all gin know one em all, nice-well,' the hologram said when it had settled.

'No amount of pay would have had me here if I'd known these Zezépfeni scum were also invited. What do you want in return?' Ngano asked, brusque as was the warrior's way.

'Petty plus haste is gon crush me and you, fight brother. This mission be special for vex dreams drag all sides cross space an' tribe.' The hologram had no discernible features apart from being a humanoid analogue, carefully proportioned not to give away its identity, but its accent was distinctly a Drifter one.

The Drifters, sometimes called the untethered, were clans that traversed the vastness of the binary system in their assorted spacecraft, trading, and occasionally raiding. They had their own codes, and while they were frowned upon by authorities on all five worlds who had their own fleets, their facilitation of commerce and travel made them indispensable assets. As such, the savviest of them accumulated obscene quantities of wealth.

'This no me reality voice. Sound power me no surrender to none,' the hologram said and chuckled, turning its eyeless gaze to Ruu'vim.

Ruu'vim, chastened, shrunk back and disconnected themself from the system. They had been trying cross referencing the oral signature through the station's database to identify the speaker. This discovery forced them to run a purge programme in case their duo-thought system, which integrated organic brain to synthetic intelligence, had been compromised.

'I don't care about any of this Dwa'ndenki shit, people,' Adelolade said, throwing off her lover's arm, which caused them to disentangle in zero g. 'I can't live like this. I'll do anything to make these terrible dreams go away. Please.'

'Corrective no easy with no sacrificial, me tell,' the hologram replied.

'But you promised us a cure!' Baba Do said. His wide nostrils flared, and then he calmed, reaching his hand across to reconnect with his partner.

'The great Obanje Kami, may him soul sing forever, preach-say, "Promise be like the oba-worm fruit; beauty outer skin, rot discovered in the bite." Me no charlatan, ngi. Fair chance is all me offer plus good reward for go carry out.'

'We can do whatever it is you need to make these strangemares end, we can do so we can wake whole again. My song voice is hoarse and magic refuses to answer me,' Xuda said.

Ruu'vim shuddered but kept to themself, folding their composite material arms to stop glitching - this started when the dreams seeped into their artificial bio-architecture, corrupting the sophisticated programming that was melded into them, and formed their unified consciousness. They were already an outcast on their home moon; a scientist who dabbled in the esoteric would never find a foothold in that society. But now they were moved from abstract studies and thrown in a room with these traditionalists. It used to be much simpler. Their vocation had been the study of chronospherics, the temporal, ever shifting shroud of Mahwè's remnant atmosphere and surface, which defied theorisation and any attempt at explanation or categorisation. There was a running joke that there were more ways to describe what Mahwè was not, compared to methods of describing what it was.

'I no force nobody. Choose free, quick, quick,' the hologram said.

'Even relic raiders fear Mahwè,' Xuda said, reorienting herself into a cross legged sitting position as she floated in the room, her garments flowing and rippling. 'No one who's ever attempted landing there comes back.'

'Coward,' Ngano replied with a snort.

'Luck for you and every, Ruu'vim's research offer perfect solution built into this craft plus five aagoo suits expensive made.'

The screen on the wall lit up with a red display of three powerful M2D class patrol vessels from Pinaa, with a calculated trajectory towards the Feja Station. That meant they had been detected. The moon's authority forbade unauthorised vessels to approach Mahwè. A metallic sound of disentangling grapplers from their hull shocked them as it travelled the length of the hull.

'Dwa'ndenki sisterfucker! The shuttle is taking off without us. I knew I shouldn't have trusted these Drifter scum,' Ngano said, kicking the wall to launch himself out of the room but the door slid shut, sealing perfectly flush as though the entrance had never been there in the first place. All that remained were the smooth silver walls and the screens which still flashed images of the approaching vessels.

'Patience. Patrol detect your transport here. I gon draw 'em away from you.'

The screen showed the shuttle which had brought them here was accelerating away. But only one of the M2D vessels peeled away in pursuit, the other two remained on course for Feja Station.

'Is it true you have no jails on Pinna?' Baba Do asked Ruu'vim.

'We heard you lobotomise your criminals and give their bodies as hosts for your AI. That's why there are no pure organics left on your world. Is that what they're going to do to us if they catch us here?' Adelolade added, raising a single eyebrow.

Ruu'vim did not reply because the premise was manifestly absurd, and they consumed vast quantities of processing power simulating alternative scenarios, none yielding a desirable outcome. But a subroutine detected a line the hologram had said about them offering a solution, and this was associated into to their visual data on the makeup of Feja Station, until it dawned on them that their classified scientific recorded oration on aagoometic materials must have been hacked, and the results used to construct this spherical vessel. Ruu'vim's great insight, in a world where sound was central to science and magic, was to theorise that time (aagoo) could be described as the frequency of longitudinal energy waves. Therefore, they had postulated in their oration of an exotic material arranged in a similar manner to the convoluted acoustic foam used for physical soundproofing as a way of dampening chrono-dysmorphatic effects. They knew the material structure would have to be uneven, perhaps in the pattern of an egg box at the microscopic scale, but they couldn't find a suitable candidate from the resources available to them at the time. It seemed someone else had cracked the practical solution to this problem. Ruu'vim was flattered that their work had been taken forward, though somewhat disappointed they'd not been the one to do it themselves.

The thought came too late and they gasped - an anomaly. Sound expelled involuntarily was an indignity only organic children should do, not a grade-three like Ruu'vim.

'The Mother has decided for you,' the hologram said.

'Kyi á yikho' Xuda cursed. *Damn it*. But it was too late.

They all felt the acceleration of their craft as it threw them against the wall, holding them fast as the screen showed it was headed towards the dreaded Mahwè. The vessel was out of their control. Ruu'vim tried to connect to Feja Station's AI but found themself locked out. They couldn't stop it from plunging into the atmosphere, just as they couldn't shut out the cacophony of panicked voices shouting at the now vanished hologram.

Xuda's mother, Afeni, had been a maadiregi who was also an instructor of the high language on Zezépfeni. The language created resonances in the atmosphere which could be harnessed for powerful magic. Afeni was often away on pilgrimages to Órino-Rin where she used this knowledge to secretly craft and weave spells for the ruling elites in three of the five worlds. Órino-Rin's resonant and variable atmosphere could be harnessed to create the most devastating sonics. Though she was a busy woman with little affection for her spawn, Afeni still found snatches of time, over many juzu to orally instruct Xuda in the rudiments of the high language. By the time Afeni ascended to join the ancestors in Eh'wauizo, the spirit realm, she had bequeathed her daughter the memorised dictionary and grammar of high language which was their most precious heritage.

A younger Xuda had rebelled and rejected the worship of the womb of the Mother Goddess.

She'd been tempted by those who believed that existence spoke itself into being, nothing becoming something out of nothing. It was good for the young to rebel, for only in the act of rejecting tradition could they come to see the value of the very customs they had cast aside. Through this way, in the practical accumulation of many juzu, the straitjacket they sought to rid themselves of would, with wisdom, transmute into the custom-made warm winter coat.

Xuda could have become a maadiregi specialising in using the high language to mix magic and tech for pay, but instead she got lost within the language itself. There was something devastatingly beautiful in the syntax and flow of high language that she would spend hours spinning verse and formulations inside of her head, abstract notations which were stunning creations in and of themselves, but lacked any real, practical application for anyone to bother paying for them. Her relatives feared she was going mad for it was not unknown for the high language to turn the brains of lesser maadiregi into mush, gradually devouring their higher cortical functions until nothing was left. Knowledge was power and power had a price. This is why most preferred to limit their learnings to the speciality of their varied industries.

Xuda couldn't tell anyone of her headache-inducing strangemares. Grotesque scenes played out every night which etched themselves as scars in her grey matter and she woke up with welts on her skin each morning. It was driving her mad and she thought the language was doing this to her, until she learnt of another, a non-maadigeri who was exhibiting the same symptoms.

Few carried a significant catalogue of high language words in their heads.

And so it was, as Feja Station plummeted like a meteor through the remnant atmosphere of Mahwè, towards their certain doom, Xuda sensed the subsonic probing of the cybernetic being from Pinaa, Ruu'vim, who was desperately trying to interface with the station's AI.

Caught up in the planet's gravity with the station spinning dangerously, Xuda tried not to pass out. The centrifugal forces acting on them pinned them against the walls of the station. Their holographic employer had erred. Whatever signals they were using to control the station couldn't penetrate the damaged chronosphere of Mahwè and so they wouldn't be able to control the descent. A strange noise, something akin to a shriek from an unnatural abattoir, rang out in the craft. It rattled through every molecule in Xuda's body, stunning her. She was shaken by its wrongness. It seemed to lodge itself into her entire being.

The station was heating up.

Ngano was praying to the god of war to grant him passage into the Huts of the Valiant.

Baba Do and Adelolade whispered soothing words of eternal devotion, promising to reunite in the next world, as they hoped they were soul-tied to one another. But what did that mean in this dead world? The screens which had showed their descent now only showed a restless greyness, as though the cameras were unable to process the images coming into them.

'They used a standard spacefaring AI from a transit tanker. Those carry bulk and are not designed with re-entry protocols. It doesn't know what to do in gravity and is unable to patch new piloting code. The ship will hold, but we will crash and burn,' Ruu'vim said, jerking everyone back to the problem at hand.

'I can get you in if you can fly us,' Xuda said.

'You have nil augmentation, and even if you could make it to a manual control panel, it would take months for you to crack the security encryptions using an organic brain alone,' Ruu'vim replied.

Xuda couldn't help but smile, even as it felt like her chest was compressed by a dreamstealer sitting atop it. She'd never been to Pinaa but knew they were averse to the use of magic, preferring technological innovation alone.

She opened her mouth and uttered the recitation of R'asasa Akooka, *The Lost Key,* in the high language.

Baba Do and Adelolade cried out in anguish, whilst Ngano gritted his teeth. Blood trickled out of their ears. The sound came out mangled, in the wrong key. Even Ruu'vim, whose chassis was built of composites and could withstand the harshness of space without a suit, shut her sonic receptors. She could still feel the overwhelming power of the language pummelling her body, for vibrations can touch. It seemed like it was going on forever until Xuda's head slumped, as she passed out, but Ruu'vim found at last they were patched into the station's AI and could take control of the craft.

Ruu'vim took charge and they crashed.

That moment was the last they saw one another alive.

The ruins of Mahwè were a temporal maze, better still, a labyrinth, and there were multiple stories, counted in powers of five, that happened on the bès the Feja Station landed there. Some Raevaagi, those griots, claimed there were thousands of versions of this tale that played out in an instant. Others argued there were infinite versions instead. The most extreme contended that the story truly never ended, rather it was locked within echoes of itself that were a hall of mirrors which reflected back to one another until the last note of the song of the Saúútiverse was sung.

The peculiar nature of time on the ruins of Mahwè meant the narrative had to be collapsed into a single wave function, a solitary co-herent narrative, rather than the played out range of possibilities, else no griot could contain it in their mind, and no audience could live long enough to listen to it all. But what was time, that untouchable essence divided commonly divided into seconds, minutes, hours, bès, juzu, and so forth, unto the Yu'uxu which is twenty-five juzu, and from there growing ever higher?

Baba Do emerged from the wreckage of Feja Station as the sole survivor. He surveyed the carnage, the pureed bodies of his compan-ions, their blood painting the silver walls of the craft. What wasn't glop were bits of bone, teeth and the composite materials making Ruu'vim scattered through the room.

How Baba Do survived could be hailed a miracle, by believers in such events.

Or it could simply be the same probabilistic property of the uni-verse that meant if you walked into a wall an infinite number of times, on at least one occasion, your atoms and the wall's atoms would be so perfectly aligned that you walk right through it as though it were not there at all.

Such vapid explanations mattered little to Baba Do as he attempted to gather the splattered remains of his love, Adelolade. He wept and wished he too had died, and he had elsewhere, in a different time, but all he knew was this single reality, the same one in which he alone had survived.

It was all so unfair.

The hologram reappeared and said, 'This is not a live link but a recording. If you are seeing this then congratulations, you may well be the first to survive entry into the ruins of Mahwè. A historic moment—'

'Kyi á yikho.' He said. *Damn you.*

'This recording cannot interact with you directly. Please wait to hear the full message,' the station instructed.

'— and if you wish to return, you must first find a precious artefact, the Codex of Qu'laaba believed to be lost in the ancient capital of. . . '

Baba Do didn't care. Though the message went on and on, and then returned in a loop, all he could do was stay in the carnage and grieve the loss of his beloved Adelolade.

Time passed, or didn't, as it does on Mahwè, until he felt hungry and the baser functions of his body compelled him to seek food and water, which the station had in abundance. He remained within its aagoo reinforced shell, until that too nearly drove him to despair. Eventually he resolved to live so he could seek vengeance on their mysterious benefactor who'd lured them here on the promise of a cure to their strangemares.

On the bés Baba Do decided to venture outside, he noticed there were five black suits on the ship and five white ones. He was not familiar with the fabric of the black suits which felt strange beneath his fingertips. There were bumps on them, something like a skin with bad acne. Disgusted by it, Baba Do chose one of the white space suits instead. It was logical to conclude that if it was strong enough to protect the human body in the void of space, it would protect him from this hostile planet.

He donned a space suit, clicked on the helmet with a wide visor, and walked into the airlock. Through the faux port window of the hatch, Baba Do glimpsed the brown, barren landscape of the planet. It was awe inspiring, even as a wave of repulsion forced his breakfast back up to his throat. He swallowed. And then he opened the door and stepped outside.

Baba Do blinked, seeing shapes that looked like people spontaneously emerging in the desolation before him. It was as though the waves of the ages were swirling around, rising and falling, churning in incomprehensible shapes. The planet changed and was unmade faster than anything his mind could keep up with. This was impossible. He closed his eyes and opened them again and saw nothing.

In this distraction, he had not realised what was broken was the fundamental quality of time as a dimension which was the stuff that kept everything from happening at once. It was orderly like a river of glue, holding events fast in their place yet simultaneously moving unidirectionally. Everyone understood the limits of what one could do with time: measure it, slow it down with a massive gravitational force, almost suspend it by moving towards the speed of light, and so forth. But on Mahwè, their ancient forbidden experiment had tempered with this order carefully sung by The Mother Goddess.

Here, with their civilisation at its zenith, the people of Mahwè had played goddess with time and reaped the whirlwind.

Baba Do's choice of the white space suit was unfortunate. For on this one world the glue of time was rendered unsticky and flowed chaotically so that, agonisingly, his very subatomic constituents were ripped into different eras, shredding him from the beginning of the universe to its very end. It happened slowly and it happened quickly, everything at once.

Baba Do died a scream suspended across the length of all time, becoming a wrong note in the Mothersound. Some menigari, those wise in matters of the spirit, have claimed this corruption is how pain and suffering first entered the universe.

In another splintered branch of the river of time, Xuda found herself as the sole survivor of the descent to the surface of the corpse world. Since everything issues from the Mothersound, this was her solo; even though the hero should have been the cybernetic child of Pinaa, Ruu'vim who, with mere minutes to impact, successfully stabilised the craft by forcing the ship's AI to reroute the non-positive fuel, thus creating an antigravity thrust in the nozzles and then bringing the ship to a soft landing.

Once on the ground, they surveyed the mess of pulverised bodies staining the craft. It looked like a child had smeared jelly on the walls. But the smell was horrible. 'What have you done?' Ruu'vim said before they slumped to the ground and shut down for the last time.

Xuda was aghast.

'We were going to crash.'

She wanted to cry out but feared the very sound of her own voice, of what it could do. Instead of saving them, she'd killed everyone in the most horrible way imaginable. Her magic had not worked right since the strangemares intensified. Not on Zezépfeni, or even when she went on pilgrimage to the incredible atmosphere of Órino-Rin. It was there she'd met Adelolade who she'd heard singing in the Divine Temple of the Talking Drum which was the largest cave set within a mountain. The others were much smaller in scale, though they all had their own special harmonics. The acoustic set-up amplified magic making the caves sacred spaces.

Adelolade, a songstress, was wealthy and independent, for the people of Órino-Rin valued few things more than a golden voice and unique music. When she was silent, she had a dreamy air about her, but when she spoke she could be highly animated.

'You are an incredible singer,' Xuda said.

'I sing better when I get a good night's sleep, but something strange and sorrowful has troubled my dreams of late,' she replied, right hand touching her collarbone.

And there in the Divine Temple of the Talking Drum, the two women had exchanged dreams, the most intimate thing two people can share. On Órino-Rin and Ekwukwe, both planets which orbited the fiery sun Juah-āju, it was commonly known that sharing one's dreams opened up the possibility they would be stolen if the other party was a dreadful dreamstealer. To share them was to show trust, even if the dreams were strangemares which no one wanted. There was the old Ekwukwe proverb which went, 'To cast aside one's strangemare is to lose the nugget of gold within.'

Good things can come from bad experiences. Discomfort was a part of life. But nothing positive was to be found in the soul shuddering despair their strangemares held in common. The rocky walls of the cave echoed their terrors back to them. And as the two women spoke they realised they had been tied into a common dream.

'There are others,' Adelolade said. 'My partner has been contacted by someone who claims to have a cure. We are going to meet them on the tenth bès hence.'

'Are they an uroh-ogi?'

'We have tried all those doctors and healers, spending a fortune in the process. No one can help us but this man who claims he has answers. Will you come?'

How could Xuda refuse this offer when her mother's inheritance had been stolen from her?

But, at the crash site, she was in shock; she could do nothing but stare at the bodies. She eventually made her way to a comms panel and tried to send a signal for aid, knowing full well the planet's field wouldn't allow that. No signals came in or left. She was on her own with nothing but the high language. It was this incredible magic that had worked in ways she'd never seen it work before when she uttered the R'asasa Ako-oka, *The Lost Key*, pulverising her companions.

Now she understood why the inhabitants of the moon Pinaa were so wary of sound magic. They were, of course, the descendants of the inhabitants of Mahwè. The events that destroyed the planet shattered their trust in the ability of people to manipulate even fragments of the Mothersound.

The hologram started up, urging her to find 'the Codex of Qu'laaba, believed to be lost in the lost capital of Jenne.'

This was her only way to get off the planet.

Multiple voices streaming different thoughts played in her head. It was as if she was hearing people other than herself conversing inside of her skull.

I have gone mad, she thought.

A cybernetic being with integrated quantum AI could think multiple thoughts simultaneously. These thoughts however disparate would be harmonised eventually like the different sections of an orchestra. One of the things Ruu'vim ran in their mind was a background check of the four others on Feja Station. Ruu'vim could assign different compartments of their intelligence to do this including a systemwide scan of government databases to identify their companions.

That was easy.

Then they'd performed an ancestral trace which kept running as the station hurtled towards Mahwè, the planet looming larger on their screens. Two parents make four grandparents who make eight great-grandparents, and sort forth, until they'd been cut off from the system as they entered into the planet's atmosphere.

Now they were the lone survivor after the loss of the four descendants of thousands of foremothers and ancestors stretching back generations. They felt sorrow and glitched, collapsing their thought streams into muddled error soundcodes.

They cleared the cache and composed themself in time for the hologram to play its message.

A mission equals purpose which increases chances of survival.

It was not unknown on Pinaa for cybernetic beings without clear life-goal to self-terminate. Usually this was linked to a degradation of the organic grey matter, especially with grades one and two types.

As Ruu'vim started up their various thought streams, they were surprised to find a voice which was not theirs embedded within.

<<Isolate and run diagnostics>>

. . .

. .

.

<<ALIEN STREAM DETECTED>>

Another lifeform here on Mahwè? Impossible. There was nothing out there but desolation beyond imagining. Ruu'vim was about to attempt a flush of the alien stream when they experienced déjà vu for the first time, which was impossible for a being that remembered everything. Someone else was on this world and as secondary diagnostics reported, it seemed they were temporally adrift.

— *Who's there?*

— *I'm going crazy. I'm going to die.* Though the internal voice was richer since it reflected the inner tone of the speaker mediated through bone, rather than air, Ruu'vim recognised it as Xuda's, which was strange, since Xuda had been pulverised in the crash.

— *Xuda?*

What in the name of The Mother?

— *Listen carefully. This is Ruu'vim. I am in your mind and you are in mine.*

— *Okay, I'm definitely nuts now. Everyone's dead. So many voices. Make it stop.*

Ruu'vim reluctantly collapsed their thoughts to a singular stream.

— *Is that better for you, Xuda? We are temporally dissociated but when you used your high language magic to help me break into the station's AI our consciousness must have become entangled. That's why I can hear you and you can hear me.*

— *I can only hear one of you now.*

— *Listen to me very carefully. We have to work together if we plan to survive this.*

— *Survive? Everyone's dead!*

— *Focus.*

— *You're dead. I am insane.*

— *Focus Xuda.*

Ruu'vim, who specialised in chronospherics, explained various theorisations on the workings of time on Mahwè. This was the reason the planet was so dangerous. Then they asked Xuda to don her aagoo suit as soon as she could.

— *It's the black suit, not the white one. They are designed to keep your atoms in a single, stable chronology.*

Ruu'vim did the same, though their body could endure outer space, the composite material was not designed for withstanding the ravages of chrono-dismorphation. They jettisoned their oxygen pack as they recycled an internal supply to sustain their meagre organics. It would be thirty bès before that needed topping up. And they did not hesitate to open both doors negating the airlock.

Gases from Mahwè's toxic atmosphere streamed in but without fleshlings on board, Ruu'vim no longer required the life support, powering it down to save energy. Their sensors registered an odd coldness as though death had kissed their suit. But what they saw as they left the vessel and walked into were the ruins of the old industrial district of Jenne, conjured back by a temporal leap. This couldn't be right at all. Nothing should be here. It was impossible to tell if this was real or a simulation as they cross-referenced the sights of old warehouses with internally saved historical records. Ruu'vim grew unsettled, worried a sonic error was affecting her system. Dissonance.

— *You're making my head hurt.*

— *Almost done. I know you're not used to running multiple thought streams but this is important.*

— *Wait, I can see what you see. Where are you?*

— *Sometime in this planet's past. I can't fix the exact juzu yet.*

Xuda nervously stepped out of her hatch into the eerie dead world.

She blinked and they appeared in front of her, seemingly spontaneously emerging from the desolation into wisps. They were ghosts, but deformed, unlike the ancestors from Eh'wauizo, who were full of vitality when they appeared, these were hollow projections. They were grotesque, as souls who had neither gone to the spirit realm nor received poured libations tended to be.

— *I've never seen ghosts before.*

— *That's because you view everything from behind your sensors and gizmos. On Zezépfeni they are a fairly common nuisance.*

— *This was a research hub.*

— *Are you still in the past?*

— *They did some sort of psychic experiments in the labs here.*

But Xuda did not hear because the ghosts had approached, a mass of spectral men, women, non-binary people and even children, pressed around her. Their faces were contorted in anger and pain as they came at her clawing. She tried to turn back and run to the ship, but she was disoriented. It should have been behind her, now she could no longer find it.

— *Don't panic.*

— *I've never seen so many at once.*

— *What do they want?*

Ruu'vim was jerked from the warehouses into a blur of temporal zones at speeds which taxed their processing capabilities. But their organic mind was buffered from this incomprehensible mesh of data.

Mahwè was simultaneously dead and undead.

It all depended on which timestream in the planet's mangled history or future you wound up in. Without the aagoo suits stabilising the observer, everything would be a blur. But even with the suit's protection, cognitively, it was very difficult to process what exactly was happening on the planet at any given moment.

Their processors were aggregating collated information. The Codex of Qu'laaba was more than an artefact. Zankara Qu'laaba was a trailblazing scientist, regarded as the father of AI on Pinaa. And while the different planets had eventually developed their own independent artificial minds, Pinaa's central AI got there first because it had been built using the insights from Qu'laaba's experiments.

Hundreds of men, women and children, including babies and infants were subjected to cruel and inhumane experiments by Qu'laaba and his maadiregi assistants. Minds were flayed, connectomes extracted, nervous systems shredded down to the last neuron, all in his quest for mastery over the mysteries of the brain. Of consciousness itself. These people had been hollowed out, so they could fill his research orations with novel ideas. Ruu'vim realised this sin was buried deep in Mahwè and Pinaa's history. Their revered ancestor had ruined lives. He had been a monster.

— *The ghosts say because of these experiments which hollowed them out and made them unwhole, stripped them of their fragment of the Mothersound, they were denied entry into Eh'wauizo. They are stuck here. Existing in all moments at once. Uncleansed and shunned.*

— *While we reap the benefits of their suffering.*

The results of Ruu'vim's interrupted background check flashed in their screenview. The five people aboard Feja Station were but leaves on a tall tree, whose fibres dug deep in history, winding down to common roots on this dead world. They might have come from different planets, separated from one another, but everyone having the strangemares was a descendent of Qu'laaba. Ruu'vim was yanked into the alternate present in which Ngano lay dead at their feet.

The sight of him made their circuits freeze, for now he was no longer a stranger but kin.

— *We are here because—*

— *I heard your thoughts loud and clear, Ruu'vim. We are here for our reckoning.*

And so the ghosts spoke to Xuda with Ruu'vim listening across broken timelines. They demanded to be heard. So many of them. Their anguish rolled through like a storm across the desert.

"Since Zankara Qu'laaba robbed us of our lives and souls, we demand the same from his descendants," the hollowed people insisted.

'If our deaths will give you peace then we accept. Let this end now,' Xuda replied, resigned. She, more than anyone else, was tired of the torment.

'There are thousands more of Qu'laaba's descendants out there. This will not stop here, my sister,' Ruu'vim cautioned.

"You will both die, as will they all. Every single one until Qu'laaba's bloodline is extinguished," the hollowed people said.

'No, please, there is another way,' Xuda replied. 'Let us pay off this blood debt another way.'

"There is no other way except blood for blood!"

"Truth!" Xuda shouted. "Let us trade blood for truth. We can be your mediums, the menigari through which you can speak. We will take your story back to all the five worlds, so they will know what was done to you. So that the truth will persist. If you kill us then your song dies with us, too. But with a medium out there in the five worlds, a host for what remains of you, then you will in effect become living ancestors yourselves. No longer trapped here, lost in time."

Silence. And then, "Two siblings. We only need one. One must live and the other must die so that this soil where we perished also tastes the blood of our enemy. Which shall it be? Choose."

Ruu'vim projected thoughts into Xadu's mind:

— *Don't offer them anything. We did nothing wrong.*

— *They did nothing wrong either. Now it is our responsibility to make it right. What choice do we have? And if we do this, at least one of us will survive to tell this tale to the Ruevaagi so that they may repeat it and we will not be forgotten. Let us at least have that.*

The hollowed people got angrier the longer the two took to think. Their collective rage, fuelled by their pain, burned the broken world red, threatening to explode like a dying star.

"Choose, choose, choose, choose, choose," they chanted.

The travelling cybernetic menigari on Wiimb-ó drew a crowd that jostled to see this new wonder. From mountain peak to mountain peak, through the cloud-stained crests, along the slippery slopes, between the passes and spurs that made up the habitable parts of this world, this wandering menigari's reputation had spread. Their fame extended throughout the system and some people came with problems, while others simply wanted to witness the spectacle of the cybernetic being sitting on a reed mat, dressed in their animal skin regalia, telling stories of the past and casting bones to divine futures.

They wore a crown of feathers on their head.

It was whispered they had abandoned a conventional research post on Pinaa to travel the system from planet to moon to planet bringing stories, healing, and lost wisdom.

Whenever the choice was made on that fateful bès on Mahwè, it was always Ruu'vim who emerged out of the fractured timelines. It could only have been them for their mind could carry far more ancestors and cope with those voices singing disparate songs all at once. They were made for this.

And when they were done divining for the public, they withdrew into the recesses of the Divine Temple of the Talking Drum. The great cave's uneven walls loomed over them. It resembled an open mouth crying out. An acute sense of déjà vu washed over them.

We remember this place, a voice in their head said.

Ruu'vim couldn't now ever see the temple with new eyes. This was the same of many places they'd never been to that now felt as familiar as the new memories stored in their drives. Before the hollowed people took possession of them, they made a bargain to also host the souls of their siblings Ngano, Baba Do, Adelolade, and dearest to them, Xuda.

Eventually, one bés, Ruu'vim too would die and then all would be free to ascend to Eh'wauizo to join the others who came before them whose voices whispered in the wind.

For now, they would continue to carry the souls of these old and new ancestors around the five worlds, healing and teaching and telling the histories, the only living being to have crossed the mangled time-threshold of Mahwè and returned.

*W*henever *a colossus of empire falls, its legacy remains. We have explored this in the previous two stories,* The Hollowed People *and* Undulation, *seeing how truth is often obscured under empire's shadow and how, eventually it comes to light, even if that requires the manifestation of the ancestors themselves. But the legacy of empire is often much more than just the lies and untold stories of past violence that must be uncovered. Violence persists where empire has not been fully dismantled. And that violence is often just mutated into a newer, different, ongoing violence that is just better hidden, clothed in metaphorical velvet, or rebranded to prevent the victims of those past violences from finding the truth or demanding full restitution. Violence to snuff out the sparks of truth that appear - that threaten to start a fire of reckoning.*

So now we come to this story by collective founding member **Eye Kay Nwaogu** *which takes place 35 juzu A1B. It examines the echo of violence from the past in service of empire and its impact on the future, as represented by children, like our protagonists. For this story, we first go back to Wiimb-ó, to a school where two students from different worlds find themselves linked by history. Echoes of actions taken long ago. Echoes of truth and violence. They must choose what to do with the knowledge, and chart a course for the future, for better or worse.*

Muting Echoes, Breaking Tradition

EYE KAYE NWAOGU

WIIMB-Ó
Site 01252. Third Juzu Class Field Trip
for Students of the Institute for Aural Archaeology

Yah-yah was almost asleep when he heard the strange, lilting call.
"Oooo...wioh-wioh-wioh!"

He laughed and rolled over, wondering which of the students in the camp was the prankster trying to mimic the call of the Akalala, a fabled bird said to fly around in daytime, but only sing at night. It was said that whoever heard the call of the Akalala would experience a major life change.

Yah-yah laughed because they were on their first ever field expedition, and everyone in third juzu was looking forward to it. Was the first field trip supposed to be a life-changing experience, or just another boring lecture with slightly more exciting scenery? At least they were on Wiimb-ó, far away from his home on Zezépfeni. The open fields like this on Zezepfeni were very few and very far between; everything was tall towers and defensive domes protected by the Rorta Kuuwa, the planetary shield. He was mentally cataloguing differences between Wiimb-ó and Zezépfeni when he finally fell asleep.

Na-Achana was finishing the last of her meal when she heard the call. As always, she had the eating area to herself, having come late to avoid her fellow students – something she always did anywhere outside of class. It was easier that way. It was not that she hated people; she was just tired of the constant looks of pity they always gave her. It was not her fault that she was an orphan, her family having been killed when she was a child, and she was being raised and sponsored by The Order of The Silent Sisters. She longed to feel a sense of belonging, to be part of something bigger, something more, but the Silent Sisters were not exactly the best definition of a family. The most they were good for was the vast library, with its millions of sonic recordings and stories. Like stories of the Akalala and the change its call heralded. But Na-Achana didn't believe in myths and fairytales. Her life had been too harsh for those.

She finished her food, cleaned up and hurried briskly to her tent.

Yah-yah was distracted. They were at the dig, a short distance from their camp. His classmates were milling around their instructor, Idongesit, a beautiful woman with sad eyes. Every now and then Idongesit would call one of them and ask them to lift a beam or fetch a tool. The skies were growing darker, but it did not seem like a rainy bés; the weather maadiregi had forecasted clouds but no rain.

Lightning sizzled in the sky.

Yah-yah looked up, startled. It never failed to amaze him how the instructors could create seals of containment around specific places, to ensure that no sound from outside would distract the students from what was being said in the class. He had heard it said by some of the senior students, but it was a different matter seeing it being done live. It was still a bit of a shock to him, standing within the circle and being unable to hear anything going on outside it, then stepping out and finding himself assailed by a mélange of sounds. The seals of containment were said to be so strong as to even block out the rumble of thunder. Yah-yah grinned and stepped outside the circle. He heard the boom as the thunder roared across the sky in the wake of the lightning, and he stepped back into the circle, to a shocking silence.

Lightning...

Thunder...

Pain!

Something slammed into Yah-yah from behind, knocking him to the ground and searing a streak across his back. He tried to scream, but the pain wracked his body and he struggled to breathe, such that when he opened his mouth his shout came up as a strangled howl. And in that moment, the person whose face filled his vision was not any of his classmates or their instructor. No, it was his father, screaming wordlessly as he was being dragged away by guards. A memory.

Then a thick inky darkness rose up from the ground and claimed him.

Na-Achana and the other students formed a circle and stared as the uroh-ogi, the healers, cut the clothes from the student that had been struck by lightning. She'd seen him before, around school. He was usually by himself, same as she was, but for a different reason. He was the only one from Zezépfeni at the Institute. The healers pulled up a glass fish tank and Abu-Oma, the senior uroh-ogi, approached the place where the boy was lying, taking deep breaths. With careful hands the uroh-ogi, extracted an alla-adigha, a small stingray-like creature, from the tank, and gingerly placed it on the young man's chest.

The sensitive underbelly of the dorso-ventrally flattened creature measured the boy's heartbeat, and the tail, which had been neutralized, tapped in time to his heartbeat. Na-Achana stared as the fish fluttered and the tail thumped. Abu-Oma said a prayer and returned the ray to the box, leaving the other healers to continue monitoring him.

"His vital signs are stable, his heartbeat is regular, and his breathing has normalized." The uroh-ogi, said to their worried instructor. "He seems to be suffering no major immediate effects of the lightning strike, except for the wound on his back. We will take him and observe him. When he wakes, we will know more."

Na-Achana didn't know him, but she closed her eyes and said a prayer to The Mother for the young man as he was taken away.

While other students congregated in groups of four and five, chatting and poking fun at each other, Na-Achana sat alone in her corner listening to recordings from the library. When she was done studying, she opened her wardrobe and pulled out a battered mutepack. It was the closest thing Na-Achana had to a memory of home, of what her life once was. it was also what had saved her life, long ago.

She had been small, only about six or seven Juzu. That age when children are big enough to talk to and send on errands, but small enough to be ignored. She was playing with the mutepack, and her father was arguing loudly with someone. She had fond memories of her father, a stout, hairy man, with a booming voice that seemed to be amplified by his beard. That day, he had seemed angry, pacing, aguing with his friends. She had held the mutepack over her head, craving the silence, and that was the last thing she remembered. She woke up in the hospital in the care of the uroh-ogi, as an orphan and a survivor. Apparently there had been a freak sonic storm, and the house had been directly in its path. The frequencies had hit just the right note, they said, to send the foundations of the house liquid and make the house crumble inward. No one had survived. They told her she had been fortunate to have something to shield her from the worst of it, but she knew they were lying.

Seven bés after the storm that allegedly killed her family, she saw the two spirit moons, Vuili-ki and Vuili-ku, for the first time in the night sky. She was much older when she discovered that on Wiimb-ó, the sonic storms ONLY occurred when the moons were fully in alignment and even then, they happened rarely, once or twice a juzu at most, not like Órino-Rin where they occurred thousands of times in one bés.

How then had one of those killed her family? That was one of the reasons she wanted to study sound-magic.

As she drifted off to sleep, she recalled the first time she heard the Rakwa-ya'yn, the Song of The Mother's Children. That was what her father and his friends had been arguing about before the storm.

Yah-yah was dreaming.

Again.

The dreams always began the same because they were memories. His sister running around with her toys. His mother sitting in the chair talking to her friends. Him playing nchokotoro with his father, winning. His father had always been insistent about him learning nchokotoro and other games of strategy. He said they would make him smarter, a better thinker. For him, it was just a way to spend time with the man he loved the most.

Just as he moved some pebbles into position to set up a win, the house seemed to shake, as massive blows thudded against the front door of the house.

His mother rose from her chair and headed for the door. "Who is it?"

The door splintered and nearly fell off its hinges. Hulking armed figures in black outfits, wearing giant earmuffs and helmets, barged into the house and whisked his father away. They told his screaming mother to come to Zezelam, to the headquarters of the Council, if she wanted to know more.

A lot of the next few months were a blur: names, faces, hearings, courts; the countless visits to Zezelam, and endless letters of appeal his mother had to write, begging to be told exactly what his father had done. They were told nothing except that his father had failed his duty.

The worst was when they placed the soundclamp on his father's neck, barring him from making sounds. It was punishment reserved for the worst of the worst, hardened criminals and those deemed too dangerous to even be allowed to utter a single sound. After then, everything became stricter, and the prison officials scrutinized everything in more detail. From then on, his family members were banned from bringing things when coming.

The only time he saw his father cry was the last bés they came to see him, after countless appeals. The prison officials spent an inordinate amount of time searching their clothes, and he could see the cruelty and savagery in their eyes. His sister had been much younger, and she was carrying her toy, a wooden eland, or kudu-kudu, artfully carved. Rather than check it over for a sign that it had been tampered with, they simply stomped on it with their ugly hobnailed boots, reducing it to kindling. Even the vilest villain in the five planets would have felt some remorse at the way his sister cried when her toy was smashed. But the guards only exchanged looks and laughed as she wailed.

Something broke in his father then, and the once strong hearty man, who Yah-yah had never seen shed a single tear, began to bawl like a baby. Yah-yah snapped, threw himself at the prison officials, swinging his fists as hard as he could. But he was barely twelve juzu, not yet a stripling. The guards laughed, and one of them pushed him hard, knocking him to the floor.

He could hear the mocking laughter as the men hooted and he had one of them chuckle, "He is defending his sister, he knows he is the new head of his family now."

The guards yanked savagely at his father's chains, pulling him away from them like a dog. Yah-yah got up and stretched his hands to run for one last hug, but a guard swung a baton that hit him in the ribs, knocking the breath from him. Even before he hit the floor, he knew that there was something terribly wrong. And he was falling backward. And backward. Backward...

His father was shouting but he could not hear anything because of the clamp. But in the dream, the words came to him as he fell.

"Yah-yah, my son, don't repeat my mistake!"

And then he hit the ground with a crack like thunder.

Abu-Oma, the senior uroh-ogi, watched the young man tossing and turning on the bed. Since being struck by lightning, he had been in a deathly sleep, and this was the first sign of consciousness. The boy's face was pale, and his breathing was harsh. Abu-Oma reached out and touched him. Suddenly, the boy's eyes shot open, and he sprang up like a creature set from free from a trap. There was something vital, something haunted in his eyes.

Abu-Oma called for the junior uroh-ogi, to come and dress the wounds on the boy's back.

Na-Achana had a headache, and it was not getting better anytime soon, which meant she couldn't study. Her head felt like it was swimming. She couldn't focus on anything. So, she decided to go see the uroh-ogi, hoping she could get something for the pain.

When she arrived, Abu-Oma was helping someone take tentative steps on the floor. She recognized him from her class expedition.

"Hey, you're the one that was struck by lightning!" She said, without thinking.

The boy and Abu-Oma both gave her sharp looks. But then the boy's features softened when he saw her.

"Sorry." Overcome with guilt, she added, "...If you need help catching up on assignments when they discharge you, let me know." And then she fled, her head still pounding.

Much later, still unable to study, Na-Achana decided to attend the evening dance, hoping the music and dancing would help her burn off her restlessness. She showed up to the square and was pleasantly surprised by all the attention she did not get. People did not huddle in corners and point at her. Feeling free, she began to move, getting a feel for the rhythm. The moons of Wiimb-ó were partly visible overhead. She wondered how many of the students could see Vuili-ki and Vuili-ku. One of the Silent Sisters had told her that people were more emotional, more excitable, when the spirit moons aligned and the borders between worlds were thinnest. She could feel it. Her inhibitions coming loose. It seemed the drummers did too, their fingers flying over the skins, battering them in the frantic rhythm, ka-ti-ka-ti, ka-ka-ti-ka-ti.

She closed her eyes; her headache receded to the background. She swayed, wiggled, lost in the rhythm. Suddenly, her father's voice, little more than a whisper, in her ears. *Do not let them get you.*

Na-Achana stopped dancing and opened her eyes.

Everyone else was minding their business, and she knew that if someone were watching her, they would pretend to be watching.

The boy she'd seen earlier, the off-worlder, was sitting all by himself across the clearing, staring at her.

He had a kind face, with thin lines around his mouth and he was staring at her like he had never seen her before. Her heart was thumping in her chest with excitement. Intoxicated with music, or perhaps it could have been the pull of the moons, she steeled herself and walked over to him.

"Are you well enough to dance?" She asked.

"No. Not yet. But I'd love to dance with you when I am." He grinned, shyly.

"As long as you don't get hit by lightning again when I'm around."

He laughed, a cute sound that she decided she liked very much. She took it as an invitation and sat down beside him.

"You're from Zezépfeni, right?"

"Yes." He said.

"How come they sent you all the way here to study?"

"My family was disgraced, I wasn't not able to study anywhere on my home world. All the bullying and name-calliing..."

"I'm sorry, she murmured, before asking. "Zezépfeni. I've heard so many stories. What's it like there?"

It was fascinating listening to him talk about his family, and home planet with its fortified biodomes, pink and green shielded sky, advanced technology and powerful sound magic. They talked and laughed and held hands and watched the other students dance as something quietly blossomed between them, drawn together by something not unlike gravity.

Bés turned to weeks, and then to lunar cycles. Their friendship, borne of mutual loneliness and the feeling of never being understood, grew wings and flew aloft.

They attended the next evening dance together.

They danced.

Na-Achana was dreaming.

She did not know she was dreaming but could sense the detachment. As though she was seeing herself living out the events while experiencing them.

In the dream, she was at home, playing with her toys and running around. Her mother was setting the table. Her father had some of his friends over, as usual, and they were arguing about a vase which they had been listening to. The men were talking animatedly, and she watched her father gesturing as he strode back and forth in the living room, his voice deep and powerful, his beard quivering with each word. She was his special girl, her father's little princess, and either because the children before her (two boys) had no interest whatsoever in the academia that was her father's passion, or because she was always following him around and as such picked up an interest, she was also the one who had her father's great love for sounds and artefacts that chronicled the ages gone by.

She picked the mutepack the vase had come in, noting the striations and marks that were etched into the leather, marks from ancient times when vases used to be large and bulky. The newer vases and mutepacks were much smaller, better able to be carried in bags. She pulled the mutepack onto her head and tried to navigate her way round the house only by touch. Her brothers had been in the house as well, appearing when summoned but otherwise content to remain in their rooms.

She heard a noise, and suddenly she could see outside, where a tall, angular man with a hard face was standing. The sky darkened and the man seemed to loom taller, bigger. The man leaned forward, and a strange, paralyzing deep bass hum emerged from his mouth. Just as quickly, like someone pulling on a shirt, Na-Achana found herself back inside her small body, glaring up into a mutepack which covered her head. Her last thought, as the building began to crumble and fall, was that she wanted to hear her father's voice.

She blanked out, but she did not faint; it was more like she had walked into a dark room: lights off, curtains drawn. So, she floundered around, feeling like she was stuck inside her own head, and when she managed to open the windows, which were her own eyes, she saw the humming man, some distance away, staring at the rubble of the house. In that moment she felt the vacuum of grief, the pain of knowing there was now a yawning void where her father used to be.

Something about the man's features looked familiar, but try as she could, she could not place it. He turned and walked away.

Na-Achana jerked awake. She looked around, finding comfort and solace in the familiar surroundings and the sprawl of Yah-yah, her boyfriend, lying next to her. Up in the sky, she saw the three moons aligned, the physical and two spirit moons. It was another time of strangeness and revelations. She knew that the dream had been meant to tell her something, that her family had not been killed by a storm. That they had been killed by this man with the familiar features and the strange voice, but the softness of the bed and the arms of her boyfriend next to her were too much of a distraction for her to focus on it.

Na-Achana cuddled closer and went back to sleep. There were only three Bés before school break, and she wanted to make the most of them.

ZEZÉPFENI
Nara'arana-3 Medical Center, Zezelam

Yah-yah entered the hospital nervously. He would not have gone, but the wound on his back had still not fully healed, and when he had told Na-Achana that he was going home to Zezépfeni for the academic break, she had insisted he consult with the famously powerful healers there.

He lay on the bed, as a tall, smooth white automaton checked monitors beside him. He realized that no one, human, machine or both had exhibited any real surprise when he mentioned that the wounds on his back had not healed. It was almost as if they had expected it. They told him they would run some tests. The bed seemed to feed into a gigantic machine, and the automaton gave him an injection, telling him it would relax his muscles and keep him from shaking and turning while the large machine scanned his body.

He felt the stillness crawl through his limbs, as the automaton tightened the straps and gave him a pill. It disintegrated in his mouth, and he suddenly felt weightless, borne aloft on clouds. Images flitted through his mind rapidly. Then he was falling backwards, arms flailing, legs cycling...

And he landed athletically on his own two feet.

Even before he straightened up, he realized he was taller, broader, bigger in the chest than he had ever been. His body felt different, and he could feel scars where he had none, and remember how he got them. The eyes he was looking out of felt different, and he felt like he was being carried on someone's back. He felt a stinging pain in his back from the wound, and even as he walked towards the house, he began to hum deep in his chest, and it was then Yah-yah realized that he was in fact looking through the eyes of his father. His father went up to a house, and his father did something he could only describe as a humming scream, raw and deep and primal. The house caved in from the roof and crumbled on the people inside it. His father was leaving when he turned back and approached the house. Bending low, he began to scream again, and Yah-yah felt himself falling backwards again...

To land on (in?) a body.

This time he was a woman. He could feel the difference in the weight distribution, the heft of breasts on his (her) chest, the subtle sway of the hips when (s)he walked, and smell the bad breath of the man walking beside her. Together, they entered a room, lavishly set out in silks and linens. He could see the lechery in the man's eyes as he hastily began to undress, and he saw that look become fear when the lady began to hum, and the man's throat began to constrict. Blood vessels stood out in relief on his pale skin, and the man began to bleed from his eyes, nose, and mouth. The woman slipped out a knife and slashed a curtain, fastening lengths of it into a rope. He felt the forced calm as servants from outside started knocking on the door, and she grabbed the knotted curtains and kicked open a window. The door was forced open, and she jumped...

Yah-yah landed in a perfect white room that seemed to go on forever.

Three figures that looked like their bodies were made of pure silver stood before him, holding bowls.

"Welcome, Sâkoukou. You have been activated." they said. "Drink, to recover data from your previous iterations." Yah-yah's first instinct was to refuse, but even before he could turn, the liquids in the bowls reduced until they were empty. A word flashed in his mind, and he knew who he was. Sâkoukou. A wolf-howler.

An assassin.

"Your father, the previous Sâkoukou, did not complete his task. That was his crime. You have been activated to find the survivor and eliminate them. That will remove the threat, restore order and bring back honor to your family. Do not fail."

Yah-yah came awake slowly.

This was not the body he had slept in.

Even before he opened his eyes, he knew he was different. More powerful. His body seemed to have gotten an upgrade, and he felt stronger, more capable. He had known he was not alone, but now he could count how many people were in the room with him. He could calculate heat signatures, seconds between breaths, and all the chemical and biological signals a body could give off.

He was breathing slowly, his air intake more measured, more de-liberate. The muscles in his arms felt different, like he could do more with them, a lot more. Sitting up, he brought his legs down from the bed and looked around. The automaton led him to a door marked "RECOVERY" and held it open for him.

He entered.

Na-Achana was walking in the school park when it happened.

She looked up at the sky and saw the milky orbs of three moons perfectly aligned. The intensity of their beaming was a wonder. And then all the sound fell away from the world, and everything stopped moving. She looked around and noticed that everything had stopped moving. Even insects in mid-flight. Suddenly, she heard a sound like someone exhaling.

"Father?"

Yes, Na-Achana.

Her eyes welled up with tears.

My daughter, I am sorry I left you so soon and in such a terrible manner. But there is something you must know now. Everything Zezépfeni teaches about our history, about The Mother, is a lie. You know this, as do I, because the truth is embedded in our DNA. Long ago, when our people were first colonized, they performed a great ritual to give us the greatest gift, the gift of knowledge that did not require hearing or seeing. They sang the truth into the very fabric of our physical bodies. Into our souls. All life originated from Wiimb-ó. Not Zezépfeni. But they continue to perpetrate this lie because it serves their agenda. And they seek to destroy any who know the truth. That is why they came for us. We are blessed by the Mother that you survived. But they will not stop. They will seek you out and come for you too. You must be brave my daughter, and careful.

"What should I do?"

You will know when the time comes. You will feel it in your blood and in your bones. You will know it like you know the truth. You are the truth.

Sound returned to the world and Na-Achana began to cry.

Yah-yah rose from the bed and stretched. It was more out of reflex than anything; working out had made him somewhat stiff. He walked into the kitchen to get some food.

And then he saw it.

A small, perfect black box. He reached out to grab the box and suddenly, everything went dark. His back felt like it was on fire.

A flicker of light appeared, and he heard footsteps. Slow, ponderous. As though something heavy was approaching. As the footsteps got nearer, he heard the clanking of chains. Suddenly the flicker of light exploded into brightness and found himself staring at... his father.

At first, Yah-yah was silent, spellbound. He did not believe that he had grown this tall, or had his father shrunk?

"Father!"

His father held up a hand.

"Now you know the truth of our family. We are Sâkoukou. Descended from the Mahwé royal guard, stationed in Zezépfeni when the flare came, we now serve them. We have been a secret held for generations. We are the poison at the tip of the spear. The ones who quietly do what must be done to protect our people. Do you know why the nanomachines in your body have been linked to this transmission? Why I appear to you in these chains, Yah-yah?"

"They said you failed to complete a task."

The image of his father flickered green.

"Yes. I failed a task I was given. I was meant to wipe out a family on Wiimb-ó. A family whose genetic code can be traced back to an ancient power that, if mastered, can destroy us all. And yet one of them still lives because I did not ascertain that the job was done."

Yah-yah stepped forward and looked down. He saw a yawning chasm, with him and his father standing on opposite sides. There was no way forward, only back.

"What must I do?"

"Complete what I did not, Yah-yah. You have been planted on Wiimb-ó for this purpose. And now she has been identified, it is time. Restore our family honor."

His father stretched out a hand, the chains on him clanking, and the walls around them became screens. There was a certain familiarity about the scene that unfolded, and it took him several moments to realize that the person in the clip was his father, walking away from the ruins of a house. As his father walked away a small figure rose and pulled off something that looked like a helmet. There was something disturbingly familiar about the child, small though it was, and when the screen zoomed in on the face and began to age her, adding a few juzu each time, he understood.

Na-Achana!

Anguish seized Yah-yah, and he dropped to his knees, the vision gone. The box sat on the kitchen table like an ancient idol.

He got up and ran to the bathroom, puking. Turning on the tap, he cupped his hands, and drank deeply. After close to a dozen swallows, he straightened up and looked himself in the mirror. The realization that he had been bound since birth by blood and destiny to some secret order on Zezépfeni hit him. As did another bout of nausea.

He vomited again all over the sink.

WIIMB-Ó
The Institute for Aural Archaeology

Yah-yah resumed after the break.

It was a different Yah-yah.

He was taller, broader. The difference in gravity on his home world had seen to that. But only those who got close enough to look in his eyes could see the real changes. His demeanor had changed, radically, and there was a certain coldness in the way he looked at people. Almost as if he was measuring them as threats. Na-Achana was the first to notice his strange mannerisms when he locked and double-checked the door when she came to see him.

Something in the way he moved ran a shiver down her spine, and not in a good way. He swung away from the door after checking it again, and in that instant, Na-Achana remembered who he moved like. The man from her dream.

The two of them spoke together.

"There is something I have to tell you..." Yah-yah began.

"There was this dream I had last session..." Na-Achana started.

Na-Achana grinned. "You first."

They sat down and talked, and the bottom dropped out of Na-Achana's world. She now knew why her family had died, and why the Silent Sisters had taken up her sponsorship. And as she sat there and stared at the face of the young man she loved, who had been sent to kill her, her mind was torn between two choices. Would she heed the echo of her father's warning from Eh'wauizo, or would she break tradition and form an alliance with someone who had been born, bred, and enhanced for the sole purpose of exterminating her and her family? Would he even let her leave the room?

On the other hand, Yah-yah was sober. His face remained impassive, his neural circuitry winking and blinking as she spoke. As he listened to the woman he loved pour out her heart, he realized that like so many of his forbears, he had been a tool in the hands of shadowy masters, killing those who had done him no harm, and preserving secrets that kept people in ignorance and servitude. While in the recovery room, he had seen files showing hundreds of other Sâkoukou, sleeper cells who were yet to be activated, and he knew that if he failed to kill her there would be others sent after her, after them. He knew he was too valuable an asset to be allowed to roam free, and that by failing to carry out the mission he would himself become a target, just as his father had. But he had not asked to become anyone's weapon, and one of the things he had learnt from his father was to stand for what he believed, even though he stood alone. His failure to accomplish the mission would mean the end of his life as he knew it, but the skills and enhancements he had received from his activation on Zezépfeni would help him adapt to almost any situation.

He removed a small bracelet from his arm, and gave it to Na-Achana.

"With this, I can always track you, and it can monitor your heart-beat and all your vital signs. If it senses you in any panic or danger, it will activate a tracker beacon, and send a warning signal to my neural implants."

The bracelet was light but the words were heavy. Na-Achana took it, the weight of the situation pressing in on her as she wrapped it around her forearm and Yah-yah pressed his thumb over it, locking it in and activating it.

"Now we can travel, spreading the truth of how the planets came to be, and teaching people to spread the word, until we can find a way to extract it from your DNA so that even if anything happens to us, the knowledge need not be lost for all time."

The old woman stretched her arms and stared at the moon(s).

"And that, my children, is the end of the story. The truth of how our world came to be."

The children got up. Some of the younger ones had fallen asleep, and the older ones picked and carried them, taking them to urinate before going into their various huts for the night. When the front of the house was clear, the old woman got up and went inside. A sudden movement caught her attention, and she chuckled.

"All these juzu, and you still want to protect me, as if we had just eloped."

"I made that oath long ago, and I intend to keep it until the bés I breathe my last."

She settled on the bed and snuggled into his arms.

"Oooo...wioh-wioh-wioh!"

There it was again. The lilting call of a bird.

Na-Achana slept, lightly, and the dim light on her bracelet blinked in time to the dots on Yah-yah's neural circuitry. Once, in the night, she rolled, and in his sleep, Yah-yah winced and grunted, quieting down only when his leg stretched out and touched her skin. The circuits in his forehead resumed their journey.

Na-Achana and Yah-yah slept together, their bodies touching, as always.

The Akalala beamed the information back to its home base in the MotherDome of the Silent Sisters. All was well.

For now.

*I*n the Sauútiverse, where everything is driven by sound, vocal performances are powerful. We have already explored some aspects of this in
Undulation, *but now we return to it, in a very different context. A music
contest.*

*600 juzu after the formation of the federation of planets, Zezépfeni
proposed a conference called The Boāmmariri (which they take from
the Sauúti word for 'truth'). It is held every five juzu as a kind of
reconciliation process, a way for the people on the different planets to
share knowledge and ideas and culture and prevent wars or problems.
A kind of Academic-conference-meets-UN-peace-summit-meets-Elders-
Council-meets-Worlds-fair-by-way-of-Eurovision-song-contest. There are
presentations, panel discussions, displays, musical performances, demon-
strations and so much more. The Boāmmariri becomes a cultural nexus
for the five planets.*

*However, Zezépfeni has an alternative reason for proposing this con-
ference. They want to know what everyone does – while keeping secrets of
their own. In some cases, secrets that affect the entire Sauúti system. But
we will come to that in another story.*

For now, the Boāmmariri itself.

*In order to choose a group that will give the opening and closing
performance at the event – a series of local talent contests are held. This is
where we find ourselves at the start of this story by* **J. Umeh**, *a founding
member of the Sauúti collective. We go back across the binary star system,
to Ekwukwe, where we meet a very special band of musicians vying for the
honour of playing at the 40th Boāmmariri, 200 juzu A1B. A story about
the joy of performing and sharing music with others. Even when that
music literally has the magic stripped out of it. Of course, the members of
the band bring their baggage and their the drama and their talents and*

their gifts with them. And lurking in the background are the hands of Zezépfeni, always seeking more knowledge, more control.

When all of these things are shaken together and allowed to run over, well, we get something special.

We get... Kalabashing.

Kalabashing

J. UMEH

1. Muji-Aah

The results have just been announced.

They are in the finals!

Muji-Aah is excited and a little anxious. The two feelings blend in the pit of his stomach into something indescribable like... *nnnnnghhh!* At least that is what it sounds like to him inside.

Last night his band, Ndi-N'suppuh, competed in the Freestyle Kalabashing contest, an expedition into musical extremes attainable only when the magical effects of sound have been muted, with the winners determined by the audience. If they win, they'll embark on a tour of the five worlds, culminating in a command performance at the 40th Boāmmariri on Zezépfeni. If they don't, they'll be broke musicians stuck on Ekwukwe. At least he will. The twins will always have options back at their home, even if the options aren't good ones. Ndi-N'suppuh spent the last of their earnings for the chance to play here. They must win. There is no back-up plan.

Muji-Aah brushes back his thick dreadlocks as he looks up at the ceiling, the distinctive silvery sheen of his skin catching the harsh electric light and giving his skin a semi-luminescent, metallic appearance that sharply contrasts the strange, dark, tattoo-like markings around his entire body. He whistles out a deep breath.

Mother God, help us.

Never in all the nineteen juzu he has lived has he experienced this level of excitement and trepidation, not even before the previous bés's semi-final performance, or his first sono-aural sexual experience on Ekwukwe. No. There has been nothing like this, the feel of having something you've always dreamed of being at your fingertips, just one performance away.

Muji-Aah has never fit in. Always felt like an outsider. His unusual skin and natural affinity for technology marked him as an outcast even when he was a child. But he knows he can't be alone. He wants to explore the system, find people like him or at least find his place in the Saúúti system. He seeks people who understand what it means to be an outcast. Which is what bonded him to the twins, the other members of the band.

When he was younger, his parents had loved and pampered him within their frugal means, but it hadn't been enough to quiet Muji-Aah's sense of aloneness. His appearance, and later, the increased manifestations of his abilities eventually forced them to admit he'd been found in an incubator, in the abandoned home of a visiting researcher-Maadiregi couple who'd mysteriously vanished. His mother, who'd worked as a cleaner for them, had agreed to look after the unusual baby temporarily. But the couple never returned, and no one came to look for him, so they raised him as their own.

At the age of sixteen juzu, Muji-Aah resolved to go out and seek his origin among the stars. He took a job as an apprentice technician at a regional spaceport in Wiimb-ó, earning his way toward a ticket until one bés he fell asleep on the job and was accidentally stowed away on a space-faring sonic-energy transporter returning to Órino-Rin after offloading its cargo.

On Órino-Rin, he was processed and placed in the custody of the Kin-Kali Interstellar Freight company where he worked and studied, still looking for ways to earn enough to explore, to seek out any others like him. His loneliness was only ever alleviated by playing music with local ad-hoc bands in the bars and clubs of the Kin-Kali spaceport. His ability to make music with any device he literally turned his mind to was always worth a few free drinks and some loose change. That was how he met the Kali twins, Kali-Mho and Kali-Yeh and they formed Ndi-N'suppuh. *The outcasts.*

He snaps out of his reverie when he hears his name. "Muji-aah! Mujiii!"

It's Vaz Irie, their self-proclaimed manager, strategic advisor, and all-around shyster with the proverbial but well-hidden, heart of gold. An aesthetically challenged and slightly balding ball of energy, Vaz always seems to be in a hurry. He often trips up on his own thoughts in conversation, struggling to stay less than two steps ahead of the general discussion.

Vaz enters Muji-Aah's quarters, focused on capturing his attention with a solid sound tablet clutched tightly in his arms.

"Have you listened through all this yet?" Vaz asked.

"No. What is that? I need to prepare for tonight... I was just thinking through the drumbeat echo sequence for our concert intro tonight." Muji-Aah says.

"Never mind all that." Vaz cuts in dismissively.

"Well, I will mind it actually. It's important. And someone in this group has to make sure the technical details are right. The Mother knows it won't be you or the twins," Muji-Aah responds, annoyed. "Did you get the equipment we asked for?"

Vaz snorts. "How many times have I told you to just trust me? I fixed your little immigration problem on Órino-Rin, didn't I?" Vaz smiles as he taps out the invocation pattern to replay the recording on his tablet. "Now, have a listen to this my young friend, and never say again that I don't deliver!"

After the brief incantation-like signature of the Kalasho Company, organisers of the freestyle kalabashing contest, the recorded deal proposal starts with the usual mumbo jumbo of legal incantations. *Just enough to put any listener to sleep as they rip you off*, thinks Muji-aah irreverently. It doesn't take long however for him to perk up and take notice of what is actually being said. Vaz nods enthusiastically when he sees the dawning amazement on Muji-Aah's face. He can hardly contain himself.

"This... this is a sponsorship deal?" He asks, still shocked.

Vaz nods, his bald head reflecting the light.

"Wait, so if we win, beyond the prize money and the tour, they will *also* sponsor us for five juzu? Guaranteed?"

Vaz nods again. "Special deal. Only for my Ndi-N'suppuh."

Muji-Aah shakes his head in disbelief. "And they'll actually provide a private star-liner for us to use to travel to each tour location?" Muji-Aah asked incredulously.

"Yes, of course, didn't I tell you to leave everything to the Vazmagical one?" Vaz replies gleefully. He draws himself up to his full height, hands clasped behind his back and wanders across the room to the far wall which is displaying a digital projection of night-time on Wiimb-ó, spirit moons and all. Vaz stands beside the weather-beaten echo-drum kit and master console that Muji-aah had been working on beforehand.

"And you can forget all this, Muji," Vaz says, with a sweeping gesture across all the musical instruments and accoutrements littering the floor of Muji-Aah's quarters. "When you... when *we* win, I'll make sure we have access to a full complement of new instruments, tour staff and crew, and they'll manage every detail, including your precious technical stuff and even details we haven't even considered. You'll just have to get used to a higher standard of living," he declares.

It's all too much for Muji-Aah so he sits down on the console chair, brows furrowed in deep thought, thin white filigrees of static electricity playing between the locks on his head. They always do that when he is excited. And right now, he is very excited.

His dreadlocks are interwoven with thin metallic wiring that is linked to his spinal cord which sometimes makes his locks take a life of their own, especially in the vicinity of certain technological devices. They also sometimes become subdued, almost limpid, in his quieter, contemplative or despondent moods, or they hiss and crackle with static energy in states of emotional turmoil, fear, excitement, anger or passion. Sometimes, as now, Muji-Aah's brain activity can become so intense that electricity arcs between his locks as they extend and surround his head like a halo of pure mental energy. The Maadiregi on Wiimb-ó called it M'majiringo. *Electromagic.*

"We need to win this." He mutters more to himself than to Vaz, who is already making his way out.

"Yes, we do. All our lives will change forever," Vaz pauses at the door, "But you weren't planning on losing anyway, were you?" He flashes a smile. "I'll get you the equipment you need for the prep rehearsals and rituals, don't worry. Speaking of which, where are the twins?"

And then a wave of the hand as he brushes his beard with his other hand. "Don't bother, I'll find them myself."

Vaz exits the room, the light from Wiimb-ó's projected moons reflecting on the back of his clean-shaven head.

Muji-Aah lets out a long sigh. His initial blended feelings of anxiety and excitement were now edging into panic. *This is it, the chance I've been waiting for. We can't lose now.*

Muji-Aah shakes his head, takes a deep breath and turns his chair to practise the echo drumbeat sequence with renewed purpose and determination. He turns off the wall projection and darkness wraps itself around him. His fingers tap lightly on the lead drum, making a soft sound as his dreadlocks reach out to connect the master console behind him, electromagically controlling the pulse of the beats emanating from five sound-caster devices.

He wills his locks towards the control console for the Anwu-Light Imagizer machine in the centre of the room. At first, nothing happens, then the Imagizer sputters to life, casting abstract shapes in the air. Muji-Aah stares at the machine willing it to transform the drumbeat sounds into complex three-dimensional shapes, as his dreadlock synaptic connectors start to pulse in time with the sound. The Imagizer begins to hum, and the shapes begin to flow in harmony with the sound.

Finally. It's working.

It is beautiful, just the way he imagined it. He can't wait till he connects it to the new master console Vaz promised to get him before the performance and then he can really show the twins what he's been working on. Kali-Yeh will probably like it. She likes every innovation he comes up with even if they don't always work with the rest of their performance. And even Kali-Mho, ever critical, would have to admit he'd done something impressive, externally synthesizing light and sound just like the inverse of Kali-Mho's own natural abilities.

Suddenly... *Static!*

Harsh and painful, like fire flowing through his hair into his brain. The thoughts of the twins spike his emotions, interfering with his electromagic ability to harmonise and control. It hurt like a hundred lava fly stings.

"Dwa'ndenki!" Muji-Aah curses, as he lurches away from the drums, severing all connections with the master console. He sinks to the hard floor.

I need to control my emotions better.

On his haunches, head bowed, Muji-Aah is still-trembling. His quietened locks trail down over his back and shoulders. He is exhausted, but he's also elated to have engineered musical synaesthesia of light and sound. He just needs to control his thoughts and get a better console.

Muji-Aah decides not to tell the twins what he is working on until Vaz delivers.

2. Kali-Mho

Kali-Mho's golden eyes stare intensely at the silky, diaphanous shapes floating and unfolding in front of him. They undulate slowly in time to the rhythm of his music, colours pulsing to the highs and lows of the arrangement of percussion and flute-like luhte'te sounds in this his latest composition. He shakes the small shekere-re hanging like a pendant around his neck, and its rattly sound joins the arrangement, transmuting into other instrument sounds as he deftly manipulates the shapes that only he can see. Kali-Mho reaches out and lightly taps a shape here, pinches and twists another there, and then rotates the entire structure by gently grabbing it and moving his outstretched arms in a circular fashion until it all starts to sound just right to him. The sounds and music change in response to Kali-Mho's motions, like he is conducting an invisible orchestra.

He hears a voice calling, as if from a great distance but rapidly approaching. "Kali-Mho, Kali-Mhoohooh!"

His concentration is broken as the sound of his name being mangled appears in front of him, a white triangle with jagged edges, right in the middle of the exquisitely intricate visualisation. Vaz Irie bounds into Kali-Mho's quarters, breathing heavily from the effort of walking more than he is used to and waving the sound tablet above his head.

"What do you want?" Kali-Mho mutters, his gold-flecked eyes flashing, irritated.

"You're not going to believe this, Kali boy," Vaz beams with breathless excitement. "Just you listen, and thank me later," he says, thrusting the tablet into one of Kali-Mho's still outstretched hands.

He taps the replay pattern and listens to the recorded proposition. Like Muji-Aah, Kali-Mho's face morphs. This time from annoyance to astonishment.

"I told you didn't I!" Vaz exclaims. "This is going to make us rich I promise you," Vaz whoops before rolling his fists in front of his bulging belly like he is playing drums.

Kali-Mho can't quite hide his joy. There is a twinkle in his eyes as one corner of his mouth curls up into a half smile. He doesn't care about the money but he cares about the opportunity. What it means. He and his sister finally had a chance to gain recognition outside of the Kin-Kali ruling family, of which they had widely been regarded as rulers-in-waiting. But they didn't want to join the family business. They didn't want to be feared or falsely flattered simply because of their name, managing a sonic-energy mining and transport conglomerate with secretive and ruthless means while maintaining a benevolent facade to protect their positions of wealth and privilege. The Kin groups worked hard to distance themselves from the ultra-violent outlaws and pirates that kick-started commercial sonic-storm mining on Órino-Rin, but beneath it all, they were still essentially the same.

So, the twins chose music instead of family and politics. They became outcasts, openly pitied and derided for their aberrant gifts which some even called signs of spiritual or genetic corruption.

"We absolutely need to win tonight. We have to." He mutters, staring in disbelief at the tablet in his hands.

"Have you told Muji-Aah?" he asks, and Vaz nods eagerly.

"He was just as shocked as you are."

"Yes, I can't imagine how he must feel. This is what he's always dreamed of."

Kali-Mho's mind flits back to the night he and his sister first ran into a slightly drunk and belligerent Muji-Aah singing about searching the universe for his parents, in a spaceport club during Kin-Kali's Wambe-beh festival.

It was the month of the Midnight sun, with both suns, Juah-aju and Zuu-vah visible in the sky, so major Kin Groups were trying to outdo each other with parades, eating, drinking, and dancing in the customary festival-of-plenty. During this time, criminals were forgiven, and punishments slight, even if someone took their revelry too far. When the twins entered the bar, their presence had induced static in Muji-Aah's hair, causing his song to devolve into a high-pitched whine. He'd accused the Kin Kali heirs of messing up his wine-sozzled routine, exposing the twins to unwelcome attention from rival Kin Groups. They'd argued and almost come to blows but eventually came to an understanding instead. They could all influence each other's music and so they decided to play together. They formed the Ndi-N'suppuh.

Kali-Mho rises to his feet and hands back the granite sound tablet. "I'll go find him and tell my sister too. Do you have everything ready for tonight? Our stuff hasn't been seized by your creditors yet?"

Startled, Vaz waves his hand dismissively. "I wouldn't worry about them Kali-boy, you just focus on winning, and I'll pay them off before they know it, I assure you."

Vaz leaves with a smile that's a little less bright than the one he came in with.

Kali-Mho waits, taking a deep breath and then he pulls on his overtunic and goes to open the door.

He nearly bumps into Muji-Aah who'd just been about to tap the opening sequence on the door panel.

"Ah, there you are." Muji-Aah says, slightly startled, "have... have you heard the news?"

Kali-Mho nods, and looks searchingly at Muji-Aah, before bursting into a large smile that lights up his face. He can even see Muji-Aah's excitement in the bright purple soundscape of his heartbeat, and he remembers that no matter what else is between them, they make good music together.

"We should tell Kali-Yeh the good news," he says with a laugh.

3. Kali-Yeh

"Kali-yeh! Kali-yeh! Kali-yeh-yeh-yeh!"

"Kali-yeh! Kali-yeh! Kali-yeh-yeh-yeh!"

The chanting of the crowd grows louder as she walks on stage to the strains of her brother's drum and flute arrangement.

She quietly mutters the mandatory chant to mute the magic triggered by her words as she steps to the amplifying voice gourd that will blast her song across the Kalabash-shaped venue. She grabs the voice gourd and takes a deep breath. Then she starts singing but nothing comes out, only a barely audible croak.

What's happening? She wonders, as light fingers of dread start to trace tiny shivers down her back. She takes another deep breath and gathers herself to try again, but this time no sound comes from her open mouth, only the small head of a black nza'nzah emerges, its eyes flashing. The black bird utters an ear-shattering screech as it flies out of her astonished mouth. It is quickly followed by another, and another, until her head is surrounded by a cloud of whizzing, screeching nza'nzahs like an evil halo.

Kali-Yeh jerks awake.

Dry-mouthed, head and pillow drenched in sweat, she struggles to catch her breath and gather her bearings. Like someone who's just been in a fight, she feels a little punch-drunk as she sits up and tries to calm her heart with one hand across her chest.

It was the same horrible dream again.

Only it seems to be getting worse. And she could have sworn she recognised a few of the nza'nzahs because they had both bird and human faces in that maddening way which only makes sense in dreams.

She's not particularly religious but Kali-Yeh starts chanting praise to The Mother. It seems to help. Kali-Yeh hopes that the dreams are only her anxiety manifesting at the prospect of performing tonight and not an omen of evil.

Kali-Yeh wonders if she will eventually have to perform before her family if they win tonight. She isn't worried about safety since the championship tour is hosted by the Sauúti Federation Council who felt it only fitting that each juzu's winners should perform at the annual worlds-unifying Boãmmariri event. They would be granted diplomatic status and virtually untouchable, not even by the all-powerful Kin Groups of Órino-Rin. Still, it would be intensely uncomfortable, not only for her and Kali-Mho but for her parents.

Kali-yeh decides to call and speak to her mother, the only family on Órino-Rin with whom she's maintained contact since the N'suppuh ceremony where she and her brother were cast out of the Kin-Kali group by their own family.

"Hello Mother, good voice to you," greets Kali-Yeh when her mother responds. It takes a few seconds for the sounds to be transmitted between planets.

"I hear your good voice." Her mother replies warmly.

The call sound fills the air around Kali-Yeh's head calming her. *Like Muji-Aah's electromagic*, she thinks fondly. Her mother's voice has always had this effect on her.

"How is my beautiful one? Did you sleep well? What about your brother? I hope he is well and recovered from last night?"

"We're all fine M'maa. I just wanted to hear your voice, that is why I called. How is D'daa?" she asks, affectionately using her childhood way of addressing them.

"Ah, your father is still voiceless and sad, but glad to know you are both safe." Her mother reassures her a little too hurriedly. "Now tell me why you really called. Are you still having those nightmares, 'Yeh?"

"Yes M'maa, it is getting worse now and I have a feeling something big is about to happen. Are you sure D'daa is well? You know you can tell me the truth, I can handle it," pleads Kali-Yeh.

Her mother is silent for a beat, "I know there is no lying to you 'Yeh, your father is not handling this well, at all but the Uroh-ogi are looking after him and I'm sure he'll be fine. He misses you and 'Mho terribly, as do I," her voice is subdued.

Her mother has known since they were children how futile it was to lie to Kali-Yeh, given the twins' abilities. Kali-Yeh could emote, and project sounds as feelings. She was also a multi-lingual, high-level empath which basically meant she couldn't be lied to, in any language. When she sang, she could amplify and project raw emotional states to those listening. Her brother, on the other hand, could see and manipulate sounds. He was highly attuned to music and could judge with precision where each beat, note or bar would fit in any composition. Being able to see and grasp each individual sound element enabled Kali-Mho to create and remix music with incredible intuitive dexterity and it was his favourite way of expressing himself artistically. It also made him obsessed with controlling the music whenever they played.

"I'm so sorry, Mother. I wish we didn't have these abilities," Kali-Yeh lamented. "Then perhaps we wouldn't be so drawn to music, perhaps we could be happy staying as part of the family and D'daa..." She trailed off.

"No 'Yeh, these gifts are special. They are from The Mother, and if they have taken you down this path, then follow and trust The Mother to guide you."

"Thank you M'maa."

"Besides, it's not always bad," her Mother laughs, "I remember the Kin-Magor funeral, where your song reduced the Kin-Teteh assassins to tears for their victim!"

Kali-Yeh smiles at the memory and says, "Didn't one of them confess the following week?"

"Yes!" Her mother howled.

"And what of 'Mho, I still remember when he made a bunch of engineers almost abort the launch of a tanker! He made the engine sound like a hundred babies crying. That was so much fun." She laughs.

"Yes, it was," her mother agrees. "And we can have those fun times again 'Yeh. Your father and I are working on ways to lift the n'suppuh order on you and your brother, but it might mean some compromises from you both," she adds hesitantly.

"What sort of compromises?" Kali-Yeh asks, a queasy feeling in the pit of her stomach.

"It's not that bad really. Kin-Teteh and Kin-Magor have both expressed an interest in an alliance with us, and with their combined influence and ours, I don't see how we can't bring you both back home where you belong once you are done with your performances tonight, at least you have enjoyed the talents The Mother gave you a little bit."

It is as Kali-yeh feared. A marriage-of-convenience into another Kin Group. The likely suitors were none other than the bad-tempered Teteh-Ntah, or cruel Magor-Rho, both of whom had teased her and her brother mercilessly as kids. What about 'Mho? And what about their music? Would they never play again?

No, it was too much.

But she only says, "Hmm. We'll think about it, M'maa," not wanting to make it any harder on her long-suffering parents. But she had no intention of returning and neither would Kali-Mho, she was sure. They had to win this contest. Kali-Yeh was keenly aware of just how fortunate they were because people born with certain 'extra' abilities were often victimised.

Fortunately for them, they did not display any signs of unusual ability at birth. Theirs had been a smooth birthing attended only by the wizened Uroh-ogi and her acolytes, instead of the usual throng of priestesses, well-wishers and other royal sycophants, who would invariably claim to have witnessed the birth of such and such from one ruling family or another. It wasn't until late infancy that subtle signs began to emerge, giving hint to their powers. By then, of course, they had been through their Afanafa name-claiming ceremonies and become bonafide heirs of the Kin-Kali.

There is a sound of sharp tapping at the door that makes her feel a jolt of induced excitement. Muji-Aah. And her brother. She could sense their joy already.

"M'maa, I have to go now. I need to rehearse for tonight. Please give D'daa our love and pray for us to win." Kali-Yeh says hurriedly.

"Alright my beautiful one," says her mother, "may The Mother speak blessings on you and your brother, and we will talk again soon."

She ends the connection.

"Come in!" yells Kali-Yeh, and the door opens to let in Muji-Aah and Kali-Mho.

"Have you spoken to Vaz?" they ask almost simultaneously.

"No and no, why?" she looks at them with a puzzled expression. Muji-Aah looks away when their eyes meet.

They tell her about the sponsorship contract Vaz obtained and her eyes go wide with amazement.

"But if we don't win, we get nothing?"

"Yes." Muji-Aah and Kali-Mho say.

She can see that they are looking at her expectantly, like puppies waiting to be rewarded. She thinks of the dream nza'nzah's circling her head and the sleazy faces of Teteh-Ntah and Magor-Rho waiting for her.

No. Focus on the positive. On hope.

If Vaz could get this sponsorship, it is a sign. We will win.

Finally, she smiles. "If that's the case, then we'd better get started with rehearsals, what are we waiting for?" They all laugh and leave, headed to the Kalabash arena. She doesn't tell them about her dreams, or the feeling of foreboding that keeps gnawing at her.

4. Vaz-Irie and The Seeker

Vaz Irie is nervous.

Not an unfamiliar state for him, but one that is becoming far too frequent now, more than at any other time in his chequered life. Vaz has just recently turned forty-seven juzu old, and although he likes to describe himself as a thirty-something serial entrepreneur, the truth is that he has failed far more times than he can recall.

But this time will be different because I have luck on my side, he thinks, remembering the night he'd decided to stop for a drink at a Kin-Kali bar during the Wam-beh festival. The night he'd run into Muji-Aah with his amazing abilities seeking opportunities to "find himself" or something like that, and insulting a pair of musically-gifted Kin-Kali outcasts when the liquor loosened his tongue a bit too much. Uncle Vaz had been right there, just in time to smooth things over, connect the right dots - that it was some kind of sonic interference - and convince them to try playing something together instead of killing each other.

He'd had a feeling that their abilities, although individually amazing, could become truly much more if put together, resonating with each other. And so, here he was, on the eve of the finale, with the three gifted youngsters ready to bring something special to the contest.

He can already see the Owo credits rolling in, if... no, *when* they win. The sound tablet is braced between his sweaty hands and Vaz is still smirking when he bumps into a large figure blocking the corridor to his quarters.

"Excuse me," he mutters, startled, "I didn't see..."

Large hands grab his tunic and haul him close to the grey-tinged and skull-like face of a Mai'karbar, a debt collector.

"Where is it?" growls the Mai'karbar, his sharp teeth uncomfortably close to Vaz's left eye.

Vaz was born and bred on Ekwukwe. He used to be an acolyte monk but his motivation for money and his willingness to try almost anything within the outermost, elastic (in his mind at least) boundaries of the law, had landed him in trouble he couldn't wiggle out of. Something to do with selling sound-powered erotic clothing he'd created with some unscrupulous Zéhemgwile tailors, that became very popular thanks to an automated mutual-attraction trigger which caused the fabric to vibrate in a most erotic manner. It had worked too well, and a couple of flash orgies in which a few people had reportedly died of ecstatic over-stimulation, eventually got him kicked out of the prestigious Ekukwe Mahadum of Theology.

Still, he remembers enough of his studies to know he is in serious trouble now. Mai'Karbar were rare and this one was no doubt sent by the Ama'Ahiyaa, a section of the notorious cabal that run Kalabash

City's underworld. He'd been taught that collectors like the Mai'Karbar don't usually say much, they only leave a trail of wounded and broken bodies in their wake. He remembers being told by shocked Maadiregi that Mai'Karbars enjoy their work and sometimes kill purely for pleasure, an abomination to The Mother.

"A little time," Vaz squeaks desperately. "Don't you see, I just need a little more time and your bosses will get all their credits back with interest, I promise you." Vaz pleads.

Four Bes ago, he'd borrowed fast credits from the Ama'Ahiyaa to buy a new control console for Muji-Aah and to invest in the Kalasho company so he could persuade them to sponsor Ndi-N'suppuh if they won, credits that were due in three bes. He knew he was taking a big risk, but his optimism and belief had convinced him to do it.

Besides, for all its high spiritual reputation Ekwukwe's underground economy was rife with credit lenders and collectors, illicit gamblers and swindlers, he was sure the Ama'Ahiyaa would have other bigger defaulters to come after before they got to him.

The Mai'karbar's lips draw thin and Vaz begins to consider his options:

One - try to break free and run? (Vaz is neither strong nor athletic even though he was taught the fundamentals of combat as a child, as all children on Ekwukwe are); or two - Use his echo, his natural magic to temporarily disable the brute (Vaz has never actually used his echo before). His mind is still spinning when the Mai'Karbar lowers his hands and starts backing away.

What?

Vaz can't believe his luck.

Perhaps the monster has decided I am worth more alive.

Vaz is about to thank the fast-retreating beast for his unexpected reasonableness when he hears the unmistakably soft rustle of a Seeker's tunic.

Ah! So that's why the Mai'Karbar beat a hasty retreat.

He turned to face the Seeker.

"My friend, you arrived just in time to save that filth from my fury." Vaz declares, clearly relieved to still be alive.

"I'm glad you didn't have to hurt anyone," says the Seeker, in a soft and emotionless voice, returning the magic beads in his hand to a leather pouch around his neck.

Seekers are relentless hunters of knowledge, particularly of the old ways, of the ancient language, Sauúti. Vaz catches a flash of withered, twisted flesh on the Seeker's briefly exposed arm.

Vaz had studied the highly secretive cult during his time as an acolyte at the Mahadum and encountered only a few of their members. They usually kept to themselves, and one could never really tell if they were male, female, both, neither, or something else entirely underneath their all-weather full-length tunics.

"To what do I owe this pleasure?" Vaz asks.

"I'm just here to make sure you don't have any problems. The Grand Seeker is interested in your group of youngsters and asked me to see that everything goes smoothly, for them," the Seeker gives a condescending sweep of the hand in the direction of the departed Mai'Karbar, "and for you."

Vaz is stunned into silence.

Why would the Grand Seeker be interested in Muji-Aah and the twins, even if they became the Kalabash champions? Surely the Seekers had better things to do?

As though sensing his confusion, the Seeker says, "Do not question, only seek to understand."

Vaz nods. Those words came from the book of prophecies which he had studied as an acolyte and had become a mantra for the Seekers. He knew he wouldn't get any further response.

"Umm, in that case, thank you."

"Thank the Mother. And make sure everything goes well at their performance. The Grand Seeker wishes it so."

Vaz suddenly remembers the rehearsal. He jerks into motion heading towards the arena, all thought of going to his quarters forgotten, as he gestures for the Seeker to come along just in case the Mai'Karbar is lurking, or they need any further divine intervention.

5. Ndi-N'suppuh

The bandmates are huddled together by the new master console on stage five at the north side of the massive, pentagonal Kalabash Arena. Muji-Aah is preparing it for their rehearsal. They are on one of five stages positioned at each vertex, of the arena, with a slightly larger centre stage at its heart.

The Kalabash Arena is built atop one of the many naturally-occurring complex cave systems that enable each individual attendee to hear the performance as though it were being played just for them, no matter where they are located in the venue.

Muji-Aah works frenetically, fine-tuning the settings he has configured and rigged up for their performance on the new console from Vaz.

"Ok, we're ready for the first check," Muji-Aah announces as his dreadlocks make their pre-set connections with the master console.

"Alright. Let's do it," Kali-Mho says, taking out his shekere-re from its pouch. The small gourd-like instrument, covered with its network of tiny string beads, rattles softly as he gently taps it against his chest. "But no surprises please, Muji-Aah, let's just play as we planned and make sure it works."

He is staring at the shapes that start to unfold before his eyes alone.

"Sure thing, big boss." Muji-Aah mocks as he catches a look of warning from Kali-yeh.

"Please," she mouths silently.

Muji-Aah nods.

Kali-Mho waves his hand, and the rattle transforms into sweeping string music in response to his gesture.

Muji-Aah's locks tremble, there is a pulse of current through his hair and then Kali-Mho's music starts playing through the speakers.

Kali-yeh starts to hum the tune of her song in time to the music.

Muji-Aah can feel the excitement in the melody. *It's working. Everything is working.*

He senses that if he can amplify the sensation with the experiment he has been working on, it will be even more spectacular. Muji-Aah wills one of his locks to engage the Anwu-Light Imagizer control and there is a flare of bright vermillion light that resolves into a sphere above the band.

Kali-Mho and Kali-yeh look up in amazement just as the entire master console fizzes out, overloaded. The arena goes deathly quiet.

"Shiii'ooorrrrrh!!" Muji-Aah curses. "Vaz promised a new console but clearly this is just another pile of junk!"

"It seemed fine to me until you decided to play another one of your tricks with it." Kali-Mho says.

"Tricks? Do you call synaesthesia of light and sound a trick? You of all people should appreciate what I am trying to achieve."

Kali-Mho shakes his head. "You're great with the technical stuff but it's when you try to get creative that things fall apart. Why don't you just leave that to me and my sister? Focus on making our music sound even better."

"Right," Muji-Aah fumes, "You want an assistant, not a bandmate. I make music just like you do. Maybe even better. And I am trying to express myself."

"With this?" Kali-Mho gestures to the lifeless console.

Muji-Aah rises, "I should have known that night in the bar. I'm trying to do something spectacular so we can win this thing and all you do is make silly comments."

"Calm down, Muji, I know you are upset and afraid but surely Vaz can find us a replacement," Kali-Yeh says. Muji-Aah knows she can sense the near panic underneath his rant, the slightest tremor in his voice and the sound of his heartbeat is all she needs.

"Sure, that's easy for you to say, Kali princess," he shoots back, irritated that she is using their connection, "some of us are not used to having someone else solve our problems."

"Hai!" Kali-Mho shouts, "we're all in this boat together, no need for that kind of talk, 'Yeh was just trying to keep it together. You need to watch your tongue cargo boy!"

Incensed, Muji-Aah turns to Kali-Mho, "Oh, look at you big bros, running to rescue your sister's from the big bad off-worlder," he mocks. "Let me tell you, I learnt more in a single bés working cargo bays than you two did in all your juzu of fancy education paid for with blood money." Muji-Aah regrets it as soon as the words leave his mouth but there is no taking them back.

Kali-Mho lunges and almost lands a fist on Muji-Aah's jaw, but Kali-Yeh pulls him away at the last moment.

"Stop it, please! Both of you," she screams at them. "Do you want this night to end before it has even begun? We need this. We can't let every adversity turn into a fight."

"We may need this, but we don't need him. Keep him away from me, I don't want anything to do with him after tonight," Kali-Mho glowers, still measuring the distance required to land a solid punch.

"That goes for me too!" Muji-Aah retorts, still visibly shaken by the near altercation. "It's not like we are going to win this thing with your shitty music arrangements anyway."

"You don't mean that," Kali-Yeh gasps.

Muji-Aah is still trembling. "I do."

Kali-Yeh looks away, her eyes wet with tears. "Fine. If that's how you feel, then let's just fix this console and get through tonight."

Muji-Aah nods and turns just in time to see Vaz appear followed by a thin, tunicked figure.

"Is that a Seeker?" Kali-Yeh whispers, turning to her brother.

"Hey, hey, hey, why is everyone so long in the face?" Vaz asks, a strained smile pasted on his face.

"We... we need another master console because the one you got us is a worthless piece of trash," Muji-Aah responds, inside, he feels a storm of disappointment and defiance.

If it's going to be our last performance together and we don't care, then I'm just going to do my thing. Whatever happens, happens.

"Can you get us one that isn't useless?"

"Is that all?" Vaz asks, annoyingly cheerful.

Sullen silence from the bandmates.

"Fine, we will figure something out," he says, casting a glance at the silent Seeker.

"Let me see what I can do," the Seeker says and silently glides away.

"Who is that?" asks Kali-Yeh.

"Ah, err... well, that is our Seeker guardian."

"Guardian?" Muji-Aah asks. "Is this another one of your schemes Vaz?"

"No." Vaz says. "They are just interested in your performance and offered to help, so let them help."

"He gives me the chills," Kali-Yeh shivers, "There is something hidden with him I just can't make out."

Vaz shrugs. "It is the nature of their Order to be secretive."

People are beginning to file into the Arena, and individuals and small groups are scattered around the floor between stages.

It will be at full capacity tonight.

Muji-Aah knows it won't matter much if they win or lose, He can't play with the twins anymore, not like this.

The huge Arena sound casters crackle to life with Kalasho Company music playing softly, as the venue fills up.

Muji-Aah spies the Seeker returning with two heavily muscled loaders wheeling a replacement master console. It gleams silver in the bright lighting. The Arena introductory music is getting louder.

Muji-Aah directs the loaders, telling them where to place the new master console and to take away the old one. It is clearly a more powerful unit designed to cope with larger venues. And it looks brand new so, even though there is no more time to test it, he begins to configure it.

Muji-Aah snorts.

Whatever happens, happens.

6. Kpakpandoh

The introductory tone stops.

Vaz watches excitedly as the lead announcer starts with the customary initial preamble and greetings to the crowd for coming to the show, then hands over to the high-priest from the Mahadum of Theology who says the opening prayers to the Mother and utters the words of binding that will limit the effect of any magic triggered by the sounds produced during tonight's performances.

> *Khwa'ra. It is acquired.*
> *Ya'yn. It is uttered.*
> *Ra'kwa. It is released.*

The Kalabashing contest originated as a religious ceremony performed by high priests and magicians on the hollow planet. They used the cave systems and their natural hollows to amplify and disperse sonic spells, with amazing effect, across vast distances and terrain. It was even said that it could be used to communicate with other worlds. The Kalabash plant which the contest is named for grows on Wiimb-ó, Ekwukwe and Órino-Rin, it is also found on Zezépfeni and is routinely exported to Pinaa. It is a versatile creeping plant all parts of which can be put to various uses, e.g.: the leaves and fruit can be prepared and eaten; the vines can be woven into tough ropes; but the gourd-like fruit is the real treasure because once harvested and dried, it's tough outer husk or shell can be fashioned into anything from ornaments to utensils or musical instruments.

It was this similarity in shape and versatility that gave rise to the eponymous freestyle kalabashing contest.

The High Priest's binding ritual concludes.

The Announcer's voice returns like thunder over the arena, "Kalabash Kway-nuu!" and the crowd responds with "Yaaah!" Again, the Announcer calls, "Ekwukwe Kway-nuu!" and again the crowd responds, "Yaaah!!"

"Are you ready to hear something marvellous? Are your ears open, clean, and eager for sounds so sublime? Let me introduce the performers, your five finalists!"

Vaz sees the Mai'Karbar in the distance, standing below another stage and he says a quick prayer to the Mother, a prayer he thought long forgotten but which comes readily to his mind now. Beside him, the Seeker doesn't react.

"First performers tonight, on stage one, our very own monks from the Mahadum of Theology, please welcome *Mothers Milk!*" The crowd erupts with applause for the home team of celestial-voiced singers.

Vaz prays harder.

"Second, from Zezépfeni, we have the *D'wiijiri Wind!*" The announcer exults.

Vaz has seen them perform incredible vocal acrobatics seemingly without pausing for breath.

"Third, we have the *Technuzu* from Pinaa!"

Vaz watches curiously as Muji-Aah's eyes focus on the enhanced bio-mechanical band on stage number three from the reclusive moon world of Pinaa. One of them appears to be a full automaton.

"On stage number four, we present the *Ipitimboh* of Wiimb-ó!" The crowd goes wild. They are clearly the favourite, which Vaz knows is due to their variety and unpredictability of content, which of course is the whole point of freestyle kalabashing.

"And finally, from Órino-Rin, we have *Ndi-N'suppuh* on stage five!"

Vaz closes his eyes and continues to pray as the first four bands play. He feels himself being pulled in by their music, but he refuses to flow, to let go. He holds on until he hears the name of the Ndi-N'Suppuh repeated.

Vaz opens his eyes to see that purple light has bathed the entire arena.

The crowd is chanting Kali-Yeh's name over and over.

Just as they had at the end of the previous night's performance. They remember. Vaz knows that is good.

Vaz sees Kali-Mho initiate the set with a tapping of his shekere're that first sounds like rattling, then like wind chimes, and then a full orchestra as he makes sweeping flourishes with his bare hands, manipulating the sounds. Vaz hasn't heard this before, not exactly.

Is Kali-Mho... improvising?

When the music dips, the crowd claps loudly.

Then Kali-Yeh steps forward and begins to sing, a sonorous ballad that seems to be coming from deep within her. She taps her feet and dances to the tune of her brother's music as she sings, and the bangles around her ankles make their own music. The audience starts to sing along and Vaz feels his lips move too. He can feel the warmth of the emotional wave emanating from her, from the music, reflecting and refracting the adulation of the crowd in every note. There is none of her usual holding back, she seems free. Freer than she has ever sounded.

As Kali-Yeh continues to sing, Muji-Aah's hair begins to tune in on the console, taking the sound produced by the twins and giving it volume, adding layers and depth to it so that Vaz doesn't just hear it, he feels it in his bones, just as he did the first time he'd heard them play together at the spaceport bar. The air is saturated with sublime music. Vaz sees Muji-Aah's hair rigidify as it seemingly of its own will connects the console to a device he hasn't seen them use before.

What is that?

Visualisations appear in the air above the crowd, bright sharp arcs of light flashing and drawing themselves out. The look of shock on Kali-Mho's face tells Vaz all he needs to know. *It is the same vision that Kali-Mho is seeing and manipulating, but now entirely visible to everyone in the arena!*

Vaz can no longer contain himself and neither can the crowd. He starts to clap his hands. The audience is now completely hysterical. Even the competing bands join in this unabashed show of appreciation.

All three members of the band look surprised at each other's improvisation, but they don't stop. They keep on playing. The thunderous applause, whistles and voices chanting "Sauúti, Sa-uu-tii, Saa-uuu-tiii...", almost start to drown out the music in the Kalabash arena. Vaz is confused when he sees Kali-Mho's projected visualisation begin to pulse in time to the crowds chant.

Kali-Mho picks the visual strands of the crowd's chanting with his fingers and starts to weave them into what looks like a horn, or cornucopia, growing up and out as the crowd chanting increases in volume fuelling its growth. The visualisation extends out of the cavernous arena and into the atmosphere. It just keeps rising and rising, getting louder and louder, and just when it seems like it'll never stop...

Silence.

Complete and utter silence descends on the arena. The crowd is still completely lost in their animated dancing and suddenly soundless chanting. The visualisation continues to sway and dance into the atmosphere. Vaz catches Kali-Mho's incredulous look. He is as surprised as the audience.

As the eerie silence continues, a misty presence, black and cold as the depths of deep space, starts to emerge alongside the visualisation. Its shapeless form contains speckles of what can only be described as twinkling stars embedded in a sheer fabric of darkness. Vaz, open-mouthed, can see that even the emotionless Seeker is visibly shaken.

Can it be... a Kpakpandoh!?

The mythical creature said to have only existed in the time before the great flare.

Is this why the Grand Seeker was interested in them?

The apparition also starts to sway and dance to the same soundless rhythm as the visualisation, sometimes obscuring then revealing the image, as if trying to intertwine itself with it.

Vaz cannot tell how much time has passed; he is lost in the music that is more than music. His heart feels like it will beat out of his chest. Then, as suddenly as it emerged, the shape starts to dissipate and disappear in the same slow-but-fast manner. Time still doesn't make any sense. Sound returns in a loud explosive crescendo of a single word.

"SAUÚTI!"

That word, almost tangible, reverberates and echoes, slowly fading along with Muji-Aah and Kali-Mho's electromagic visualisation.

Then, finally there is silence. Real silence. The performance is over. And Vaz, like most of the audience, is in tears.

7. Family

"What was that?" Muji-Aah asks when they are back to Vaz's quarters.

Kali-Mho replies first, still visibly shaking. "Something special."

"Yes. Special." Muji-Aah echoes. He'd had no idea what was going to happen when he'd engaged the Anwu-Light Imagizer. In fact, he'd expected it to fail just like before, expected their abilities to interfere with one another and cause everything to come tumbling down but it hadn't. Instead, they had played, carefree, without worry, without overthinking anything, each of them thinking it would be their last time and they had... resonated.

Vaz sits and sinks into the bed, his round belly riding up his shirt and facing the ceiling like a beached fish. "It must have been the mythical Kpakpandoh, attracted by that wondrous performance," he says.

"We didn't even plan any of it." Kali-yeh says, looking at Muji-Aah. "We were just doing what felt right."

"What felt right," Muji-Aah repeats, and he can see their eyes brighten when the twins come to the same realisation he has. "We work better together when we are each doing what feels right for each of us."

Muji-Aah's new M'majiringo, or electromagic projection of Kali-Mho's improvised musical visualisation; and the deep emotional fuel of Kali-Yeh's singing, had all intertwined and interacted with each other to create something so unique and compelling that it attracted a mythical celestial being.

"A Kpakpandoh." Vaz repeats. "No wonder the Seekers had sent one of their own. They must have known it was possible. They will probably follow us everywhere now, perhaps to study or recreate what you just pulled off."

"Yes," Kali-Mho says. "We need to be careful about that."

There is a tapping at the door and Muji-Aah goes to get it. When he turns back and closes the door, he is cradling a miniature sonic stone tablet and there is a smile like Wiimb-6's crescent moon across his face.

"They just made the announcement. We won," he says.

"We won?" the twins ask in unison.

Vaz jumps up from the bed.

"We won!" They all cry out at the same time and run toward Muji-Aah. They crash together in a group hug. The smell of hair and sweat and perfume residue from performance powder collide in his senses and make Muji-Aah feel giddy with something that sounds like *wheeeooooiun!* inside him, something he hasn't felt since he left the loving parents who'd raised him on Wiimb-6.

It is a good feeling. A feeling like family.

They stay that way together, holding onto each other for a long time. Vaz is crying, perhaps from joy at finally having something go right or relief about being able to pay his creditors, Muji-Aah isn't sure.

"So does this mean you guys don't want to break up the band. That you want us to stay together?" Kali-Yeh asks and Muji can hear the yearning in her voice.

"Yes." Muji-Aah replies, a half second before Kali-Mho does. They exchange knowing smiles.

Vaz jerks up, wiping the tears from his face and regaining a jovial mood. "Ah. Who was talking about breaking up after the Vaz-a-wonder got you that special sponsorship deal, eh? Please! Better stop joking with my life like that. In fact, please record your acceptance of the contract right now!"

Muji-Aah laughs as he taps the recorder sequence on the stony surface of the tablet they received, whistles the input tone and says, "Muji-Aah, Kway-nuu," to signify his agreement to the terms and conditions of the sponsorship which he'd already heard earlier.

To the stars.

He hands Kali-Mho the sonic stone tablet who repeats the sequence to record his agreement and passes it on to Kali-Yeh to do likewise.

Kali-Yeh stares at the tablet in her hands, looks up to Muji-Aah and smiles at him. He feels his heart flutter when she says, "Kali-Yeh, Kway-nuu.".

She hands the device to back to Vaz who lets out a deep breath, places his hand on his chest and says with an exaggerated air, "Praise to The Mother. You children almost gave Uncle Vazie a heart attack twice in one night."

They laugh, the Ndi-N'suppuh. The outcasts. They laugh together. Like family. And they keep laughing as Vaz orders wine and they discuss the upcoming tour and performance at the 40th Boāmmariri, their elation and their hopes ringing into the night.

*I*n the previous story, we met the Kali twins, heirs to the Kin-Kali sonic energy mining and transportation conglomerate, and talented musicians. Now we go to their home planet, two hundred juzu after the events of "Kalabashing", where the Kali twins have become pseudo-mythological figures. Here we encounter a very different kind of story about music in the Sauútiverse.

A planet of high mountains and deep valleys, with thick atmosphere, that gets progressively thicker the deeper you descend, Órino-Rin is perhaps the most physically unique of the planets in the Sauútiverse.

The population mostly live on mountainous landmasses, and elevated areas since the thick, viscous atmosphere near the surface makes it hard to see, breathe, hear or move. This makes the planet vertically stratified

according to wealth as all the best living areas are at the highest points and the less desirable accommodations are below. The dense atmosphere also makes sound amplified and resonant, leading to unexpected new magics. There are vast natural geological formations that give rise to unexpected sounds so that it is said that the planet itself is always singing.

And then there are the sonic storms. Random blue plasma-like energy discharges (sometimes called magical lightning) in the atmosphere that make intense sounds and last for a long time. They also increase in frequency and intensity the closer you go to the planet's surface. They can have catastrophic impacts on any unprotected physical or biological structures and environment. Mining (capturing) the energy from these storms is a key revenue source for the planet as the raw energy can be exploited for use in magic and technology. Particularly interplanetary travel.

As alluded to in Kalabashing, commercial mining of sonic storms used to be practiced by pirates criminals which evolved into organized crime families referred to as kin groups. And by the time we get to the events of this story, those crime families have evolved into corporations, or Korps. Despite the new name, the power games stay the same and the desire for control of this valuable resource drives much of what happens on the mountains and valleys of Órino-Rin.

Enter Ruk, or Ruk'ugrukun kel Az'zagru, our deaf protagonist of this wonderful story by collective founding member **Xan van Rooyen.**

A citizen of Órino-Rin in 400 A1B, about 200 juzu after the events of the previous story, Ruk has a unique ability similar to that of the Kali twins combined, but perhaps more potent. Ruk is unable to hear sounds and lacks a perceptible sound aura or 'echo' of the Mothersound but can feel the sounds made by others, interpret the fundamental vibrations of the world, of people. And Ruk can even manipulate them, though this ability comes at a price, the price of pain. He is a runaway from his nomad tribe, working in the clubs of Órino-Rin as a kind of DJ, performing un-restricted, illicit music-magic until, as we find out in this story, he gets caught in the web of a Korp power play and is forced to make a difficult choice.

Lost in Echoes

XAN VAN ROOYEN

*Magurgurma: a lost Word from The Mother, a sonic tatter carried
by the cosmic wind, shaped by storm and whittled by planetary forces,
snagged by needle of earth and stone. A demigod born of a broken
whisper.*

—from "Threnody for a Mother-Fragment", a story of the Ts'jenene

Like blood in water, the music ribboned through the dense atmosphere of the sub-meridian club. Ruk'ugrukun *felt* it: a subtle
change in the texture of the air—a thicker current winnowing past his
out-stretched fingers, triggering the afferent sensors where he'd once
had nails. The nanotech heightened his natural sensitivity, as if his body
were a drum and the world a fist pounding on his skin.

Patrons danced, gyrations loosening flakes of sound from the sonic
auras encasing their bodies in invisible scales. No two auras felt alike:
this one a sting and judder beneath Ruk's skin, another an itch on
his shoulder or an ache between his toes. His own, little more than a
subdued murmur—a small mercy for those born Taq'qerara.

The frequencies pummeled his ribs, captured and channeled by the
biotech enhancing his nervous system. With his nanoware active and
his usual pain ameliorated, he could endure the tumult, sculpting songs
from the sonic dandruff patrons shook free. Like this, he could weave

subtle healing frequencies into the music already spilling through the speakers.

Ruk glanced down at the writhing crowd from his vantage point on the DJ dais. Nausea roiled through his gut, bitter gorge rising up his throat. Hadn't he run away to escape this? And yet here he stood, bathed in the implicit adoration of the club-goers high on the poly-rhythmic panacea of his devising.

Braced for the beat drop, he still winced when it happened—his masochism born of guilt and the need to atone. He'd failed his family, but here he did what he could to alleviate fear and angst and tribulation, to replace exhaustion with euphoria in those desperate to escape reality. A few hours gentle reprieve was better than none.

Ruk shuddered and curled his fingers, magic sizzling through his sinews. He was trying to do the right thing even if it might be too late to earn his people's forgiveness, to repair the trust he'd shattered when he'd broken the rules governing his power.

The club would be closing soon as one sun set and the other rose somewhere far above the mire of the city's lower levels. The patrons would have to emerge groggy and disorientated, disgorged from reverie but hopefully rejuvenated. Ruk surrendered to sensation as he embroidered the air with a final rising melody over the pounding bass.

The dancers contorted, limbs plucked by melismatic tendrils of power, faces seized in ecstasy. When it was over, the club-goers staggered, released by magic but still drunk on music: their auras more consonant, their souls soothed.

Perhaps if the club owners understood what made Ruk's sets so popular, they'd pay him more, but he was glad he earned enough owo to keep his head above the meridian murk, the threat of eviction as constant as the sonic storms battering the planet.

He deserved nothing more. And he certainly didn't want to draw attention from the Korps that ran the city. He already abused his power for his own gain, he didn't want to become a weapon in Korp hands.

Having reduced the efficacy of his implants, Ruk fled before the house lights incinerated the gloom. He headed down the narrow street leading to one of the numerous elevators. Mist tinged teal and vermilion by the sun-swap billowed in ropy coils, snaking around him like a hungry constrictor. Clouds tumescent with yet to be harvested sound-energy kept the cold trapped in the valleys cut between the planet's peaks. Ruk shivered in the frigid air as heavy footsteps thumped behind him—the sensation ratcheting through his bones.

The elevator doors opened and figures draped in white boubou emerged, their faces obscured by breathing apparatus and their auras resonating in the stagnant air, already shedding frequencies. On Órino-Rin, the very air chafed auras raw, leaving weeping gaps in the personal orchestration enveloping every human.

Korp members, Ruk surmised. Or maybe members of an upper echelonlowering themselves for the thrill of partying in the slums. But the clubs were closing now, the inhabitants of the underworld slinking back to their dens to recover from yet another night of sensory ravaging.

Ruk cast a suspicious glance over his shoulder. The figure behind him stood with feet planted, legs like boa'oba trees, and arms folded across a barrel chest, the hilt of their dagger on display at their hip. Their aura thrummed and unease curdled Ruk's insides. His hands balled into instinctual fists, muscles tensed and ready for flight or fight. He had nowhere to run, hemmed in by walls and flesh.

The white-clad person at the elevator gestured with a flick of gloved fingers, the movements stiff and awkward but at least discernible. With the breathing apparatus, there was no way for Ruk to interpret their expression, but the hand gestures were at least a passable attempt at Sign. Not the visual language used in the city, but the dialect exclusive to his people: the Ts'jenene.

Ruk shook his head, using his hands to tell them they had the wrong guy.

They spelled out Ruk's name, phoneme for phoneme: Ruk'ugrukun kel Az'zagru. And then, the sign he most despised, a swirl of wrist and flutter of fingers naming him Taq'qerara. They knew what he could do.

Come with us, they signed before their hand drifted to the weapon on their hip.

Ruk's shoulders slumped in defeat. Meekly, he allowed himself to be ushered into the elevator. He worked for whoever offered the better pay, trawling the clubs scattered across all eight extensions of the sprawling city, deliberately never loyal to any one Korp. For the sake of self-preservation, he kept everyone at a distance.

In the elevator, the one who'd signed pressed their wrist to the biometric panel, paying a sum that made Ruk giddy with disbelief. The doors closed and the elevator began to rise. They were packed in tight, shoulders brushing and vibrations clamoring—a sharp stone caught in his shoe rubbing away restless echoes that swirled and lingered in the confines. He resisted the urge to reach for the aural effluvia, to hook them with a careful finger, shaping them with Mother-given signs into magical melodies. Instead, he buried his hands in his pockets, jaw clenched at the waste.

As they rose up the extension, so the clouds thinned and the sky brightened, but Ruk's heart grew heavy with dread. When they switched elevators at the meridian station where the atmospheric density decreased, Ruk sucked in a dizzying breath, savoring the lighter air few could afford to live in. They were still a long way from the towers where the truly wealthy made their homes.

Once inside the next elevator, the white-clad group finally revealed their pristine faces. Each had the chrome of the Kor'ebibi Korp embedded in their left temples.

Ruk tasted blood as he choked on his fear.

Magurgurma, upon the mountain: impaled and impregnated by a bombastic storm. From the dissonant clash of forces—air and earth—

tumbled two daughters. Each carried within them a fragment of the Mother's word, a healing utterance, and yet they could not staunch the wound of the one who birthed them.

—from "Threnody for a Mother-Fragment", a story of the Ts'jenene

Ruk had seen Órino-Rin from above.

He'd grown up a nomad, in a home floating through the proximal zone between spires and storm clouds.

The planet was a sea of verticals, wave upon wave of needles all pointed at the sky where the suns courted each other in a fiery dance.

It was the larger star that Órino-Rin orbited and that now illuminated the morning with its superior glow.

Squinting against the glare, he remembered his childhood view of the planet where still uninhabited mountain peaks punctuated those capped with cities, all connected by rhizomatic highways. These the Ts'jenene traced for ease of their own aerial navigation, drifting in their tent-ships from one city to another in search of trade.

But Ruk had never set foot on one of the spires.

Now he stood at a floor-to-ceiling window east of central Moki-gu. The city spilled like an impaled pwezapwe—its eight tentacle extensions trailing down the mountainside, latched to the bedrock in defiance of the atmosphere.

Again, a tide of nausea rolled from his toes to his temples as he gazed down.

A disturbance in the atoms, a vacillating vibration of approaching feet—small, light, determined.

Ruk turned to face the newcomer, their aura already gnawing like broken teeth at his nerves.

Short, petite, spine straight, hair an ebony torrent, eyes twin black holes of jet and glimmer.

The vertigo will pass, the person signed with deft fingers. *I'm Iya Kor'ebibi.* She used a sign audaciously similar to the one reserved for The Mother, before shaping the phonemes of her kin name.

Ruk tried not to react to the almost-blasphemy. He was in the presence of the Kor'ebibi matriarch, one of the most powerful Korps on the planet. He, who was less than one of the scuttling memedede bugs infesting the squalid crannies of every extension. And, unlike the memedede bugs, Ruk was not all that hard to kill. He would not survive this woman's ire should he provoke it. He inclined his head in a polite gesture of greeting.

Iya Kor'ebibi glided toward the wall opposite the window where the light from the sun turned her sharp-cut suit a blinding white, lapels gleaming silver to match the kin patterns embroidered in shiny thread on cuffs and hems. Ruk squinted against the rays reflecting from elaborate display cases housing a variety of artifacts, a timeline of the five planets rendered in slivers and shards.

One statuette caught his attention, the figurine fully intact and meticulously carved from wood most likely sourced from Wiimb-ó. He recognized it as one of the legendary Kali-twins, Kali-Yeh perhaps, given the typically female anatomy. While Ruk knew the Órino-Rin-born twins had been living, breathing people capable of incredible feats of sound magic, he'd always questioned the part about their ability to tear through the veil of unreality. Hearing the legends as a child, he'd always wondered if the twins also carried splinter-sounds from Magurgurma, and if so, had their shards festered as his did?

Iya Kor'ebibi caught him studying the figurine, her gaze searing as she began to sign. *I'm a big fan of your work. Your abilities are almost as impressive as theirs.* She gestured to the Kali figure.

Ruk shook his head, palms sweaty as her aura continued to trill across his skin. *I'm honored. I didn't think you'd enjoy the extension clubbing scene.*

Cute. She brushed her chin with index and middle fingers, her mouth a thin slit of a smile. *I meant your* other *work. I keep my eyes on the maadiregi, in all extensions, especially my own.*

He'd never meant to reveal the power that had earned him venerated status with his tribe, but the tech required to soften the blow of sound even as it amplified internal sensation was expensive and could only be installed by a maadiregi, an engineer trained in the ways of both magic and technology.

Desperate, Ruk had sought out a maadiregi with questionable scruples and an even more malleable aura. And so he'd once-again broken the first tenet governing the use of the Taq'qerara's power. It had been easier to pretend he felt nothing when he didn't have to look his worshipers in the eyes. Even so, abusing his power had only amplified his guilt. He'd promised himself then it would be the last time he did it for selfish gain.

But he was weak, and the magic came too easy.

Iya Kor'ebibi regarded him with a raised eyebrow. She had delicate chrome laced across her forehead in a fractal topography reminiscent of the scars marking Ruk's own face, a cauterized geometry worn by the women of the Az'zagru tribe. At fifteen, when the tribal healer had cut and sung his breasts to thin lines of keloid, the patterns had been altered and *she* became *he*. If only the uroh-ogi could've also excised the Mother-sliver embedded in his soul; if only the healer could've sung away the power he didn't deserve.

Surprised by an unusual wave of homesickness, Ruk flexed his fingers. *I don't know*—but Iya Kor'ebibi grabbed his hand, tapping her thumb on the sensors in his fingertips before continuing to sign.

Don't lie to me. I know what you did. I know what you are. That sign again naming him Taq'qerara.

Ruk crossed his arms, as if he could hide his hands and his guilt.

Do what I ask and you'll never know poverty again. Iya Kor'ebibi's face turned granite and steel. *You'll never have to worry about rent or food. You'll be able to keep your head above the clouds and upgrade your sensors.* So she'd noticed his fingers capped in rusting tech. *All I ask is that you do for me what you did to the maadiregi.*

What you're asking me to do is illegal, he signed.

Her lips peeled back to reveal blunt but perfect teeth, incisors capped in silver to match her forehead. The laughter trickled over Ruk's skin like drizzle.

Didn't stop you before, her fingers moved deftly.

What you're asking me to do is... wrong. He knew it, felt it twist deep down in his organ meat as a familiar self-loathing simmered to the surface.

Now you care? she signed, as if she knew the rules he'd broken, the bonds he'd severed the moment he'd touched another's aura without their consent. And wasn't he still doing that near-nightly in the club, even if he was doing it for their benefit? If he truly wanted to make things right, he would forfeit his power altogether and never shape another soul-sound again.

But Ruk couldn't seem to help himself. Why give him this power only to stifle it? And yet, the wrongness of what he'd done—and continued to do—flogged his insides.

For several moments, Ruk floundered. When had deceit become routine? When had lies replaced his Mother tongue? He'd only wanted to escape his tribe and their constant demands, the pain he'd had to endure answering others' pleas, the disappointment he would've been when they discovered how he'd ground their trust and hope to ashes. But what if this was the answer to his own prayers—one final sound-shaping granting him so much owo he'd never be tempted to touch another person's aura?

Did he even have a choice?

If I refuse? he asked.

She tilted her head, long hair swaying, fingers dancing across her throat.

Instinctively, Ruk swallowed then sucked in a mouthful of rarefied air, hypocrisy fermenting in his gut as he nodded, his conscience already bleeding.

> *Magurgurma, bleeding out: a trail of echoes slip-sliding down cliff and soaking into valley; fractured echoes whipped away by fingers of blue lightning, flung across the sky to burrow through ears and settle in the bones of the Ts'jenene—wanderers of the firmament, captives of the echoes. An honor to be so soul-burdened; an honor to be born Taq'qerara.*
>
> —from "Threnody for a Mother-Fragment", a story of the Ts'jenene

The body lay inert, imprisoned by sound.

Ruk felt it before he saw it, a pattering against his ribs as if someone were playing his bones like the wooden slats of a mari'imba. The person lay supine, pillows cradling their shoulders and propping up their knees. They seemed at peace, face slack beneath the intricate tattoo spilling from their right temple to disappear beneath the arrow-cut neckline of their colorful dashiki. Blue, black, and red—like the web of ink decorating their skin.

Ruk could almost believe they were merely asleep instead of being held captive, except for the headphones clinging to their ears like the city itself clung to the mountain. Sound magic to render a body inert and disrupt the signal from the comm chip embedded in their wrist.

Taji'iba Kor'ochoyo, Iya Kor'ebibi signed out the phonemes. *Heir-apparent to the Kor'ochoyo korp. She's the one you need to—* The matriarch made a swirling motion with her hand as if stirring a pot.

Kor'ochoyo. One of the few families who stood between Kor'ebibi and dominion over all the other Órino-Rin Korps.

Why? Ruk asked, gaze flicking to Taji'iba.

War, so old-fashioned, Iya Kor'ebibi began. *But unavoidable, and I'd rather spare the city unnecessary bloodshed.*

The Korps were known for territorial disputes, but as long as the casualties remained below the cloud meridian, city officials rarely did much to contain the violence.

I've always preferred more subtle strategies. She continued. *The scalpel, not the hammer.* She smoothed down the baby hairs at her temples as she regarded Ruk with a measured gaze. *You will be my scalpel. Change Taji'iba, like you did the maadiregi.*

Ruk wiped the sweat from his hands before moving his fingers. *That was a small, temporary change.* He'd never made significant or lasting adjustments. Only minor tweaks to get him what he wanted without raising too much suspicion in his victim.

This must be permanent, Iya Kor'ebibi gave an emphatic twist of her wrist. *I need this to be slow. I need Kor'ochoyo to crumble from the inside and* she *will make that happen, thanks to you.*

I can only tweak what's already there. I can't alter the nature of a person. Ruk suppressed a shudder as he approached the bed. To permanently alter an aura—a soul—would sever their connection from Mother, perhaps even deny the person access to the afterlife.

Iya Kor'ebibi wore an affable expression, but her gaze was calculating. *You do it every night in the clubs.*

What he did with the music, picking up dropped fragments and recombining them into entirely new soundscapes—that was different. He did it to help the patrons, to minimize anguish, to heal sore hearts, and return those who'd lost the beat to a steady rhythm. A paltry attempt at making up for all the times he'd abused his power.

Ruk shook his head as he touched the fingers of his right hand to his forehead and pulled them away again. The pattering of Taji'iba's aura became knuckles knocking at his bones, while Iya Kor'ebibi's continued to grate at his flesh like a lover's teeth eager to devour, a disorientating mix of pain and pleasure.

Iya Kor'ebibi stamped her foot to get his attention, the vibration tickling the soles of his feet.

Unlike Taji here, she pointed at the body on the bed. *I wasn't born into power. I've fought for every scrap and clawed my way to the top.* Her gaze drifted to the windows. *You might not believe that I was once like you, some city ...* she hesitated before using the sign for rat, for vermin *... drowning below the meridian, but I believed in my ability to bend the world to my will.* There was a threat in her gestures. Ruk would bend to her will or be broken. *Now it's your turn to seize this opportunity.*

An acid effervescence scorched his insides as Iya Kor'ebibi sashayed closer. She smelled faintly of thiouraye, a traditional mix of wood shavings and spices common among the Ts'jenene yet so highly prized among the city-dwellers.

On this world, you don't get what you deserve, she signed, every gesture slow and deliberate. *You get what you take, so... take it.* She snapped her fingers into a fist before jerking her chin at the unconscious body.

Her words looped through Ruk's mind, a ligation of dark intent and even darker understanding. He squeezed his eyes shut, breathing deep against the battering of the women's auras.

He opened his eyes, decided.

One more time, and then never again. He stamped the last shreds of his conscience into the guilt-ridden mire of his past knowing he could never be forgiven for what he was about to do.

You can't be here for this.

She raised a questioning brow.

Your aura is... distracting. He wouldn't let it be the blunt-force trauma he'd inflicted on the maadiregi. *And it might be dangerous for you to be so close when—*he hesitated before swirling his fingers, trying hard not to grimace at the gesture.

Fine. I'll leave you two, but we'll be watching. Iya Kor'ebibi pointed to an orb recessed in the ceiling, a single eye ensuring he did as commanded.

Ruk perched gingerly on the edge of the bed and raised his hands. Braced for the onslaught of sensation, he increased the sensitivity of the sensors and let himself explore the sonorous landscape of Taji'iba Kor'ochoyo.

> *Magurgurma, decayed and tacet: waiting for the Taq'qerara, for the one Mother-touched and born of silence, who might hold the echoes, reshape the sound, and one bés wake Magurgurma who will sing the Word and make Mother whole again.*

- from "Threnody for a Mother-Fragment", a story of the Ts'jenene

Ruk sank into an ocean of vibration.

A thrill in his marrow and winnows of electricity swimming through his blood—he exhaled, smoothing the staggered thudding in his chest into an aching hemiola as he and Taji'iba became entrained to the primal beat all children of The Mother carried within. Even as the Taq'qerara, as hollow as a gutted kalabash, Ruk felt the throb that was the heart of the universe, of The Mother.

Taji'iba was a stew of oscillation and Ruk rode those wave-forms, sliding up every peak and delving into every trough, her aura so like the jagged landscape of Órino-Rin.

Echoes upon echoes, filling up his hollows.

Ruk relinquished the last of his control and his senses flared, finger-tip sensors channeling his natural ability.

He luxuriated in her sound, marinating in the ebb and flow of her soul as he traced the stitches of her symphonic tapestry, analyzing themes and composing the variations that would leave her changed. Her aura was layered in melodies looping lazy serpentines through harmony both consonant and dissonant. Moments of darkness balanced with light, a harshness gentled with gliding harmonics—for every punch, a caress—a morass of profound complexity. How dare he think to muddy such an exquisite rendition of Mothersound.

He couldn't do it. He wouldn't, even if it meant being tossed from a city balustrade and shattered against the cliff, feeding the scavengers before being eroded to dust by the planet's heavy air, to be swallowed by the spreading silence drenching the valleys, subsumed into absence. He didn't expect he'd be granted entry to Eh'wauizo and allowed to walk among the spirits of his ancestors.

He deserved to rot and decay, to vanish, forgotten and unmourned.

Ruk withdrew, delicately untangling himself from Taji'iba's aura. He signed so those watching would see, *Not yet, I still need time,* before angling his back to the eye above and slipping the headphones from Taji's ears.

Taji'iba blinked open dark eyes. Her gaze flicked across the room before settling on Ruk, mouth pressed into a tight line as her body tensed.

"You're not Kor'ebibi," she said and Ruk read the shapes of her lips.

He shook his head, wondering how to explain if she didn't know Sign.

"I've seen you in the clubs. Extension Six. I've..." she added something Ruk didn't catch.

Kor'ebibi hired me, he signed the phonemes refusing to use the gesture so close for Mother to name the matriarch. *She wanted me to change you so you'd sabotage your Korp.* He added the stirring motion of his hand, hoping Taji would understand.

Her expression darkened, lines knitting across her forehead in a scowl as she tapped her wrist where the comm chip shimmered beneath her skin.

I didn't. I couldn't, Ruk signed, careful to keep his gestures hidden from those who were watching.

Taji raised a subtle finger to the ceiling and whispered, "They'll kill you."

I deserve it. I am not a good person.

"Are any of us?" Taji asked. "But even the worst people can still do good things. So how about..."

A change in air pressure, the retort of heavy steps, hands on his shoulders, and the pleasurable resonance of Iya Kor'ebibi's aura. Ruk groaned, his sensors still heightening all aural sensation. He turned them down, tension draining from his shoulders as the ache of aura-exposure was attenuated.

Is it done? she asked, glaring at Taji'iba.

Ruk hesitated, casting a surreptitious glance at Taji who had managed to smooth her expression into one of docile compliance.

I tried. We'll only know with time.

The accompanying Korp members hauled Taji from the bed as Iya Kor'ebibi perched beside Ruk. Her hands had only just begun to shape her words when blood splattered her face and peppered her white suit crimson.

Ruk watched the stains spread, breath caught in his throat, heart seized in a fist of fear. Sticky heat dribbled down his own face where he too had been spattered.

Bodies slumped, flesh hitting hard floor with a thud Ruk felt in his jaw. Finally, he turned, following Iya Kor'ebibi's gaze to Taji. She stood over the corpses, a dripping Ọbẹ in her hand, no doubt slipped from one of her captors who'd assumed she'd be compliant. She pointed the blade at Iya Kor'ebibi, speaking words Ruk couldn't parse though each felt like gashes in his skin.

"You won't get out of this building alive," Iya Kor'ebibi said, signing simultaneously for Ruk's benefit. "Neither of you. My people are watching." She raised a finger. "You're both already dead."

"So are you." Taji advanced, her intention clear.

The blade glinted in the rays from Juah-āju slicing across the floorboards. Ruk braced for a scream, for pleading and tears, but Iya Kor'ebibi canted her head, revealing the vulnerable flesh of her throat.

"Before I go, tell me why," she spoke out loud and with her hands, her question directed at Ruk. "You could've had everything."

Ruk studied his fingers, trying to understand why he'd failed to do what had been so easy so many times before.

It would've been wrong. It wasn't what my power was intended for. I want to do good. I want to do better. How he wished he'd taken a different route home, that he could fold back time and return to the life he'd known before. Perhaps he never should've left the Ts'jenene and instead admitted his failings, endured their wrath and disappointment.

"You have so much power," Iya Kor'ebibi said. "What a waste."

Taji slit the woman's throat with the Kor'ebibi blade and eased her onto the bed as her last breath bubbled red across her lips.

Ruk felt himself screaming, the scrape and shear of ragged breath in his throat, the formless syllable catching at his teeth as it spewed from his tongue. The scent of fresh iron filled his nose along with the sharp tang of excrement as the matriarch's body surrendered to death.

Battling involuntary tears with eyes burning as if they'd been scrubbed with black pepper, Ruk reached for Iya Kor'ebibi's hand. Her aura was quietening now, the sensation dulled to the patter of an echo.

He wasn't familiar with their customs, he didn't know what rites the Kor'ebibi family might grant their recently deceased or how they might call to the spirits of Eh'wauizo to come and claim one of their own.

"You weep for her?" Taji wiped blood from the knife before stowing it in a stolen sheath on her hip. "Her Korp has hurt people all over this city," Taji continued. "Without her, the Kor'ebibi Korp will fall. Things will be better."

With Kor'ochoyo in power? His fingers trembled.

Taji'iba regarded him, gaze intense. "You could've done as she asked and ensured my family failed."

I didn't want to use my power, not for this. Ruk staggered away from the bed.

"We all makes choices." Taji's tone was indiscernible with his sensors dialed down, her expression inscrutable.

I've been trying to help people.

"Me too. I killed a tyrant. The people of Moki-gu will thank me. Well, some might not." She grinned at that and folded her arms.

I never wanted any of this.

Taq'qerara. Sound-shaper.

To be Taq'qerara was to be a walking wound assaulted by sound, with scabs scraped raw by every murmur.

He studied Iya Kor'ebibi, her throat a second mouth peeled open in wet ribbons, watched as Taji'iba picked drying blood from her fingers as if they were no more than specks of dirt. His own skin itched with magic and shame, guilt and a gnawing sense of duty.

He was meant to search, to give and give and never want more than gratitude in return, until the bés when he fulfilled the prophecy and returned the syllables dropped and scattered from Mother's tongue. It had never been enough. He'd always wanted more, thought he *deserved* more, and resented being denied the opportunity to use his power as he saw fit. He wasn't worthy to bear the mantle The Mother had bestowed upon him.

Ruk flinched when Taji's hand touched his shoulder.

"As long as you have power," she said. "There will always be those who want it for themselves, or to exploit it."

You included? He flicked his fingers, hoping she could sense his animosity.

She shrugged. "I can see many ways we could use you. For good, as you claim to want."

He bristled at that but had no time to respond. Her lips were still moving.

"Power will always be a double-edged sword." She traced the tattoo on her face with her thumb. "We're all fallible, despite our good intentions." Her gaze dropped to the corpse of her rival. "Not matter how hard we try, we all fail. And having good intentions doesn't exonerate us from that failure, and you—"

Ruk looked away, not wanting to read the words on her lips.

Instead, he slid to the floor between puddles of gore. A rush of footsteps, shouts reaching him like blows to the shins. Kor'ochoyo forces summoned by Taji'iba come to the rescue, and now Korp members were no doubt slaughtering each other just beyond the closed doors.

You don't get what you deserve, Iya Kor'ebibi's words echoed in his skull. *You get what you take.*

Take, take, take. All he'd ever done because he'd been asked to give.

When he'd first been named Taq'qerara and placed upon a skewering pedestal, his people had come to him in supplication, their adoration like sonic caresses soothing his aching flesh. *You must search, must find, release, heal, you must fulfill the prophecy.* Their adulation became like nails, leaving him bloodied and suffocating beneath the weight of their expectation.

Perhaps he could indeed use his power one last time.

He would remake himself. He would un-become what he'd never wanted to be—a scar to finally seal the hurt, numbing his senses to the world.

The Mother had made a mistake before and Ruk had had to correct his anatomy.

It had been another mistake to make him Taq'qerara. But no more.

As the sound of fighting escalated, assaulting every nerve, Ruk used the pain to sink deep within himself. There, the sliver that had invaded him. A splinter sloughed from Magurgurma and blown like a feathered seed to lodge within him: Mother's orphaned utterance.

The lost syllables became a sonic storm within the confines of his flesh as violent and tumultuous as those lambasting the planet. His body convulsed—a symphony of cataclysmic sensation, and yet, the agony helped him to focus.

Take it, take it, take it.

His mind met with the slicing heat of the echo. He took hold, wrenching the fragment from where it vibrated in agitation in the thicket of his soul. Perhaps it would be enough, he thought, as he plucked and unraveled, tearing the parasitic sound loose from its improper host.

Take it—and let it go.

He relaxed, every strained sinew releasing tension as he loosened his grip on the sound fragment. It slid and slithered through his insides, a trail of raw iron in its wake as it clawed up his throat and across his tongue, cracking teeth in its desperate need for liberation.

Ruk opened his mouth in a scream he couldn't hear and felt the echo of terror from others in close proximity.

Glass shattered and the tower lurched. Ruk opened his eyes when strong hands wrenched him to his feet.

"Go now if you want to live." Taji'iba yelled into his face even as the floor tipped beneath their feet. He saw her lips move, but felt nothing. Not even the faintest ghost tickle though she continued to scream orders at the various Korp members scrambling for purchase while the tower swayed.

Ruk wanted to live.

He gathered his limbs and ran.

The music pulsed through the dense atmosphere of the club. Ruk felt it in the coils of his guts, an extraneous thumping behind his ribs and buzz in his back teeth. He raised his arms in mimetic movement of those around him, scarred fingers capped in gel tips painted black.

He danced, every gyration no doubt loosening flakes of sound from the sonic auras of the dancers, but he heard nothing, his body buoyed by pleasant tides of throbbing bass.

He glanced up at the DJ weaving music and magic through the sweat-soaked air, watching as they raised their arm in anticipation of the beat drop.

He still braced for pain, still flinched whenever someone opened their mouth, but he was no longer assaulted by the sounds he couldn't hear, his soul a gentle ripple in the sea of silence in which he floated. When the DJ's fist dropped, a flood of cooling relief soused Ruk's veins.

He'd managed to escape, and here he stood—ignored and unknown —one more murk-dweller spending precious owo on a sensory soothing in a club now owned by the Kor'ochoyo Korp, the walls daubed blue, black, and red.

Kor'ebibi was no more. Iya Kor'ebibi had been crushed in the rubble of her own tower, destroyed by a sophisticated magic attack some sources speculated. Others suspected the Kor'ochoyo Korp had deployed a high-tech energy weapon to bring down their enemies in a terrifying display of ruthless power.

Only Ruk and Taji'iba knew the truth.

He checked the time. The transport would be leaving soon, his seat secured courtesy of the Kor'ochoyo Korp.

Wreathed in blissfully numb silence, Ruk rode the elevators up and out of the extension, disembarking at a mid-tier station where an assortment of ships awaited myriad cargo. And there, the one marked in Korp colors that would take him to the flotilla of Ts'jenene crafts drifting above the city.

Home, he thought. Home to face his people, their ire and whatever reparations they deemed necessary, though he wouldn't be returning an utter failure. Ruk strode toward the waiting transport, hesitating when the now familiar quake juddered up through his feet, a constant quiver across the skin of the planet as Órino-Rin cracked its spine, mountains shivering.

Ruk smiled before finding his seat. Magurgurma had been stirred to waking.

In most of the stories so far, Zezépfeni has been cast in an unflattering light – first in their ambitions to empire with Mahwé, and later in their neocolonial aspirations. Their attempts to control knowledge and narrative even while they claim to be equals with the other member-planets (and moon) of the post-independence Sauúti Federation. So, is Zezépfeni the overarching antagonist of the larger Sauúti story?

No.

As a collective, one of the things we agreed on is that every group in the Sauútiverse is the hero of their own story, they see themselves as aspiring to something noble.

To understand them better, it's important to consider their position. Zezépfeni is the only circumbinary planet in the system, and is farthest from the stars at the center of the system.

The planet orbits the center of mass of the two suns, moving very quickly, with a non-elliptical orbit and large axial tilt that causes rapid changes in seasons. It is also impacted a lot by the outer asteroid belt, due to its proximity. This causes frequent meteor strikes. All this makes it a difficult world, and the last to be settled by the original Sauúti civilization that originated on Wiimb-ó. It had to be fortified by technology and magic for it to be habitable. Their distance and the pre-existing planetary protections meant that the people of Zezépfeni were the least affected by the massive solar flare that destroyed much of the five worlds. This gave them a head-start on recovery as they had less to rebuild from and more access to information that was not completely lost. Because of this, the people of Zezépfeni initially perceived themselves to be the direct descendants of the original race and better at sound magic than all others even though this was not historically accurate. And even after they realize the truth, they cling onto that image of themselves as the protective older sibling, because they need to believe that to justify what they have done.

Another thing we agreed on was that while there were no overt antag-
onists, we did want to have a larger, hidden threat to the entire Saúúti
system, an ominous presence that leaks into some of the stories in hard to
identify ways, until it is made real.

That is where Zezépfeni's scheming brings us to the Nga'phandileh. Being the closest to the outer boundary of the system, Zezépfeni are the first to
discover a secret about the nature of the Saúútiverse. That Nga'phandileh,
powerful beings of unreality that exist in a parallel dark dimension, want
to enter their space and claim it. And just like the people of Zezépfeni, the
Nga'phandileh too are motivated by more than mindless desperation for
power. Even the monsters seek a kind of justice as you will come to see.

So, the leaders of Zezépfeni take it upon themselves to keep this a ongoing war a secret and maintain the reality border, constantly seeking new
knowledge, new powers to help them hold the Nga'phandileh at bay.

Now, in this fast-paced, epic story also set in 400 juzu A1B by founding collective member **Akintoba Kalejaye**, which sets up a lot of what is
to come from this world, we dig into the details of this border. We meet

the people that control it, the warriors that protect it and of course, the creatures of unreality themselves that threaten it.

This is Hologhiri.

Hologhiri

"Understanding is not the same as comprehension,
But they do not reject each other,
The old and new are fundamentally different,
But they do not disdain each other,
To find the future, the old must correspond to the new,
To gain true knowledge we must follow paths of both
understanding and comprehension,
Find the word and find the voice,
Find knowledge and observe the future."
—The Arcadeum Pluralis

1. The Failing Wall

The sky raged pink and green on Zezépfeni.

In the hall of a large stone temple, its walls pulsing with energy, twelve figures wearing dark red robes sat in a silent conclave. Wires and circuits jutted out if their bodies like vines. Their robes pulsed with the same energy that ran through the walls. They spoke to one another, not with their voices but through thought. The subject of their discussion could not be uttered, secrecy could not be broken.

Their facial expressions changed rapidly, the only evidence of their communication. From shock to anger. From indignation to frustration. And then, collectively, resignation.

Finally, one of the figures waved a hand, and suddenly, they were in the middle of a dark sphere, the spectrum of color leeched away. Not even faintest trace of color remained within the space. There was only light and dark. The space hummed.

The motion of the figure's hand coincided with movement of lips. "They are breaking through," the figure said. "The Hogiri Hileh Halah is failing."

Another figure responded, "We have lost eight Jurors in the last hundred juzu and that trend is accelerating."

The first figure waved a hand once again and suddenly, the now-monochrome stone hall disappeared, revealing a broken landscape of barren rock, and burning purple skies. The glowing symbols of the sphere pulsed.

The figure's eyes began to emit both blue and red fire. "What was lost will be found. No matter the cost, we will man the Hogiri."

2. Ignorance

There are many places and spaces which exist in the bubble of reality. Some places are different as light and dark, and others are both as similar and different as shades of the same color. But similarity does not connote consonance.

Far away from where the dark figures sat, in another turbulent place, reality itself was being put to the test.

Dark holes littered the sky, piercing heavy, multicolored clouds.

Creatures of pure shadow advanced in uncountable number upon one being of pure light. The dark beings screamed and bellowed a mélange of horrifying sounds as they attacked from every side.

The lone being was bored.

With small movements, each one a tiny arc of light, the being obliterated the assailants in their number as though it was a chore. Black blood was spilled, blood that evaporated as soon as it left their bodies.

The creatures continued to attack mindlessly as they disappeared in their millions for every action taken by the being of light.

Staff Sergeant Baryoh Rinu observed this battle but did not understand it. He saw in both slow motion and at an impossible speed. He observed from close-up, almost intimate, as each individual creature's existence was erased, and from far away as swathes of the dark creatures disappeared with a single stroke. Nothing the creatures did mattered; their rage was futile. The light-being turned its face from the battle, holding the creatures at bay with a single hand.

Baryoh felt everything too. The mass of rage from those whom the light had abandoned, and the boredom of the light-being, a white noise devoid of emotions. Baryoh became overwhelmed and his mental state swirled into a cocktail of things he could not process.

He screamed.

And then...

The sound of a horn blaring.

Baryoh woke up.

The same dream every fourth night. Dark creatures battling a bored divine being, losing over and over again. It had been many juzu, and yet, always the same dream.

Baryoh stared at the ceiling of his room, awake. He was drenched with sweat. He didn't need to look at the clock to know the time. He'd joined the military when he was just sixteen juzu old, an orphan without any living relatives. He'd worked his way up, every promotion earned with sweat and blood. Mostly his, also the blood of comrades lost to the conflicts of those who knew only greed and nothing of sacrifice.

Baryoh sighed as he rose and went to the bathroom. Another mission was at hand. As the leader of the 87th Battalion of Wiimb-ó's West Nilean Army, he considered the men and women of his unit his family. They'd been together for almost twelve juzu and he treasured their lives above any accolades of military success.

SERGEANT BARYOH FINU

He showered and dressed up quickly, pulling on his brown body armor with the insignia of a hyena blazoned on it. He stood tall; muscles still firm. Most officers his age had retreated from active combat, preferring to send others to fight.

But Baryoh wasn't most officers and he'd refused a promotion to command twice. He despised their politics. His eyes had seen death, had glimpsed the gates of Eh'wauizo, and he wasn't afraid to look again.

He stepped out of his quarters and walked to the command center, the glare of the twin suns in his eyes.

Baryoh and the other fifty-five soldiers of the 87th battalion were standing outside a tall grey and green building, waiting for their orders.

He stood facing them, observing the expressions of excitement, trepidation, disinterest. They were going to battle again. An important mission, they'd been told.

The door behind him opened, releasing a blast of cool air.

"They are ready for you," an officer with plump cheeks said and indicated to be followed. Baryoh signaled to his second-in-command, the only older and more experienced man in the unit, Corporal Dhisuh, who nodded back. They both made to follow the officer, but Dhisuh was stopped. "Command expects only you...Sergeant," the officer said, smiling.

Dhisuh frowned but Baryoh nodded at him, "Its fine. Return. Tell the unit to get their gear from the armory."

Baryoh walked into the building alone.

They were on a military transport vessel, thick green forest sweeping by beneath.

"Boss, why all the secrecy from command?" Dhisuh asked.

Baryoh did not change his expression even though he'd been uncomfortable since he was called in. "No need to worry, we just need to provide support to an ally, nothing we haven't done before. Let's just focus on getting it done and bringing them home," Baryoh gestured towards the other chatting soldiers.

The Corporal tapped his bronze badge and nodded. "Understood boss."

The vessel began to descend into the carpet of green below. When it came to a halt, the soldiers exited and settled into formation, neatly lined up like a well-oiled machine.

A thin woman wearing a uniform with a bright gold Lakean army badge approached them in short, casual strides. It was General Baa'cha, the woman who had forcefully taken control of the neighboring country of Lakea, just north of the isolated continent of Suraral. She was surrounded by heavily armed military guards. Baryoh squinted as corporal Dhisuh muttered, "are we really here to help this despot?"

Baryoh grunted.

Please be quiet Dhisuh. You'll get yourself killed.

The General stopped ahead of them and smiled shiftily as she welcomed and thanked them before inviting Baryoh and Dhisuh to her mission command tent for a briefing. The sinking feeling in Baryoh's stomach deepened. He'd been told by his superiors to help the General in whatever way she needed.

When the briefing was done, Baryoh realized that his superiors had loaned them out as mercenaries to help the General quell a rebellion.

"You expect us to do what?" Dhisuh blurted out, unable to contain himself.

Baryoh gave him a glare and Dhisuh went quiet. Baryoh knew they were stuck between their orders and the blood-thirsty madwoman.

Best not to anger her now.

"Excuse the outburst, General," he said, "mission briefing received. We'll surround the rebels and secure surrender. When do we start?"

General Baa'cha smiled, revealing sharp white teeth. "Immediately, once you receive the location."

Baa'cha signaled to her right, and an officer with thickly muscled shoulders handed a stone table to Dhisuh who touched it to play the sonic map embedded in its grooves.

A look of shock evolved on his face as he heard it. "You want us to sweep the Xiffarh Utuwah zone?"

Baryoh's eyes went wide. The Xiffarh Utuwah zone, which meant the zone of death in the native language of the region was a remote forest in the North of Lakea. It was called the zone of death because many explorers had perished there, even the Zezépfenians had largely left it alone during their occupation of Wiimb-ó hundreds of juzu ago. The only inhabitants were the native Hipamo people, a reclusive tribe of nomadic herders that kept to themselves.

Baryoh could tell Dhisuh was fuming.

Why would Lakea need us to quell a rebellion in an unarmed, remote province? Something strange is going on.

Baryoh put his hand to his lips before Dhisuh could let out another outburst, then he turned to the general, "we are ready."

General Baa'cha's sharp smile cut wider. "Good boy. You know what to do, follow orders and you will go far."

Baryoh clenched his fists.

"We will provide mission support to you from the top of the hill," General Baa'cha said. "To ensure no dissidents escape."

Baryoh unclenched his fist and saluted, trying not to let the General see the turmoil behind his eyes.

We are in Dwa'ndenki shit now.

They walked quickly back to the battalion.

Baryoh took up position in front of them.

He spoke quietly but firmly. "I ask you all to follow me, as you always have. I will get you home safe, but you must know this is no longer a normal mission."

When the chorus of murmurs died down, he smiled faintly and continued. "I don't know what is going on either but let's be careful. Our mission now is to survive and get out of here."

The soldiers saluted Baryoh. He saluted them back, a true salute with no pretense behind it.

Hours later, they were cowered behind their vehicles as a hail of sonic disruptor blasts whizzed by. Everything that could go wrong for them, had.

Baryoh returned fire, corporal Dhisuh bleeding by his side. The bodies of his soldiers lay around, empty of life.

They'd arrived at the mission location and found a group of the nomadic Hipamo tented for the night in makeshift buildings. Old men, children, women, and young men carrying sticks, praying to The Mother. When they'd calmed the people down and informed them that they were not enemies, they'd contacted the General who told them to kill everyone they encountered. Baryoh refused, but the General only laughed and responded, "You're not as smart as I thought you were, boy. Your superiors already told me this would happen, but it doesn't matter, your presence there is enough. I have what I need." That was when fire began to rain from the sky, the General's Maadiregi using their sonic magic to flood them with flame. They barely had time to take cover under their vehicles. There was heat, death, and then the sonic disruptor fire started.

There were fifty-six of them defending forty unarmed Hipamo while facing an attacking army of over a thousand.

Baryoh grit his teeth. His gut feeling was right. They had been betrayed by the West Nilean Military command, offered as scapegoats to be blamed for the Hipamo massacre so they could help the General and get rid of him in one fell swoop. He knew command saw him as a threat because of how much the other soldiers looked up to him, but this was evil.

Well, he thought, *they will find out why they call us the Battlefield Hyenas.*

They had started the hostilities, but he and his men would finish it.

Because never let go of any meat in our teeth.

They gave as good as they got.

Exchanging one life for more than a dozen of the enemy. For every soldier of the 87th Battalion he saw fall, Baryoh felt pain, as if he was the one dying over and over again.

After an extended period of fire and the loss of more than forty members of the 87th, Baryoh was weary, the survivors were wounded, exhausted, and running out of ammunition.

I promised to return them to their families.

I've broken that promise.

All his previous strategies, his victories, his sense of loyalty and honor had led them to this: a dead-end. Death by betrayal.

Corporal Dhisuh fired a burst of sonic disruption and coughed out pieces of blood and lung tissue. His puff of white curly hair was dyed red with blood. His eyes rolled back in his head, and he grabbed at Baryoh's leg.

Baryoh looked down and screamed, "Dhisuh, you are not allowed to die! That's an order. I will follow you to Eh'wauizo and punch you in the gut if you do."

The Corporal smiled, leaking blood, and croaked out, "Yes boss. But you must leave with them," as he gestured towards the Hipamo innocents huddled in a corner behind an overturned vehicle.

He knew Dhisuh was right. He had to protect the innocent.

He barked at his remaining soldiers. "Grab the injured, we are retreating!"

And then he gestured to the remaining Hipamo people to follow. The forest was ablaze in an inferno of ash, dust, and acrid smoke. One of the Hipamo, a girl dressed differently from others looked at him and she said something in a language he didn't recognize while pointing into the deep forest.

The Xiffarh Utuwah zone. Sure why not.

"Go!" He shouted. "Follow her."

When he looked down to grab Dhisuh, the corporal's eyes were glazed over. There was no life in them.

Baryoh suppressed the urge to charge the murderous enemies.

May The Mother guide you into Eh'wauizo, my friend.

He ripped the bloody bronze badge from Dhisuh's chest and moved quickly, blasting fire to cover the retreat.

Baryoh looked up. It was dark, and saw there were three blood-red moons in the sky.

Where in The Mothers name did the two extra moons come from?

A tree exploded ahead of him and he refocused on retreating. The forest was a raging inferno as the Lakean army continued to fire. Reaching a clearing, Baryoh turned round and noticed that the rest of the Hipamo refused to go any further into with the strangely dressed girl.

Superstitious people.

He shouted but they didn't budge. They were afraid. But death was coming. Around them, seemed to be a creeping silence.

Fine.

Baryoh told the two least injured of his soldiers to take the Hipamo the long way around and out of the North Forest while the rest of them drew the Lakean Army fire in the direction of Xiffarh Utuwah, following the girl.

The soldiers protested but Baryoh insisted. When they began to move, he looked at his remaining soldiers with resignation.

"I failed you."

One of them, a woman named Isi who'd lost an eye in a battle with him many juzu ago, shouted, "Boss, the hyena does not cry when it is wounded, it takes the lion with it to a glorious death!"

The rest of the unit raised their weapons and Baryoh forced himself to smile.

Fighting to the end. This is my family. And we will make them pay for every life in blood.

They marched into the Xiffarh Utuwah zone, firing their weapons behind in loud, rapid bursts to ensure the enemy followed them and not the escaping group.

The Lakeans took the bait and responded in kind.

Baryoh was injured.

He'd been struck by a sonic disruptor blast to the side and thigh and was hobbling, carrying Isi on his shoulder. Another soldier limped behind him. He was out of ammunition. He didn't know if Isi was still breathing but refused to abandon her body in some forest her ancestors didn't know.

I'll bring you home.

The air was filled with a thick, rolling black fog. Baryoh didn't even notice when the perfect silence overtook him until he couldn't hear himself draw ragged breaths anymore.

And then the colors of the dwindling fauna began to fade.

What the...?

The Lakean attack had all but ceased. There was the occasional explosion of monochrome tree bark and soil as they hunted him down but the shots were wider, coming from much farther away.

They are afraid to enter.

Desperately tired and hovering on the edge of complete exhaustion, Baryoh continued. They were surrounded by fog, wrapped in silence.

The soldier beside him fell and didn't rise. Chest horrifyingly still. No longer breathing. The fog rolled like a liquid. Baryoh looked around. Only he was left standing. Baryoh let out a howl and stopped, setting Isi's body down against nearby rocks.

Rocks?

He noticed all the fauna were gone and there were no trees, grass, or sand. As far as he could see, there were only dark metallic rocks that pulsed purple with energy.

Baryoh winced in pain when he stood up.

The blast to his side had penetrated his body armor and his thigh throbbed. Blood was dripping steadily through his trousers.

I don't have long.

Everything seemed still, too still, frozen. He looked back and saw a mass of debris suspended in the air where a sonic blast had hit, as if something had completely frozen the moment in time.

I'm seeing things.

Trailing blood, he continued into the fog. When he rounded a corner, he suddenly burst onto a smooth platform overlooking a mono-lithic mountain-sized structure that was darker than the purest black.

What in the Mother's name is...

He collapsed to the ground. Blood pooled around him. His vision dimmed as he continued to crawl forward until he couldn't feel anything anymore. He stared at the alien structure.

How beautiful and quiet.

As his vision flickered, he saw the strangely dressed Hipamo Girl staring at him, smiling.

Darkness settled over his consciousness.

3. Awakening

The rocks absorbed Baryoh's blood.

A child dressed like one of the Hipamo, but not quite, materialized from liquid fog and walked up to the unconscious Baryoh with an excited smile, "Candidate 0173AQ for the Hulor Iwui located. Restarting the command protocols for the 27th sector."

The Child's face froze for a few seconds and then turned to a frown, "Error, Error, Error. Unable to connect to Vibrational dimensional Conveyance Portal for sector 27 echo spire. Exploring other Solutions. Connecting to the Corpus Asteroidium Origin base for pickup."

As the child uttered the last statement, the monolith started to vibrate. The fog began to recede into the structure, and the other rocks all around it rose into the air. They advanced toward the monolithic dark structure and fused with it. A massive shock wave of sound, vibrational energies, and light erupted as the monolith bellowed into operation, flashing with signs, and sounds. The child vaporized and was also absorbed into the structure which shrank and then merged with Baryoh's body, sinking into his chest.

Far away, in a place filled with rocks like those surrounding the monolith in the Xiffarh Utuwah, three robed figures walked together into a massive ship made of grey stone with an assortment of signs and sigils on its body.

One of them said, "The Command Quarters for the lost sector 27 is broadcasting on Wiimb-ó. The command quarters seem to have been activated. We have been sent to investigate."

The other two nodded in response, their faces obscured by pulsating metallic masks. They entered the massive stone slab as it erupted in a melodious vibration.

Symbols lit the air around the stone ship as it shimmered, hummed, and then disappeared.

> *"The fire burns,*
> *It burns without end,*
> *Illuminating the darkness,*
> *The darkness of wisdom,*
> *The light of ignorance,*
> *The fires of unknowing burn indiscriminately,*
> *What we know, and what we have discovered must remain*
> *in dark,*
> *While we willfully stoke the fires of innocence."*
> —The 36th sonic record of the Susu Nunyaa

4. Council

When confronted with that which defies their senses, their security, or their reality, people congregate and confer upon one another.

In Zezépfeni, where the sky was a perpetual pink and green, the Ramarire council sat in the conclave. Nine of the most powerful people on the planet, bearers of the most secret of secrets, of things known to only a few in all existence.

They sat to deliberate events on Wiimb-ó where a long-forgotten potency had awakened.

Robed, they sat around an ancient stone blazing with pulses of green energy. It thrummed softly. They were visibly riled up. The Energy Stone started to glow as the entire space around them lapsed into colorlessness once again.

One of them spoke. "It cannot be that the be the Hulor Iwui, the accord of rules, which fell a long time ago..."

Another interjected, "The Susu Nunyaa detected the energy signature of the command quarters for the 27th Sector on Wiimb-ó..."

Yet another robed figure jumped in. "But the command quarters will only respond to a descendant of the Hulor Iwui. Not just a child but a personification of the Iwui itself."

"Don't repeat what we all already know. What must be determined is whether or not Hulor Iwui has truly returned. What are the Pluralis saying?"

"Calm down," the previous replied, palms facing the ground. "We destroyed Hulor Iwui once, we can do it again."

The first jumped back in.

"Yes... the Hulor Iwui must not return."

The figure at the head of the conclave, who'd convened its meeting, asked, "So...what have we done?"

All others lapsed into silence.

The first bowed and addressed the head figure. "Horchichii, all-seeing prelate, we have sent the Jurors of the 13th, 16th, and 7th

boundary to retrieve whatever caused the energy distortion. But if it is truly the Iwui as we fear then..." he trailed off.

The Horchichii looked up at the sky, "We are the guardians of reality, we shall not allow any that threatens the order. That Command Quarters will obey or be buried along with that which awakened it."

The Ramarire went into a silence of agreement and understanding.

Horchichii waved his hand and faded away from the stone hall.

The others also rose and faded away as the turbulence in the skies continued to rage.

It had been decided.

5. Jurors

The wispy blue and white atmosphere of Wiimb-ó was surrounded by flaring spatial energies as lines and dots materialized around the planet and arranged themselves into arcane symbols. A slab-shaped dimensional ship of grey rock appeared, unfolding spacetime ahead of it. It was an Okor Horjuaaye, a secret Zezépfeni vessel that used one of the most closely guarded words of the Sauúti high language to unfurl spacetime and travel great distances in an instant without being detected.

The vessel thrummed.

In the Horjuaaye control room, a hologram teeming with graphs, symbols and images was being watched by the Jurors of 13, 16th, and 7th Hibodeh dispatched by the Ramarire to investigate the source of the anomaly on Wiimb-ó.

"The massive energy readings were emanating from the Northern continent. They've reduced. There is only a small leftover reading detectable." The ship's AI announced in a droning voice.

The jurors approached the hologram, their robes and armor illuminated in its light.

One of them, a tall, muscled man, spoke.

"So, Mm'hiri, are we sure this is not just a very powerful Maadiregi?"

Mm'hiri removed her mask. Her face was oval, skin dark and smooth, almost childlike but with impossibly wise eyes. She gestured towards the hologram. "No ordinary Maadiregi can cause these spatial distortions."

The third juror removed his mask and laughed, "If some stupid person has absorbed the command quarters, they will not be able to handle it. So let us wait and enjoy the show." He gestured at the array of screens showing energy streams all over the planet, converging on the northern sector of the Lakean Territory.

Mm'hiri looked at the screen and frowned. She knew what would happen next if she didn't act.

She closed her eyes and spoke a single word in the high language. The word unfolded visibly in front of her, a manifestation of fundamental particle vibrations. Her word evoked the energies invisible to the senses, emerging out of the empty, into the fabric of time and space. The vibrational energies circled her body and she disappeared from the ship just as the tall man ripped off his mask and shouted too late, "Mmhiirih, don't!"

Mmhiirih appeared in the darkness of space, her eyes blue as waves of energy flowed around her body like water. She clicked her tongue and gestured toward the planet.

Chronal lock.

The energy receded from her for a moment and then poured forward like an endless tide of blue and black lava.

The energy covered the entire planet and slowed its rotation until it lost color and came to a complete halt. Everything, the atoms, the people, animals, trees, and even the light completely stopped.

Mm'hiri looked at the chronally locked planet beneath her, clapped her hands and appeared back on the ship, her countenance changed. She was pale and wobbled as she tried to walk.

The tall man rushed towards her, his brown robes the color of fertile soil, swaying. He held her. "Why Mm'hiri? That could have killed you!" Mm'hiri held up a hand "No, Hajalar, it had to be done. if we did nothing, you know what will happen to that planet, those people, and Hoku'naeri will..."

"Yes. Me." The third juror, Hoku'naeri smirked, his eyes flared orange and red with fire. "You know I would not approve. I always do my duty, as should you. We are to keep our existence a secret as required by the Pluralis. You should have let the planet be destroyed. If it was truly what we think it is, another Juror, it would have survived anyway." The fires in his eyes died out. "Your actions were unnecessary, reckless." Hoku'naeri looked at her derisively, "the Hulor Mm'hiri have always been weak. Unwilling to do what is necessary. A house of water indeed."

Mm'hiri was about to respond when Hajalar cut in, agitated, "the energy readings have not stopped."

The Hoorjuaaye ship appeared above the Xiffarh uttuwah zone. Everything was white, grey, and black. All frozen. Even the smallest insect. An impact crater was visible in the forest, its center a roiling mass of black lightning and gas, immune to Mm'hiri's powerful sound magic. The Jurors were surprised but they did not show it.

"Let's investigate."

Symbols lit up around the Horjuaaye, as the cylindrical lights of a levitation beam lowered the trio softly to the surface to the middle of the impact crater. They saw a man in a tattered green and black military uniform, his head shaved clean, and his smooth dark skin covered with rapidly healing wounds.

Hoku'naeri was no longer smiling, "He is not affected by Mmhiri's magic even though she used the high language."

"It would seem so." Mmhiri responded matter-of-factly.

The man's soft breathing was interrupted by spasms and jerks, like he was dreaming.

"So are we carrying out the order?" Hajarlar queried.

"No, not here. If he is a fellow Juror we must follow procedure." Mm'hiri replied.

6. Mitotor

Baryoh was in a familiar dreamscape.

A singular being of light was disinterestedly holding ground against an endless mass of attacking dark creatures.

He felt the desperation of the creatures, fighting like their very existence was at stake.

He felt the disregard the light-being had for their desires, mowing them down in swathes.

But for the first time, he could hear and smell everything, like the dream had crystallized into reality. The light being was talking, sounds emerging from its stiff lips. Sounds that he couldn't understand entered his head like a lover's intimate whisper. The dreamscape began to glitch, like a bad recording. Lines appeared across his vision, tangible and solid. The vision of the light-being and the creatures disappeared but the lines remained, flickering. The whispers too. As Baryoh strained to listen to the words and touch the lines, he felt a tug on his wrists. He looked down and saw a child dressed in the traditional garb of the Hipamo. The child looked worried. It yelled at Baryoh but he couldn't hear what was said. Suddenly, the child stopped and gave Baryoh a determined look. Sparks of electricity shot out of the Child's body, traveling into Baryoh. Pain. And then finally he heard the child. "It is not time yet! Don't listen to her! The light will claim you if you do!"

"Dhishuh!" Baryoh yelled as he exploded back into consciousness. He was sweating and hyperventilating.

I'm alive?

He took a deep breath to calm himself and took in his surroundings.

He was in a dimly lit space, a cubical room with smooth stone walls. There was a small orb of light softly levitating in the upper middle section of the cube. The stone walls were too dark to be any stone he'd seen before, and they absorbed every ray of light. The orb continued to undulate gently mid-air.

Wherever this is, it can't be Lakea.

He suddenly felt heavy, burdened. There was something within his body that had not been there before. The feeling made him appraise his own body. He was still wearing his military gear, holes, tears and all. But no more wounds.

The weird feeling intensified when he saw deep scarification marks drawing out complex symbols on the skin of his arm, like traditional tribal markings. Raising his shirt and body armor, he saw that the marks ran from his heart to his left arm, covering half his chest. The marks seemed to dance and move as though they had a life of their own.

What in The Mother's name is happening?

Confused, he closed his eyes and saw the monolith from the Xiffarh Uttuwarh zone. But it no longer looked aged and worn, it was active and pulsing with light, gasses swirling around it. The monolith no longer looked strange to him, evoking intense feelings of intimacy.

I don't understand.

But it didn't matter. Strange markings. Visions. Whatever. It didn't matter. He had to get home. He could not let the bodies of his soldiers be abandoned in the Mother-forsaken forest, away from their ancestors.

He opened his eyes and his training kicked in.

Move. Collect information. Make a plan. Escape.

Baryoh stood up and went to touch the walls. They were cold and hard with no obvious door or exit point along them.

Suddenly, a cheerful child-like voice said, "Finally! you are awake!"

It was the voice of the child from his dream.

Apprehensive, Baryoh responded. "Who are you? Show yourself!"

"Relax Iwui, they must not know of my existence. I am on your side!" The cheer in the voice was gone.

Baryoh finally realized the voice was coming from inside his head. It said, "Yes. You can communicate with me mentally. Just be calm."

Summoning all his leadership resolve to hold back panic, Baryoh tested the voice.

Explain?

A child materialized in the stone chamber, the same child from the forest and his dreams. It was a girl, only about six or seven juzu old, with unnaturally black eyes and circuits running through her iris. Her hair was plaited tight to her scalp and she had an innocent smile plastered on her face. Then her voice in his head, "Don't worry, I am a personalized mental display, only you can see me. I have moved the command quarters inside you. They are here for it."

Who are you and who are they? He thought back.

The child knelt. "*I am Mitotor wah Milezii, the machine mind of the echo spire manning the 27ᵗʰ Sector of the Hogiri Hileh Halah, loyal, till my last circuit is destroyed, to the Hulor Iwui.*"

Baryoh's mind was spinning. The words made no sense. "*What are you talking about?*"

Mitotor Wah Milezii rose and chuckled. "In simple terms, I am an autonomous AI programmed to serve you. My soundcode is linked to you. I know you do not remember me, but, in time you will."

Baryoh pondered a moment.

What do you mean you moved the command quarters inside me? You mean the monolith?

"Yes, the 'monolith' is inside you."

How?

Mitotor grinned, "A combination of ancient magic and advanced technology that would take me a long time to explain to you."

So, you are an automaton? From Pinaa?

"Automaton? How? No, I don't have a real physical body. I am an autonomous artificial mind." Mitotor smacked her hands together in front of her like she was dusting them. "Unlike your captors. Who are very much real."

The three jurors stood in front of the transparent cubical structure and watched Baryoh. He could not see them.

Hoku'naeri laughed, "The fool has gone mad. He is talking to himself. I told you he could not handle the power of the command quarters!"

Harjalar remained silent, observing.

Mm'hiri focused on Baryoh with pity in her eyes. She only looked away when Hoku'naeri asked, "Shall we begin the Njuputar inquisition?"

"I know you won't understand all of what I am about to say, but please listen, it's important," Mitotor was agitated, waving her hands as she spoke quickly. "This room is inside a ship belonging to the Arcadeum Pluralis, a secret order of the Zezépfeni government. They pretend to share knowledge with the rest of the five worlds, but their true objective has always been to keep all others all in the light of ignorance while they reap the benefits of knowledge in the dark. They have set their sights on you because you now possess something that they are incapable of wielding. And, that which Zezépfeni cannot control, they destroy. You must be prepared for what is coming, master Iwui".

Baryoh shook his head. *Who is this Iwui? That's not my name.*

"You are the Iwui. The rules. Bound to defend the Hogiri Hileh Halah against the displaced ones."

Baryoh was confused. But also, beneath that confusion lay a nebulous certainty, like all that had transpired was meant to happen, like there was nothing truly strange about it all. He decided to treat it like another mission.

Without warning, the stone walls started to dissipate as if they were vapor.

Mitotor stopped abruptly and disappeared from his vision. "I have withdrawn back into your mind for now. They cannot know I am with you."

Baryoh steeled himself.

The Stone walls gone, Baryoh saw three figures seated on floating slabs in a brightly lit room of stone, metal, and clay. He could see translucent lines running through their bodies. One of them, a woman of intense beauty, cloaked in blue, drew his gaze and he could not pull his eyes away.

7. Counterbalance

On Zezépfeni, Dadebisi and Horchichii, two members of the Ramarire council sat in front of each other surrounded by creeping green and yellow flora. They drank hoguro, a brew made of tree sap, from smooth clay cups. The pink and green sky periodically surged with what looked like lightning. The two men seemed not to notice.

Dadebisi wore white trousers and a large thick tunic with gold accents that flowed down and draped over his arms. His orange eyes did not disguise his desire for power. He rolled the material of each tunic sleeve, bunching them up around his shoulders. "The Hulor Mm'hiri knows what must be done. And even if she fails, Hulor Hoku'naeri will surely not."

Horhichii, his face wrinkled and his clothes plain despite his position as the head of the Ramarire, didn't respond, he continued to drink in silence.

Finally, he said, "Did you know that over a hundred asteroids, big and small, hit the Rorta Kuuwa, our planetary shield between the first rise of Juah-āju and the setting of Zuúv'ah? Without the Rorta Kuuwa, many of us would die every juzu. Billions subject to the whims of the universe. And yet, we have not only survived. We have thrived." He barely moved his lips, but everything reverberated with his voice. "Shields. They are essential."

Dadebisi dropped his cup and averted his eyes.

"You, Dadebisi, have been the shepherd of the Arcadeum Pluralis, our shield against ignorance, for hundreds of juzu. In that time, I have not challenged your authority in that domain. You have grown and thrived along with your children, grandchildren, and great-grandchildren. But now..."

Dadebisi fell to his knees. "Horchiichii, I have it under control. I dispatched the best of my people, I assure you."

"Silence!" He thundered. "If indeed, it is the Iwui returned, can the whelps of the Pluralis do anything but flounder like chicks in the wind?"

A wave of power flowed from the Horchichii's body, seizing Dadebisi and lifting him above the ground. He groaned in pain.

The Horchichii continued "I am not ignorant of your desires, of your ambition. But know this, I opened the gate in front of you to be who you are. I can lock the gate behind you and open it for another."

The Horchichii folded his hands behind him and looked away from Dadebisi who was bleeding from his mouth, eyes, and ears.

"Reality is in order, chaos will not be entertained or allowed. There is so much more you do not know at play. Even you, conniving as you are, are but a mere aspect of my designs."

They were suddenly surrounded by images of chained gigantic creatures, titanic beings the sizes of cities, and ancient weeping statues.

Then, everything shattered, like glass.

The two men were back seated on their chairs, Dadebisi's eyes filled with terror. He was still bleeding and the cup of hoguro in his hands had spilled onto his white robes, staining them.

The Horchichii waved a hand Dadebisi's blood retracted into his body, wounds completely healed.

"I want you to send your pet. The one you snuck in from the R'ejimah Korps projects. Send the Hulor Mm'uoh, the accord of souls."

Dadebisi's eyes widened but he didn't express his surprise. He bowed. "As the Horchichii wills it."

The Horchichii smiled and continued to drink his hoguro.

> "When we ask, 'what is chaos?',
> Most would answer, evil.
> In the same manner, good will be ascribed to order,
> But, if chaos heralds change, which is constant,
> And order heralds stagnation, which is abhorred,
> Then ask yourself, what does The Mother think?
> Would The Mother prefer order or chaos?
> Ask yourself this.
> And then consider what The Mother would do if she did
> not like your answer."
> —47th record of the Susu Nunyaa

8. Chicks In the Wind

Baryoh blinked, adjusting to the light. The ceiling of the room was too high to be in a ship of any sort as Mitortor had said. The attention of the three figures in front of him didn't waver but he was most persistently drawn to the eyes of the woman. Her blue robes seemed to flow around her like a fountain.

And then, she spoke. "We will now commence the Njuputar Inquisition as is the requirement of dealing with potential Jurors reincarnate."

The two men nodded and grunted in response.

Her voice was pleasant, at least.

She continued, "in line with the Precepts of the Corpus Asteroidium, you are offered a chance to speak."

Baryoh kept silent. He didn't want to give them any clue of Mitortor's existence or that he wasn't as ignorant as they imagined.

"Understand that silence will be deemed as consent, your silence serves no end."

One man cut in. "Mmhiirih, you waste our collective time, the savage doesn't understand, he has nothing to say, let's kill him now."

"We must follow procedure, Hoku'naeri," the other man said.

"Harjarlar is right." The woman said. "If you understand, then speak who are..."

Baryoh cut in, "You are speaking a language I have never heard but I can understand you."

The three were taken aback.

Mm'hiri's demeanor morphed into one of curiosity.

"Do you understand this," Harjalar took in a deep breath and let out a single word in another language. "Ngbwuru"

Baryoh felt his feet sink into soil that suddenly appeared. Panicked, he shouted, "root, it means root."

"That's impossible." Mmhiri gasped.

Hoku'naeris eyes lit aflame. The air around him rippled with heat shimmer. He stood up; finger pointed. "He understands the high language. A soldier from the remote regions of Wiimb-ó with no education. I knew we should have let him perish on the planet without all this unnecessary process."

"You would let an entire planet die without verifying?" Mm'hiri said, rising to her feet too, her liquid aura now turbulent. "Hulor Hoku'naeri, I am in charge here. Remember your position. We are here to investigate, not destroy."

Baryoh stepped back, wary as Hoku'naeri flared vermilion. Things seemed to be getting out of hand.

"Mm'hiri, will you not regret this?"

Mm'hiri began to visibly tremble. She looked livid. "Hoku'naeri, do you dare?"

Harjalar stepped between them. "No. You will not engage a fellow brother of the Hogiri. Hoku'naeri, remand yourself to your quarters now."

Hoku'naeri sneered. "Cowards. Whatever. Just know that I will do what is needed, with or without you."

He spun and walked into a wall that opened to give him access.

Baryoh felt unsettled but slightly relieved.

So, they aren't even unified among themselves.

Baryoh watched as Mm'hiri's liquid aura settled. She sighed.

Baryoh took his chance, "Why have you kidnapped me? What do you want?"

Mm'hiri and Hajarlar looked at one another and then she asked him a question. "Have you seen the light that breaks the darkness?".

Intuitively Baryoh knew she was referring to his dream. The one he'd had for many juzu. But that felt too deeply personal to be right. He responded with another question, "What is the Hogiri Hileh Halah, and what is the 27th sector?".

The two shared another look.

"You awakened the spire. You instinctively understand the high language. It seems you are truly one of us. We will help you remember. But you must trust us." Mm'hiri said.

Baryoh shook his head.

"How can I trust you? You made everything on my planet stop, snatched me up like some sort of trash."

"That was our mercy. We saved you and your planet." Mmirrih said.

"Mercy?" Baryoh spat. "Mercy is only given from an aggressor, do not call me your brother."

Harjarlah stepped toward him, "we are bound by a duty that transcends blood ties. If you are who we think you are then we will take you where you belong. But first, you must understand. This is part of the inquisition process. Don't resist, I will transfer a part of my knowledge to you."

In Baryoh's mind, there was an urging to agree.

Mitotor?

Harjalar came close, his eyes the color of earth. Green and brown. Four globes of sand spontaneously manifested around him. An orb of swirling brown light shot out of Harjalar's head and entered Baryoh before he could dodge it.

Mitortor's voice, clear in his head. "Don't resist!"

Hajarlar flinched, as the orb settled in the crown of Baryoh's head. Baryoh saw streams of grey energy escape his pores, like those of Mm'hiri. He felt something crawling in his mind, like billions of ants struggling to find space in his mind.

Information, too much information.

His mind went blank as his eyes rolled back.

Everything went dark.

And then...

Baryoh saw himself in a perfectly blank space as images began to manifest themselves around him, like pictures, or memories. Suddenly, he heard Hajarlar's voice.

"When the universe was young, all life was in harmony. All beings shared a balance that has been lost to the ages. Understanding was available to any who sought it. Then they came. An endless stream of them. Things that defied knowledge, that mocked reality itself. Those aberrations to whom life and emotions are both a lamp in the darkness and a flame to be extinguished. We called them the Nga'phandileh. They hide in the cracks of creation. To keep them at bay, the old ones, the first Sauúti civilization who bequeathed the five worlds to us, shattered the outer planets and using magic lost to time, they used the debris to create a wall around us, the five planets of Sauúti, The Hogiri Hileh Halah."

The entire space trembled. The stars in the background started going out one by one as Baryoh tumbled through a flood of images. Hajalar's voice stuttered but continued.

"But after the great flare that killed off the ancients, this wall, the Hogiri Hileh Halah, was forgotten. Until it was discovered by the old Mahwé-Zezépfeni empire. By then, the darkness had begun to seep in. A secret order was formed, and they created the 27 Hibodeh, or sectors, of the Hogiri, manning each one with the strongest of our magic wielders and the best of our technology. They are tasked to defend the Hogiri and stop the Nga'phandileh at any cost. But, the Nga'phandileh have since overrun several sectors... sector 27, whose command quarters you now carry, was one of them. Your predecessor..."

The voice and the visions were suddenly cut off.

Baryoh felt an intense headache as he was yanked back into reality. The first thing Baryoh felt was an intense pain in his leg and the smell of burning flesh. Somehow, he was on the floor. Disoriented, he saw Harjalar snarl and scream at some enemy that was out of sight. He had been in enough ambushes to understand.

Attack. We are under attack.

Pain rolled over him. His leg was aflame. He scrambled to put it out, but Hajarlar screamed, "Do not touch that fire!"

Beside him, Mmiirih moved her hands, and a liquid blue sphere enclosed the fire on Baryoh's leg. The fire started to die out. Explosions rang out all around them.

Baryoh sat up and strained his eyes to adjust to the smoke.

The word *Juahrir* vibrated through the smoke, lighting up the environment, and a ball of rolling flame materialized and exploded right in front of Harjalar, dispersing his aura and propelling him into the air. Through the smoke, under the power of the word, Baryoh saw Hoku'naeri.

Baryoh had no weapons. Harjalar was unmoving on the ground and Mm'hiri, looked exhausted, with burns all over her clothes.

Mm'hiri moved and stood ahead of Bayoh and unconscious Harjalar, shielding them.

"Hoku'naeri, you would kill your fellow Jurors just to please the council?"

Hoku'naeri yawned, waving his hands dismissively in front of him. "Mm'hiri, save your breath, I have only one target, get out of the way or die with him."

Hoku'naeri looked directly at Baryoh. "I am Hulor Hoku'naeri of the 21st Hibodeh," he bowed in mockery, "Savage, you have no right to carry that command quarters in you. Give it to me and I may spare your planet. Or are you ready to die for something you don't even understand?"

Baryoh looked to the faltering Mm'hiri. She seemed too tired to fight.

He grabbed a rock from the ground.

"A friend once told me that the hyena does not cry when it is wounded, it takes the lion with it to a glorious death. Are you read to die?"

Hoku'naeri's smirked. "Fool. On the bés a monkey will die, all trees become slippery."

The nagging feeling at the back of Baryoh's mind intensified. All his senses screamed at him. All three jurors, including Harjalar who was just rising, jerked to attention and went still.

"How?" Mm'hiri cried out.

Even Hoku'naeri was baffled. "How did it get so close without us detecting it?"

That was when Baryoh heard it, the clear sound of a Shekere-ke, a beaded dry gourd, accompanied by a dissonance of voices. Pain, anger, despair, unfulfilled desire.

Another massive explosion, followed by the sound of metal grinding against stone. In a moment of abject terror, Baryoh recognized the sounds.

Those sounds come from my dreams

The multitude of dark creatures. Theirs was a cry of rage that despised life itself. A cry that was a hunger. A cry that wished to consume all consciousness.

9. Nga'phandileh

The walls of the room exploded inwards abruptly in a burst of stone and fire.

A stream of black, ash-like particles that seemed to move on their own entered, and debris, air, and light started to spill out.

Mm'hiri, shouted, "Ngbwuru," *root*, in the high language while pointing at Baryoh. Her aura wrapped around him and held him in place.

The others had done similar to anchor themselves.

Baryoh heard a cry coming from the maw of the tear in the ship. Beyond the walls were the flickering lights of distant stars and empty space. At the entrance, a creature flickered in and out of vision. It looked like it was both there and not there. A large moist eye stared directly into the ship, opening and closing. Baryoh could feel its desire, it wanted them more than Baryoh thought anyone could want anything. Its desire, its obsession was so massive and tangible that Baryoh felt his sanity slipping from just looking at the thing. His instincts told him immediately that this was only a small part of that creature.

The eye blinked. Baryoh could feel the creature licking at the edge of his mind, tearing at the walls of his psyche. His vision went hazy. The creature crept into the ship. The massive eyeball was replaced by incorporeal bleeding tongues, voices speaking profane things.

Despite the carnage, the sounds were not very loud, and the colors of the entire space kept receding.

The three jurors huddled together. Even Hoku'naeri, all pride gone, "What is that thing doing here?" He whispered. "It is meant to be at the first Hibodeh."

Baryoh joined them. They waited, shaking with fear.

The creature suddenly cried out. A grey pillar of light had materialized and cut through the creature. Baryoh could see someone encased in it, floating through space.

The Nga'phandileh roared. Baryoh noticed that the air had stopped leaking out of the ship. There was a look of relief on the jurors faces. They knew what it was. The shekere-re sound rattled persistently. Baryoh heard a voice speak in the high language. "Aalúmdalaa." *Boundary.*

The bleeding of colors stopped.

The grey pillar of light disappeared, and a tall, thin black robed man with shiny black skin and wearing a terrifying mask of bone that obscured even his eyes. appeared. His entire body was adorned with beads. Some even looked like they had melded into his skin. The man did not speak. His every movement was followed by the sound of the shekere-re rattles.

Hajarlar rushed forward but the man paid no heed to him. Instead, he focused on Hoku'naeri, who fully assumed the mien of subservience, his left hand on the ground, his head bowed. "Elder brother, Hulor Mm'uoh, I welcome your help and attention, but we have everything under control." Mm'uoh looked around the ship with disdain.

Harjalar huffed. "That Nga'phandileh only follows him around stubbornly bent on consuming him first. If it is here, it is because he is here."

The Hulor Mm'uoh, still silent, looked at Hajarlar. There was a Shekere-rerattle, and then a word, "Bukhiso." *Raise.*

The air shifted, Hajarlar was lifted and slammed into a far wall. And then he said, "ha'ahshii," *silence,* and Hajarlar's head drooped, his eyes blank.

Baryoh gasped.

I don't know which is worse. Him or the creature.

The Hulor Mm'uoh finally turned his attention to Baryoh who gripped his rock tighter.

Hoku'naeri snickered and Mm'uoh cocked his head without saying a word projected a thought at Baryoh. "So, you are the Iwui".

The voice and its shekere-resound materializing in Baryoh's mind, made him feel violated.

Mitortor abruptly materialized in front of Baryoh. She was frantic. "This is the Hulor Mm'uoh, the Accord of souls, he is dangerous. We must escape immediately."

A shekere-re shake.

And then, "I see you, machine mind."

Mitortor's projection stepped back. Even though she didn't possess a physical body, her electric fear was visible.

"Eternity is unflinching in it distaste for consciousness. People possesses an immortal middle, a fire that burns with varying levels of brightness deep within them," Mm'uoh looked at the hole in the ship. "That thing outside follows the brightest souls and nothing has been more delectable to it than me but now..." The shekere-rerang out again, now with more intensity. "Now, it wants you. But I have seen you and you are weak. Unworthy." Mmhuo smiled softly as if talking to a loved one, "I will leave you to it. Fight, struggle and rage, provide it with a great meal."

Mm'uoh turned away leaving Baryoh feeling strangely offended.

Hoku'naeri groveled and gave Baryoh a derisive smile. "As you wish Hulor Mm'uoh".

Mm'uoh seized Mm'hiri and Harjarlar with a rope made of pure grey energy. Then he said another phrase that materialized in front of him as a vibration. "Weyha ahywe." *Space tear.*

Space trembled and broke like glass, revealing a bamboo door leading to a place Baryoh did not recognize. Its skies were pink and green and purple, dotted with tall buildings. Floating rocks hovered in the distance.

Mm'uoh walked casually through the door, pulling Mm'hiri and Hajarlar after him. Hoku'naeri followed, smiling at Baryoh. "I will return to Wiimb-ó... eventually."

Space trembled, the word flickered, and the bamboo door was gone. Baryoh was alone.

Everything quaked as the Nga'phandileh resumed its attack.

For the first time in a long time, he felt afraid. He was faced with an enemy he couldn't comprehend. In a place that was unfamiliar and unfavorable.

Mitortor?

"Yes, master Iwui."

What now?

Focus returned to her eyes. "The Nga'phandileh will not leave, it does not relent or rest. We can't fight it master Iwui."

Baryoh stared at Mitortor, considering his options as he felt Dhisuh's badge move in his chest pocket. No matter what else was going on, he was a soldier, and this was a battle. He knew what was needed in a battle. Determination. Grit. And reliable comrades. "You call me your master, but I do not need a slave," he said out loud. "I need a fellow soldier."

"Master, this is hardly the time..."

Baryoh, cut in. "This is exactly the time. We stare down an impossible enemy. In this moment I need you to be my comrade, Mitortor."

Mitortor stared for a moment and then smiled. "You are more like him than I thought. My friend died but my friend lives. I'll fight with you, Iwui."

They held each other's looks for a moment and then Baryoh turned to see the Aalúmdalaa vibration, the boundary, at the place where the ship had been torn was flickering. "So, how exactly do we fight that thing?"

"We don't. Not here anyway. According to my records that is the Relehbi Orii, a Limye-class Nga'phandileh, the one that hungers for the spirit."

The ship quaked as the vibration of the Aalúmdalaa word dimmed further. The hole in the ship widened and Baryoh stared into a visage of endless mouths lined with teeth as far as he could see. His vision darkened; colors started to blur.

In his mind, Mitortor yelled, "Focus! Don't get lost in the causality field of the Relehbi!"

Baryoh shook his head and tore his eyes away. Lights around them flickered and explosions rang out. "We cannot fight it here. We need to even the playing field. We need to return home."

The 27th sector? Didn't those Jurors say it was lost?

"Maybe it is, but it's our only chance. There is a perpetual kinesis energy mechanism there. We should be able to use to fight back."

"Then what are we waiting for? Let's get out of here!"

Mitortor moved quickly as holograms manifested all around her. Alarms blared as the ship's AI resisted her attempts at an unauthorized takeover of its controls.

Mitortor sneered. "A basic vessel control AI trying to stop me. Cute."

The lights went green as she locked in.

Baryoh asked, "Won't this thing just follow us?"

"The Relehbi cannot bend real space like this ship can, but it can move faster than the speed of light, in an unreal dimension parallel to our reality. That's how it keeps up with the Hulor Mm'uoh. We will have time, but I don't know how much."

"We'll have to make it work. Let's go!"

Baryoh shouted and looked back into the hole of hungry mouths and teeth just as the Aalúmdalaa word disappeared. There was a sound like breaking glass. The Relehbii began to flow into the breach.

"We will be waiting for you," Baryoh whispered as the ship shimmered and disappeared, leaving the echo of the Relehbii's hellish sound ringing in his ears.

10. Return

On Zezépfeni, Mm'uoh stood in front of Horchichii and Dadebisi in the darkened hall. He cocked his head, looking up at the ceiling.

"You let him go." Dadebisi protested.

Mm'uoh remained silent.

Beside him, Mm'hiri, Hoku'naeri, and Hajalar stood, also silent. Mm'hiri and Hajalar's garments were disheveled, and they sported bruises and burns.

The Horchichii looked at them and said, "Chicks in the wind".

Dadebisis face went red.

"Return to your Hibodeh and confine yourself there you are needed again." The Horchichii commanded. "The house of the Iwui will return to us or be destroyed."

Mm'hiri opened her mouth as though she was going to say something but thought better of it. She waved her hands, clicking her fingers to a rhythm. A bamboo door materialized in front of her, a portal to a place of different hues of blue. She walked through it and disappeared into her domain. Hoku'naeri and Hajarlar did the same, disappearing from the hall.

The Horchichii turned to Mm'uoh "You, prepare for the return of the Relehbi."

Mm'uoh who had been unconcerned by Dadebisi floundering till this point finally looked up from his musing at the Horchichii. His shekere-re rang out.

"A mere doorman deigns to give orders to the guardians of the reality. What makes you think you can control me?"

The Horchichii met Mm'uoh's gaze, and a shadow of a smile tugged at the edge of his lips. His eyes lit up for a fraction of a second. Mm'uoh suddenly grunted in pain as blood began to drip from his mouth.

"Very well," Mm'uoh said. "Power answers power. For now."

He bowed mockingly at Dadebisi, whispered a single word and walked through the grey smoky pillar that appeared in front of him.

"This is how it starts." The Horchichii looked up at the ceiling and grit his teeth. "Has the era of erasure come for this epoch as well?" he wondered out loud as the nervous Dadebisi continued to squirm beside him.

Time and space are things of inanity,

There are events that happen outside time, outside space,

Events so important that existence cannot be separated from them,

But we have no way to apprehend, measure or understand these events,

In the same way, the Nga'phandileh are not beings of time or space,

Flickering in and out of reality but stubbornly clinging to existence,

If we did not know better, we would say that these things from the outside,

We would say that they are angry, they are searching for someone, for something,

We would say we know of what they search for,

We would say we know they will never find it,

We would say that we know they will turn their indignation to us since we are the ones who replaced them.

—Recovered Sound Fragment from Mahwé.

11. The Displaced

Large chunks of rock, metal, and dust drifted through an asteroid field. The rocks were held together by impossibly large chains which glowed softly in the background darkness of space.

The chains all linked to a massive stone-and-metal structure rippling with sound waves. Beyond the asteroid field, a curtain of light shimmered faintly, except for the occasional burst.

THE DHAMUYAH-MAISHAH ECHO
SPIRE.

The structure, the Dhamuyah-Maishah Echo Spire of the first sector in the Hogiri Hile Halah, pulsed and was engulfed by grey light. Gears were engaged, engines activated. The structure started to thrum rhythmically as it received its command quarters and resumed active operations.

Inside the spire, in a room with walls of pure white marble into which glowing gourds and beads were embedded, Hulor Mm'uoh sat still in a rattan and cast-iron throne. The robes that now sat on his body showed an emaciated figure, an discolored grey skin with bandages and strange features, his bone-mask now removed. He was neither asleep nor unconscious but performing his duty. His mind was connected to the spire, repelling the unreal, while his body slumbered.

Suddenly, the gourds in the wall began to vibrate. Mm'uoh lifted a hand without raising his head and snapped his fingers. A large hologram unfurled in front of him revealing the livid face of Dadebisi.

"How dare you? Who do you think you are? You were supposed to return with the command quarters, instead we get nonsense about worthiness and your insolence. The Horchiichii is questioning my ability to lead the pluralis because of you."

Silence.

"Answer me!"

Nothing.

Dadebisi raised an eyebrow. "So, you are forgetting who you are. Let me remind you."

The hologram shifted to display an array of glass biochambers where male bodies of different ages floated in a clear viscous liquid. They all bore a resemblance to Mm'uoh. Dadebisi pointed to them. "We have prepared the Accord of Souls up to the 43rd generation, you are merely a temporary Juror. A replica. AJR4.304."

At that, Mm'uoh flinched and sat up. "You call me a replica, then replace me if you dare. I am tired, tired of this pointless, endless tribulation you call duty." Mm'uoh's shekere-rebegan to ring out. "Even if you replace me, I will return to this throne. I will return."

Mm'uoh's eyes glazed over. He rose from his throne, gazing out toward the asteroid field. "I seek a higher purpose now, a higher truth. Mortals are weak, they are bound by rules. They die, they are forgotten. But memories... memories never die."

The entire space around them started to vibrate as Mm'uoh continued, "Imagine an event so terrible that it cannot be called a genocide... it is beyond that. It is a deletion of all beings in existence at the whims of one."

The vibration around them increased in intensity.

Dadebisi started sweating profusely. "The Mother will strike you down for this blasphemy! Stop talking at once, you mad man!"

Mm'uoh ignored him and the vibration. "The souls, the consciousnesses, they are gone. But where do the memories go?" The vibration became a ringing as though his words were being rejected by reality itself. There was the crack of glass. Mm'uoh remained unfazed. He laughed.

"The memories go nowhere, they remain, they are twisted, they hunger. Do they not deserve their vengeance? Do we not deserve our fate?"

Dadebisi screamed "Stop! you fool! Can you not hear a warning echo of the Mothersound? You will doom us all to The Mother's wrath!"

Mm'uoh's walked back to his throne. "Creatures outside reality that cannot be stopped, destroyed or unheard. Creatures of unreality trying to return home. Who are we to refuse them?"

The vibration reached a crescendo. Glass shattered. Mm'uoh stopped talking and blood leaked from the edges of his mouth.

Mm'uoh sat back on his throne, bowed his head and went back to his duty, his consciousness no longer in the room. Behind Dadebisi, an assortment of bodies lay on the ground, the bio chambers housing them had been shattered and broken by the vibration.

Dadebisi gasped and hurriedly ended the transmission.

The Maisha Echo spire continued to thrum softly.

12. Sector 27

Baryoh frowned as he looked at a holographic recording of the attack while the Oko Horjuaaye made its way through the very fabric of space-time. He saw the hull of the Okor Horjuaaye explode, a space opening up, but not what caused it.

Why can't we see the creature? He thought to Mitotor.

Mitotor replied. "This is the nature of unreality, only consciousness can appraise it."

But it was there... mouths and teeth. He shook his head.

"Yes, it was, but like a quantum particle, the appearance of an Nga'phandileh is determined not only by its own nature but also that of the observer and they can only be observed by a conscious being."

Baryoh shook his head again and his stomach rumbled noisily. He was hungry and he needed to pee.

Mitortor, still in his mind, looked at him for a moment then laughed. "If your bowels are bothering you so much then just say 'Túr Dhanu'."

Baryoh looked at her curiously but said it anyway. The urge he had to urinate suddenly disappeared with a feeling like a tickle. Baryoh jumped to his feet, shocked.

Mitortor howled with laughter.

Baryoh moved towards her with mock anger. *What was that?*

"You are a Juror with natural access to the high language, and an ability to manipulate the Mothersound so I'm helping you use it."

Baryoh shook his finger in front of her not-quite-real face. *It's weird. Don't do it again.*

And then he thought, *I am still hungry though*, trying to hide his smile.

"Okay, this time say 'Mhu Hounje wah'"

Baryoh paused, staring at her and said, "Mhu Ounje wah hib baryii". A fragrant cube of energy, materialized in front of him and he bit into it.

Mitortor sulked. "You changed it, no fun."

The Okor Horjuaaye jerked suddenly. Baryoh and Mitortor stopped smiling.

Did we hit something?

Mitortor shook her head, "No, we were stopped by the relativistic defense shield of the echo spire. We are home."

Baryoh looked out through a port in the stone ship and saw a field of asteroids set against a border of darkness. The light of the two suns seemed to just stop at a point, unable to travel any further. He'd been plagued by visions of white lines in his dreams but now he was sure they were not hallucinations. He could see them, tears in space. And then he saw the echo spire. A massive space station melded into a gigantic asteroid. It looked battered, ancient, and non-functional.

Even though she had no physical body Mitortor seemed to sag. She had taken on a faraway look. "That is the Hundongweh Echo Spire," she said, "and this, this is sector 27."

Baryoh felt a sense of familiarly with this strange place. The echo spire was completely dark, all nearby asteroids floating silently away from it. Mitortor went silent for a while and her face scrunched up.

What's wrong?

Mitortor responded "I have been trying to activate the echo spire reception conduit but its unresponsive."

She sat down and hugged her knees, her voice quivering. "I'm sorry master Iwui. I can't get us in, I have failed you."

Baryoh laughed. *Mitortor. No. You haven't failed me. The only way to fail is to give up and you're not giving up on me now, are you comrade?*

"No."

Baryoh stood tall, projecting a determined visage. *We came here to fight that thing on our home turf, so we shall. If you can't get in the usual way, find us another. Any other. But just don't give up.*

Mitortor looked up, the light back in her eyes. "Yes comrade."

She went silent again and then after a moment, "There may be another way, but it is dangerous."

More dangerous than waiting here for the Rehlebii to kill us?

"No."

Then do it. I trust you. Do what is necessary.

She froze, her projected image shimmering in front of him. "Really? Even if I'll have to cycle the space-time fold engine of the ship on and off and try to use it to cut through the relativistic barrier?"

"I don't know what that means but yes, even then, comrade Mitotor." He said out loud.

She smiled. "You're insane, Iwui, but I like it."

The Okor Horjuaaye's engines roared as Mitotor engaged the propulsion engines. Baryoh strapped himself into a seat and braced.

The ship lurched forward and crashed right into the barrier. On impact, fires flared all around them and alarms blared. Baryoh's vision swam as everything shook around him. Mitotor engaged the spacetime fold engine as though they were going to transport away but instead, locked their position in and cycled it on and off before they could phase. The ship and the barrier protested with a stone and metal groan louder than anything he'd ever heard.

The ship cut its way past the barrier. Flaming and spewing smoke into open space, the ship fell into the gravity well of the echo spire.

"We're through!", Mitortor yelled. Baryoh looked out the port and saw the echo spire get bigger and bigger.

"Brace!"

Baryoh steeled his nerves and grit his teeth.

They hit the spire. There was a sound like the bones of the universe cracking. Everything shook.

Baryoh blacked out.

The vast emptiness that was the Relehbii was approaching the outer reaches of the system. It became more excited the closer it got to its target. It could already sense the delicious memories, the delicious consciousness, the reality of the things it had once been. Eager, it picked up its speed continuing to beeline towards its prey.

13. Yalago

Baryoh's eyes shot open.

There was smoke and ash and debris all around him. He could hear something like incessant whispering.

Mitortor blinked into existence, staring at him with concern.

"Iwui, how are you?"

Baryoh shot to his feet. *Fine. I'm fine. Situation report?* He thought to her.

"We're on the spire, but the situation is worse than expected."

Baryoh spat out a glob of bloody saliva. *Of course it is.*

Mitortor walked out of the hole in the wrecked ship and into the spire. Baryoh followed.

"While you were out, I have been trying to activate the spire's perpetual kinesis energy mechanism." They entered a place like a hall, darkness and shadows pervading. "There has been no response. This is really worrying because there are only two scenarios in which the mechanism won't respond. One, if it has been obliterated, which isn't likely since we are standing here. Or, two, something is funneling away its energy at the source."

Right. So?

"According to my records, there is only one entity, an Nga'phandileh capable of consuming that energy, The Limye-class Nga'phandileh, LM1280, the Yalago, The time thief, A chronal anomaly."

Baryoh shook his head.

The Mother must be testing me because this is getting ridiculous.

He exhaled and then, to Mitotor, *we already faced impossible odds, this changes nothing.*

There was panic in Mitotor's voice as it bounced around his head. "You have no idea Iwui, if it is the Yalago, it can probably see us already, it is waiting for us. For you."

Baryoh walked to the dark red walls of the hall and touched them. The whispering from the walls seemed to surge. He looked at the residue on his finger. *Clay. Just like my home.* He turned to Mitortor. *Nothing changes. I will attract the attention of this creature, so it stops absorbing the energy while you get the perpetual kinesis thing started. If we can use it to fight one Nga'phandileh we can use it to fight two. Right?*

"Right."

The entire station was suddenly rocked, and they heard a crash and scream from afar.

The Relehbii is here.

"The relativistic shield won't hold it for long."

Baryoh looked away from Mitotor toward the massive doorway at the end of the hall. He felt a strange sensation, like a tingle in his chest. He shouted, "You've been here for some time, why not show yourself?"

Two massive eyes filled with stars opened on the ceiling of the hall as a creature extruded itself from the walls and the ceiling. It was humanoid, with no facial features. The hunch on its back was pulsing and spilling a pus-like liquid that glimmered in the dark. Instinctively, as with the Relehbii, Baryoh knew that was just a small aspect of the full creature. The tremors from outside hit again. The creature stared at him and Baryoh suddenly felt a wave of exhaustion.

"Iwui, that thing is already stealing your time just by its being in your presence."

Baryoh blinked himself awake and suddenly took off in a sprint. Around him, the whispering seemed to grow louder.

The entire space rumbled as the Yalago moved but it did not move like the Relehbii, it was really there, its movements labored by gravity, its ugliness reflected in the glass and metal surfaces as he whizzed by. It contradicted what Mitortor had told him about the Nga'phandileh.

In his head she explained, "Yes, the observer-Nga'phandileh inter-action is no longer valid because the Yalago has been tethered to reality by the Khuvutar chorus".

Baryoh frowned. *What in The Mother's name is a Khuvutar chorus now? Mitortor, you and I need to have a conversation about concealing mission-critical information.*

Her tone was subdued. "Not hiding. Protecting."

Baryoh leapt over a fallen pillar and kept running.

"The Khuvutar chorus is how we level the playing field. It is power-ful sound magic, drawn from a tone of the Mothersound that has been woven into this echo spire. It invokes the universal laws of equality, forcing any entities within its influence to operate under similar rules of physical reality."

Baryoh could hear the Yalago behind him but, it was not hurried, it reminded him of an adult chasing a baby.

"Now it has been bound to reality, it is subject to rules like every-thing else. Rules you should be able to manipulate once I activate the kinesis mechanism."

Ahh. Hulor Iwui. The accord of rules.

Baryoh burst into an open space filled with trees, grass, and a rapidly flowing river of what looked like pure silver. A broken bridge hovered above the water. Everything was illuminated by the light of fireflies. The steps of the Yalago sounded close but the silver river looked turbulent and was moving too fast for him to swim in.

Why is there a forest in the echo spire?

The walls adjacent to Baryoh suddenly exploded as the Yalago arrived. The place where its face should have been was nothing but twisted space. The Yalago inched closer. The whispers got louder. Baryoh saw the white lines across its body. They pulsed bright and suddenly, the whispers became a clear voice coming at him from everywhere. There was a rumble like a mighty engine being activated. The Yalago stopped moving.

"The kinesis energy mechanism is active Iwui! You should be able to sense its power and see the rules! Speak!"

The rules. He could hear the rules. The rules that bound all things, the rules that made up all things. He'd heard them in his dreams and in other places. But he had never heard them this clearly.

There were many rules of the Khuvutar chorus binding the creature, he listened to them but one stood out most of all. *Dwudinsh. Inequality.*

Baryoh looked at his hands and saw that he was emitting white light from his pores that wrapped around his body like an aura. He raised his hand, searching his mind for a word in the high language but before he could find it, the creature ran forward and crashed into him. They fell into the thick silver water. His breath was knocked out of him, and his vision darkened as he struggled against the rapid current. It was too strong.

Baryoh gulped in mouthfuls as he struggled to orient himself. He struggled and struggled but he grew tired against the weight of the water. He could feel his arms slumping and he was tempted to just stop. Stop fighting and let himself drown, let it all end. The madness of the bés was all too much.

Dhisuh's badge was torn out from his pocket by a rip current and started to swirl away from him, its bronze finish glinting in the water. And then he remembered. He remembered his comrades from battalion 87 slumped over, their lifeless bodies still in battle poses. They fought. Hyenas till the very end.

No.

You only fail when you give up.

Baryoh grabbed the badge and growled with a mouthful of water as the command quarters in his chest roared to life. The bright light from his skin intensified and from the depths of his memory he shouted, "Hayhiihyah!" *Reversal.*

A shockwave emanated from Baryoh and the river came to a halt. A white scroll of light shot out of his arm and latched onto the surface of the river. It started flowing in the opposite direction, but this time, less turbulent, more controlled. Baryoh lifted himself up and floated on the surface of the water until he reached the other side. He sputtered, coughing out water and stood to his feet. He heard a roar and saw the Yalago approaching, wading through the river.

There was a door behind. The command quarters inside him whirred when he turned and saw it like there was something calling to him from within. The whispered rules had become a song in his ears.

Baryoh ran through the door and entered a massive room. This room was still pristine, free of damage. It was completely transparent, floor, walls, and ceiling were glass-like. The distant lights of the stars glimmered. At the center, Baryoh could see a crystal throne fused into the ground like it had extruded from it. The singing in his ears got louder, urging him to sit in.

The doorway behind him trembled noisily as the Yalago seeped through it into the room still chasing. Baryoh's eyes narrowed, and his ears pricked up as he evaluated the thousands of rules being spoken and sung over the creature. "Cigbuhn, malazgwa, awachisha, abiima, dwudinsh." *Pain, struggle, desire, requisition, inequality.*

"This thing," Baryoh said. "You are a prisoner here, bound by rules to flesh, to pain, to desire, to be eternally unequal to your true form. You need me to free you. Let me sit or you will be imprisoned here forever."

The creature stopped moving and stared at Baryoh as he inched closer and closer to the crystal throne.

Suddenly, above, a massive eyeball appeared outside the transparent ceiling.

The Relehbii!

Baryoh broke into a run. The Yalago, its hesitation shattered, gave chase. The ceiling caved in as the Relehbii's formless mass of mouths and teeth crashed into the room, raining sharp glass. The stars outside the echo spire were gone, only silence and emptiness pervaded the entire space outside the spire.

Baryoh jumped into the throne just as the Relehbii hit the floor him, the Yalago only a half-step behind. A black light shot out from the base of the throne into Baryoh's body and connected with the command quarters in his chest. The song of the spire became impossibly loud in his ears. And then a white light swallowed his vision.

14. The Accord of Rules

Baryoh was back in his officer's quarters on Wiimb-ó.

He sat up and blinked.

How?

Everything was quiet. Baryoh rose to his feet and touched the chair, the window the walls. He felt his own face and saw the mist of his breath. It was real. But the Relehbii, Mitotor, Yalago, the Jurors, they were all real too. He shook his head.

"You are interesting." A said from behind him. It was familiar. Too familiar.

Baryoh spun around, instinctively reaching for his gun, but it wasn't there. The figure stepped out of a corner and into view. It was him. But at the same time, not him. The face was the same, but the eyes were too indifferent, too uncaring, too empty. "So, an orphan from Wiimb-ó is the new Hulor Iwui."

In that moment, Baryoh knew it was his predecessor the first Hulor Iwui of the 27th Sector of the Hogiri Hileh Halah.

Baryoh sank into his chair. "I should have known. Everything seemed too scripted. Like I was a pawn in someone else's game." He fell silent, staring outside.

The first Iwui looked at him quizzically. "Most people would be barraging me with questions but you are waiting."

Baryoh kneaded his forehead. "Well, since you seem to have planned all this, I know you intend to tell me what I need to know to fulfill my role in it."

The first Hulor Iwui smiled. "Since you are so sure, then grit your teeth and receive my gift. I will awaken your gene memories, maybe then you will be prepared for what is coming. For your duty."

Baryoh shrugged. "Duty. I can handle that."

"A good solider, still. If you fail in this duty, I will be waiting, watching. I will take everything from you, including your very being and give it to another."

Baryoh scoffed. "If it's truly who I am, then I won't fail."

The first Iwui nodded. "I expect nothing less."

Without warning, the eyes of the first Hulor Iwui went black. Visible vibrations in the air shot out of him like as tendrils. They drilled into Baryoh's body, levitating him. He heard a thousand voices at once, telling him everything. And he understood.

On the Hundongweh echo spire, Baryoh's body began to convulse in the chair.

The Relehbii's tendrils of emptiness grabbed and began to pull him up towards its gaping maw. Baryoh's aura spilled out of his body unceasingly, his face contorted a thousand ways. The Relehbii flinched at the pinch of a memory, one of the many it had stolen. Thousands of light-lines suddenly materialized in the emptiness, solid like the sharp edges of a diamond. The Yalago growled and lunged for Baryoh's body, but the Relehbii did not pay it any mind. Even among the Nga'phandileh, there was a pecking order, and the Yalago could not contest food with the Relehbii.

Still unconscious, Baryoh growled, "Zahkronyu". *Champion.*

The vibration of the word wrapped itself around the Yalago. The Yalago began to squirm as the space around it caved in. The flesh encasing it began to melt away. The three figures drifted up and out of the throne room, into open space. Yellow light entered the Yalago's eyes as it remembered its true name and its true nature and it recognized Baryoh, the Hulor Iwui, the blazing white entity that had bound it to reality and made it mortal, that figure that had made it feel.

The Yalago spoke in a language that had been lost from reality. "Stop! That is mine."

The space around the Yalago completely collapsed as dark spheres lined with glittering stars rushed out of its center. The echo spire trembled. The Yalago, unbound, finally, saw the full size of the Relebhii.

The Yalago was the size of a star collapsing on itself in a parallel dimension, but the Relebhii was an emptiness, a lack of space, the dearth of everything that stretched over reality itself, encompassing the entire 27th sector and corrupting everything it touched with the essence of nothingness. But the Yalago did not care. All it wanted was revenge.

A conflict between the Nga'phandileh is not physical.

It is not a conflict of behemoths crashing into one another causing destruction. A conflict between the Nga'phandileh, however rare, is a conflict of existence, one that takes place in parallel to reality, corrupting the very space and time next to which it transpires.

The Yalago emitted a black light that restrained the Relehbii from consuming Baryoh. Annoyed, the Relehbii turned its attention to the Yalago for a split second. The black hole at the Yalago's center collapsed further as the Relehbii wrapped itself around the region of reality-unreality occupied by the Yalago and squeezed, consuming it.

Baryoh's eyes shot open.

They were clear, his pupils replaced by a string of white lines. His aura flared out as the nothingness surrounding him receded. His lips barely moved as he spoke in the high language, "Iykadheim kyi efraiu." *Recover lost data.*

The words materialized in front of him, white hot pure vibrations like those that had existed at the birth of the world. Baryoh floated gently in the space between reality and unreality. The Relehbii recoiled, still crushing the Yalago within it. Emboldened, its tendrils began to slowly reach for him once again.

Am I still Baryoh... or am I Hulor iwui?

Baryoh cocked his head to the side.

It doesn't matter.

You made a mistake coming to the Hundongweh Echo Spire, where the preserver of rules and laws presides.

"Iykadem ya'yn." Baryoh-Iwui said. *Restore all.*

A ripple of golden light escaped his lips and began to expand and race out, spreading through space in all directions, echoing his words. Everywhere the golden light passed, space was repaired. The echo spire station re-assembled itself to its former condition. The asteroid reconstituted and started to glow with a milky light as chains and ropes of white light shot out and connected with each other until it was a web of connected lines of rules, the echo spire at its middle.

The restoration of real space was forcing the Relebhii out of reality, ripping away its expansive emptiness. The creature squirmed and screamed. It could not be killed, but it was being weakened so much that even the weakest of the Nga'phandileh could demand its existence. All the destruction and corruption it had inflicted upon reality was being undone. The Relehbii did the only thing it could, it gathered itself and fled. Baryoh-Iwui saw a tiny mass of darkness like an evil orb shoot away and move beyond the flickering wall of light, its only evidence a slight flicker. A humming sound like the singing of millions of rules came softly to him as the wall became fully engaged activating the sound that would keep the Nga'phandileh out.

Baryoh-Iwui turned to what was left of the Yalago, which had been compressed into a nebulous black hole that was little more than the size of a pearl. "Time never dies," he whispered.

Lines of rules surrounded and encased it. Its swirling form condensed into a solid orb with a surface like metal. Baryoh-Iwui took it and slid it into his pocket.

Iwui... Iwui, can you hear me?

Baryoh descended back into the transparent throne room.

Yes.

Mitortor's projection was standing close to the entrance, staring at him. He walked up to her and placed a hand on her not-quite-real head. "Old friend."

Mitortor's eyes lit up for a moment, then she bowed. "Hulor Iwui, I am embedded within you, and I will always serve you. But, my master, it is no longer your time."

Baryoh-Iwui laughed. "Yes. Of course. From now, you are on your own. Take care of my child."

And then, as an echo in Baryoh's head. *And you, take care of her. She is more important than you know.*

Clarity suddenly returned to Baryoh's eyes.

He looked around the throne room for a moment and then he smiled at Mitotor. "Thank you, my friend, my comrade."

Mitortor smiled her cherubic smile. "So you have awakened your memories?"

Baryoh nodded.

"Ready to resume duty?"

Yes. But first I need to return home, to my home, to my men. And I need to make sure justice comes to some greedy, conniving generals.

"Alright then. I'll fix the ship."

Thank you.

Baryoh saluted her with a smile and turned to stare out of the glass throne room, focusing on the twin lights of Zuúv'ah and Juah-āju in the distance, listening to the sound of restoration as it propagated through the system.

In Zezépfeni, the Horchichii sat in his garden. He looked up into the sky and a pink-tinted golden wave of light passed above the planet. He frowned.

"That troublesome Juror is truly back. This just got more interesting."

He took another sip of Hoguro.

In sector one, seated on his throne, Hulor Mm'uoh's eyes shot open. He pricked up his ears, listening closely as the sound of the golden wave of restoration rules swept away from the asteroid field boundary and deeper into the system toward the inner planets.

"Finally," he said. "A purpose worth fighting for. An opponent worthy of my struggle."

He stood up and began to laugh as the echo of his shekere-re rattling rang throughout the spire.

A nd so we've reached the end.
From the very start of this imagined science-fantasy universe to its present, we've had twelve stories set over a timespan of more than 300000 years (or juzu) of imagined history.

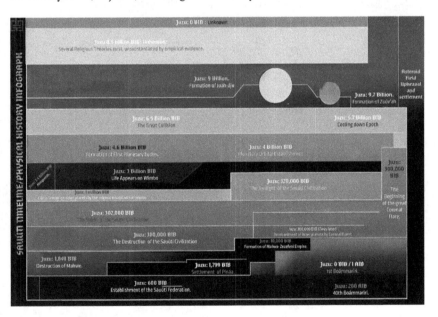

We've met the creator goddess, The Mother, both in myth and in the everyday lives of the people of the Sauútiverse. We've met heroes, villains, schemers, warriors, musicians, ancestors, AI, monsters, ghosts, and even creatures of unreality, across the five planets and beyond.

But every end is also a new beginning.

This is just the start of the Saúútiverse. The part where we invite you to join us. To tell stories with us, to fill in the gaps in the timeline with stories of your own, using this rich and layered setting as a sandbox. The worldbuilding already exists, all you have to do is use it, or if you wish, add to it. The Saúútiverse, just like our own universe, is ever-expanding. For every African or member of the wider African diaspora, you are welcome to join us, become a contributor to this world. The Saúúti collective is about more than just stories. It's about community about creating a universe together. We own the rights to the world and the setting but you will own the rights to your stories.

You can lean into the magic or the technology or both. You can bring in as much of your own cultural touchpoints as you wish, integrating them into the fabric of this world. You can do almost anything you want as long as it doesn't directly contradict what has already been established. We want love stories, horror stories, science fiction stories, mundane stories, action and adventure stories. We want all kinds of stories in the Saúútiverse.

So if you are African or from the wider African diaspora (interpret as widely as possible) and you want to create stories of your own set in this world or just delve deeper into the Saúútiverse, well, you've already read the stories, now read the abridged story bible here: https://syllble.com/sauuti/

And if, or when, you have an idea for a story of your own, you can contact us at: sauutiverse@gmail.com.

All you need to do is: sign the contributor agreement, send in a pitch, write your story, send it in for a review. That's it. It'll be part of the Saúútiverse. And official Saúútiverse story. Just like all the stories you just read.

Exciting, isn't it?

We think so and we hope you do too.

So join us.

We'll be waiting.

AUTHOR BIOGRAPHIES

Eugen Bacon is an African Australian author of several novels and fiction collections. She's a 2022 World Fantasy Award finalist, and was announced in the honor list of the 2022 Otherwise Fellowships for 'doing exciting work in gender and speculative fiction'. Her short story collection DANGED BLACK THING made the 2021 Otherwise Honor List as a 'sharp collection of Afro-Surrealist work'. Recent books: MAGE OF FOOLS (novel), CHASING WHISPERS (short stories) and AN EARNEST BLACKNESS (essays). Eugen has two novels, a novella and three anthologies (ed) out in 2023, including SERENGOTTI, a novel, and the US release of DANGED BLACK THING. Visit her website at eugenbacon.com and Twitter feed **@EugenBacon**

***

Tobias S. Buckell is a New York Times Bestselling and World Fantasy Award-winning author born in the Caribbean. He grew up in Grenada and spent time in the British and US Virgin Islands, which influence much of his work.

His novels and over seventy stories have been translated into nineteen different languages. His work has been nominated for the Hugo Award, Nebula Award, World Fantasy Award, and the Astounding Award for Best New Science Fiction Author.

He currently lives in Bluffton, Ohio with his wife and twin daughters. He's an instructor at the University of Maine's Stonecoast MFA in Creative Writing. For more, visit his Press Kit. To see an exhaustive list of what he's published, visit the bibliography page.

Tobias Buckell's fiction and media rights are represented by his agent: Hannah Bowman.

***

Oghenechovwe Donald Ekpeki is an African speculative fiction writer, editor and publisher from Nigeria. He has won the Nebula, Otherwise, Nommo, British & World Fantasy awards and been a finalist in the Hugo, Locus, Sturgeon, British Science Fiction and NAACP Image awards. His works have appeared in Asimov's, F&SF, Uncanny Magazine, Tordotcom and others. He edited the Bridging Worlds non-fiction anthology, Year's Best African Speculative Fiction anthology and co-edited the Dominion, and Africa Risen anthologies. He was a CanCon guest of honour and a guest of honour at the Afrofuturism themed ICFA 44 where he coined the term/genre label, Afropantheology.

***

Stephen Embleton was born in KwaZulu-Natal, South Africa and is a resident in Oxford, after the 2022 James Currey Fellowship at the African Studies Centre, University of Oxford. His first short story was published in 2015 in the IMAGINE AFRICA 500 speculative fiction anthology, followed by the 2016 Edition of Aké Review, the debut edition of Enkare Review 2017 and more. He is a charter member of the African Speculative Fiction Society and its Nommo Awards initiative. His then unpublished fantasy novel, BONES & RUNES, was a finalist in the 2021 James Currey Prize for African Literature, and published in the UK in 2022. He was awarded the James Currey Fellowship, University of Oxford 2022. Stephen is the editor of The James Currey Anthology 2022, featuring short fiction and non-fiction with contributors hailing from Botswana to Nigeria, Ghana to South Africa – writing from the Continent or in the diaspora. He is the editor of the 2023 edition of the posthumously published final novel of Flora Nwapa, THE LAKE GODDESS. Stephen is one of the ten African writers making up the Sauúti Collective.

***

Dare Segun Falowo is a writer of the Nigerian Weird. Their work draws on cinema, indigenous cosmologies, pulp fiction & the surreal.

Their short fiction has appeared in the Magazine of Fantasy & Science Fiction, The Dark Magazine, Baffling Magazine and others. They have also contributed to the anthologies of black speculative fiction: DOMINION and AFRICA RISEN. Their lysergic science fiction epic, CONVERGENCE IN CHORUS ARCHITECTURE was longlisted for the British Science Fiction Award for Short Fiction. Dare currently lives in Nigeria, between Ibadan and Lagos, where they are trying to find their truth in text, symbol and spirit.

Their first collection of stories, CAGED OCEAN DUB, was published in June 2023.

***

Fabrice Guerrier is a Haitian-American science fiction and fantasy writer and founder of Syllble, a pioneering science fiction and fantasy production house and publisher that creates fictional worlds by connecting diverse creative writers, visual artists and inspired creators from different countries, backgrounds, and cultures through artist collectives. His vision is to bring a new era of storytelling in Hollywood and the publishing world by building vibrant collectives of underrepresented creators producing together within unique fictional universes, publishing the best original work that emerges and growing these worlds through creative collaborations, content creation, and transmedia. He was selected as a 2022 PEN Emerging Voices fellow finalist and a PEN Haiti fellow by PEN America. He was inducted into Forbes 30 Under 30 list and named to Root magazine's 100 most influential African-Americans.

***

T.L. Huchu's work has appeared in 'Lightspeed', 'Interzone', 'Analog Science Fiction & Fact', 'The Year's Best Science Fiction and Fantasy 2021', 'Ellery Queen Mystery Magazine', 'Mystery Weekly', 'The Year's Best Crime and Mystery Stories 2016', and elsewhere.

He is the winner of an Alex Award (2022), the Children's Africana Book Award (2021), a Nommo Award for African SFF (2022, 2017), and has been shortlisted for the Caine Prize (2014) and the Grand prix de l'Imaginaire (2019). THE MYSTERY AT DUNVEGAN CASTLE, the third instalment in his Edinburgh Nights fantasy book series, is due out in summer 2023. Find him @TendaiHuchu.

***

Somto Ihezue is a Nigerian–Igbo editor, writer, and filmmaker.

He was awarded the 2021 African Youth Network Movement Fiction Prize. A British Science Fiction Award, Nommo Award, and 2022 Afritondo Prize nominee, his works have appeared in Tordotcom, Fireside Magazine, Podcastle, Escape Pod, Strange Horizons, Nightmare Magazine, Cossmass Infinities, Flash Fiction Online, and elsewhere.

Somto is Original Fiction Manager at Escape Artists. He is an acquiring editor with Android Press and an associate editor with Apex Magazine, and Cast of Wonders. Follow him on Twitter @somto_Ihezue.

***

Adelehin Ijasan is an eye surgeon ('ophthalmologist' is a mouthful for most people) and writer. His short stories have appeared in The Best of Everyday Fiction, Takahe, On the Premises, The Tiny Globule, Page and Spine, Pandemic publications, Omenana, Sub-saharan Magazine, The Naked Convos, Kalahari Review, Canary Press, Our Move Next anthology and FIYAH. He was nominated for the Commonwealth short story award in 2014 and, more recently, was on the Nommo award long list for speculative fiction. He also made the Locus recommended reading list in 2020. He can be found at www.adeijasan.com.

***

Akintoba Kalejaye hails from Nigeria. He is a lawyer, comic writer, and graphic artist. Akintoba has brought to life over 20 comics under the umbrella of the award-winning publisher Comic Republic, including the critically acclaimed VISIONARY and METALLA both inspired by Yoruba mythology and Nigerian way of life. He's also the mastermind behind other thrilling comics like BEATZ, ITAN, VANGUARDS AFTERMATH, and ERU #8 to name a few. Akintoba's contributions to the comic world have garnered him numerous accolades, including winning "Best Traditional Comic" at the 2017 Comic Connect Award and earning a nomination for "Best Writer" at the 2023 Glyph Awards. Akintoba's work has caught the attention of Universal Studios, who are currently adapting some of his comic creations into live-action TV series and movies.

His 15 years of legal practice have sparked a deep interest in international copyright law, leading him to embark on a fellowship with Harvard University's prestigious CopyrightX program.

When he's not crafting storylines or practicing law, Akintoba enjoys programming, photography, and video games. His source of inspiration remains his wife Adanna (a doctoral candidate) and their three young children, Demi (six), Tara (four), and Kunle (two).

***

Cheryl S. Ntumy is a Ghanaian writer of short fiction and novels of speculative fiction, young adult fiction and romance. Her work has appeared in FIYAH Literary Magazine; Apex Magazine; Will This be a Problem and Botswana Women Write, among others. Her work has also been shortlisted for the Nommo Award for African Speculative Fiction, the Commonwealth Writers Short Story Prize and the Miles Morland Foundation Scholarship. She is part of the Sauútiverse Collective and a member of Petlo Literary Arts, an organisation that develops and promotes creative writing in Botswana.

***

Ikechukwu "Eye Kay" Nwaogu is a writer and editor from Nigeria.

He credits his siblings with teaching him to read, and his parents with teaching him to tell stories. In 2016, he was awarded a Tony Elumelu scholarship to study screenwriting at a film school in Lagos. That same year, he was Writer-In-Residence at the Ebedi International Writers' Residency, Nigeria's premier Writing Residency, in Iseyin, Oyo State. In 2018, his manuscript, THE BOOK OF LOST WORDS was a finalist at the inaugural edition of the GTB Dusty Manuscript Contest, where contest judge and Brittlepaper editor-in-chief, Ainehi-

Edoro-Giles, praised his work. In 2019, he was shortlisted again for the Quramo Writers' Prize, for the same manuscript.

His writing interrogates identity and bias through the lens of experience. His writing has been published in various anthologies and publications, most notably The Noirledge Anthology Of Short Fiction, and Horror Without Borders. His hobbies are listening to music, lots and lots of reading, and the occasional swim.

***

Climber, tattoo collector, and peanut-butter connoisseur, **Xan van Rooyen** is a non-binary storyteller from South Africa, currently living in Finland where the heavy metal is soothing and the cold, dark forests inspiring. Xan has a Master's degree in music, and–when not teaching–enjoys conjuring strange worlds and creating quirky characters. You can find Xan's stories in the likes of Three-Lobed Burning Eye, Daily Science Fiction, and Galaxy's Edge among others. They have also written several novels including the YA fantasy MY NAME IS MAGIC, and adult arcanopunk novel SILVER HELIX. Xan hangs out on Instagram and Twitter, so feel free to say hi over there @xan_writer.

***

Wole Talabi is an engineer, writer, and editor from Nigeria. He is the author of SHIGIDI AND THE BRASS HEAD OF OBALU-FON (DAW/Gollancz, August 2023) and INCOMPLETE SOLU-TIONS(Luna Press, 2019). His short fiction has appeared in *Asimov's*, *F&SF, Lightspeed, Clarkesworld* and *other* places. His work has been a finalist for the Nebula Award, the Caine Prize, the Locus Award, the Nommo Award and been translated into seven languages. He has edited four anthologies: TALES FROM THE COMING NIGHT (2022, a translation anthology in Bengali), AFRICANFUTURISM(2020, nominated for the Locus Award), LIGHTS OUT: RESURREC-TION (2016) and THESE WORDS EXPOSE US(2014). MOTH-ERSOUND: THE SAUÚTIVERSE ANTHOLOGYis his fifth work as editor. He likes scuba diving, elegant equations, and oddly shaped things. He currently lives and works in Malaysia. Find him at wtal-abi.wordpress.com and @wtalabi on twitter.

***

J. Umeh is a published author, blogger, music producer, film reviewer. He lives and works in the UK as a technology architect and consultant. As a creative artist, technologist and former biologist, Umeh's interests spans the confluence of technology, art and humanity and this is a theme he explores in his first speculative fiction work *Kalabashing*. Umeh is passionate about the co-evolutionary tension between emerging technologies and intellectual property (e.g. copyright), and he is a regular conference speaker on these topics, which are also reflected in a lot of his non-fictional works.

- Aagoo: a technical term for time in the Sauúti high language (aa-goometric materials are materials used to manipulate or control time).
- Adundun: tiny beasts that sleep upside down and whose cry it is said can turn the hearer into stone.
- Akakikikaka: a resting reptile native to Wiimb-ó with yellow eyes which are said to have magicial powers and poison glands used to make weapons and potions.
- Akalala: a fabled bird said to fly around in daytime but only sing at night, native to Wiimb-ó.
- Ama'Ahiyaa: a cabal that runs Kalabash City's underworld on Ekwukwe.
- Arcadium Pluralis:
- Aze'aze: giant firefly with the head of a goat, native to Ekwukwe
- Baa'gh: a crab-like sentient and intelligent species on Mahwé who have a unique way of evolving by consuming other creatures which they call Nududu.
- Bés: a standard "day".
- Boāmmariri: a conference between the planets held every five juzu to share knowledge and ideas and culture and prevent wars or problems.
- Boriiwili: spirit entities from Eh'wauizo that can be summoned to aid in magic.
- Chekele'le: creature like a hyena, native to Ekwukwe.

- Chrono-dismorphation: The distortion of time in a place which makes it unstable, such as the environment of Mahwé after its destruction.
- Corpus Asteroidium: The governing body of the Jurors that protect the Hogiri Hileh Halah
- Djazi-séshwe: masquerade-style performers and dancers that use masks, disguise, sound to enhance performances.
- Dreamstealer: a creature from folklore that sits on people's chests and steals their dreams and can kill – said to be sent by evil people.
- Dwa'ndenki: a sea slug, also used as a curse word.
- Echo Spire: a fortress at a sector of the Hogiri Hileh Halah. The primary residence of a Juror that protects that sector.
- Edà: the inner substance of a person, ego.
- Eh'wauizo: the spirit realm, dimension of the dead and ancestors.
- Ekwukwe: one of the five planets.
- Enhwaunu: like a sloth, holds onto caves upside down like a bat) with fine white fur.
- Erii: continent on Wiimb-ó. Its northern region is mostly desert.
- Fuúzimwazii: turtle-like amphibian sea-creatures. They use echo-location and communication like dolphins and whales. Live mid-water. They have carapace shells with hollows that amplify their vocalization sounds.
- Geréwiig: a brown-black veined hard-wood (like ebony)
- Hibodeh: a sector of the Hogiri Hileh Halah protected by a Juror.
- Hogiiri Hile Halah: a wall bounding the Sauuti system protecting it from the Nga'phandileh
- Hulor: title given to the jurors that protect the Hogiri Hileh Halah.
- Impudu-pudu: a monstrous flying creature on Ekwukwe
- Irëgi: name used by AI on Pinaa for people with significant latent magical ability. Derived from maadiregi.
- Javuiili: uninhabited physical moon of Wiimb-ó
- Juah-āju: larger one of the two stars in the binary

- Juhaianith: the cave habitats of the mythic enhwaunu.
- Juror: a class of powerful warriors assigned to protect the Hogiri Hileh Halah.
- Juzu: a standard "year"
- Kalabash/Klalabash: A plant which grows on Wiimb-ó, Órino-Rin, Zezépfeni and Ekwukwe (where it is called Klalabash). It is a versatile creeping plant all parts of which can be put to various uses, e.g.: the leaves and fruit can be prepared and eaten; the vines can be woven into tough ropes; but the gourd-like fruit is the real treasure because once harvested and dried, it's tough outer husk or shell can be fashioned into anything from ornaments to utensils or musical instruments.
- Kin Groups: semi-criminal family groups that control territory and sound mining operations on Órino-Rin
- Kndliluni: a type of court/theatre or general performing area.
- Korps: later names for business entities that control territory, mining and trade on Órino-Rin. Evolved from Kin groups.
- Kpakpandoh: mythical creature said to have only existed in the time before the great flare.
- Kunkun: a ferocious, carnivorous large cat native to Wiimb-ó.
- Kuu'uum: caves in Mahwé which serve as the Baa'gh colony home after the solar flare.
- Kyi á Yikho: a curse phrase meaning "to be relegated, damned, expelled, shunned to the void."
- Lakea: a region in Wiimb-ó just north of the northern sea above the isolated continent of Suraral
- Layoshwelo: a spiral
- Liliche – a kind of bioluminescent lichen
- M'majiringo (also called Electromagic) – ability of a person to make electronic devices do their bidding.
- Maadiregi: a title given to anyone who uses knowledge of the high language or sound magic and technology professionally for payment e.g., engineers, technicians, architects.

- Magurgurma: A demigod, part of the mythology of the Ts'jenene people on Órino-Rin.
- Mahadum: a type of university.
- Mahwé: one of the five planets – now uninhabited, after being destroyed by an experiment in time magic.
- Mai'Karbar: a species of vicious bloodthirsty creatures used as enforcers by criminal groups on Ekwukwe.
- Mamba'ba: like a mamba, giant snake native to Ekwukwe
- Mamenyeh: a place where sacred relics are housed, shrines to ancestral spirits of the people of the Paramikule Zékunekude and surrounding region on Wiimb-ó.
- Memedede: tiny bugs, pests, like cockroaches
- Menigari: a title for seers, spiritualists and mediums who are sensitive to the spirit world and able to constantly perceive the realm of the ancestors.
- Meridian: a part of Órino-Rin's atmosphere where the atmospheric density rapidly increases with increased depth, the atmospheric gas becomes thermodynamically supercritical.
- Mothersound: the primal sound or big bang sound that created the universe. It is believed that every creature and thing in the universe carries an aspect or fragment of this sound within it.
- Mutepack: mobile device used to mute sounds
- Nakoko: mythical a beast according to the Baa'gh on Mahwé. A creature believed to consume time.
- Ndi-N'suppuh: The Outcasts. Also the name of a band from Órino-Rin.
- Nga'phandileh: creatures of unreality that inhabit a parallel 'dark' dimension
- Ngõgda tree: an "upside down tree" native to Wiimb-ó.
- Nilea: a nation of Wiimb-ó
- Ntum'tum: bloodthirsty insects native to Mahwé.
- Nududu: name given by the Baa'gh on Mahwé to any species which they consume in order to gain properties and evolve.

- Nza'nza: a small, sparrow like bird
- Ọbẹ: a short knife
- Og'beh: the group of four leaders of the Baa'gh on Mahwé
- Órino-Rin: one of the five planets.
- P'hobawawa: a one-eyed bat that is native to Ekwukwe.
- Paramikule Lézalude lush, green region near Zékunekude on Wiimb-ó.
- Paramikule Mézilede: arid region near Zékunekude on Wiimb-ó.
- Paramikule Zékunekude: a chiefdom-based village in the vast equatorial district of Abzizi-Lukhi on Wiimb-ó.
- Pinaa: Inhabited moon of Mahwé
- Pwezapwe: a spider-like creature
- R'asasa Ako-oka: The Lost Key. A magical recitation from the high language.
- Ra'engi: trainer/mentor.
- Raevaagi: a title for the "bearers of histories", messengers/bards/storytellers/orators/history holders.
- Rakwa wa-Ya'yn: "The Song of Our Mother's Children"
- Rakwayn: the sacred space of the ruevaagi
- Ramarire council: secret council on Zezépfeni that is in charge of maintaining their dominance.
- Rorta Kuuwa: planetary shield of Zezépfeni, that protects it from meteors.
- Sâkoukou. A secret genetic order of assassins descended from the Mahwé royal guard, now in service of Zezépfeni.
- Sauúti: The name of the original race which evolved on Wiimb-ó and from which all humanoids descended from. It is also the name of the "high" language which they spoke. Also used as a collective name for the system of the five planets.
- Seekers: relentless hunters of knowledge, particularly of the old ways, of the ancient language, Sauúti. They are independent, unlike the Susu Nunyaa

- Shekere-re: a small percussion instrument consisting of a dried kalabash with beads woven into a net covering it. Makes a rattling sound.
- Soundcode: equivalent of computer programs which are created using manipulated sound only.
- Strangemare: a nightmare
- Suraral: an isolated continent of , much like Australia. The people of this continent are called Surali.
- Susu Nunyaa: The elite order of Zezépfeni tasked with seeking knowledge and interpreting new words of the lost Saúti high language.
- T'Songesonge: a region of Ekwukwe.
- Tahlata: a ceremonial face paint paste made with ash and melon oil
- Tai-te-Kawa: determination rite used by the AI on Pinaa to identify children with innate magical ability.
- Taq'qerara: a rare and special individual that can manipulate echoes, reshape the innate fragment of the Mothersound in all things, including people.
- Thiouraye: a traditional mix of wood shavings and spices common among the Ts'jenene.
- Tikolokolo: a spirit gremlin of Ekwukwe
- Tor-Tor: Death ritual of the Baa'gh on Mahwé, during which new Og'beh eat the old ones alive.
- Ts'jenene: nomadic group that lives on Órino-Rin.
- Ura-aru: a hypnotic-chamber that uses repetitive, tight focus and low-frequency vibrations to put people into suspended animation. Used to permanently imprison people without killing them off.
- Uroh-ogi: healer, a title given to anyone who performs healing of people and animals professionally for payment e.g., doctors, nurses, healers, veterinarians.
- V'hushalele: a magical spear used by the character Sina.
- Vuiili-ki: one of the spirit moons of Wiimb-ó

- Vuiili-ku: one of the spirit moons of Wiimb-ó
- Vwesu'erosu: The faithful ones. Previous rulers of the Lomanoo city in the deserts of Erii on Wiimb-ó.
- Wiimb-ó: one of the five planets
- Xiffarh Utuwah zone: zone of death, in Wiimb-ó.
- Yikho: the void or non-existence. Similar to "Hell" but refers more to the void/blackness/emptiness – "Hell" is not used in the Sauútiverse
- Yu'uxu: the name for the phenomenon of noticeable increase in stellar activity between the two stars Zuúv'ah and Juah-āju every 25 years which interferes with electromagnetic waves. The solar flare that destroyed the original Sauuti civilization is thought to be an extreme version of this.
- Zéhemgwile: the guild of tailors.
- Zezélam: capital and spiritual centre of the planet Zezépfeni. It is a city-state housing the Temple, home to the Susu Nunyaa.
- Zezépfeni: one of the five planets
- zje'lili fish: equivalent of jellyfish
  Zonne: an old technology from the Surali of Wiimb-ó, used for navigation.
- Zuúv'ah: smaller one of the two stars in the binary at the center of the system.

MORE STORIES SET IN THE SAUÚTIVERSE

An Artificial Intelligence's Spirit-walk through Eh'wuaizo
by Adelehin Ijasan

Where Daylight Bows to Darkness
by Cheryl S. Ntumy

Listen, Don't Touch
by Cheryl S. Ntumy

The Alphabet of Pinaa: An AI Reinvents Zerself on an Inhabited
Moon
by Eugen Bacon

The Mystery of the Vanishing Echoes
by Eugen Bacon

Children of the Storm
by Eugen Bacon

Separation
by Stephen Embleton

How To Win The G'idiidigbo Challenge: A Practical Guide
by Wole Talabi

Descent by
Wole Talabi

The Heretic Harmonic
by Xan van Rooyen

Thief
by Xan van Rooyen

Threnody For the Tetekute
by Xan van Rooyen

With more to come. The Sauútiverse is ever-expanding.

also available from

Android Press

Science Fiction & Fantasy Punks

www.android-press.com

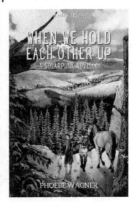

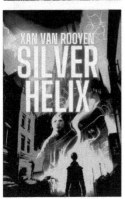

Printed in the USA
CPSIA information can be obtained
at www.ICGtesting.com
LVHW010727310124
770075LV00049B/247